CW00517819

The East Erie Company Presents:

We Buy Used Marbles: Tales of Terror

K.P. Maloy

ISBN: 979-8-8689-7927-9 (Ebook)

ISBN: 979-8-8690-4025-1 (Paperback)

Printed in United States

Designed by Hemingway Publishers

Cover art by Amy Josh

For more information about this book and other titles from Hemingway Publishers, please visit our website at www.hemingwaypublishers.com.

This book is dedicated to
Anyone who has ever quit
On their passion
Or belief in themselves…

Try again.
It is never too late,
Until it is.
Trust you to be You.

Contents

We Buy Used Marbles

Chapter 1

"That's a funny sign," Preston Jackson said to his mom.

"Mmm, hmm." Her eyes on the road, his mom replied without even trying to catch a glimpse of the sign screwed into the telephone pole.

"Why would someone want to buy used marbles?" the young boy of ten asked, again appealing to his mom.

"Buy old marbles?" Janay Jackson replied. Having not seen the sign, she was unaware of the context; she also did not know that the sign had specifically expressed an interest in used marbles. What the married mother of one was aware of, however, was that they were going to be late for her son's first knothole baseball practice if the driver in front of her did not start driving an appropriate speed, which to her, was at least five miles over the posted limit. The police gave you nine.

"Yeah," Preston continued, "why would someone buy used marbles?"

"Someone who lost their marbles, maybe," Janay joked. She had rushed home to get to Preston, but the late afternoon traffic caught up with her and now had everything moving slower.

"Well, that's what the sign said."

"What sign?"

Preston sighed. "Mom, the marble sign back there. I told you."

"I'm sorry honey, we must have already been too far past it for mommy to see it through the eyes I have growing out of the back of my head."

"Grandpappy had old marbles," Preston remembered. "One time he showed me."

"Your grandpappy loved to play marbles." The loving mom glanced at her son; he was a good kid. "You know, some of those were probably mine."

"You played with marbles?"

"Well, not like your grandpappy, I suppose." Janay tried to recall the last time she had seen a marble, and all she could recall were the few times playing with them on the floor with her dad. Mostly, she had liked the marbles that were blue and looked like the world, but her other favorites were the ones that had the yellow and brown swirls. Janay's absolute favorite had been a shooter that was colored like a yellow rose with a beautiful brown swirl in the middle.

That was the one that she most associated with her dad and the game itself.

There was one time, she supposed maybe the first time she had ever seen them, when her pappy had sat with her on the floor, teaching her the ins and outs of the game. Her dad had large hands, and even now, frustrated by slow traffic, the tenderness of the moment and the vivid image of his long thumb tweaking the marbles just right dented her heart and brought a twinge of emotion for the dearly departed man.

Funny how the thought of something as mundane as a marble can invoke real emotions; such is the power of memories.

"How did you play with them?"

"The game?" Janay asked, immediately answering her own question after a second of thought and another quick look at her little man. "You would draw a circle in the dirt or sometimes use a piece of string to make a circle. Then, you would each put a couple marbles in the middle and take turns trying to plunk the other guy's marbles out of the circle. If you were playing keepsies - and everyone played keepsies – then you would keep any marbles that you knocked out of the circle. It was stupid but it was so much fun."

"What's keepsies mean?"

"It meant that you got to keep any marbles you won."

"That's serious."

Janay laughed out loud. "Playing for keeps is always serious business. That's why you had to state that from the beginning if you were playing for keeps. Know the rules going in. Good idea in life, too, I suppose, establish everything up front."

"Did you get his marbles when he died?"

"You know we don't like to talk like that," Mrs. Jackson said, scolding her son in the nicest of terms.

"I'm sorry mom."

"It's ok."

Preston looked out the window. There were many times when he and grandpappy had time for playing games. He knew that his grandpappy loved playing with marbles as much as any of the other games that they played together, even if the old man did not always have special stories about each of Preston's choices. "But do you think we have any marbles at the house?"

"I don't want you selling any of our stuff to any stranger on a sign."

"Mo-mmm." The word as spoken had two syllables.

"I'm just saying." The light turned green, and Janay was not happy when the slow driver did not immediately start moving. She waited for the count of five, well maybe three, before honking her horn. "Come on! Jesus."

"Mo-mmm." The same two syllables but with a different meaning.

The mom, already stressed from the commute, shot her only child the quickest of glances. Preston did not need to be told twice; that one look was meant to shut down the discussion. Without much more conversation, they raced to the practice field where Preston was less than five minutes late. Before dropping him off, Janay wished her son luck and assured him that she would be back for at least the last forty-five minutes of his two-hour practice.

She had some errands to run.

After that, they didn't talk about finding lost marbles again.

Chapter 2

eing the first day of practice, and Preston's second year with the same team, showing up five minutes late was not of much consequence. He would still have the same number as the year before, 8, and he already knew three-quarters of the team. It did not take him long to reconnect with his old buddies, and over the course of practice, he started making bonds with the new ones, the 9-year-olds.

"Are all the practices that hard?" David Hardy asked. He was one of the new kids, and he was small even for his age; still, even the 12-year-old players could tell that he would be one of the future stars of the team if not the entire league. The littlest kid on the team had a great eye at the plate, a decent arm that would only get stronger, and the ability to catch every ball coming his way.

"Ha," Troy Hershey said. He was one of the oldest boys and the team's leader this year. "Just wait until it really gets hot out."

"Yeah," another teammate said, "this was cake."

Preston knew David from the tennis practices his parents made him take last winter. Being himself one of the youngest on the team – even for a 10-year-old he was young – and being smart enough to see that David was already a better baseball player than him, Preston gravitated toward the new kid when the group broke their respective ways.

Preston didn't see his mom waiting for him because she had not yet returned.

"Where are your parents at?" Preston asked. He had met the Hardy's once and on a few other occasions seen them pick David up from the tennis club where they played; like his absent mom, he did not see them here.

"I rode my bike," David said. "We live pretty close by."

"That would be sweet!" Preston tried to imagine such freedom. "Your parents must trust you."

"My parents are both working right now, so I guess they have to trust me."

"Oh." Preston's parents worked, too, but most times they were able to take him wherever he needed to go; sometimes his Aunt Gina took him places, usually during the day.

"Where are your parents?"

"My mom had to run some errands, but she's the one picking me up."

"Oh." David looked at the parking lot. "I can wait with you."

The parking lot did have cars leaving, but with the next round of practice for the next team starting in fifteen minutes, the lot was active. Cars would switch places with one another, new ones in, old ones out, but the lot itself would stay mostly full until dark.

The last team usually got to practice with the lights, at least once the season really got going near the end of June, but there was still one more team until then.

"You're really good at baseball," Preston said.

"Thanks, I play a lot with my brother."

"What team is he on?"

"He's in high school now."

"Oh."

"I think he played for the Kiwanis, though."

"Oh, those guys are annoying." Preston liked playing baseball, a lot more than he liked tennis, but not as much as he liked swimming in his own pool. Baseball, though, was fun enough, and he liked the comradery of his team. He even had some friends on other teams, and he enjoyed getting to meet new people through them. There were, however, a few teams that he never liked playing, and the purple and black Kiwanis' team was one of them. He did not have any real friends on the Kiwanis, but he did know Danny Green as the weird kid one street over who never wanted to play with any of the other kids in the neighborhood.

"Yeah, sounds like my brother," David laughed. "He's annoying alright, but he's pretty good at baseball, though. He's going to play on a traveling team next year, dad says."

"That would be cool: Travel around and just play baseball." Without trying, Preston imagined all the best parts of life on the road.

"It will be pretty cool when he's out of the house for the summer." The boys laughed together.

"I don't have any brothers or sisters."

"You aren't missing much."

"Besides some extra baseball practice, I guess."

"Yeah, I guess."

The two boys laughed and watched as the next team started to take their place on the field.

"What are you going to do tonight?" David asked.

"I don't know." Preston looked up the hill, the way from which his mom was expected to arrive. They had a pool, and he would certainly be jumping in there almost as soon as he got home. After a day of play and practice he knew the water would be refreshing. During baseball season he was not allowed to swim before practice or especially before a game, so he always appreciated every opportunity to splash away hours of fun afterwards. Tonight, though, he doubted he would stay in the pool long. His mind was back to thinking about marbles and searching his house for them. "Have you heard about the guy who buys used marbles?"

"Old marbles? No. Who is he?"

"I don't know, but he has a sign," Preston nodded without really smiling. "It has his phone number on it and everything."

"What do you think he does with them?"

"Who cares, if he'll pay you for them." Preston laughed, but he doubted that he would ever sell any of his grand pappy's little glass globes. "I don't know."

"I think we have some old marbles." David scratched his head.

"I bet that man has got a lot of them, though."

"He must have if there's money involved."

"I wonder what he does with them?"

"I don't know."

Preston and David talked for a few more minutes before the familiar car came into sight driving down the hill. It took less than a minute from there, and Preston's mom was pulling into the lot.

"Well, thanks for waiting with me," Preston said before turning for the car.

"No problem, man. I'll see you Thursday I guess," David said, getting on his bike. Their next practice that week was just two days away, on Thursday.

"I'll see you!" Preston ran to his mom's car without looking back. Once he was in the car and the door was closed, his mom was quick to speak.

"Buckle your seat belt." Her words were short and terse, and her skin glistened as if she had been sweating.

"Ok." Preston complied without arguing, a fight he learned he would never win. His mom immediately pulled away.

"So, how was practice?" Now that they were moving, Janay calmed.

"Oh, this year is going to be way better than last year!" Preston was genuinely excited. The only kid that he didn't like from last year's team was now thirteen and moved on to a different level of play. "I'm better than all the new kids except for one, and I already know him: David Hardy, from tennis practices."

"That's wonderful sweetie."

"Yeah. Plus, he'll never want to play third base, so I don't need to worry about that." On their team, Vince Diaz played third base, but he was twelve and next year he would be moving on. Preston had his eye on that spot.

"Well look at you." Janay Jackson was calm, but she still wanted to get home before her husband. Not that they were in a race, but the facts of life meant that the first one there was not the first one to have to explain the events of their day or why they had been late picking up their son from practice.

"I thought you were going to come watch."

"Well," Janay paused, an omission not technically being a lie, "my appointment ran over."

"Oh." Preston said, not really caring one way or the other. "Are you bringing me Thursday or do you want me to ask dad?"

"Why would you ask your dad?"

"I don't want you to always have to worry about it, mom."

"I'm not worried about it."

"Our practice is at one o'clock."

"On Thursday?" Janay looked over at her son.

"That's our next practice."

Preston's mom sighed loudly and slowly through her lips. *Why Thursday?* "Ok, your Aunt Gina might have to take you then."

"I told you I can ask dad."

"Preston Gerard..." Mrs. Jackson shot her son the same glance as before, the topic killer. Their conversation did not end there, but for the rest of the ride, they no longer talked about the ride, this one or any other coming up.

There was also no talk about marbles, used, old, or otherwise.

Chapter 3

――≡ 1 ≡――

hannon Louise Tate was frustrated. Though she was only twelve and still had a lifetime of disappointment ahead, her current mood came about after only earning $12.50 working at her lemonade stand. Yesterday was a little better, $23.50, but after subtracting the $10 - *Keep the change* - from their nice neighbor – she did not know his name, just that he spent a lot of time working around his yard – the results of the two days had been about the same.

The young entrepreneur supposed that today was technically better in that she had not spent as much time working her booth as she had the day before, but the results were paltry and hardly what she was expecting for all her hard work.

Her parents were great, and she loved them, but this current lesson in *learning responsibility and the value of a dollar* was going too far. Her parents had been nice enough to start her off with everything that she needed; her dad built the little stand from old pallets, and her mom had invested in the first 25-pound bag of sugar, a case of lemons, and two sleeves of 50 plastic cups each. Being a nice guy, her dad also included enough lids to match and a box of 500 straws. He told her that to someone in a car, having a lid on their lemonade would be a value-add, whatever that meant.

Being a restaurant manager at a successful downtown establishment, Shannon Louise's dad also stressed to her the importance of being nice. *No one ever stops at a lemonade stand expecting hospitality, so if you exceed their expectations, chances are they will come back, and you will have yourself a repeat guest. Remember the difference: a guest gets an experience; a customer gets a product and a receipt, and they can return it; an experience can neither be returned nor refunded.*

Her parents had given their daughter all the information she would need, and then they allowed her to make the following decisions for herself.

Her first choice was the type of lemonade to serve. Her mom had explained that there were basically two ways from which to start. Her daughter could make lemonade using a standard mix. This would be easier to use and allow for less waste. The other option would be to have a freshly squeezed lemonade. This would be more work but would come across as a better product and could thus be sold at a higher price.

The choice hardly seemed like a decision: Of course Shannon Louise wanted to sell the better of the two types of lemonade.

Two days in and the young entrepreneur was regretting her choice. Squeezing the lemons, even with the fancy press her mom used almost daily, was a lot of work. Cleaning up the contraption was also not very fun, and Shannon Louise had already pinched her finger once cleaning it.

Dealing with the sugar was almost as bad. Her dad had been nice enough to break the big bag into three smaller containers, but even these were still awkward for her to carry. Plus, the sugar was sticky! Shannon hated being sticky! Then there was the problem with trying to figure out how to make the two taste just right when mixed with water. By the time she had the proper concentrations of both, she had two batches of lemonade, more than enough for her first day, but not enough for two days.

Cleaning up the mess at the end of the day was also not fun: More stickiness.

Her other major decision had been how much to charge for each cup. Starting with the fact that her local UDF sold Gatorades for $1.50 each – technically $1.89 or buy 2 for $3.00 – Shannon Louise was set on charging $1.50 per glass. Both of her parents, while not telling her what to do, had each given her that look they shared, the look that let her know they disagreed with her or were in some way disappointed.

Though only twelve, Shannon Louise was a great kid who made her parents happy, but even she recognized what this look meant from each of them. In her young mind, if she was going to be making the good stuff – and serving it with a straw! – then she was going to charge as much as a Gatorade. Her parents had suggested that $0.75 was a better price; even after reminding them that she was going to be making the good stuff, freshly squeezed lemonade, they did not seem convinced.

What was the point of selling the good stuff then? She had asked what their price would have been for the pre-mix, $0.50? She was not happy when they seemed to accept that.

Fifty cents per glass! In her head she screamed.

Shannon Louise had a very specific goal for this summer: She was going to earn $500. Math was one of her favorite classes in school, but it did not take a genius to realize that to make $500, fifty cents at a time, would require selling at least 1,000 cups of lemonade.

One thousand cups of lemonade!

Again, it was enough to make her scream in her head. Plus, she knew that to reach her goal, no matter the price, she was going to need to invest in more of everything. Just to make her goal, at fifty cents, would mean having to buy 900 more cups.

Nine hundred more cups!

No, Shannon Louise had done the math.

Her parents had already set her up with one hundred cups and the good stuff, fresh lemons and sugar. To her thinking, selling the first 100 cups of lemonade, the good stuff, at $1.50 a pop, put her at $150.00 right out of the gate. That left her with another $350 to hit her goal. She would need more cups and lids, and four hundred of each would put her even with the box of straws. The price to get those items would be $67.00. More of the good stuff, she assumed, would cost her at most the same, and maybe a little bit more than the supplies. Her assumption was $150 spent, so back to zero.

Back to zero!? How!?!?

From there, though, everything else would be, as her uncle always said, gravy. 400 more cups sold at $1.50 per cup would put her at $600, $100 over her goal!

So, to make her summer complete, Shannon Louise set her sights on selling five hundred cups of lemonade. *500 Cups!!*

Still, it was a long summer, and, again, she did the math. She had nine weeks of summer, time between last bell and first bell minus the week vacation they had planned in August, so that was about 56 cups a week; or, 8 cups a day if she actually had to work every day; or 11 cups a day if she was going to try and, as her uncle always suggested, get her two days off in a week.

Her goal was 12. If she could get 12 cups sold in a day, then she could feel good: $18. Something about it all made her feel sad, but she trusted her math. The summer would work out and she would be better than where she started - and a grade older!

What had she done so far? $36 in two days. Her brain tried to square the fact that she was on her average goal and yet still felt underwhelmed by her sales each day.

Tips.

There was no mystery at all. Each day *had been* crappy, but tips also made each day seem better. Not sure what to do with the information, Shannon Louise nonetheless put it away for safe keeping, just like the contents of her lemonade stand for the day.

Chapter 4

ad, do we have any old marbles?" David Hardy looked at his dad, Chuck.

"Marbles? What do you want marbles for?"

"There's a guy that buys them."

"He buys marbles?"

"Yeah, I guess."

"I don't think you should be talking to anyone who is buying marbles, dear," David's mom, Nancy, said. She was one of the nicest moms in David's group of friends, and most considered her the most attractive mom, too. At home she took a backseat to the boys in her house, including her husband, Chuck. Realizing early that her son was too short for a career in basketball, it had been her idea to get David into tennis lessons. Her husband had at first objected, but she countered by pointing out the higher chance rewards of a tennis career than the same shot at basketball fame; in the end, she was still the hottest mom on the block, and meek or not she could get her way on occasion.

"Why would he buy marbles?" Chuck's question was set in a different tone.

"I don't know, maybe he wants to set some kind of record or something."

"Or maybe he wants to take advantage of a bunch of kids by undercharging them for something that is obviously worth something more than glass." Chuck looked at David's older brother and mom before looking back to David. "Think about it."

"Makes sense to me," older brother, Todd, said.

"Yeah, makes sense to me too, dad," David agreed. He was not the smartest of his friends, but there might not have been any of them better at understanding the dynamics of relationships. No sense arguing when his dad and brother agreed on something, especially not with the admonition from his mom already stated.

David knew that sometimes during an at bat the hitter needed to sit on a pitch.

He might not have had any marbles of his own, but he wasn't dumb.

Preston was only ten, but even he understood that the conversation at dinner was different than usual. His mom did not look at his dad, and his dad seemed preoccupied with his phone. Neither of them even asked him how his first day at baseball practice went.

It sure wasn't like last year.

What could have changed in a year?

He liked the meal that his mom cooked, she called it Salisbury steak with green beans, and it was one of his favorites. His mom was a good cook, and he was not especially picky.

"Practice was good today," Preston said. The uninvited remark came after talking to his dad, but he was not directing his comment at either parent.

"Oh yeah," Haynes Jackson said, looking up from his phone, "good first day?"

"Oh yeah!" Preston wasted no time saying. "It's great being a year older. I'm better than all of the new kids, too, except maybe my friend David."

"That's good to hear," Haynes said, putting his phone down. "Same coaches and everything?"

"Yeah, same coaches."

"That's great, buddy."

"I know. I caught all my fly balls."

"That's great, slugger."

"So, what are you going to do tomorrow?" Janay asked, changing the subject.

"Swimming!" Preston said.

"Sounds like a plan," Haynes said.

"Are you off?" Janay looked at her husband.

"Yeah, we talked about this," Haynes said. "I have to work Sunday, so I'm off tomorrow."

"You have to work Sunday?"

"We talked about this." Haynes looked at his wife. "Remember I said I was thinking about playing golf...?"

Preston's mom said nothing in reply.

Preston chewed his food and thought about mentioning the marbles again, but he knew that now was not a good time for that. He might not have been the best player on his team, but like his newest friend, Preston had few problems reading the room. He knew that if he cleaned his plate, his mom would give him at least half of the last piece of his favorite meal and maybe even some warm pie and ice cream.

That, of course, depended on him keeping his mouth shut about the marble man and cleaning his first plate clean.

He went to sleep early that night, but his belly was full of pie and ice cream. His mom must have been happy with him, because she gave him three scoops of ice-cream in addition to her portion of the delicious pie.

The only child did not say anything else that day about the guy who buys used marbles, but Preston could not get the bizarre idea out of his mind.

Chapter 6

Teddy Hahn was out earlier than usual on Wednesday morning. The elderly Price Hill native was content to do his shopping at the local Kroger, the one over on Delhi Pike, but today he was going downtown to the historic Findlay Market. Staying open through good times and bad, the market was again a great place to buy some local produce, homemade candles, novels, and, in Teddy's case, a couple bone-in ribeye steaks.

His old Chevy was great for driving around the western side of town, but the senior citizen was beginning to doubt that it was still able to keep up on an outside track. Traveling from the west side of Cincinnati to its market district in the downtown section of the city called Over-the-Rhine, or OTR for short, was less than fifteen minutes; for Teddy, the trip took closer to thirty minutes; parking alone added what seemed like ten minutes more.

Fortunately, he had almost a full tank of gas in the car.

When he pulled into the parking lot, he was surprised to learn that the market did not open for another hour; he was too early. Happy that he had not paid – he did not know how to use the parking app, otherwise he would have paid before finding out that the market was not yet open – Teddy was still not enthusiastic about walking around OTR on a Wednesday morning, and there was no way he was going to just sit in his car; besides, he figured he would probably be expected to pay just for that privilege.

Deciding that the market was not for him today – though maybe the slightest bit relieved for the excuse to avoid the overwhelming crowds he had been expecting to find there - Teddy was neither upset nor happy about making the drive and turning around empty-handed. Though the outcome indicated a waste of time, the retired plumber saw the trip as a learning opportunity; if nothing else, today he learned that Findlay Market does not open until ten o'clock.

Plus, he never minded a good drive: no better way to clear your head.

As he backed his car out of the parking spot to begin his return trip home – with a planned stop at his neighborhood Kroger market store - he was certain he would never make that mistake again. He was also surprised to see a store dedicated to selling comic books; by the signage, it appeared the place was also a bar.

Reliving the events of the morning in his head, Teddy was about half-way home when his drive got sidetracked.

Driving slower than average, Teddy had just crossed under the railroad tracks and crested the small hill beyond when traffic grew dense as cars were bunching together. On the downward stretch of the road there were too many cars, so he was unable to merge left to continue heading west on River Road. Forced to take the exit to his right, he slapped hard the steering wheel before committing to the next choice by staying in the left lane of the two-lane exit; better to take a shortcut through the edges of the Incline District and southern Price Hill than to go straight through the heart of it all by going right up to Warsaw Avenue and then Glenway Avenue past that, a street that was generally too busy for him.

The exit Teddy took led to a road which was steep and very curvy, a route that suited the speed to which he was accustomed to driving but one that kept him from obtaining even that velocity. When he was brought to a stop, however, it was not his fault, driving faster would not have gotten him anywhere any more quickly.

Traffic was stopped waiting for a construction closure.

The signal worker was on his phone holding the STOP sign facing the few cars waiting their turn. Because of the impending bend in the road just ahead, it was impossible to see exactly what was causing the delay. Cars were not yet heading their direction, so he could tell at least that much.

It took him only a few seconds of waiting before he saw the sign.

Similar to the one that young Preston Jackson had also seen, but not the same one and not at the same place, the sign was nonetheless identical: *We Buy Used Marbles*, followed by a local phone number, the same one as on the sign seen by young Preston and countless others. The white sign with colored orbs could as easily have been advertising balloons. The block let-ters had probably been spray-painted, but the shakiness of the colorful work almost made the inking seem as if done by hand.

Teddy turned his head away from the sign as he laughed out loud.

"Well now that might have just made my day."

He was still chuckling to himself when he noticed the construction worker now talking into his radio; his other hand still held the cell phone idle. Whatever the conversation was, it did not last more than a few seconds before he returned to his phone and the few cars waiting were now joined by two more behind Teddy.

Marbles. Teddy thought to himself. *Why on earth would anyone want to buy old, used marbles?* He knew that the answer was as old as civilization itself: money. If there was money in comic books, then Teddy supposed that there probably was some potential for real money to be had in just about anything nowadays.

He again looked back at the sign.

Though himself a retired old man, he knew that even he was at the tail end of the generation that widely liked playing with marbles. Back in the day, some of the older kids took their game playing seriously, and the scramble to best others and collect their marbles could be fierce. He had himself of course played, but most of his gaming was in the form of contributing marbles to the kitty; his losses were always someone else's gains.

Still, he had other victories when he was just a few years older, like the time he put his trusty green baby on the line and bested Clay Patton, winning the eighth grader's own prized blue swirl. He supposed that there had been others, to be sure. He could clearly picture some of the marbles that he used to keep in the little sewing bag his mom gave him. It was a soft material with a sturdy medal frame sewn inside the opening, allowing easy access and tight security with an always reliable and incredibly simple clasp of two overlapping nubs. And the marbles he used to have, blue ones – including Clay Patton's treasure that was never recovered or returned – green ones – like his own never lost baby – red ones, brown ones, black ones like 8-balls, even ones with swirls of many colors.

Oncoming traffic finally started its march past them; first one, then another, then after a few seconds a steady stream of cars following behind their slow-moving lead. Teddy was relieved to know that there would be an end in sight for this traffic stop, but he now had a nag in the back of his mind trying to recall where he had stored those little round treasures. Not only was he curious after all this time to see again his forgotten possessions, but he also had a sense of curiosity as to their actual value. Guessing that he potentially had as many as two dozen keepers, the old man could not help but wonder what they were also worth. If he didn't sell them, then his kids would probably just turn around and do so if and when he ever did die, and the marbles sure weren't doing him any good sitting in a little velvet bag.

But where?

Somewhere, he was sure of that.

The sense of urgency came over him as quickly as he now felt the need to act. His first thought was to take a picture with his phone, but he could not get it out of his pocket without unbuckling his seat belt, and that did not seem like an option. Still, he tried to get the phone out, but it did not work.

With great anxiousness now, his actions driven by simple curiosity and complex psychology, he opened his glove compartment and pulled out the first piece of paper he could grab, an invoice from the last time he had his car in the shop. He looked for a pen in the same place, but there was not one there.

The last car from the long parade drove past them, and now frantic, Teddy looked in the side pocket of his door. He always threw small items in there, lighters, gum, and pens. He pulled one out as the sign man again started talking into his radio and disregarding his phone.

We Buy Used Marbles

The area code was a familiar 513, the most common one in use for the area. The next three numbers seemed like an odd combination to Teddy, and he was careful to write so as to be able to read his handwriting, which was sometimes a problem even for him.

The first car in their line wasted no time in moving as soon as the signal was given. Teddy could feel his heart racing more than normal, and he wondered what his doctor would think about this much excitement in his life; probably tell him that he's losing his own marbles.

The last four numbers were surprisingly easy to remember, 2468, so he scribbled them quickly, recording them and starting his car in motion before anyone had to honk their horn.

The trip to the grocery store was otherwise uneventful, and before he even returned to his house, Teddy was positive that he had a good idea where his old collection of marbles could be found. He doubted that he would sell them, but he decided that it was at least worth a listen.

Taking in his groceries themselves took three trips. When he was younger, he would have tried to get everything in one trip; now, the retiree decided that maintaining a healthy back and heart was best done through multiple circuits back and forth. Even before putting away the last of his groceries, Teddy went into his bedroom closet and dug through everything to get to a box towards the back.

Along the way, he saw a few things that he could probably do without. Stacks of mason jars that his late wife used for her preserves. More than enough shoes to last the rest of his lifetime. A box filled with old magazines; another one with a wider variety of forgotten tokens, forgotten items that he set aside specifically to be looked at more thoroughly later. Once he found what he was looking for, though, so many other memories came floating back.

First, the bag was more purple than red, and it was truly better made than he remembered. For all the times he had undoubtedly opened and closed it, the clasp still felt perfect and tight. There was some slight wear around the corners of the metal framework, but as much was to be expected. The item was at least made to be durable and withstand the rigors of use, even if it was designed for an old seamstress and not a risk-taking boy.

Not wanting to risk losing the bag regardless of his decision on the marbles, Teddy grabbed a mid-sized mason jar and dumped his balls of colored glass inside the container of clear glass.

All the best ones he had remembered were there, as well as others that brought back more old memories and names. Roger Thoms used to be the owner of this red devil, and Dicky Rust had cried about losing his yellow swirl. The marbles were also heavier and more beautiful than he remembered. Not sure of the last time he had even seen marbles, Teddy was nonetheless convinced that, like nearly everything nowadays, marbles of this quality were not made anymore.

He went out to the living room and picked up the phone.

Surprising himself by remembering the number without referencing his note, Teddy was equally surprised when the phone was answered on the second ring.

"Hello today."

"Hi," Teddy said, "um, hello."

"How may we help you today?" The voice on the other end of the line sounded friendly and relaxing. Nothing about the voice put him on alert or seemed in any way ominous; in fact, quite the opposite, he was happy that it sounded so much like an average man working at some sterile business.

"I'm, ugh, I'm calling about the marbles." Teddy almost hung up the phone. This all seemed ridiculous.

"The used marbles, yes."

"The old marbles, yes," Teddy repeated. "I mean these were used already by the time they ever got to me, so yeah, I suppose that they're old and used."

"Very good."

"So how much are they worth then?"

"Well, that depends," the voice began, about to launch into a familiar speech, "on how they are viewed by our appraiser. The real money, for you, I can say, is with the keepers, the real gems that are still floating around out there. If you have some of those, then you can make a pretty penny indeed."

"Pretty penny…?" Teddy sensed the con, small return and probably not worth the time it took to call.

"It's a figure of speech," the voice paused, "it actually means a lot of money, kind of the opposite of a penny."

"So how do you tell then?"

"We have an expert who issues the appraisals."

"And what does he do then…"

"She, not that she cares. Gets it all the time."

"Um, sorry, what does she do then, just look at them, makes an offer, and then pays that day?"

"Just that easy," the voice assured him.

Teddy thought for a moment. He was not getting a straight answer as far as amounts, and it was hard to gauge if the return was worth the time of the trip. "If I decided to come in, how does it work? Do I make an appointment, then?"

"We are open seven days a week," the receptionist stated. "Fairly standard business hours. We don't stay open past dark, though."

"And the appraiser?"

"She is here now."

"But does she keep regular hours?"

"Oh yes," the voice said as if humored, "our employer requires us to keep regular hours. She does not like to be out after dark, however, so it's always best to come earlier in the day."

"So where are you at, then?"

The receptionist gave Teddy the address as well as a familiar landmark to help focus the spot in his mind.

"Price Hill Chili? Of course I know where that's located! I love that place. You're located right there?"

"Basically. Just south of there and around the corner."

"Well, that's not far from my house," Teddy said. "I might even come up there today, then."

"Well then, we will expect to see you."

"Can I get that address one more time?" He looked down at the piece of paper with the number written on it.

"Absolutely."

"Great, just let me grab a pen." Amazed at all that he had already packed into one early day, Teddy wondered how much else he could handle in the afternoon. He pulled out the drawer and got a pen to record the address of the location right down the street from the familiar eatery that he visited at least twice a year. He would of course eat a late breakfast and have a cup of coffee or two before even deciding whether to go visit the marble store.

Everything he did from this point on, including visiting the marble store in a few hours, Teddy Hahn would be doing for the last time in his life.

Chapter 7

A t about the same time as Shannon Louise was setting up her lemonade stand for the day, Preston was getting ready to take the first of
what would be several swims that hot Wednesday in June. Preston was
two years younger than the girl one street over, and operating a lemonade
stand would never be in his future.

Preston had no idea what his future would hold for him, and he was not
really set on any predetermined career path. He loved science classes and
learning about discoveries of the unknown, but math was not his strongest
subject. The second-year knothole player was also creative, and he had the
ability to make up stories and think out possible scenarios regarding almost
any situation, but he struggled through English class. Not worried about
the future, and unwittingly fatalistic regarding his own path through it,
Preston enjoyed the fruits of his parents' labor by staying cool in the pool.

Swimming had been a part of his summers for the last four years, since
they moved into this house. He had memories from their old place, an
apartment across the street from a Meijer and behind some place called
Dantes, an old nightclub or restaurant or hotel or something. That apartment complex also had a pool, an in-ground and much larger than the
above-average above-ground pool that they had all to themselves in the
backyard.

It did not matter to Preston: A bad day swimming was still better than
a good day at school, or most days at practice.

For the first time that day, Preston thought about the guy who buys
marbles. He really wondered why someone would pay for them when no
one played with marbles anymore. It was possible that they could be used
as artillery in a slingshot, but he did not know anyone who even knew anyone who had one of the mythical toys from yore.

With his mom working and his dad out playing golf for several more hours if not most of the day, the house was his.

He tried to think about where his mom would have stored such a collection of presumably fragile glass. He knew that some of his grandfather's stuff was up in the attic, and he could get up there, but not without any real trouble, a ladder and climbing and stuff. There were other places to try looking, first.

His initial swim of the day done, Preston dried off and went inside. After stopping in the kitchen to eat a Pop tart, Preston went out to the closet at the bottom of the stairs. His parents called it the coat closet, but he knew that it had some other things lurking there in boxes and up on the shelf. It was a great waystation for items going to the attic, and he knew that some boxes stayed longer than others.

The top shelf was high and would require dragging out a chair from the kitchen. First, though, he went through the items that were easier to reach. There was a box that had old sweaters and gloves and things in it. Items that would ideally summer out of sight in the attic would instead just wait their crowded turn here in place until needed again next winter. There was also a tall garbage can container that was filled with a bunch of rolls of wrapping paper. The impressionable youngster did not recognize the wrapping paper last used by Santa himself, but it was there to be seen.

Besides the vacuum cleaner and a bunch of shoes – including an old pair of Nikes that he was sure his mom threw away! – there was nothing left to discover in the closet without a chair. Had he gone through all the coat pockets within reach he would have found two twenty-dollar bills, a five, three singles, and a handful of quarters. And one pack of gum. And one set of keys that his dad presumed lost four months ago.

Dragging the chair over was a hassle. The chairs were large and made from heavy wood, and the hallway had a narrow space walking through the kitchen doorway as well as another tight spot where a table stood in the middle of the hallway collecting all random things. It did not take very long, but it required effort and thought, and it would need to be returned the same way going back. Not a big deal, just a hassle.

The top of the closet was easy to reach standing on the chair. His head was too tall for the doorframe of the closet, so he had to have the chair pulled in far enough so that his head was comfortably inside the space, too. A third of the shelf was filled with film for their old projector and the projector itself. Preston remembered watching these old relics, and he knew that there were some funny home films from his parents when they were kids as well as a couple old baseball games. The projector was way too heavy to lift out by himself, at least safely, and he did not want to take a chance at ruining the film.

Preston was positive that the marbles would not be found there.

The rest of the shelf was nothing special. Another box with gloves and winter hats was on top of a box of new boots that his mom was going to return one day. There were also some folded-up blankets and another box containing filters and extra pieces for the vacuum cleaner. One last box had his aunt's name on it and was filled with something called forty-fives that looked like little CD's, though the hole in the middle was way too big.

Nothing worth moving the chair out of the kitchen and back.

Walking the chair carefully past the hallway table made him think about looking there next. Inside he found a treasure of old photos. In one of the drawers, he also found an old metal box of his mom's that he remembered playing with as a younger kid. One drawer had a bunch of mail stuffed in it, and another had things like string and needle and thread. The main drawer - though less deep it was the longest - was filled with a random assortment of various things. Some pictures, some mail, a pair of scissors, a small box just large enough for a few small pictures, were all found randomly in the drawer.

But no marbles.

Not easily discouraged, Preston next moved into the kitchen. There were two places there where2 he thought to look.

The first of these was, like the desk drawer, a lone kitchen drawer dedicated to, as his mom called it, all the little crap in the house; her name for it was the junk drawer. That drawer was a collection point for all kinds of things, from paper clips and tape and nails and a hammer and more scissors and some change – which Preston put in his pocket, $0.79 – and a tape measure. There was even some mail stuffed in that drawer too, but no marbles.

The second place he looked in the kitchen was on the square table they had in the back corner of the room. On top of it were several knickknacks and other ornamental items like an old-fashioned lamp, but the table was more like a cabinet because although square, the bottom had an opening with a door hiding the secret space inside where there were two shelves of more random items. The stuff that Preston found here was more like magazines and fancy glass jars and vases. He thought that there had once been a box in there, and that was where he had been hoping to find the marbles, but he did not find either.

Before leaving the kitchen, he realized there were also shelves around the top of two of the walls, and on one of those was a jar in which his parents randomly put things. Pulling the chair over was less of a hassle since he was already in the kitchen, but the reach was slightly higher than was the shelf in the closet; still, he was able to reach the jar and look inside. The jar, a country crock that was very dense and very heavy, was easy for him to examine without emptying the contents everywhere. He did find a very cool dice with more than six sides that he put in his pocket, but he did not find any marbles.

Done searching the kitchen, Preston decided to make himself a glass of purple Kool-Aid. He saw a couple more jars on the counter that he had not thought of before as possible hiding spots and he looked there; nothing was inside that crockery except some pens and a little knife that his mom used one time for digging out a splinter from his hand.

Leaving the drink on the table, he walked around the corner to go to the bathroom, passing the basement door on the way. He had to pee badly, and he rushed to lift the lid and the seat the way his mom liked. He was also, at his mom's request, careful to aim his little squirt into the big hole. Though she never watched, she did make enough of an impression on her young man that he never wanted to grow up to be one of those men who couldn't control his flow.

After closing the seat and the lid – he learned, too, that his mom did not like it when he left the seat up, and she also questioned him when she found the seat down, so he just closed the whole thing – he flushed and washed his hands. He turned to grab a towel and noticed the clutter on the table holding a plant and some magazines. The bottom shelf was open, and that was where the magazines were scattered. The part holding the plant, though, was in a trough, and Preston could see some random objects there. Curious more than anything, he moved the plant to one side and found a Sharpie as well an old army man: another addition to his pocket. He slid the plate to the other side and found several rubber bands, more pens, but no marbles, not even a random one.

Without incident, he walked back to the kitchen to grab his glass of purple goodness before moving his search next into the dining room.

The first place he checked there was the large hutch where his mom kept their good plates, the ones they used to use during the holidays. That was when more of his grandparents were still alive, and the holidays had still been more a celebration. The wooden cabinet was so well stocked with plates and silverware and fancy, folded napkins that he doubted he would find the marbles there, but the large storage space in the bottom section offered the possibility of hope; plus, it is where his mom kept what she used to consider some of her greatest treasures.

No marbles.

The next opportunity for hope, and this one also seemed real as Preston began, was the much fancier though smaller liquor cabinet that was on the other side of the room. Though young, he knew that this piece of furniture was an antique and certainly of some value. The fact that his parents really did not drink alcohol in the home meant that there was a lot of extra room for more knickknacks and other hidden treasures. A quick look through all the shelves and drawers revealed no marbles, but the young boy did find an old watch he had received for his birthday two years ago. It was cool because he could play a couple different games on it, a toy none of his friends had; it was bad because changing the battery was a major hassle that his father had been meaning to do for several months before Preston lost interest and then completely forgot about the thing. More carefully than he had the change, and in the other pocket, he took the watch, too.

The last place in the room was really no hope. There was a delicate wooden shelf that was built specifically to stand in the corner of a room and display little curios, a lot of which his parents seemed to own. There was no place there to find his grandpa's marbles, but he looked through each shelf for a lost stray.

The top shelf had an empty alcohol bottle, and the label was old and made the thing look like an antique. There was a picture of him and another one of his mom and his grandpappy sitting on a dock by some water. There was on the next shelf an old plate and a handprint in plaster that was his hand from kindergarten.

Looking at it made him laugh because he could still remember the day when he made the imprint and how gross his hand felt afterward.

Without much thought to his actions, he looked at the items on the lowest shelf and saw an old teacup, which was the only item that could possibly hold anything. When he picked up the cup, he could hear the sound before he saw the sight of a lone, solitary marble clanking around inside.

A marble!

His prize!

Exactly the thing for which he had been looking; well, almost the thing, one of them anyway.

A single marble was a reason to hope and continue his search, but it was not the true prize of his quest. This one was a beauty, though. Larger than he remembered most of them being, this marble was a shooter colored yellow like a rose with a beautiful brown swirl in the middle. The yellow and brown colors were deep and vivid; there was a swirl of chaos beneath an otherwise smooth surface.

The young boy's mind was amazed by the process of making such a thing even as he had no idea how it was possible. He had been to Cedar Point and could remember visiting the glass blowing exhibit on the Frontier Trail, and those creations were impossible to believe without seeing them happen, too. Something about the simplicity of the orb, though, really captured his attention and stoked his imagination.

Looking at it intensified his desire to find them all.

He stuck the single marble into his pocket and moved on to the next room.

The living room connected to the dining room and then on to the hallway that he had already searched. He looked in every place that was possible in this room but all he found were a bunch of old records, the large, standard ones as well as some more of the smaller ones, too. He found some sheet music for their piano, some blankets, a bunch more magazines, and more pictures.

He took time to look through the photo album and could not believe how dumb he looked as a toddler.

Why was I always making faces? Argh!

His interest in exploration renewed, Preston ran upstairs and began the slow process of searching the second floor.

When he was done, he still wouldn't have his hands on the real target of his quest, the bag of marbles his mother inherited from her dad, Preston's grand pappy.

Chapter 8

"**H**ello today."

"I saw this number on a sign."

"The sign, yes. How may we help you today?"

"Is this the marble place?"

"Is that what *you* saw on the sign?"

"Um, yeah." The caller, a female, was much too anxious for all this talk. "I have some marbles."

"The marbles, yes."

"So how does this work? Do you want to meet me somewhere?"

"Oh no; we would not want to do that. We have a location, a brick-and-mortar store, as you say."

"Oh."

"We have an expert who issues the appraisals."

"So, I can just bring them in and get my money that day?"

"Just like that."

The voice paused before continuing. "I don't have a receipt or any-thing."

"People never do."

After again being reassured of the ease and discretion with which the transaction would be processed, and after getting directions to the store surprisingly close to her current location, the 32-year-old, an adult child still dependent on her parents, hung up and decided to waste no time in making this happen. She sent a quick text to Jake, her most regular dealer, and let him know that she would be looking to score in the next few hours. The car ride to the marble guy's store was at most ten minutes away, and it took her less than ten minutes to change her clothes and gather her things.

The most important of these things, the Crown Royal bag of marbles, was more unwieldy than heavy and not something she could even begin to think about stuffing in her pockets. It forced her to take a bag, which she assumed would probably also be a good thing for carrying the product she would be buying with some or all that marble money.

Her first time seeing the sign was about two weeks prior, driving home from work just like today, when she finally was able to write down the number. The sign seemed funny and out of place, and there was a childlike quality to the colorful orbs on the white painted board.

Two things happened to impress upon her that first impression and then to make necessary the call. The first of these was that on the same afternoon as she saw the sign for the first time, she saw the exact same sign on a different road entirely. She traveled both roads semi-frequently, and never before had she seen the signs; then, on the same day, she saw the curious message twice.

On that first day, the second time, she had been on her way to run an errand and help a friend of hers who had just moved into a new place; she did not have any time to think about writing down the number if the thought had even occurred to her then.

She knew her parents – at least her mom - had a lot of old marbles. She no longer lived with her family, and she did not really talk to them that often, but she was on good enough terms to still have a key to their house. Her problems with drugs and making bad decisions had hindered her life, she would even be the first to admit, but so far, she had done nothing irrevocable; one DUI notwithstanding. Yesterday, though, finally, she had been able to find the perfect time to sneak in and take what she considered hers.

For her, it was not even that dramatic; without thought or feeling, just the knowledge of how and where, she acted and snatched away the bag nearly full of marbles.

On the way to the store, she tried to guess how much money she should expect from the sale. Really, any amount was worth it. The bag of marbles had just been sitting in a box in the basement, and there was nothing recent to indicate that they would ever be missed, so there was no real guilt over the act, just a calculation for potential reward. She knew that they had at one time been very important to her mom, and maybe her dad, too, but that was a lifetime ago: hers.

The lowball offer she expected was $10, but the least she decided she would accept was $20. With the story about the sign and the bag of marbles, she figured she could probably talk her dealer, Jake, into trading the bag for $20 worth of his product. Best case, she thought that maybe she could get $50 from an actual antique dealer as these people were presumed to be.

Parking was easy, and she wasted no time feeding the meter before crossing the street and going up to the store.

From the outside, the narrow building fit seamlessly on the otherwise busy corner. The room she entered was small and non-descript, without any sort of décor or style. Plain and an older shade of white, there was a small window and counter on the long wall. This seemed to be the only room accessible through the main door.

There was a single sign above the window: *All Sales Are Final.*

The window slid open. "Hello today."

"I called."

"How may we help you today?"

She pulled the bag of marbles out of her purse. "This is the marble place, right?"

"Is that what you saw on the sign then?"

She nodded her head. Holding the bag forward, she set the marbles down on the slim counter in front of the open window. The solid sound of the bag coming to rest on the wooden countertop indicated that the contents had some heft. "How much can I get for these?"

"Well, that is quite the bag," the man's eyes lit up, as was his custom. He could not appraise the marbles any differently whether they were hidden in a bag or scattered about a tray; his job was as the receptionist. "Bound to be some good ones in there. Let me get our appraiser."

"Appraiser?"

"Yes, she will take a look at what you have there, and she will make you an offer." With that said, the receptionist closed the window.

Anxious, the woman fidgeted, moving her bag of marbles from hand to hand, all the while glancing about the expressionless room. Was this a set up? She had heard of police departments - and local ones at that - using the ruse of free cars, football tickets, or refund money to lure wanted criminals into such a trap. Paranoid though her only criminal record would show an expunged possession charge and a single conviction for DUI, hardly worthy of entrapment, she considered leaving the room before the appraiser could come back to the window.

Not having a lengthy record and being lucky often went together hand-in-hand.

She was not perfect, and she had broken the law many times even if she did not have the paper trail to show for it. What stopped her from leaving immediately, though, was the realization that the sign had not really been directed at her; anyone driving past could have seen it. Still, she had technically stolen these marbles from her parents; nonetheless, there was no way that any law enforcement agency would waste their time chasing marbles.

Right?

The very thought was almost laughable.

The only door in the room, the door from the street, opened.

"I apologize for your wait," this new woman said. Her accent was more or less local, to the Midwest if not Ohio, and her attire was appropriate for the neighborhood. The skirt she was wearing was black and covered her long legs, and the top was a dark burgundy blouse with a paisley pattern. A silk scarf tied around her waist matched the scrunchy holding her curly black hair into one contained tail. "I was stopped on the street just now by a vagrant. Can you believe the nerve of people nowadays?"

Changing the bag of marbles to her other hand and still fidgety, the younger woman could only nod her head.

"My name is Deb Vilitch," she held out her arm, her hand open to shake, her voice calm and professional, "I am the appraiser."

"Um, nice to meet you," the woman replied, embracing the more elegant hand outstretched before her. Distracted trying to recall why the perfume she now smelled was familiar, she held the woman's hand too long.

"Yes, well," Deb Vilitch said, pulling her own hand away, "let's get down to this, then. I presume you have the marbles in the bag."

"Yes." She shook the bag to indicate how full it seemed.

"Ok, let me take a look, then."

As she handed the appraiser her bag of marbles, the seller noticed the window again sliding open. The receptionist, the same man as before, extended a thin wooden drawer through the opening. His task complete, the window again closed.

"Thank you," the appraiser said without regard to the closed window, taking the bag of marbles and wasting no time in pouring them into the wooden tray. Because this slender frame was lined with crushed velvet cloth, the sound of the marbles clacking together was muted. Before the last one was out of the bag, however, the woman's eyes widened and almost seemed to glow with excitement. "Oh my! You have a few very high-quality pieces here, and quite a few superb pieces overall, in fact."

"I do?"

"Oh yes." She looked up for a moment, giddy from the display. Her eyes twinkled. Her attention went back to the tray and the marbles inside. Her aptitude for appraisal rested not in her ability to determine the resale value of colored glass orbs, but in her talent for seeing the intrinsic value the colored little balls held for others, their rightful owners.

Viewed through her eyes, the marbles displayed a glow, some more than others, and some not at all; those last ones she simply saw as the glass toys we all see. She supposed that all marbles started out like those that she did not see as special; and she was positive that if she ever visited a factory that made marbles then she could probably look at them all day and never see one glow. Those same little trinkets years later, though, after they had been used in a conquest of fun and games, themselves the treasures to be gained or lost from competition, could amass a glow almost enough to cause her to squint and look away.

She never did that, of course, because she was a professional working for a boss who did not lightly forgive mistakes.

Her ability was not just confined to marbles, of course; she could sense the strength of the memories attached to almost anything. Like a star, the radiance could build to such a glow and then be gone in an instant, so immediate can death be to a memory, or, even, the memory of a memory. Some memories, of course, transcend death, but Deb Vilitch was equally sure that if a bag of truly ancient marbles were ever brought into her chamber, then they too would be faded and resemble their normal, colorful selves, viewed to her as if to any.

Antiques and in their own way priceless, but to her and her concern, they would be without worth.

Without any memory of a thing then there is no inherent value in that thing, at least not to her eye, and certainly not for the purposes of those to whom she answered.

This bag of marbles, however, was special and glowing brightly; even the least significant of the lot were still a degree above average; the appraiser was impressed indeed. Her fingers picked up the one that was the brightest. To most people, like the woman selling them, it looked like a slightly over-sized marble that was cloudy white with a green swirl through the middle of it. Though certainly beautiful on its own, it was not necessarily the most beautiful in the bunch; the subjectivity of beauty itself withstanding. To the appraiser, however, this was one of the finer ones that she had seen in quite some time, perhaps ever. There was no heat to the touch from the light, but the round glow was still present in the appraiser's vision as she looked up from the brilliant thing.

"Is that one worth anything?"

"This one?" the appraiser replied, her attention again drawn back to the stranger before her. "Yes, this one is certainly worth something to someone."

Unsure of the intent of the appraiser's words, the woman shifted her feet. *Did this woman just accuse me of stealing these?*

"Honestly, this entire collection is most impressive."

"So, you'll buy them all?"

"Well, that's usually how it works. I appraise some marbles higher than others, but we will take all of them off your hands, even the ones that are really nothing more than glass."

Paranoia returning, this woman just wanted to get her money and leave. "Ok, so how does this work?"

"Give me a moment."

The appraiser did not move, but her attention again went back to the collection before her. None of the other pieces had the same value as the first one she picked up, but there were only a few duds in the entire bunch, and most were superb. Altogether, there were 92 marbles to appraise. It took her less than a minute to speak, and in truth, less than that to arrive at her number.

"Ok then."

The window again slid open.

"We are prepared to offer you sixty-five hundred dollars for the lot."

"Six thousand five hundred dollars!?" For the first time in a while, her attention was truly engaged. Her own eyes widened as she imagined how high she could get from that kind of money; drugs and getting caught up on some bills. To her, that kind of money could be a game changer, maybe allow for an upgraded car. Surely, she had misheard the woman, though.

"Yes, if that is acceptable to you."

"Six thousand dollars, cash?"

"Six thousand five hundred, if that is acceptable…"

"Acceptable? You have yourself a deal lady."

"Marvelous," Deb said, a genuine smile stretching across her face. "I assume cash also will be acceptable."

"Cash? Yes! Of course!" The seller did not have any reservations about expressing her joy.

The receptionist extended forward a short stack of money, all $50 bills, a piece of paper, and a pen.

"Just sign the receipt, and we have a deal, today."

The paper seemed straight-forward, nothing more than a line documenting the sale of 92 marbles for a price of $6,500.00: No fine print, just a blank signature line. Besides the line for her autograph, she did not see a place for her to simply print her name. Laughing to herself, she considered signing something fake, but at the last second reconsidered: no sense risking that kind of money for anything, especially her stupid name.

Deb Vilitch smiled as the woman signed the paper, the sale complete. The real transaction was still being processed but would itself be complete within the hour.

"So that's it?"

"That's it, unless there is a next time."

"Can I keep the bag?"

"We have no use for it."

She picked up the money and the bag, sticking everything together as a bundle. Without a thank you or a goodbye, she rushed out the door. With any luck, her guy would be home and holding and she would be back at her own place within the next hour.

The sale was complete, and the transaction would not haunt her like a room of vacant memories; she had no attachment to the round things, and to her they would not be missed.

Chapter 9

P reston decided to go swimming instead of searching the attic. He had already looked through the hallway closet upstairs, and he also spent an hour going through the closets of his parents. It surprised him the things he found there, but he found no marbles.

His mom had a lot more clothes than he ever imagined, and she also had a box with some vibrating dog bones or something. His biggest surprise in the closet of his father was a loaded gun. He knew that his family owned a gun – his dad would sometimes mention something as being worthy of getting the gun – but he had never actually seen it. He also did not know it was loaded, but luckily, he didn't learn by accident.

Swimming was not as fun as usual, and his second swim of the day lasted less than fifteen minutes. It was a warm day, hot but not yet muggy like it would be by midsummer or especially August. The water was refreshing, but it could not wash away his disappointment at his lack of success in finding the marbles.

For all his effort, he only had one marble.

Preston got dressed, stuck the marble in his pocket, and then went for a ride on his bike.

The Jacksons had their share of disagreements, but Preston's parents were united in their stance on where he could and where he could not ride his bike. The youngster could ride anywhere within the family's designated block of streets.

They lived on the corner of Benz and Zula, and their parameters for his bike were generally clear. He was allowed to ride as far south as Rapid Run Road, as far west as Covedale Avenue, and as far north as Cleves Warsaw Pike. These streets were busy thoroughfares, but each had sidewalks, and his parents did allow their son to ride along those paths as long as he never actually took his bike out into traffic or on these roads.

His boundary to the east was a little less clearcut.

Technically, he was only allowed to go as far as Coronado Avenue, but along part of that street there were other side streets that were still residential, including Zula; these were gray areas that his parents would not have preferred him testing, but that were not really a concern as far as traffic. To them, the biggest issue limiting his range to the east was Glenway Avenue, a major thoroughfare on the west side of Cincinnati, it was not a smart place for a kid his age to be riding a bike. As far as the Jackson's were concerned, if their son could even see Glenway Avenue while on his bike then he was in trouble. Overlook Avenue was another street that connected Rapid Run and Glenway, cutting across before the two eventually met, and was itself a hardline that bounded some of those other gray area streets between those other two.

Preston took for granted that he lived in a neighborhood where he could ride his bike alone. His parents did not like the school district he lived in – they often commented on how if they lived down the street like his best friend then he too would be going to a different school that they were more excited about - and they often commented on how it was convenient to live close to a busy street like Glenway Avenue and all the shopping there but still live in a neighborhood with relatively peaceful streets.

Still, the young boy knew his boundaries, and except for some of those side streets at the southern end of Coronado, he did not test those limits.

Preston always listened when his parents were on the same page.

Aimlessly pedaling, Preston turned left on Coronado and was about halfway up the street when he came upon the girl at the lemonade stand. She looked familiar from school, and he thought she was pretty, but he could not remember her name. He did know that she was a grade or two ahead of him in school. He pushed hard on the pedal backwards, causing him to stop and leave a little skid on the street. That's how the cool kids did it.

"How's business?"

"Not too good today, to tell you the truth." Shannon Louise was not wearing her sunglasses yet, but she was already done with the day. Except for this familiar kid on the bike, no one had stopped all day.

"I'm sorry."

"Are you in fifth grade?"

"Yeah, this year I am," Preston said, happy to be considered as such before attending day one. "You're in middle school, right?"

"Seventh grade."

"That's cool!"

"Woohoo," Shannon Louise replied, twirling her finger for effect.

"My name is Preston."

"Nice to meet you, Preston. I'll tell you my name if you buy a lemonade."

"I don't have any money on me," Preston said.

"That's ok," she said as if she was not surprised by the disappointment. It was obvious he wanted to come across as apologetic. She reached for a cup and filled it halfway before handing it to the younger kid on the bike. "My name is Shannon Louise."

"Hey thanks!" Preston said, happy to take the drink.

"No problem. I appreciate the break from nothingness that you provide."

"No problem," Preston said. "So, is your last name Louise?

"No, that's my middle name, but my mom insists on calling me by both. My last name is Tate. You can call me whatever you want, though."

Preston took a drink but kept one eye on the young vendor as she spoke. "This is really good, too! I bet you sell a lot."

"You would think so." She smiled at the compliment, but the truth of the remark was still a painful reminder that not all things go as planned.

"What's the middle school like?"

"You get used to it pretty quick." Shannon Louise already had one year under her belt.

"I bet the eighth graders are the worst."

"Actually, it was the seventh graders. The eighth graders were too busy with themselves to worry about lowly sixth graders, but the seventh graders could be real jerks."

Preston took another drink. "It's a big building, though."

"You get used to it. If you can ride your bike around and still get home, then you can figure out your way around the middle school."

"Yeah, that's true."

"Where do you live, anyway?"

"Over on Benz."

"Oh."

There was a pause in the conversation, and Preston felt pressed to fill it. "Have you ever heard about the guy that buys used marbles?"

"Used marbles? Why would anyone buy old marbles?"

"My mom said that it's someone who probably lost their marbles, I guess."

"There must a market for them," Shannon Louise said, considering the idea. She seemed to remember seeing a bunch of marbles at some point in her life. "You could go online and check."

"Yeah, that's a good idea."

"Do you have any marbles?"

Preston reached into his pocket and pulled out the single treasure.

"Oh, that's really pretty."

"It kind of looks like your eyes."

Shannon Louise looked from the marble to the kid. *Did this fifth grader just hit on me?* It reminded her of the time that Billy Hampton asked her to dance by telling her that she had pretty eyes. She had not been interested in him, either. Objectively, though, she knew he was not wrong.

She handed the marble back to Preston, who took another look at it himself before putting it back in his pocket.

"How did you hear about the marble guy?" Her mind was distracted by the money. Suddenly she was wondering how many marbles it would take to fill a lemonade cup. How many cups of marbles would it take to get to $500 for the summer?

"There was a sign on my way to baseball practice. It said, We Buy Used Marbles and then a phone number."

"Just used marbles?"

"I think that's what it said."

"What was the number?"

"I don't know. My mom didn't stop."

"Well, if you see it, write it down next time," rapping her knuckles lightly on the top of her lemonade stand, "and if you bring me the number, I'll hook you up with another glass of lemonade."

"Deal!" Preston finished his drink.

"Deal."

"Do you have a garbage can for my cup?"

"I'll take care of it." Shannon wondered about the ethics of washing the cup and reusing it, since it had been a freebie and all.

"That really hit the spot!"

"It's the good stuff."

"You can say that again. Thanks!"

"No worries," Shannon Louise said, the sun above now bothering her to the point of putting on her sunglasses. "See you next time."

Chapter 10

Thomas Abell could not remember the last time he was proud of his little girl.

For starters, it had been close to two decades since she had been that little. It was hard to believe how the time between fourteen and hopelessness had flown past even as it was hard to believe that some of the worst moments had ever ended. In high school he had known about the underage drinking and the drug use, at least he thought that he understood based on his own experiences at that age.

Moderation and even experimentation he could understand.

His little girl showed no restraint.

College had been a tremendous waste of time and money, and in the end all it had really resulted in was a huge debt and an STD. His daughter did not know that her father was aware of that filthy fact - a disease and an experience which she had thankfully put in her past - because he had found out through a billing statement sent by their insurance company in the annual statement.

So many other little disappointments and betrayals, sordid and illicit actions the 64-year-old dad had already forgotten some; still, he could recall the most recent disappointment.

At times when she was a problem, or when he knew of her problems, he always blamed himself. If not the late age at which he had fathered a child or some punishment for fathering a child prior to committing to marriage with her mother, then surely some lapse in his parenting skills was to blame. He and his wife had a happy marriage, had been so for as long as their daughter could remember, and he had so many fond memories of the problem that had at one time been his little girl.

His wife, Mabel Abell, nee Whittaker, shared similar guilt. Like her husband, she too had waited until later in life to have children, and she had also kept herself busy, working her way up the corporate ladder to a position as vice-president of foreign acquisitions for a local multi-national corporation.

Mabel was a winner, and she felt a personal shame in the antics of her adult daughter, a clear loser. No grandchildren to spoil, no accolades from work or degrees from college to brag about. Nothing to show for 32 years of parenting.

By far it was her worst investment of time or money; by far it was her worst defeat.

As a kid, Mabel had also been a precocious winner. Her father had been an ace marble player in his day, and his little girl had a knack for the game as well. Though her heyday was during the waning years of the era when playing marbles was still popular, she had so completely dominated the competition in her neighborhood that she was a local legend in her own right before the age of eleven. Local TV celebrity Ruth Lyons even featured the marble ace once on her program, and that was where the moniker she wore so proudly as a kid was first coined: Mabel the Marble Marvel.

Mabel the Marble Marvel so completely wiped out all the competition on a seven-block radius around her home that she quickly outgrew the game and moved on to a game with another round ball, golf. Any good marble worth having in the neighborhood was in her possession, and for a long while she would have said her bag of marbles was her most prized possession.

Then, she got good at golf, middle school became high school which became college which in turn led to graduate school and pretty soon the bag of marbles just became one of the many things she lugged from place to place, new apartment to new home.

If asked, Mabel honestly would not have been able to tell you the last time she even thought about her bag of marbles or the moniker she had once worn like a superhero wears a cape, but all those memories and all that pride and confidence and everything else that went into the glue and gray matter creating Mabel Abell was nonetheless inside her still. Occasionally, she would hear the name of that old tv program or see a game like Sorry that had little round balls made of glass – definitely not marbles – or even think about her own daughter and it would open a tiny window into reminiscing about the old days, but mostly what she had was a near bottomless well of the confidence that sprang from those victories she had as a little girl, the little neighborhood marble champion, Mabel the Marble Marvel.

No matter any other shortcomings in her life or no matter the depth of her disappointment in her daughter, Mabel knew that she would always have that confidence and expectation of being a winner.

Not even her downtrodden daughter could take that away...

Chapter 11

D eb Vilitch closed the door of her office and placed the tray of marbles on her desk. The desk was an old one, but it was original to the room and had not followed her from her last assignment in Toledo. The other most visible piece of furniture in the room had come with her from northern Ohio, and it had been with her in every city before that.

About a yard tall and slightly less square, squat enough to fit easily through a standard doorframe, the dark wooden artifact had a stone top that was smooth, black, and reflective. The sides of the pedestal were made of wood, reddish brown, and polished smooth save for the engravings and designs carved about the four sides. Although it appeared to be a simple piece, the closer one looked the more details emerged to be seen, more levels and raised edges and craftsmanship.

Though not obvious, the top was removable and inside was concealed a void. The object would not have looked out of place in a church or a museum or even in the bedroom of a moderately nice house. Looked at from afar, one could even suggest it being a column suitable for holding a vase of flowers.

Inside the small office, the altar merely looked like an unused counterspace.

The depth of the work, however, was within.

Not wasting time sitting in her chair, the appraiser turned to the altar and removed the stone top.

The stone slab was square like the top plane of its stand, and the color was as black as obsidian. Though heavy, the demon appraiser had no trouble sliding it out of place and then onto the ground where she leaned it against the wooden piece itself.

Perfectly circular, the void had a diameter that filled almost the entirety of the artifact, nearly touching the four edges at its widest arc. Almost paper-thin at one point four times, the wooden sides were not as thick as one would have assumed.

None of that was of note, however, once the slab was fully removed.

Empty to the ground, the squat, square pillar with the circular opening held at the bottom what looked like a fiery pit of brimming molten stone. One did not have to look directly into the cylinder of the thing to feel the malevolence and heat burning within. Deb Vilitch looked inside, basking in the warmth of its depths' reach. She could spend hours doing so, and often she did, just gazing into the mesmerizing surface, at once as unsettling as it was comforting.

Now, though, at times like this, when she had her own offering and truly working, the anticipation and eagerness for acceptance – a disappointment that was always expected to show – was palpable.

The appraiser turned her attention back to the tray of marbles on the desk.

To her, each marble's shine was just as apparent as it had been minutes ago when the sale had taken place. Not that she really cared about such things, especially nowadays, but it was obvious to her that the seller had little if any connection to this collection. Regardless, this batch of marbles was going to make for the most wonderful transaction.

The goal of her, concern, was not to make a profit in the conventional sense; with a well-financed benefactor, money was never an option.

The ends to these means was something else.

Her eyes made another quick glance across the collection in her hands. This was a fine set indeed. Before she turned back to the artifact, she grabbed one of the shiny marbles, not the brightest one in the bunch, but certainly one of the better memories enshrined there. With a paranoid look over her shoulder, towards the pedestal and not the door, Deb Vilitch snatched up the single marble and without thought slipped it into her mouth where it would disappear forever as surely as if it were consumed by the fiery void within the artifact.

The momentary ecstasy in her brain exploded and she thought that she could never be more satisfied. Mabel the Marble Marvel! The Ruth Lyons Show! A childhood period of dominance! What a special connection to each there had been. *Oh, this was going to be quite the offering!*

In a second that euphoria passed, and she scrambled to gather the tray from the desk. Turning quickly but with a grace that would never allow a spill, the appraiser offered no words before dumping the entire tray of marbles into the void, the pit of eternal fire in which they would be consumed, destroyed, and their associated memories forgotten.

The fire did not burn any brighter once its offering was accepted, but as the last of the orbs sank below the surface and seemingly through the floor, there was satisfaction from her actions.

The transaction was complete.

As if paying a penalty for the indiscretion of taking one of the morsels for herself, the relief from a job well done was interrupted by the buzzer indicating it was time for another appraisal.

Though there was an emptiness from having the satisfaction of the last transaction cut short, she knew that such was the nature of the beast. Having learned long ago not to count her losses, no matter how painful, she was just happy to have more food for the fire. Good providers were given thicker skin, more insulation from the void while being more embraced by the fire itself.

It was shaping up to be a pretty good Wednesday after all.

Chapter 12

O n Wednesdays, Mabel Abell had lunch with her team in Conference Room A. Long a tradition, the gathering was always a productive way to keep her group working toward the common goal of exceeding all expectations. It was also a great way to build comradery and open communication between the team members themselves. The company floated the tab, but Mabel would always have her assistant present one treat as if it was a gift from one of her own personal accounts.

"And these," Tabitha Sorrenson, Mabel's trusty assistant said to the group, carefully placing one perfect, domed pastry in front of each team member, "are the Chocolate Torts from Taste of Belgium up at Findlay Market in OTR. Mabel picked these up specifically for us today."

Tabitha had actually been the one to make that trip to the market.

"Look at the gold-leaf detailing!" one team member pointed out.

"They are just amazing," Mabel said. "Todd and I go to Findlay every weekend, and he just loves these things. Because I also must manage his waistline, I only allow him to purchase them on special occasions."

The team laughed in unison.

"Anyway, this for us is a special occasion. We are here to celebrate a little victory today." Mabel stood to better address the group. Her own ego was the largest in the room, but her secret to success was to suppress projecting that from herself and stamp out the very idea from those beneath her. By always approaching subordinates on their level, she never tempted them to soar at hers.

"Teamwork and leaving your ego at the door have always been hallmarks of success for every team I've ever led. Teamwork is counting on each other and doing so without ego is critical for us to acknowledge bad ideas. We all have bad ideas, and we all have failures, but there is no bigger failure than failing to admit the failure of a bad idea.

"Now, last month I had a bad idea," Mabel paused, a few people chuckled, a couple chided, one looked down, "I know, I know, but I did. One of you came to me, privately, and expressed your concerns in a professional and competent way. You convinced me to see your perspective, and we abandoned my idea and pivoted another way.

"Some of you know where I'm going with this."

Half the group nodded in acknowledgement and the rest nodded simply in agreement; one of the thirteen could feel their cheeks beginning to blush in anticipation.

"This week, some numbers came in and confirmed that the pivot was the right move, and not only saved our division a loss but also netted us a pretty healthy gain." Mabel turned her attention toward her young colleague and wondered if she had ever been so proud of another person, certainly never of her own daughter.

Mabel paused, but not for effect.

She could not recall the name of her daughter and doing so suddenly seemed very important.

Looking away from the person with whose eyes she had just been looking – they themselves would later describe the moment as if everything behind their boss's eyes just went blank – Mabel uncharacteristically started playing with her thumbnail, using it to pick at her teeth.

Her attention was now completely turned away from the group seated around the table in Conference Room A.

"Mabel… is something wrong?" the questioner was not the person with whom she had broken eye contact, but the team member who had been most closely seated to the vice president.

Mabel did not acknowledge the question. Uncertainty in herself had never been an issue for Mabel, but now she was seemingly filled with the stuff, any rational thoughts she had were now drowning in doubt. There were other things she could not remember, other details and events that she would never again recall, other names and places and even attitudes. Mabel's ego, for instance, had left the room, never to return. Sense of self, the warm blanket of childhood memories, dreams and aspirations all gone with it.

Like a house of cards, the removal of even the most minor memories or connections can cause the crash of a mind, of a self, maybe even of a soul. Mabel's marbles were the bedrock upon which her very sense of being was built. Without those memories and associated accomplishments, who was she?

Who was her daughter? She had a name.

Mabel did not look at her team anymore, even as they all eventually stood to surround and comfort her, each trying to make sense of whatever it was that was happening to their beloved boss.

Was she having a stroke?!

What are we going to do?

Call 911!

Mabel did not look at any of them. Determined to remember, though without the will or confidence to do so, without the memories even there to be found, the winner formerly known as Mabel Abell, Vice President of Foreign Acquisitions, and, in a much younger though no less important life, Mabel the Marble Marvel, was taken down in a game of marbles by a daughter who's name she would never again recall.

Chapter 13

===== 1 =====

T eddy Hahn looked at the address in front of him and confirmed it with the address he had written on the paper. It was hard for the old man to believe that this was the right spot.

In his mind, he had been picturing an antiques store or a place where he could at least browse at items as if in a pawn shop or something. That was not the case at this place where he was told to come sell his marbles.

There was one word that came to mind when he looked at the outside of this building and its unmarked front door: abandoned.

Undeterred, and with his two quarters already in the meter, Teddy tried the door and, when it opened, walked inside.

The new word that came to mind was sterile. The paint and everything seemed a little faded, even for being white, but the place did not seem dusty, and it certainly was in no way cluttered. Like the woman before him, he also noticed the sign above the window indicating that all sales were final.

The window opened and the receptionist smiled. "How may we help you today?"

Teddy extended his jar of marbles. A standard Ball jar, the 16-ounce size, was about half-filled with colorful balls of glass.

"Well now, that is quite the jar!" the receptionist said.

Teddy chuckled slightly. The man's enthusiasm broke the awkwardness of the introduction, and Teddy let his guard down as to this sterile room being certified or not by the Better Business Bureau. He smiled at the receptionist. "Yeah, I guess I collected a few over the years."

"I can see that."

"And these are the real deal, too," Teddy said proudly, as much trying to justify their value to him as opposed to goosing higher their monetary worth to the business. "Not a one of them came from one of them *200 marbles for twenty bucks* deals that you can find on the Internet, neither."

"So, do you already have an expected price for these based on your own Internet search?"

Teddy lost his grin; *Ok, this is how they get you.* He was not quick to answer. "No, not exactly."

"Well either way," the man said, waving his hands as if he could care less. He shrugged his shoulders before continuing. "Bound to be plenty of good ones in there, anyway. Let me ring our appraiser."

"Appraiser?"

"Yes, she will take a look at what you have there, and she will make you an offer. I'm certain I would have mentioned that on the phone." With that, the receptionist slid the window shut.

Unsure how to process the interaction or jibe it with the setting, the old man again looked around at the empty room. In his mind, Teddy had been expecting to find a pawn shop or some other antique-type place where he could just as easily spend whatever money he earned from selling his marbles. Probably better this way.

Price was another thing he considered. Teddy had gone online and found that there were indeed some rare marbles out there, some true antiques, but he doubted that his were any of those. He did have one specific marble about which he was curious, one that he had found in a box he once purchased at an estate sale and that he now had in a pocket separate from his own collection. He would have called it an alabaster cloud taw if he had seen it as a kid, but to his adult mind the antique appearance, faded color, and larger size appealed to him. It would not have surprised him if that one marble was worth more than all his own hard-won pieces put together.

He had a few victories at other auctions, so it was reasonable to assume that such could again be the case. There had been one time when a box of books he bought for ten bucks at a garage sale netted him sixty bucks for just one of them on E-Bay.

Without much to look at, Teddy took time to consider his marbles in the jar.

He was not lying to the receptionist when he said that he had come by his marbles honestly. There had been a couple starter marbles that he inherited from his dad and older brother once the older sibling outgrew the game, but the rest were ones that Teddy claimed and then used to acquire more. His circle of friends was limited, and they had lots of options besides playing marbles with any prolonged consistency. From what he could recall, most of his real playing had happened in a three-year span that ended around the 7th grade.

Teddy had losses, too; in life and in marbles he had experienced loss, and he did his best to take what lessons he could from defeat as much as victory. Being at least a decade older, he also would have been familiar with the name Mabel the Marble Marvel, but their days of playing never coincided. To his way of recollecting, though, his run had ended on a pretty good streak and his collection of marbles was by the end as large as it had ever been throughout what he would have considered his playing career: what he now had in his clear Ball jar representing that treasure, that legacy.

What was the price for something like that, those memories separate though yet intrinsically linked to the marbles? Looking at the colorful orbs of glass did bring back a flood of memories, but Teddy did not think that parting with one would mean losing the other.

The only door in the room, the door from the street, opened.

"I apologize for your wait," the appraiser lied as she walked in the room. She did not mind when her clients were made to wait just the slightest bit. Of course, she would never allow one to wait so long as to lose their nerve or grow overly impatient and leave, but there were some, like this old coot here, who needed this time to reminisce. To her way of looking at things, this was akin to letting things warm up a little bit, maybe enhance whatever else was already there. "I had to feed my meter right quick. I advise and hope that you did so before entering. You know how they are about that nowadays."

"Oh, I know what you mean," Teddy said. "That's how they get you. Parking on a public street should be free. It's a free country."

"I could not agree more." She paused just long enough to extend her arm and open hand. "My name is Deb Vilitch; I am the appraiser."

"Nice to meet you, ma'am." Teddy was gentle when embracing the woman's grip, but he was quickly taken by the sturdiness of her grasp; not painful or overbearing, but firm and unyielding. "Teddy Hahn."

"Yes, well," the appraiser said, pulling her hand away, her eyes already drawn to the glowing jar of joy in the man's other hand, "let's get down to this, then." Already wispy from her previous intake, Deb Vilitch reminded herself to gather her emotions and play her poker face with this one. The man's collection was impressive.

"Here's what I got," Teddy said, holding up the jar of marbles.

"I see that," she said, raising her eyebrows in a quick twitch, "let me take a closer look then."

As she took possession of the jar, the window slid open, and the receptionist handed out a tray identical to the one as before. Without much hesitation, but with a good amount of care, the appraiser emptied the contents of the jar across the felted confines of the area.

"Well look at some of these gems," she said, her voice betraying the slightest bit of anticipation, "you have had these in this jar awhile I take it."

"I stored them in an old bag, actually. I just put them in the jar because I wasn't attached to the glass the way I was to the bag."

"I understand. Regardless, though, how old were you when you quit playing if you don't mind me asking?"

"You know, I was just thinking before you came in, I guess, and it must have been around seventh grade, maybe the summer going into it, when my friends and I started caring more about football and cheerleaders than any of the other things we also used to do back then to pass the time. Hard to collect swings on a rope, though, I guess." He laughed out loud just the slightest bit.

The appraiser picked up one of the marbles. It was a green shooter with a white planet swirl. A nice marble. Again, like the one she consumed in her office, this one was not the brightest in the bunch, but it did have an above average glow. "Like this baby here. I bet you did some numbers with this one."

Teddy looked at the little marble, taking it into his palm as she allowed him to again have it so close to his grasp. "This one I think I called the Green Typhon. It's got what we used to call a planet swirl, but all the war movies back then talked about typhons, and I guess I thought that sounded a lot cooler. I used this one to win that one there," he pointed toward the lower corner of the pile scattered across the tray, "the brown aggie in the corner. Mason Lowry never played again after that. Most of us stopped playing not too long after that, I guess. Suppose that's why I still have them all; I ended on a hot streak." Teddy again laughed out loud. He was having a good time with this marble lady.

Deb Vilitch, the appraiser, the marble lady, demon, did not need this customer to tell her which marble was the one associated with the Green Typhon he was holding in his hand. As the man spoke, retelling his tale and backtracking through the network of his brain to retrieve that specific memory, she could watch as the glow from that one marble increased by a factor unmeasurable to almost anyone else on this plane of existence. The two marbles together had already increased in value.

"And that other green one there," Teddy said, "that one was my absolute favorite, my Green Baby, and I used it to get most of these marbles."

"I see."

Of course, in a perfect world, Deb Vilitch would have spent this long with the man talking about every single one of the marbles in his collection in the same way. In the end, however, a perfect world for her…, concern, was one that was inherently imperfect, and she was not ignorant to the fact that some customers could be lost by again connecting so ethereally with their possessions.

It was a fine line she walked with these people, and there were none better at walking it than Deb Vilitch, the appraiser. Personally, she did not mind the moniker of marble lady – better than the stamp lady or the furniture lady – she heard too many others in a week to fit so many placards on her official, impossible to get, business cards.

She held out her hand, palm upward, lest the man confuse her intent to pry from him the marble in his hand. That she had to do so little encouraging for him to willingly drop it into her grasp did not change the matter.

"That one there," Teddy said, pointing to a blue boulder in the center of the pile, "was probably my second-favorite. I had a lot of favorites, I guess. I got that one from my daddy and he said that it was old when he got it. I never played with it much, though; didn't want to take a chance on losing it."

"I see," she said. This was not a lie nor a euphemism; she had immediately been able to identify the most important marble in the group. It was impressive how the already bright orb was able to increase in brilliance as the man spoke of its value to him. She could not lose this one. "Please just give me a minute, and I'll be able to make you an offer."

For the first time since interacting with the receptionist, Teddy again felt on guard. For the first time, the lack of a second door concerned him. Was this woman about to walk away with his marbles? Was she going to pass them through the window and try to pull a switcheroo?

To his surprise, though, the appraiser remained in place and simply turned her attention to the tray of marbles in front of her. Her hands appeared to handle each of them, touching them at least, but without taking notes, it seemed impossible that she would be able to record any pertinent information about any of them. Teddy also noticed that she did not seem to be placing any of them aside as if special.

After a full minute of silence, the marble lady again spoke. There had been sixty-three marbles to appraise.

"Honestly, sir, this entire collection is impressive."

"Well thanks. I worked hard at something at one point in my life to get them, I guess."

"Ok then."

As before, the window slid open.

"We are prepared to offer you fifty-three hundred dollars for the lot."

"Well now that can't be right!" Teddy exclaimed. "You wanna give me five thousand dollars for this jar of glass marbles?"

"You can take the jar with you, sir." The appraiser smiled.

"We actually prefer it," the receptionist added.

"Well for that kind of money, I'll go clean up your sidewalk! Hell, I'd even clean your toilets!"

"So, we have a deal?" Deb Vilitch again extended her arm to shake the man's hand.

"We have a deal."

"Marvelous," she said, "I assume cash will be acceptable...?"

"Cash is king."

"Just sign this receipt, sir," the receptionist said. He already had a $5,000 bundle of fifties and 3 crisp $100 dollar bills in a stack.

All defenses dropped, Teddy signed the paper, took his copy, and picked up the money. He had held enough paper in his life to know that it was all real, and if it was not the right amount then it was certainly close enough as far as he was concerned. He supposed he would need to consider the taxes, but his accountant could deal with that next April. He dropped the money in the now empty jar.

Deb Vilitch smiled. "Thank you for stopping in sir, we will see you next time, I'm sure."

"That's all my marbles, so to speak..." Teddy stopped in mid thought. He was not having any ill effects from the sale; those would happen after the transaction was complete. He remembered the other marble he still owned, the one from the auction, the one in his pocket. He pulled it out, anxious to learn its worth. "I almost forgot about this one. I guess I did."

The smile never left her face, but the twitch in her eye again betrayed her. She was done with this seller, and she was ready to complete the true finality of this deal, after siphoning off her own little nibble, of course. The marble in this man's hand was nice, and it was an antique, and he probably could get some decent money for it on the Internet; to she and her employers, however, with he having no real connection to the thing, this marble was practically worthless, just pretty glass. Maybe during hard times, she could wring out some emotional value from the piece, but now was not those times; besides, compared next to the collection already in the tray, this lone marble may as well have been a splinter of glass.

To make him happy, she took it in her hand and examined the antique marble. "This is a European made Aggie. Honestly, we don't deal in that market too much. You could probably do better online."

"You won't even make an offer?" Teddy was not mad, and he was certainly not greedy, but a part of him still felt hurt and rejected by the lack of an offer.

"I wouldn't want to insult you, sir. The ones you had in the jar were worth so much more."

In some part of Teddy's brain, this made sense; in some part of his being - deeper than his brain could hope to reach - the scream of this truth's horror echoed unheard.

The appraiser bit her lip. Her new appraisal was the worth of this man leaving sooner than later. "It is very beautiful. I could buy it myself and have it set as a necklace. How about twenty-five dollars?"

"Twenty-five?" The amount would have seemed like a lot before he had over $5,000 in his jar. He scratched his cheek, confused by the turn of events.

"You really could do a lot better on the Internet. There is a specific market for them, just not ours." She handed the marble back to the man.

"I understand," Teddy said, taking the marble and dropping it into the jar with the cash.

"Thank you for understanding."

"Oh, no problem," Teddy said as the woman led him to the door.

"Well, you have a nice rest of your day, then."

"You too, ma'am." Teddy walked out the door but stopped long enough to turn back one last time. "I'll tell my friends about you!"

The appraiser smiled and thanked him, but she knew that was not going to be true.

Unfortunately for them, their business model did not generally allow for first-hand referrals in that way.

Chapter 14

"Y ou're telling me they just what...had all that cash ready to give you? No questions asked?" Jake Branch was not your happy, neighborhood weed dealer. His brand of predatory behavior took his customers to a deeper level of isolation than could be offered from a chronic supply of nature's grass. Dealing primarily in pharmaceuticals and high-grade opioids like heroin and fentanyl, Jake was responsible for more death than one man should ever be allowed to dispense.

For the first time, he saw the extent of the cash that this woman had brought into his house. When she had reached out and said that she fell into enough cash for a serious hook up, he had assumed that maybe she had a hundred or two hundred dollars to blow. The amount of money she was pulling out of her Crown Royal bag, though, was so much more than that.

"Just like that," the woman said. She had injected a couple times before, but never had the effects been so mild and long lasting. Every other experience had been, for her, a quick trip through euphoria before passing out and waking up wanting more, often with the taste of vomit in her mouth or evident by the mess around or even on her.

Now, this time, the more seemed to just keep coming.

"For a bag of marbles?" The man was less concerned about the woman on the verge of overdosing on his couch than he was about her bag of money ending up in his hand.

She nodded her head. Everything felt good; every part of her being and body tingled. It was nice to have that balance in her life, her body and her mind quiet.

"And what was the address again?"

WE BUY USED MARBLES

56

Confused, the woman slowly blinked her eyes. She looked around to see if she was still in this man's house. They still seemed to be in the same place.

"Where is this place?" He wished that he had confirmed this information before letting her get too far gone. He knew the area she had mentioned before, but at the time he had not really been paying attention to the details of her story. He also knew that street corner and could not recall ever seeing a store that would buy or sell marbles. There was a trading card and coin store down the street where he had sold for cash some merchandise that he himself had traded for a little smack, but he could not picture such a store on that section of street, especially on the corner.

He doubted the coin store bought marbles.

Maybe they had left and went elsewhere? She thought to herself through the fog of delight. *It was possible that they were somewhere else. Anything was possible now, it seemed.*

Lightly, as far as he was concerned, he slapped her across the cheek.

Her eyes opened fully, but the gaze was still mostly vacant. "Where?"

"The. Marble. Store," he said, articulating each word. "Where is it."

Oh that. She smiled again before mumbling the address.

Pulling it up on his phone and losing momentary interest in her, he saw the exact corner he had been picturing. Though he still could not visualize the place, he did not really go that way too often and marbles were not on his radar.

Not until now, anyway.

When he spoke, it was almost to himself. "That's what I thought you said."

His attention was again fully on the bag of money; *there was more where this came from.* Robbery was not his specialty, but he had a dependent friend who excelled at breaking and entering. Worst case they get interrupted by what, an old guy secretary or some accountant lady?

First, he'd make a call to his best friend, then he'd show the unconscious customer the good time she didn't know she was missing. If she was nice, he might even send her off with another little push before turning her loose on the streets; she would not be leaving with her bag of money, though; their brand of friendship was not going to last that much longer.

"Jim, this is Jake, want to make some easy money tonight?"

Chapter 15

Deb Vilitch wasted little time scurrying into her office. As soon as the door was closed, she set the tray of marbles on her desk. With her back to the altar, she picked up the two marbles associated with the seller's story, the green typhon and the brown aggie. Their glow had not dimmed by any considerable amount since the man told his tale, sold the marbles, and left on his way.

Her mouth watered, lusting for the morsels in her hand. She knew that taking any memento was prohibited, and taking two was just plain greedy, but she could not help herself.

She weakened her resolve by consuming the one earlier, and it had been so surprisingly tasteful! Even more than she had expected or hoped. She would need two more just to equal the complexity and power of that previous taste.

She popped both marbles in her mouth at once, swallowing each whole.

The rush through her body was surely worth any eternal time thinking otherwise. So strong and so fresh, certainly fresher than her previous delight, and in some ways just as satisfying. Perhaps more satisfying! With such levels of pleasure weakening her knees and causing her to immediately sweat, she did not try to gather herself for a full minute before remembering her job and standing erect.

She wiped her forehead with her arm before again doing so with her hands, one hand for each side of her face.

Composed, and with a still glowing pile before her, she turned and removed the stone top from the pedestal. Without thought or ceremony she dumped the contents inside and watched as the last one disappeared into the fiery void forever. Only tales escaped this pit, and such stories were never told by those on the other side.

Chapter 16

S hannon Louise finished putting away the last of her business for the day. Her last bit of business coincided with one of her daily chores, and along with the dirty dishes she included in the dishwasher her lemonade pitcher, stirring spoon, and anything else sticky before pushing start.

For what seemed like the fiftieth time that day she again washed her hands.

She wondered if the stickiness would ever truly come clean.

$22.00. Another average day in terms of money, but $6.50 of that total had been either *keep the change* or just a plain *here's a tip, kid*. So, the reality was that her sales numbers were underperforming. She also noticed that her box of lemons was now less than half, and some of the lemons seemed crushed and not firm as had been the ones on top. The sugar was holding out, but even that would need to be replenished sooner than later, certainly before the cups.

Frustrated at the pace and the fact that the cash she already made was essentially already spent, the young entrepreneur turned her attention to finding the marbles that she knew existed somewhere within the confines of her home.

It took less than fifteen minutes of searching to find the bundle she sought. Just as she remembered, there were at least fifty colorful marbles in the clear baggy; there were eighty-three.

To her untrained eye, even the plain ones had flair.

Like the other woman we already met, Shannon Louise took the marbles for herself without regard to matters of ownership; unlike that tortured soul, though, she did know for a fact that neither of her parents cared a hoot about the bag of marbles that happened into their way by chance and happenstance. Hopeful that any money made would at least help to offset the costs of resupplying her summer business, Shannon tucked her newest investment in a safe place and washed up for a night of reading and watching television.

All she needed now was that kid from over on Benz showing up with the number for the marble guy. With any luck, her chance encounter with Preston would allow her to retire from her business a few days or maybe even weeks earlier than planned.

Chapter 17

T he kid from over on Benz, Preston, finished his last swim of the day. Tomorrow was a practice day, and he would not be allowed to swim until afterward. Practice was earlier tomorrow, so he would at least be able to swim at some point, but he was more concerned about being able to get the number for the marble guy. The thought occurred to him in the pool, and it was the idea of not wanting to forget that made him get out and dry off.

Before he even got dressed, he found a piece of paper and a pencil, both of which he stuffed inside his baseball glove. Smart beyond his years, Preston understood his weaknesses and tried to minimize them whenever possible. As a 10-year-old, he did not exactly think in those terns, but that was nonetheless how he processed some of his actions: keeping the pen and paper there would not only give him something to write the number on, but, perhaps as importantly, would also remind him to look.

He doubted that would be a problem, though. Shannon Louise the lemonade girl, the cute 7th-grader two years his senior, seemed genuine about also wanting the number for the marble guy. He supposed that he had other reasons for wanting to have an excuse for again talking to Shannon Louise – a free glass of the good stuff - but his true motivator was simply to have a partner in crime, so to speak, someone else to at least stand there and help make the all-important first call.

It was easy to picture that girl being his partner in crime. Preston could also imagine his other newest friend, David from baseball, remembering their talk and being excited. He did not suppose that bringing friends would make his marbles – if he ever found them – to be worth less because he had also supplied more. If anything, it was easier to imagine the marble guy giving him a little extra for bringing in more business.

Either way, with a group, on a friend date, but preferably not all alone, the young 5th grader was going to see what the marble guy was all about. If nothing else, he had at least one good item to offer for sale, and he was still confident of finding more.

Both of his parents were home, so they all ate dinner together. They had been commenting on the news, specifically a story about a local man who was killed that afternoon in Indiana.

"So what, he just drove until he ran out of gas...?"

"That's what the news said."

"And how did he die?"

"Just wandered out into the road," Haynes shook his head as if he knew the man. "They said he was old, so he must have just gotten confused and stumbled into traffic."

"Poor guy."

"Yeah, really makes you think." Preston's dad was not sure about what lesson he was pondering, but it did give him an appreciation for his age and his ability to keep his car filled with gasoline.

"It sure does."

"What happened to the man?" Preston asked.

"Nothing, Kiddo," Haynes said, insulating his son from the truth.

"Nothing good," Janay said, certain that their son was not stupid and had heard enough to already surmise the truth.

"And how was your day?" Haynes asked, changing the subject while turning to his son.

"It was pretty good."

"Do any swimming?"

"Yeah, a little."

"Remember, no swimming tomorrow."

"I know dad," Preston said, "not until after practice."

"What time is your practice?"

"One o'clock."

Haynes looked at his wife. "I can probably get off to take him if you can pick him up."

"I was actually going to see if you could get off early to pick him up after practice." Janay looked from her husband to her son. "We talked about this, and I already asked Aunt Gina if she could take him."

"Oh," Haynes said. "Yeah, I could probably do that."

"Able to just come and go at work whenever you want to now...?"

"I'm actually starting to get real fed up with this job," Haynes wiped the last bite from the corner of his mouth. "I updated my Linked-In profile and signed up for ZipRecruiter."

"What?!" Janay seemed surprised. That her husband had been threatening as much for the last two months did not mean that she had taken any of it seriously. Could their family afford him taking a new job?

"We've talked about this."

"I know, but I'm surprised you've actually taken steps."

"Oh, I'm taking steps." He tried to play, but his wife seemed more serious about the matter.

"Well don't take any leaps until you know where you're going to land."

"I have never, not had a job."

"Well don't start now." Shaking her head, she took a small bite of her meal. It no longer tasted as good. "I mean, it took you two years to get that job."

"I've never not had a job."

"That's not what I'm saying."

"That's what it sounded like."

"We've never not had bills, that's what I meant to say. My apologies."

"I've been there for two years. I'm ready for a new challenge."

"A new challenge…?"

"Yeah."

Janay looked at her husband, locking eyes with him. She had suspicions about his faithfulness, and she supposed that he had a few questions of his own, but now those doubts were mingled with concerns for the day-to-day well-being of her family, at least of she and her son. "And this is your decision?"

"Of course," Haynes said, looking up, surprised and indignant. "What are you trying to say."

"Well, it wasn't that long ago that you were reprimanded for…" she looked at her son and then back at her husband, "well, you know what for. This isn't more of that or some unfinished business from before…?"

"You are too much sometimes."

"Just sometimes?"

"Most times."

"So, this is just you wanting a new challenge?"

"That's what I said. New challenge, fresh start, however you want to classify it."

Shaking her head, Janay tossed her napkin on her plate and stood from her chair. "Preston, you can get up when you finish your cauliflower."

"Ok, mom." Preston loved his mom's cauliflower casserole. Finishing the few remaining pieces would not be a hardship.

"Your aunt will be here at 12:30, so make sure you have yourself ready tomorrow."

"We're going to get there way too early."

"Then you won't be late, will you."

"And plan on me picking you up at three o'clock, slugger," Preston's dad added.

"One of us will be there when you're done."

Preston did not see his parents exchange nasty glares. "Will Aunt Gina drive the same way you went the other day?"

"I suppose so. There's only so many ways to get there."

"Ok."

"Worried about getting lost?" Haynes asked.

"Yeah," Preston said, telling himself that it was not a lie; every drive with Aunt Gina was an adventure.

"Which way did you go?"

"The same way you would go from here."

"Oh."

"You'll get there just fine," Janay said, her attention again focused on her son. "Just be ready when your aunt gets here."

"I will be mom."

"Ok," she bent over to kiss her son on the forehead, "I'm going to take a shower and then go to bed. I'll call you at noon tomorrow to remind you to get ready."

"I'll be ok, mom."

"Ok, well then I'll just call to say how much I love you."

"Ok, mom. Love you too."

When his mom was gone and safely upstairs, Preston broke the silence with his dad. "Do you know where mom put all the stuff she brought from grandpappy's house? Is it all up in the attic?"

"Like what are you looking for?"

"I think that he used to have a bag of old marbles. I just wanted to look at them again."

"Yeah, I kind of remember seeing that," Haynes said to his son.

"Where do you think they're at?"

"I don't know. Did you ask your mom?"

Preston considered his answer. "Yeah, she didn't know either."

"Probably up in the attic, or maybe in her closet. She keeps lots of things jammed in there."

Preston nodded but did not confirm what they both knew. "What about in the garage? Do you think she put anything out there?"

"I doubt it. Your grandpappy had lots of old books and things, and the garage is too hot and cold for storing things like that out there."

"So, the attic is better for that?"

"Well, not much better, but yeah, probably so."

"Oh."

"I'll tell you what, kiddo. If we have time, I'll take you up in the attic on Saturday or Sunday and we can look through some old dusty boxes together. How does that sound?"

"Pretty good, dad, pretty good."

"Sounds good to me too, son." Haynes reached across the table and rubbed Preston's head. "And tomorrow plan on it being me who picks you up after practice."

"Ok dad."

Chapter 18

"Christ, this was a mess," the highway patrolman was pulling down the caution tape while the sheriff's deputy was picking up the traffic cones and burnt-out flares.

"You can say that again," the deputy agreed. "Never seen anything like this."

"I see accidents every day, but yeah, this one was different, alright."

"I told the sheriff that we had everything cleaned up, you know, all the pieces and everything, but I don't think we could ever really get all the pieces. You know."

"Oh, they'll be finding pieces of that guy until Labor Day."

"Do you think it was a suicide?"

"I thought about that, but did you see all the money the guy had just sitting there on his front seat?"

"Yeah," shaking his head, the deputy again tried to make sense of it all. "Over five thousand dollars in a mason jar."

"I think I'd spend that before I'd just end it all by walking into traffic."

"Yeah, none of it makes sense, though."

"All that money, and cash, at that."

"And no gas."

"And no gas."

"But don't forget about the marble."

The highway patrolman laughed. "Yeah, don't forget about the marble."

"Probably the key to the whole case."

The two lawmen stopped their somber chores to look at one another and laugh. The urge, desire, and need to release what was inside was simply too much to hold back any longer and laughing was better than crying.

Had they known the truth, they probably would have continued laughing just to keep from going mad.

Chapter 19

"It's just a door."

"I can see that, but what about the alarm?"

"I don't think it has one." The man showed the inactivity on his handheld electromagnetic monitor. "No electricity, no alarm."

"This place is holding serious cash, though. It has to have an alarm."

"So you say."

"Oh I say." Jake looked over his shoulder to ensure they were still alone. The back door was situated almost perfectly for a break-in; there was little light and no visibility from either the road or the alley. The closest parking lot did not offer a particularly good view, either. "So, let's get a move on, then, if you are so sure."

Jim pulled a little tool from his pocket and began to work at the lock on the door. He trusted his buddy to come through on this tip, but nothing about the ease of this caper screamed big payday. No cameras. No electronics on the door. No security lights around the perimeter of the crappy building. Nothing to indicate the presence of any treasure, much less cash.

At the end of the day, they were taking the word of one of the man's stupid junkies.

The lock surrendered quickly, and Jim was careful to finish opening the door with as much ease and silence as possible. Before touching anything else, he put his gloves back on. "We're in."

Jake was first into the building, his gloves leading the way. Entering from the back, the men were privy to a view of the business that the customers never witnessed.

Though not as barren as the front waiting room, the back space was not much to look at and, in most ways, worse. A couple of filing cabinets stood against one wall and a desk against another. Two closed doors were next to each other on the near wall. The only window in the room was on the far wall, and it was the sliding window that opened into the waiting room. There was a phone on the wall next to the window and four wooden trays stacked on the counter under it. Between the window and the phone there was a little button that rang a buzzer in the back office.

There were no cameras needed to watch the action unfold.

Jake walked over to the filing cabinets while Jim started rifling through the desk. In one drawer, Jim found a stack of blank receipts. In another drawer, he found a bunch of pens. The bottom drawer, the deepest one and as big as the drawers in the filing cabinets, was filled with jars of liquid that looked like homemade wine. Always willing to try anything, but unsure of the contents – and needing to take something – Jim grabbed one bottle. He walked away with all the drawers still at least partially open.

Jake did not have better luck with the filing cabinet. One drawer was completely empty. Another drawer was filled with garbage: discarded wrappers, an old McDonalds bag, Tupperware with moldy food inside. In none of them did he find anything of value or anything to even indicate that this was an operative business.

"What did you say they do here?" Jim questioned his friend. This venture was turning into a big turd burger.

"They buy old marbles."

"Old marbles?" Had his friend mentioned this detail before? He doubted it. The entire notion now seemed ridiculous, and he could not imagine the idea ever being taken seriously. Was he taking this risk for marbles?

"They buy old shit, ok," Jake replied. His blood was growing hot as he felt under the gun to deliver something. He looked around the room and noticed the drawer under the counter over by the sliding window. "Check this out!"

His steps buoyed by the discovery, Jake hastened to cross the room. "She said that the old guy opened a window and slid the cash through. It's got to be here."

"Not a very big drawer." Even from across the dark room, Jim could tell that there was nothing exceptional about the slim drawer under the counter. Even the counter itself was not very deep.

Disregarding his friend, Jake pulled the drawer open with enough force to break the lock he assumed was holding it shut. Instead, the drawer was not locked, and the would-be thief pulled it all the way out and off its tracks, sending the contents strewn across the wooden floor.

"Some paper clips and rubber bands and gum wrappers?" Jim asked, taking note of the new trash scattered on the dirty floor.

"God damn this place," Jake sneered. He picked up the phone, heard a ring tone, then replaced it in the cradle. He pointed angrily at the two doors. "In there."

Jim was the closest to that side of the room, so he first reached to open the door on the right. The knob turned easily and without much fuss; the door creaked slightly as he opened it fully. He shined his flashlight inside. "It's the shitter, bro, and it's disgusting."

Jake looked over his friend's shoulder; the bathroom was indeed disgusting. The smell alone was appalling, even to these two hooligans, and the sight of the stained toilet filled to the brim was not the most unappealing aspect of the little room. "If she's not already dead when we get back, I am going to kill that lying bitch."

"Yeah, man, whatever they got going on here isn't worth our time."

Jake looked back across the room at the sliding window. With no exterior windows on the ground floor, they had been unable to look at the front room of this building, the room on the other side of the sliding window, but that detail did seem to match up with the story she told him about this place. "One last door; one last crack at glory."

"Yeah, I'm sure this will be where all our dreams come true." Jim was not smiling as he spoke. He was over this caper before looking in the bathroom, and now he also felt mildly nauseous.

Jake opened the other door. The first thing his eyes set upon was the wood and stone pedestal in the center of the small room. If it did not have value, then it would at least look cool next to his patio bar.

Jim was right behind his friend, and he immediately set eyes on the desk.

Both men split towards the object of their attention.

Jake was the first to reach his destination, and he ran his fingers across the smooth surface of the black stone. The wood was also polished and smooth, but it did have texture in the form of designs and swirls and patterns carved across its surface. The artifact seemed sturdy.

Setting the found bottle of dark liquid down on the flat surface, Jim went through the desk with the same efficiency as he had the one out front, and his reward was similar. The biggest difference was that in the top drawer of this one he found a vial of perfume and a large bag of breath mints. The large brute did not need to spray the perfume in the air to know that he was not fond of its rosy aroma. He let the vial drop back into the drawer before taking three of the mints and shoving them in his pocket.

Jim looked back to Jake; his friend was crazy if he thought they were walking out of here with the big piece of furniture currently holding his attention.

"Let's get the fuck out of here, man," Jim said, already on his way to the door. No longer interested in a souvenir, he left the bottle of liquid on the desk.

"Hold on a second."

"Bruh, we aren't carrying that thing out of here."

"Come on, we can't leave here with nothing."

"It's probably bolted to the floor."

"I don't think so." Jake indicated this by tilting the thing ever so slightly off its base. Nothing, no gas, liquid, or light spilled out from the momentary gap created between it and the floor.

"Come on."

"You come on," Jake said, standing his ground. He was not bigger than his friend; breaking and entering was the area in which his friend was the specialist, too; still, of the two, there was no disputing who was the leader. Jim was a bad man, but Jake had the best connections when it came to pharmaceuticals, hallucinogens, and especially smack. If the dealer wanted this thing the thief would not be able to stop him, and they would be leaving with it.

Jim dropped his shoulders and walked back across the room. Stopping with the artifact between them, he grabbed the object higher than had Jake, causing the top stone to slide slightly off square.

"What the...?" Jake began.

"It's not attached," Jim said, helping the stone to move some more, revealing the first gap of the void within. "I think it's hollow!"

"That must be where they keep all their goodies," Jake declared, certain as if stating facts. "They make all the rest of this look like crap to throw us off."

Jake's words made Jim think of the bathroom and the revolting feeling that seeing and smelling it had brought upon him. Those same feelings again began to rise from his own void within.

The glow from inside the artifact did not spill out into the room, but it did fill the cylinder inside with a red hue. Jim's eyes continued to grow as wide as the hole he was revealing, and he was unaware when Jake's own hands began assisting in the total removal of the top from the base. Working together and without words, they set the top down and leaned it against the squat wooden column. Locked onto the fiery motion within, their eyes at no time left what they had already seen inside.

The pool at the bottom of the thing looked impossibly hot to be in the wooden object, and each was certain that any sense of its depth was an illusion. Bubbling and gurgling, the red stew of fire and rock conveyed action and heat that a mere glaze of liquid cannot contain, but it was clear from looking within that the top of that movement seemed to be as deep as the object itself.

"What the Hell is that?" Jim asked.

"It's...everything."

Unable to look away, Jim watched the action inside and understood exactly what his friend was saying.

Together, they both watched, transfixed by the beauty of confusion and desire and fire all swirling together in a fiery pit. Neither man felt satiated by the warm glow, and each was as sickened to their stomach by the motion and horror of what lay inside as they had been when looking at the bathroom.

Not catatonic, but not capable of looking away or even leaving, ever, both men simply stared into the void waiting for something to happen. They had no grand ideas; their proximity to death and its deepest reaches offered no epiphanies; indeed, each stood engulfed and transfixed by the sight as if hollow, themselves already void like the true depth of the cauldron below.

In fact, the two men were still standing there many hours later when the appraiser and the receptionist showed up at dawn's first light.

"Look at these two fools," Deb Vilitch said to her assistant. The appraiser and the receptionist got along, but they were not friends. A lifetime or two of working together had made them familiar with the ways of the other, but each would stab the other in the back to further the cause of the company.

"Haven't seen this in a while."

The appraiser shook her head. She did not have a morning coffee or any personal effects that she carried on her daily commute. "Nope."

"Do you want a hand?"

"I don't think so." Deb walked behind the closest one and looked closely at his face. His eyes did not try to register her presence or the movement around his space. With one hand high and the other hand low, she upended Jim into the artifact's gaping mouth. The top half of him was gone before his feet were even above the rim of the opening, but his body stayed whole as it was quickly swallowed like spaghetti in the pit.

Jake's eyes twitched at the sight of his friend's demise, but the glitch in his system was from the swirl of molten activity being momentarily obscured and altered by the body it had just consumed. His turn was next, but he felt no fear; that emotion had burned away a few hours earlier.

Now, if he could feel – or even tell tale of – one thing, it would be a sense of relief.

Were his mind actively aware, it would know that he was about to become one with the fervent activity below.

What he didn't know, as most people going to the same destination usually don't, was that once there he was going to have his own special place reserved and checking out was not an option.

When his eyes made their splash into the flow, all was beautiful; by the time his feet followed, that beauty was gone and all that remained was desolation.

Chapter 20

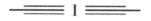

P reston would not have been able to quantify it, but never in his short life had he been as prepared for something as he was ready for the drive to practice on Thursday. He had a piece of paper. He had a pencil. He had his baseball glove. All he needed now was his aunt Gina to drive the right route.

"You know the way to get there, right?" Preston asked.

"Oh, I know the way." Aunt Gina was early, and her car smelled good. It also had a funny smell too, one that was different than the honey blossom spray that she used in her apartment as well as here in her car, but even that other smell was not horrible; Preston was pretty sure that his neighbors had some candles they burned on their porch that smelled the same way.

As she made her first two decisions behind the wheel, turning left and then turning right, Preston started to feel confident that everything was going to be ok. He considered asking his aunt if she had ever heard of the guy who buys marbles but thought better of it; if he mentioned it to her then there was a chance she would mention it to his mom.

At the next intersection, his aunt went straight. His mom always turned right.

"Aunt Gina…?"

"Yeah babe."

"Mom always turns there."

"Your mom has thought that way was a shortcut since we used to ride bikes," Gina said, waving away his concerns while keeping one hand firmly on the wheel. "It's quicker when you're on a bike, because you don't have to deal with this hill, but it's actually a longer route."

"Oh," Preston said, dejected. He knew that arguing with his aunt Gina was more pointless than doing the same with his mom; if he made his aunt mad then he would have to hear about it once from her and again later from his mom, too. Plus, he knew from experience that adults never like to turn a car around once they're heading in a direction.

As if racing her sister, Gina edged the gas pedal down enough to climb the hill as if it was flat. At the next intersection, she turned right and allowed the car to build up more speed as it sped back down what was basically the same hill. Preston did not really notice it, but as they approached the next intersection, Aunt Gina pointed across his face and towards the side window.

"See that red truck there," she said, the pride in her voice apparent, "we were behind that guy and now he's still waiting for two cars before him to go. "For the life of her, your mom will never learn that one."

Preston looked back as the intersection went past his side of the window. He was again familiar with where they were on the map, and he knew that the marble sign would be coming up soon. He readied his paper and pencil. His baseball glove was not the best desk, but he found a flat space that was more than large enough for a phone number; the young slugger already knew the subject matter on the sign.

As the road curved and turned and descended onward down, Preston sat alert.

"What is this?" Gina asked no one aloud. "Construction…?"

"We had this the other day," Preston said. They had seen the sign before stopping for the traffic. "It must be longer, today. We weren't this far back before."

"Oh," Gina said. Intent to not wait, she considered a different route. She had an idea that would probably not save them any time, but if it meant not waiting then she was all about maintaining constant motion. She put the car in reverse.

"Wait!" Preston exclaimed, his heart almost jumping out of his chest.

His aunt decisively stopped all movement of the car and put it in park. "What the dickens Preston!?"

"I'm sorry."

"Are you ok?"

"Yes," he said. Though happy that their retreat was halted, he immediately regretted his outburst. There was a good chance his mom would hear about that one.

"Then what the heck, kiddo?"

"It's stupid."

"You know you can tell your favorite aunt all about stupid."

"There's a sign for a comic book shop and I wanted to write down the name of it. That's why I brought this piece of paper."

"Oh," Gina said, now putting the car in park. "That's cool. We can wait, and I'll even drive slowly if you need me too."

"Thanks Aunt Gina."

"No problem little man." Gina winked at her nephew. "So, who is your favorite auntie…?"

Chapter 21

══ 1 ══

P ractice was more intense than it had been on the first day, but Preston was inspired by how much better he was hitting the ball than last year. Everything about the game seemed easier and all the little things that the coach asked them to do – like backing up a teammate on a throw – made more sense. He was shocked when he even got a few reps at third base!

This was one of the days when the joy of playing baseball outweighed floating in a pool.

After practice, his dad was there waiting so he felt rushed when David approached him in the dugout.

"How's it going, Preston?"

"Good. My dad's here. How are you?"

"I'm good. I wanted to see if you wanted to come over after practice on Saturday. Maybe you could bring your bike, then we could just ride home from here."

"My mom would never let me do that," Preston said. Though his mom was fine with her son having friends over, she was too protective of him to allow a sleepover like that, especially if they were going to be riding bikes home from practice.

"Oh," David said, disappointed.

"She would let you come over, though, if you'd be allowed. We could put your bike in the trunk, and then we could ride around my neighborhood."

"I would probably be allowed to do that!"

"I'd have to ask my mom, first."

"Ok."

"What's your phone number? I already have a piece of paper." Preston pulled the paper out of his pocket. He had left the pencil in his aunt's car, but the coach had a pen on top of his stack of papers.

After giving Preston his number, David noticed the other number on the page. "What is that number for?"

"That's the marble guy! My aunt slowed down so I could write it down! I don't think she was paying attention, though, because I told her that it was for a comic bookstore, and she never asked about it."

"I forgot you told me about the marble guy."

"Yeah," Preston said, looking through the dugout at his dad waiting for him. "But hey, I have to go; my dad is here."

"Ok. Call me when you talk to your mom."

"Ok, you check with your parents, too."

"They won't care."

"And find your marbles and we can go check this guy out."

"Ok! I will!"

Chapter 22

W hen Preston got home, his dad dropped him off and said he had to go back to work for a few hours. Only half listening, all he could think about was calling the number on the paper, the one written in pencil, not his friend's number written in pen. Once he was alone in the house, before he changed into his swimming trunks, he went so far as to pick up the phone and dial the first three numbers; each time, just as quickly, he hung up.

Unable to proceed, Preston decided to take a swim.

Baseball practice had been good, and he was confident that this year he was going to be better than some of the 11-year-olds. He knew that playing third base was still a stretch, at least starting, but already the coach had given him time at his favorite position. Not only that, but his entire team was somehow better than they had been the year before. He thought of all the 12-year-olds from last year's team, and he was surprised to realize that not one of them was irreplaceable. For everyone who left, a new player came along, and in almost every case, these new people were now better.

Not that the best 9-year-old like David could replace a 12-year-old like Rodney Friesinger, but all of last year's 11-year-olds were better than any of the older kids they effectively replaced.

In some ways he was proof of that himself; he had improved.

Confidence is a great thing for kids, and the small victories that Preston had today would be crucial in building every day that came after. These little successes in something as basic as Knothole Baseball would become memories around which he could build a life, as long as it lasted.

Preston was excited, too, about the two new friends he had already made this summer.

True, David was just a teammate, and so a friend by happenstance, but he supposed that sometimes chance works out the right way and things maybe do happen for a reason. That kid was cool, and Preston really hoped that his mom would let the new friend stay over Saturday after practice. Shannon Louise was not really a friend, but she too had been pleasant, and Preston liked the way the older girl talked with him. He also thought about how things worked out with his aunt and the phone number for the marble guy; his day was coming along about as good as any day he could have hoped to imagine.

Unencumbered by any adult thoughts or inhibitions, Preston spent the next twenty minutes splashing and swimming and floating and just relaxing in his parents' large above-ground pool. Today was a great day, and it was hard to imagine it getting better.

His thoughts returned to Shannon Louise and her lemonade stand. She had seemed serious about the phone number, and she had been willing to give him a free glass of her good stuff lemonade just to talk about it. It was not impossible to imagine that she would be willing to make the call to the number of the marble guy, too.

Doubting it was much, Preston again wondered how much his solitary marble might be worth.

By the time he was out of the pool and drying off, Preston had already decided on his next course of action.

Wearing his favorite t-shirt, Preston stuck the piece of paper and solo marble in the pocket of his shorts and set off on his bike. He still had at least two hours until his parents were home from work, and for a kid his age on summer break, that could be a lifetime.

He saw the lemonade stand before he saw Shannon Louise. She was inside washing her hands, and he noticed that her stand did not seem as tidy as it had been the day before. When she came out of her house, she was carrying two wet towels.

"Sticky mess?"

"Oh my gosh, I hate being sticky," Shannon Louise declared. "I just sold two cups of lemonade, and the kid spilled his all over my counter."

"That sucks. I'm sorry."

"Not your fault."

"Didn't he have a lid?"

"The dad didn't want one; the straw neither!" she said while wiping the cashbox under the counter first. "He was worried about the landfills or something."

"Didn't help your lemonade stand."

"Yeah right! But you know what really sucks? The dad expected me to just give his kid another one." She waved her hands in the air, the towels flowing wildly. "Can you believe that? They spilled it. They didn't want the lid. So it's somehow my fault and I should give them another one...?"

"They could have at least helped clean up."

"Right!?" She started wiping the top counter of her lemonade stand, her second attempt at removing the sticky-icky-ness. "I told him no, I wasn't giving him another one for free, and the dad was mad. I ended up giving the kid half of a cup and a lid and a straw. I think he was still mad when he left. He didn't tell me to keep the change."

"Your pitcher is almost empty."

"Yeah, this was my best day!" the young entrepreneur exclaimed. "I bet I made at least thirty bucks with tips."

"Oh wow! That's a lot of money."

Shannon Louise shrugged her shoulders. "It's above average."

"I had my second baseball practice today."

"Oh yeah." She was politely interested.

"Yeah, we're going to be way better this year than we were last year."

"Nice." Her wiping complete, Shannon used the half of the wet towel she had been preserving to again wipe her hands. They still felt the residue of stickiness.

"I got that phone number, too!"

"The marble guy?" She stopped wiping and looked at Preston.

"Yeah."

"Did you call him?"

"No, not yet."

"What are you waiting for?"

"I don't know."

"Do you want to call it now? We can use my phone."

"That would be awesome!"

"I found my bag of marbles, too." Shannon grabbed her money box in one hand and the towels in the other. She motioned for Preston to follow her towards the house.

"Sweet."

"Don't say that word. Please."

"Ok." Preston did not know that the word sweet made his new friend think about being sticky, but if the word bothered her then he could oblige by not saying it.

Shannon Louise had also done her homework. Though unsure of any real value within, she knew that her bag had several of the classic marbles that any collector would desire. She had cat's eyes – in boulder, shooter, and pee wee form – she had swirls and twirls and aggies and clay marbles and alabaster ones and even one made of ivory, though she did not know that. Her bag also had one marble made of steel; although she took that one out because she was certain that it would cheapen the value of the entire collection.

When they were in the kitchen, Shannon Louise did not hesitate to pick up the phone. She looked at Preston. "Break off the digits."

"What?" Preston asked, truly confused.

Shannon Louise sighed. "What's the number, kiddo."

The word hurt, just a little. Preston knew he was a kid, but the word enforced the idea that they were different, somehow separated. He pulled the paper from his pocket, again, and handed it to her without saying a word. "It's the one in pencil."

Already moving on and not even remotely aware of how she had just stabbed the dreams of her little friend, Shannon Louise dialed the number and prayed for a few days early reprieve from the lemonade stand. It was not impossible to imagine earning a week's worth of wages with one transaction.

Though pragmatic, she was still only twelve, and a kid could dream.

The phone answered on the second ring.

"Hello today."

"Hi," Shannon Louise said with all the confidence in the world, "I'm calling about the old marbles."

"The used marbles, yes."

"Yes," she said, picturing her bag full of them, each one surely useful if not exactly used. Was there even a difference worth considering? "What's the deal?"

"The deal?" the voice said, almost seeming to laugh out loud. "We buy used marbles. That's the deal."

"I mean, how does this work? Do we come to you?"

"That's usually how it works."

"Usually?" Shannon Louise did not want to miss out on an offer.

"We do not make house calls, not usually, no."

"Not usually," the young girl questioned, "but sometimes?"

"Do you want us to come to your home?"

She paused for a moment. Would that be a better option? If they had something like a backwards Doordash, then she could do nothing and have her cash and her couple days off delivered to her door. But that option might make her parents mad. They could understand trouble in the world, but not trouble in the house.

"I don't know, I suppose that depends. Do you have a store?"

"We have an address and a real bricks and mortar location and everything, yes."

The young girl did not recognize the sarcasm in the man's voice. "Ok, break off the digits, then."

"I'm sorry, what did you say?"

"Your address. What's your address. "Shannon Louise looked at Preston, her head shaking. Without transition, her expression changed, and her eyes grew as wide as her smile. "Guerley? Like Glenway and Guerley?"

Preston of course knew all about busy Glenway Avenue, but he had never heard of the other road.

"Great! And how late are you open?" Shannon pointed at the phone with her free hand, her head nodding with excitement. "Ok! Bye!"

"What did they say?" Preston asked before the older girl had replaced the cordless phone back in its cradle.

"They're basically right up the street from us!" She seemed genuinely excited.

"Where's Guerley?"

"It's just Cleves Warsaw, but on the other side of Glenway."

"Oh," Preston said. Though close, anything beyond Glenway Avenue may as well have been on the other side of town.

"What's wrong?"

"I'm not allowed to ride my bike that far."

"But it's literally just like two blocks away."

"I'm definitely not allowed to go on Glenway much less cross it. My parents would kill me just for looking at it."

"What they don't know won't kill them."

"I'm not worried about them being the ones who get killed."

"Your parents won't really kill you, you know."

"You don't know my parents. One time they took away my bike for a week just because I said the word, Glenway."

Shannon Louise laughed. "Well, I'm going right now, after I finish closing up my stand for the day. You aren't going to make me go by myself, are you?"

"That doesn't seem like a good idea."

"So...you are coming?"

Preston shifted on his feet. According to the clock on the kitchen stove, he still had almost an hour and a half until his parents were expected home.

"Let's let fate decide," Shannon Louise suggested.

"What do you mean?"

"Do you know what fate means?"

Preston nodded affirmatively, but his face betrayed his doubt. "I've heard of it."

"It's basically like when you are swimming in a river. You can decide where you want to swim in the river, but the whole time you are in it, the current is taking you wherever it is going, too. That's like fate; sometimes life just takes control for us even when we think we have control of it ourselves."

That made sense to Preston; he supposed. "Like once you're in a roller-coaster, you're going up that hill...?"

"Exactly!"

"Makes sense to me."

"Perfect."

"So how do we let fate decide? I can't just hope away my parents killing me if I ride my bike that far."

"First things first," Shannon said, happy with herself for the ideas filling her brain. Determined to trade the bag of marbles for some extra days off, the young girl could almost smell the money she would be getting. "Do you have your marble with you?"

"I haven't found the other ones, yet."

"Yeah, but do you have the one with you now? The one you showed me yesterday?"

"Yeah," Preston said, absentmindedly touching the marble through his shorts.

"See!" Shannon exclaimed, slapping the top of the counter with her open palm. "That's fate right there."

"It is?"

"Of course. If you didn't have the marble, then that would have been fate telling you to pack it up and go home; forget about the marble guy and try again a different day. But you were ready for it; that's fate telling you to go for it today. See how that works!?" To her, it was not a question but rather a statement of fact, as well as a convenient excuse for the smaller boy to be her partner in crime, so to speak.

"Oh!" Preston said, now enlightened. "I still can't ride my bike past Glenway."

"I got a plan for that, too." Shannon Louise was on a roll. "We can ride our bikes until we get to Glenway, and then we can walk our bikes across the street. Technically, your parents couldn't kill you because you won't be riding your bike on Glenway."

Preston thought about her logic for a second, and it all made sense in a way his young brain could justify.

"What do you say? Want to help me clean up and then we can go?"

"Ok! Sounds like a plan to me."

Preston helped his new friend take down her business, surprised that she did this multiple days each a week. Like her, he hated being sticky, and when they were done, he actually had to take his time and wash his hands with soap, certain that all traces of stickiness were gone before feeling clean.

"Have you ever played with your marbles?" Preston asked.

"I know that it was a game or something, but I never really thought about it much less played it."

"I played before, with my grandpappy."

"With your one marble?"

"No, he had his own marbles that we played with."

"Was it fun?"

Preston shrugged his shoulders. "It was fun with him. My mom said that people used to play something called keepsies, and that sounds like it would be fun."

"Keepsies?"

"Yeah, it's when you get to keep the marbles that you won. Guess it was like gambling for kids."

"Keepsies?"

"Yeah, that's what she called it," Preston said. He remembered an important fact. "She said that you had to call that before the game started, though, otherwise it wouldn't count."

"Well yeah, you can't change the rules in the middle of a game. No one likes that."

"That's what she said: Know what's what before you do what's what."

"Your mom sounds like a smart lady." Shannon Louise smiled at Preston, and they hurried to finish cleaning up.

By the time they were on their bikes and riding down Coronado, he still had well over an hour until his parents would be home.

When they reached Cleves Warsaw and turned right, he was riding on a sidewalk that he had only travelled on a few times in his life. It was a short ride before they crossed the next street, Rulison, and from there Glenway was basically a small parking lot away. It felt strange being within sight of the street he had been taught to fear getting near, but with the courage of his older friend leading the way, Preston followed Shannon Louise right up to the crosswalk.

Once there, she stopped and got off her bike.

"We can walk them across, then you won't technically be breaking any rules."

"I'm not even supposed to be able to see this street," Preston said.

"Well, you can close your eyes if you want, but just stay close to me. It should be that door right over there." She said this last part while pointing across the street.

Considering the choice of dying by a parents' hand or getting run over by a car, Preston took his chances and kept his eyes open as he crossed the street. Even if his parents did kill him, they would surely be more merciful than a full-size sedan.

Without incident, they made it across the busy street safe and sound.

Once across the street, Shannon Louise led them to the door. "This is it. Are you ready?"

Preston nodded. He did not know if he was ready or not, but he knew that he was not comfortable just standing on the sidewalk so close to such a busy intersection waiting for a parent to drive by and catch him this close to the finish line. "Let's do this."

Without another word, they opened the door and wheeled their bikes inside.

Chapter 23

A s his teammate and Shannon Louise were entering the shop to sell their marbles, David Hardy was looking for his own glass beads. Unlike Preston, though, David already had a good idea where to find them.

In a house dominated by boys, his mother was protective of the things she considered valuable. Although the marbles were not considered precious because they were a commodity, the mixed collection of shooters and boulders and peewees were once important to David's maternal and paternal grandfathers, and therefor family treasures to be kept safe.

Nancy Hardy did not have many things that she considered her own treasures. Her boys were the most important things in her life, and everything flowed down from there. The garage was filled with tools and sports equipment for every season. Baseballs and wooden bats for her sons, softballs and aluminum bats for her husband, and every type of lawn equipment lined the walls. The recent addition last Christmas of a weight bench eliminated the ability of either parent to park in the garage anymore. The basement did have a laundry room that was her domain on that level, but except for a bunch of blankets, all kinds of sheets, and a summer's worth of extra towels, she did not keep anything of sentimental value there.

David had also once looked in his mom's closet one day. For no reason other than boredom, as most kids eventually do, he had gone into his parents' room and snooped through their things. His dad's closet had a lot of interesting items. He found a couple shotguns; though younger than Preston, more so then and not just now, David could tell at the time that the guns were unloaded. In the closet that one day, he had also found a box of magazines that his dad collected. It surprised him that his dad had so many magazines with pictures of girls, but at the time the pictures did not interest the young child one way or another. His dad also had a shoe box filled with odd gags, golf tees shaped like naked women and funny playing cards.

In his mom's closet, however, David found nothing interesting. In fact, her closet had been so well organized and precise and delicate that he did not even try to look for any hidden gems there. He had not seen a lot of closets in his day, but until seeing a celebrity closet one day way in his future, David would never see another closet where every inch of space seemed to have a functional purpose. He did not know that her full-length mirror opened to conceal jewelry, but there was no collection of family heirloom marbles to be found there if he had.

No, David knew that what he wanted could only be found in one place.

Their house was not as large as either the Jackson or Tate households, and their living room and dining rooms were connected as if one larger room. The effect made the otherwise two small rooms seem like a larger space. The only visual delineation between the two spaces as any way being different, was the presence of a large hutch in the middle of the long room.

In that wooden antique were held special plates and other fragile things. Like the one that Preston's parents owned, this cabinet was slightly larger, though with a similar design, hidden cabinets below and glass door shelving up top. It was in the bottom cabinet that David found the box of marbles.

A reclaimed cigar box, there was nothing fancy about the inside of the space, no felt lining or cloth bottom. Inside, the marbles rolled as freely as they could, back and forth they could tumble when he turned the box to either side, but there were enough of them that they were layered about two or three high. He guessed there were maybe a hundred marbles inside.

David took the box and closed the cabinet door. He walked to his room and put the box on his bed. Next to his backpack, the one he would use to take his things during the sleepover on Saturday. For the first time, the 9-year-old had doubts about taking the thing. He did not think that either of his parents would miss the marbles so much, but he was wondering about the box. Even if his mom never looked inside the thing, surely she would eventually notice that the entire box was gone.

Walking out of his room, David left the box of marbles on the bed and went to the kitchen. In the bottom drawer he pulled out one of the quart-size Ziplock baggies that his mom used for storing leftovers. Once he was back in his room, he opened the box and dumped half of the marbles from the box into the clear bag. When he was done, there were still more than enough marbles left to cover the bottom of the box. He had no idea what the difference was between the marbles in his bag and the ones left in the box, but the young baseball player understood averages, and he was confident that the bag contained a sample indicative of the whole.

The clear bag also fit nicely in the zippered pocket inside the main compartment of his backpack.

After returning the box into the cabinet, David grabbed his baseball glove and went outside to practice throwing balls at his practice netting, a cool device that would allow the balls he threw to bounce back in his direction.

After just a few minutes of playing, David forgot about the bag of marbles in his bag. They would be there Saturday when he needed them, and he had no use thinking about them again until then, just like he was sure that his parents never thought about them when they were safe in the box.

If there was one thing he believed about his practical parents, it was that neither of them was going to notice a few of their marbles missing.

Chapter 24

For a day that started auspiciously, the rest of it had been like a slow day in Hell.

Without even small talk between them, the coworkers sat at their respective seats waiting for something to happen. Occasionally, Deb Vilitch would stand from her desk, walk over to the artifact, remove the lid, and stare inside. Unlike the two hooligans she dispatched in the morning, the demon could control her time looking, or not looking, into the void.

Staring at the pit did not bring her any joy or even any satisfaction, but it was something she could do with her time besides sitting at her desk waiting for something to do. She never offered the same distraction to her coworker, the receptionist.

Officially, they were open every day of the year – even for that holiday at the end of December – from dawn until dusk, but each knew that if a late customer walked in just as they were about to close and head home, they were expected to stay and complete the transaction.

There were worse jobs they could have been assigned, especially the receptionist, who did not have Deb's eye for valuing used things. There were also some better ones, though, too, jobs with a higher level of engagement and excitement. Sometimes, she imagined what it would be like to work for the Claims Division or an exciting group like The Trackers, a team that her skills could possibly use, but she understood the futility of complaining about an assignment. The best way to move on, she had heard, was to keep your head down and put in your time.

With no activity and only one lousy phone call, the time put in today seemed like an eternity.

She heard the bell chime, indicating someone walking through the front door. The appraiser took out a breath mint and waited. When the second chime, the one in her office, rang, indicating her turn to engage, she stood from her desk, wiped away any wrinkles that had formed on her skirt, and walked out her office door.

Without even looking at her coworker, Deb made the short walk to the back door and stepped outside.

The fresh air was always a welcome part of her day, as was the brief time she was able to spend in the sunlight. Lingering outside would have been strictly forbidden on company time, but there was not really a rule about how quickly she walked around to the front of the building. Knowing there was a fine line between doing her job and getting a visit from someone in Operations or Legal, the appraiser did not stop as she slowly walked to the front door.

When she entered through the only door in the room, Deb Vilitch was surprised to see two customers instead of the usual one; she was also taken aback by the young age of the two people waiting for her arrival. The demonic appraiser was equally caught off-guard by the two bicycles standing in her lobby; only the quickest double-take toward the bikes and a quick twitch of her eye betrayed this distraction.

"My name is Deb Vilitch," she said, though without offering to shake any hands. "I am the appraiser."

"Hi. I'm Shannon Louise, and this is my friend Preston."

"Hi," Preston said. He seemed calm, cool, and collected on the outside, but he was none of those things. The bike ride had only been a short one, just like Shannon Louise said it would be, but besides being a hot day, he was also nervous and on edge from walking his bike across Glenway Avenue. It was a very busy street, and the intersection was an especially chaotic one for drivers; even so, waiting for a red light and walking through the crosswalk was no big deal. The action would still get him killed by his parents, but he did not see any issues with cars once they were stopped. He did have the marble in his pocket, his bike was safe, and his parents had no idea he was here, so maybe he was cool and collected if not exactly calm.

"We have some marbles."

"Ok, let's take a look, then."

The pass-thru window slid open, and the receptionist extended the tray, which the woman took. The window again slid closed.

Shannon Louise held her bag tight and looked at her young friend. She knew that her bag of marbles was a lot more extensive than her friend's own measly, single marble, but she was curious to see what the potential was for her lot before getting her appraisal. Logic dictated whatever Preston's marble was worth, her many marbles would easily be worth several times more. She could already picture enough days away from the lemon-ade stand to not feel any residual stickiness on her hands, imagined though it may be.

"Show her what you got, first," the older girl said to her new friend.

Reaching into his pocket, Preston pulled out his marble and without saying a word extended it towards the appraiser.

"Oh!" Deb Vilitch said, surprised and amused but not entirely disap-pointed with the single marble glowing in front of her. "Look what we have here."

The appraiser took the shining marble from the hand of her smallest customer, and like him, she did not say a word. She held the small object up and looked at the entirety of it. "Absolutely beautiful coloring, marvel-ous swirl, and perfectly smooth for a shooter with so much experience on it."

Shannon Louise watched all of this, fascinated. She was waiting for the woman to pull out a magnifying glass or an iPad to look up the value of the prize. She herself had looked up Preston's marble as she remembered it, and she knew that he could possibly get as much as eight dollars for it even if the average would be south of $5. If she could average that much for her own bag, then she could almost retire for the summer.

"Ok then,"[i] the appraiser said.

The window again slid open.

The much older woman looked down at the little boy who would never be her friend, ever. "We are prepared to offer you one hundred and twenty-five dollars for this marble."

"A hundred and twenty-five!" Shannon Louise exclaimed, uncontrolled, her imagination immediately running wild through her mind. Was she about to have summer off for the rest of her primary school career!?

Preston did not know what it meant to talk about an out-of-body expe-rience, but he was in the midst of having one. Though he did not visualize himself functioning from the perspective of outside of his body, he did not feel in any way in control of his actions or his words. Did this lady just say she was going to give him over one hundred dollars? Could he even spend that much money?

"I assume that is acceptable to you?"

Preston nodded his head.

Deb Vilitch looked at the little boy. It was always best when the seller vocalized the acceptance of the sale, but that was a technicality; such was the reason for the paperwork. She looked to the widow and the man sitting there; she nodded her head once.

Preston saw the man hand the short stack of bills through the window, twenty-five crisp, $5 bills, and he still could not believe his luck.

"Just sign the receipt and we have a deal, then," the appraiser said to her first customer of the day. Recognizing that this little guy was having a slight case of stage fright, she helped motion him to sign the paper next to the pile of cash. "Just like being famous and signing an autograph."

"What's the receipt for?" Shannon Louise asked, pointing to the sign above the window. "It says all sales are final."

"Tax purposes," the woman stated. "We are a cash business and have strict obligations to the IRS, not to mention having to account to our own concern. I can't just have my boss think I'm taking cash home every night."

The little girl nodded. Made sense to her; besides, she was about to get paid.

Preston had no idea what he was doing, but he carefully wrote his name on the piece of paper as if it was a legally binding document. Before he took the cash, he looked at the older woman and waited for her acknowledgement before picking it up, folding it in half, and stuffing it as deep into his shorts as his pockets would allow. His heart was beating faster than when they crossed the big road, and he was sweating more now than when their ride was done.

The appraiser stuck the lone marble in her pocket. The window stayed open.

Deb Vilitch turned her attention to the 12-year-old lady, Shannon Louise. Hidden in a thick, dark bag, it was impossible to see what this little girl had to offer. Maybe this would be a very good day, indeed. The mornings' offerings would add some balance of favor within their weekly ledger, and the little boy's marble, though only one, was a decent piece. Maybe this little girl was going to make their entire week.

Shannon Louise held out the bag. She had not taken an inventory of each marble, but she knew that she had eighty-three of them.

The appraiser took the bag and motioned that it had some heft to it before carefully emptying the contents into the tray the receptionist had provided for Preston's transaction. Before the last marble was out of the bag, however, the appraiser lost all interest in the collection. Like empty calories, there was not a single piece with any real worth.

"Oh," the appraiser said, clearly unenthused.

Shannon Louise did not fully understand the initial expression, but her young mind could nonetheless read that something was amiss. Just like her luck to have something go wrong. "What?"

Deb looked up, realizing she had for a moment been unprofessional in letting her feelings show. "Give me a moment, please."

"Ok. Do your thing." For the first time, Shannon Louise took notice of the room and its lack of décor. She looked at the sign above the window, and again she wondered about signing a receipt if you could not return the item. That said, she realized that she was the one selling the thing, so maybe it was in her best interest if the lady decided to give her money and then settle on the value was not there.

None of it mattered if she could buy some time away from the lemonade stand.

"Ok then," the appraiser said. The collection in front of her was a fine one if she were running an antique store, or if the worth of the things was in their age, but that was not the case. Any offer she made for these marbles would be a courtesy to the little girl for making the trip here with her friend. Perhaps she would even tell others, bringing them by to sell their own goods, some of which were bound to be better than this glass that would inevitably end up in the garbage. Her job was not to burn the trash, and it went against her nature to provide a courtesy, but her instincts for business dictated her making an offer. "We are prepared to offer you thirty dollars for your marbles."

"Huh?" Shannon Louise managed.

Preston felt the lump of cash in his pocket, glad that he had gone first but uncomfortable at this turn of events.

The appraiser bit her lip. "Thirty-five, and that's really as much as we can do."

"Thirty-five?" Shannon repeated. That was like two days of lemonade stand money, so not nothing, but certainly not the windfall that Preston's own sale would have implied. Had she gone first, would she have been satisfied with the amount? She did not know the answer to this unasked question, but the perspective of disappointment was already set.

"Yes, if that is acceptable to you."

Shannon Louise considered the offer. Before yesterday, she had absolutely zero connection to the marbles in the tray, but after looking each one up on the Internet, she now felt a closer bond with them. "Um...I have eighty-three marbles and you're only offering me thirty-five dollars?"

"Eighty-two marbles."

Shannon Louise was about to protest when she remembered the steel marble; she had counted that stupid one when adding up her total number. She felt as if all the wind left her sails.

Deb Vilitch looked at the two tykes before her. She had already gotten all she needed from this group, and anything else was just mercy, which was not her business. "Listen, sweety, you seem like a smart cookie, and I'm sure you know how to find your way around a computer. My suggestion to you would be to spend some time and sell these there, that way you can maximize your profits."

"Like sell them all individually?"

"Yes. I'm sure you could make a lot more money that way."

"But isn't that what you guys do?"

"We buy used things."

"Things?"

"Marbles."

"Well, mine are used. They're really old."

"Yes, well our specialty is not necessarily old marbles."

"What's the difference?"

The appraiser stiffened her posture and re-set her focus. Because of their age, she had momentarily let down her guard and given these two the slightest window into her deeds. It was time to cut this interaction short. "Any difference is your choice to make. We can offer you thirty-five dollars, and that last five will likely come out of my pay."

Shannon Louise blinked. The number was not far off from what she had initially been expecting, but after seeing what her friend got for his lone marble, she was not going to be happy about this deal. It was still two days of work, almost, and she could not ignore that, especially for a bag of glass that meant nothing to anyone.

"How about thirty-six...?"

"Thirty-six dollars? That will make you happy?" Deb Vilitch seemed genuinely amused.

"Not happy, but ..." she knew the word placated, but could not recall it, "but I can live with that."

"Ok, thirty-six dollars is what we can offer you then, if that is acceptable to you."

"Ok, I'll take it."

"Alrighty then," Deb said as the receptionist handed out the paper to sign and the seven bills plus the one extra.

Shannon Louise looked at Preston before signing her own receipt. She was in no way mad at her buddy, but she did not understand what made his lone marble worth so much more than her entire collection. She could have taken off more than a week with the kind of money her friend just earned.

She signed the paper and took her money.

"Thank you both for stopping in," Deb Vilitch said. "Please tell your friends to check their basements."

"Yeah," Shannon said, "we will."

The appraiser looked at Preston. "And you see if you can't find more of those little babies around the house. I'm guessing you could probably find a few more if you really tried."

"I will!" Preston said, happy and eager.

"Well fantastic then," the appraiser said, moving to open the door. "Let me get that for you two."

Money in their pockets, Shannon Louise and Preston walked their bikes out the door, across the street, and then pedaled back down Cleves Warsaw until they came to Coronado, where they turned, all without speaking. When they pulled back into Shannon Louise's driveway, she was not in the mood to talk.

"Do you want to come over and go swimming?" Preston asked.

"No, I have to get some stuff done before my mom gets home."

"Oh, ok." Preston dropped his head before getting an idea. "I could give you some of my money."

"What?"

"I could split my money you."

Shannon Louise smiled at her little friend. "I appreciate that, but it's your money, fair and square."

"Are you sure? We could go halfsies."

"Halfsies is like keepsies; it only counts if you say it ahead of time."

Preston thought about what she was saying, and it made sense.

"Thanks for going up there with me; I wouldn't have gone without you; and I'm glad it worked out for you."

"It sure did!"

"I'll see you around." Shannon Louise said as she opened the door. She paused before going inside. "Think about what you're going to tell your parents before you let them see all that money."

"What do you mean?"

"Well, if they see all that money, then they are going to ask you questions. That's what parents do in case you haven't figured that out. You aren't about to tell them how you got it, are you?"

For the first time, Preston considered the totality of the situation. He took a marble from his house. He took his bike past busy Glenway Avenue. He talked to a stranger, and in a strange place, nonetheless. He sold something that was not his.

"Yeah, I see what you're saying."
"Yeah, well, anyways, good luck."
"Thanks."
"Hope you don't need it."

Chapter 25

=== 1 ===

Although she was seeing another man every day after work, Janay Jackson was not having an affair.

Concerned with her health as well as her marriage, the mother of one had recently enrolled at a local gym and had signed on to six weeks of one-hour training sessions, four days a week. Her trainer was a buff guy named Kellen, and he was a flirty pretty boy, but she recognized the playfulness of his comments for what they were and instead focused on making herself feel better about her self-image. If her husband ended up recognizing her efforts and put his own renewed emphasis on their marriage, then all the better, too.

If not, well, then she would be stronger and in a better place to move on.

The motivation, however, was her own well-being, nothing more.

Motivation had rarely been a problem in her life. At times, like anyone she supposed, there were peaks and valleys in her enthusiasm for improvement. There had been other hobbies aimed at raising the level of either her physical endurance or appearance or more ephemeral things like learning a second language or taking lessons in calligraphy. While her incentive for different things did not always have the momentum necessary to become a life habit or remain a constant, her ability was in her willingness to try.

Janay owed this willingness to accept challenges as a trait she learned from her father. Marbles were a joy for her dad, and not necessarily for her, but she did enjoy playing the game with him growing up. Even as a young girl, younger even than her son now, Preston's mom understood what the game meant to her father by listening to him regale her with stories of the time he took this marble from one kid or lost another marble to a different challenger. Her father was a genuinely nice man, but when he told those stories about old battles in the circle, she could – if she tried – still recall a different light in his eyes as he spoke about the past playing a silly child's game.

Genuine, simple joy.

He had his own way of keeping his daughter interested in playing the game, too, and when her beautiful marble was unceremoniously banished into the void, it was not even the first time that she had lost the precious token.

Janay had one marble of which she was especially fond, a shooter that was colored like a yellow rose with a beautiful brown swirl through the middle. One day, Janay's dad let her win the marble from him, making it her marble. Her day had been made. Just seven at the time, she could not imagine a better prize ever being won. The victory meant so much to her little heart that she went to bed that night with the marble under her pillow.

The next day she then learned a lesson of loss.

Just as easily as she had won the marble, her dad was able to win the thing back. The loss stung, and she went to bed that second night feeling about as bad as she had felt good the night prior.

However, the next day it was she who instigated the playing of the game. This time when she won the beautiful prize from him, the victory and treasure seemed so much sweeter. Not only did she again sleep with the marble, but she held it in her hand looking at it with what little light came through her window, unable to fall asleep for at least an hour past her bedtime.

Such was their little game with the marble. Sometimes her dad would win it back from her; always she would play until it was again hers. They did not play as often after that first week of intense competition, but it was a fun thing that they shared for the rest of her time in his house, and, even occasionally, after.

The longest she had ever been without the marble was in college.

Janay had been dating a fellow student, and he carelessly misplaced the item as if it was just a piece of glass to roll as it pleased and land where it may. Together they had looked on their hands and knees for the small thing, yet the search ended with an argument and harsh words. Janay stopped seeing the man after that, though she did not stop looking for the lost marble, at first diligently and then only once in a while when drinking alone.

Janay then met Haynes and the two of them eventually moved into their own place. Before leaving her old apartment, filled with so many dreams and at least one cherished marble, Janay cleaned the empty place like a tenant has never before detailed an apartment, the entire time hoping to find the lost glass.

Her hope had limits, though, and she left her clean, sanitized life behind and started down a new path unknown.

She did not have the marble as a thing she controlled, an object she could produce at will or by whim, but she held close those memories and lessons no less close; if anything, her resolve to recall them was intensified by her loss of the possession.

Janay and Haynes had been living together for about six months, and were just a few weeks from becoming engaged, and close to embarking on the first steps towards becoming expectant parents, the earliest steps, when Haynes unpacked the contents of a vertical organizer Janay had used to hold pens and remote controls and other random items that collect on a coffee table.

One of the items that had been collected there and hiding at the bottom was Janay's prized marble.

Haynes had never seen the thing and had before then only heard mention of the round object once, and in passing. That night, though, they sat up drinking wine until after midnight as Janay recounted story after story which her father had handed down through her memories. Not all of those stories on that night had been about marbles, but that was the subject that got the proverbial ball rolling, as it were.

It had been years since she even thought about the little thing forgotten in her own grammy's teacup on a curio shelf, but if asked, she would have been able to still describe the little object perfectly, so much was it a part of her life at one point along the way. Unlike Mabel the Marble Marvel, who's collection of marbles was a foundation for a life, or unlike Teddy Hahn, the unfortunate motorist who got confused and wandered into traffic, the marble cast away from her life was not so much a foundation as it was a cornerstone; its loss was not enough to bring down an entire building, yet still enough to damage the stability of the structure.

When the marble disappeared into the pit, she was in the middle of a squat thrust, Kellen encouraging her to get just one more rep.

"Come on! You got this! J all day! J all day!"

Janay did not get confused or forget what she was doing, but the weight on her shoulders suddenly seemed to increase. Her focus on completing the task evaporated, and she could feel her back begin to bend forward.

"Whoa! Whoa! Whoa!" Kellen said, stepping in behind his client to help ease the load on her shoulders, keeping her from collapsing in a heap.

With the help, Janay was able to set the bar on the rack in a controlled manner.

"You ok there, J?" Kellen asked. He rarely called her by her full name.

"Yeah," Janay said, her mind clouded and foggy as if from lack of sleep. "I don't know what happened there."

Kellen draped his arm around her waist. He did not rub her or do anything as forward as pull her closer to himself, but he kept his hand on the small of her back as he talked. "You were doing great until that last rep. You sore anywhere?"

Janay shrugged her shoulders and lifted her arms back. "No, I think I'm good."

Kellen moved his hand up to her far shoulder as he moved behind her, bringing his free hand up to the other side. He began rubbing her shoulders and mid-back.

The rubbing felt good, not in a sexual way, but as a stress reliever. She could feel the first bit of a headache coming on, but as much as she wanted to excuse herself to take an Excedrin, she was unable to pull away from the man's strong hands making her back feel like putty. She looked back over her shoulder and smiled at his cute, sweaty face.

As if in a dream, the man's eyes seemed to twinkle, and she felt herself blush. "That feels amazing. You should have a side hustle."

"I am a full-service trainer," Kellen said, smiling wide and winking.

Her head light and swooning as if being held up by balloons, the massage was relaxing to the point of making her feel the need to sit down. Were her legs now weak and wobbly from the exercise or was there something else? "I think I need to sit down for a minute."

Kellen stopped rubbing her shoulders but moved his hand lower, down again to the small of her back, where he helped ease her onto the weight bench beside them. "Is that better?"

"Yes," Janay said, her thoughts clearing even as the haze around them seemed to grow thicker. "I don't know what came over me. I think I'm done for today."

"You want me to go see if there's a massage room available? I could get us fifteen minutes of alone time now for that treatment. Might be just what you need."

Janay looked up at the trainer and smiled. The thought of spending fifteen minutes alone with this man appealed to her very much, and she almost agreed, but a group of guys came into the room and brought her back to a different version of reality.

Once, as a teenager, Janay had been in a car accident with a friend and had gotten a concussion. The disorientation and foggy thoughts now reminded her of what she could recall from then.

Had she bumped her head?

"I really think I need to take a rain check."

Kellen looked disappointed, but his frown did not linger. Flashing his smile, he had another prospect scheduled in thirty minutes. "No problem, J. Go get some rest, and I'll see you tomorrow."

"Yeah, I just need to drink some water or something."

"Good session today."

"Thanks." Preston's mom smiled, but for the life of her, she could not remember anything about her workout except for the last rep, the one that she couldn't get, the one that occurred as the shooter that was colored like a yellow rose with a beautiful brown swirl, was consumed by the void.

Chapter 26

⸻ 1 ⸻

P reston was home before either of his parents, and he took the $125 from the sale of the marble, kept it folded, and stuck it in the box where he kept his LEGO instruction manuals. If there was one place where his mom would not find the money anytime soon, it was there.

He had never considered that having money to spend would be a problem, but Shannon Louise had made a valid point about parents questioning everything, and more specifically his parents asking about his new riches. Even if he managed to spend it on something useful, like a new baseball mitt, there would still be the question of where the new item originated. Answering any questions about things he bought with his money would be as hard to answer as any questions about the money itself.

Preston had never heard the term money laundering, but his young brain did imagine faking a business like a lemonade stand to convince his parents that he had earned the money.

That's about where his mind was when his dad surprised him by walking into his room.

"Hey Sport"

"Hey dad."

"Has your mom been home, yet?"

"I don't think so," Preston said, standing from off his bed, "but I didn't hear you pull up, so it's hard to say."

"Well, her car's not in the driveway."

"Yeah, I haven't seen her."

The two men of the Jackson house walked out into the kitchen as Janay was walking through the kitchen door. "Hey hey, the gang's all here," Haynes said.

"Hey," Janay answered. Like a sore tooth that had been pulled, the headache was gone but the feeling of something missing remained. Her

K.P. Maloy
⸻ 103 ⸻

thoughts seemed less foggy, but her mind was still distracted by the lack of pieces from the whole. Unlike every other day before leaving the gym, today Janay was still wearing her workout clothes.

Haynes looked at his wife in the tight leggings, surprised at how great she looked; nonetheless, he was still confused about why she was dressed that way. "Did you go to work like this?"

"Like what?" Janay looked at her husband, oblivious to what he was referring.

"Your outfit. You look like you just came from the gym."

"Oh, I was at the gym."

"Since when?"

"Since about four o'clock."

"You got off work two hours ago?"

Janay nodded.

"When did this start?"

Janay was confused. She thought she had just answered that question. "What do you mean?"

"When did you decide to start going to the gym again?"

"I don't know," Janay said, truly unsure of exactly when she had started her regime. "I guess I started meeting up with Kellen at the beginning of May."

"Who the Hell is Kellen?"

"He's my trainer."

"Your trainer?"

Janay nodded.

"And how is it that we are just now hearing about, Kellen." Haynes said the man's name with all the scorn you would imagine.

"I don't know."

Haynes shook his head. "I knew that you were being sneaky about something."

"About what?"

"About Kellen, your workout buddy apparently."

"He's my trainer," Janay said. "It's not like he rubs my back *every* day."

Haynes was about to speak up when he looked over at his son and thought better of it. Biting his lip, he changed the subject completely. "So, any plan for dinner?"

"With Kellen?" Janay said with the slightest of giggles. "Oh no, just normal stuff tomorrow, arms and core. Maybe I'll take him up on that massage."

"Massage?" Haynes fought hard to avoid blowing his cool.

"Sometimes a rub down after a workout feels good," Janay said, lost in remembering how relaxing she had felt not that long ago.

"Well, I was talking about our dinner, tonight, with your family, not some dream date with your arm and core guy."

"He does my leg days, too. He's a full-service trainer."

Haynes nodded his head, the steam almost visibly pouring from out the top. "Well, some of us have been at work all day, to pay for Trainer Mike…

"Kellen."

"Whatever."

Janay looked at her husband, unsure why he was so angry. She looked at her son and smiled. "I have everything cut up to make veggies and pasta tonight if that sounds good to you."

Preston nodded his head. He did not know what was going on with his parents, but he could tell that his dad did not like this guy, Kellen. His mom did not seem worried about any of it, though. "That's my favorite!"

Janay smiled at her son. Such a good boy.

Preston did not hear his parents speak again until dinner, but even then, their conversation had been limited to talk about the food. He did not hear the name Kellen mentioned again.

"Baseball practice went good today. I even got to play third base for a little bit."

Haynes smiled at his son. They had already discussed this on the car ride home. His mom looked at her son and smiled. "You are growing up so quick."

"Thanks mom," Preston said. "We're going to be a lot better than last year. I can already tell."

"That's great. We're really proud of you."

"Yeah, like we talked about today," Haynes said, "you just keep on practicing, and you'll keep on getting better."

"I know, dad."

"If you want, we can go look for those marbles after your practice tomorrow."

Preston did not swallow the food in his mouth but stopped chewing and looked at his mom, waiting for her to cause a commotion over his going around her by asking his dad about the marbles. This was exactly the kind of thing he had been hoping to avoid; now, here it was.

The confrontation he feared was here; it was happening now.

Except nothing happened.

Janay did not seem to take any notice of the subject, or if she did, the mother did not care as much as her son would have expected; still, he found it better not to challenge the issue further.

"Hey," Preston said, ready to change the subject, "I was wondering if David Hardy could come over and stay the night Saturday after practice."

Haynes immediately answered, "I don't care, but it's up to your mom."

Preston swallowed his food, looking to his mom for an answer or even a reaction from the previous comment about the marbles.

"I don't care, sweetie."

"Really!?"

Janay smiled. "You seem surprised."

"I guess I am."

"Well, I don't know why."

Content to not push his luck, Preston stayed quiet through the rest of dinner. He did not talk about his new friend, Shannon Louise; he certainly did not mention crossing Glenway Avenue for the first time; and he sure as heck did not mention anything about a shooter that was colored like a yellow rose with a beautiful brown swirl in the middle.

His dad used to say that what someone doesn't know won't hurt them.

Turns out his dad did not know everything.

Chapter 27

S hannon Louise woke up later than usual on Friday morning. When she went downstairs for the first time that day, she slipped on the last step and stubbed her toe on the bottom edge of the baseboard. At breakfast, there was not enough milk for her to have a bowl of cereal. Then, she left her pop tart in the toaster oven too long and it burnt both of her pieces. She peeled away all the burnt edges and decided to settle on just the delicious inner fruitiness, the best part anyway; she burnt the roof of her mouth on the first bite.

Frustrated almost to the point of tears, the young entrepreneur considered not opening her shop for the day and just going back to bed. Surely her day had to get better.

By noon, after only forty-five minutes of being open, Shannon Louise was in tears and closing her shop early for the day. Three people stopped to get lemonade within the first hour, which was a record start to any day so far; all three of them complained and asked for their money back.

Their money back!

Why!?

She knew why. Her fresh lemons were going bad, and the taste of the good stuff was nowhere to be found. She couldn't even stay open if she wanted to, the taste was so bad. Merely frustrated at that point, the young entrepreneur closed her shop and quit on the day, determined to make her dad drive her to the restaurant store just as soon as he got home from working at his own restaurant for the day.

The tears came when three more potential customers stopped and asked for lemonade as she was taking the last items inside.

Today would have been a record day for sure.

Shannon Louise just knew that she could have made more than $36 today, and it all just made her so mad.

Chapter 28

1

Preston had a great Friday.

Like his older friend, he too slept in later than was usual. The day was extra hot, and muggy for June, and he made good use of his pool. Swimming reminded him of how Shannon Louise had seemed upset after leaving the marble shop. He wished that he had known what to say to make her feel better about the situation, but he figured that it was strictly because she had made less money for all her marbles than he got for his lone sale.

Short of giving her money, he did not know a way to ease that pain for his new friend.

Between swims, he considered riding his bike over to see her, but each time he started out to get on his bike something came up to stop him.

One time the phone rang.

Another time he saw a stranger walking on the street and stayed inside like his parents taught him.

The last time he had started pedaling and just felt too hot to ride any farther.

One thing he was thankful for was that he did not have practice today. He was not ready to practice through those dog days like last year, not just yet anyway; plus, he had gotten more used to swimming than he had last year. It was hard to imagine hot days like this without taking a refreshing dip in the pool until after practice or a game.

Thinking about practice did make him think about his friend David coming over tomorrow.

The piece of paper with his friend's number on it was stuffed in the same place as his wad of cash. Taking the time to count his money for the first time, he was amazed at seeing all the $5-bills in one place. His $5-bills.

Twenty-five of them. He could spend one every day and still have some left over after the Fourth of July. The trouble was, nowhere in his allowable range was there a store to spend any money. To actually have fun that way, he would either have to go somewhere up on Glenway Avenue again or else ride way over to 8ᵗʰ St, neither of which was a realistic option. Even the closest UDF was much too far, not that he knew how to get there on his own.

He took the piece of paper with the two phone numbers and returned the money to its hiding spot. Walking over to the phone in his room, he dialed the number written in pen.

David answered on the third ring.

"Hello, Hardy residence."

"Hey David, this is Preston."

"Oh hey!"

"I wanted to see if you could still come over after practice tomorrow. My parents already said it was cool."

"My parents are fine, too, as long as I don't need a ride later that night."

"No, my parents said you could stay over."

"Sweet."

"Yeah, sweet."

"Well, I guess I'll see you at practice."

"Yeah, twelve til two tomorrow."

"Yep."

"Yep," Preston repeated. "I'll see you."

"Preston! Wait!"

"What?"

"I found my marbles. Maybe we could call that number."

"David, we already called it! My friend Shannon Louise and I called it and went there yesterday."

"Shannon Louise?"

"Yeah, she's this cool seventh grader that lives up the street. She got less money than me for her marbles, but she still got like forty bucks."

"Forty dollars! No shit?"

Preston laughed. "You won't believe this, but I got over a hundred dollars for mine."

"A hundred dollars! No way!"

"Way. It was actually one hundred and twenty-five, all five-dollar bills."

"For one marble?"

"One marble."

"I have like a baggie full of them."

"Well, either way, you'll make some money, that's for sure."

"How did you get there? Did your parents take you?"

"Heck no, they don't even know that I went. They would kill me for sure."

"Did your friend have someone drive?"

"No man, this place is like real close to where we live. We can ride our bikes there."

"Sounds like a plan."

"But my parents cannot know what we're doing."

"They won't hear it from me."

"Ok. Maybe I'll have some more marbles by then, too."

"Awesome. Do you think your friend will want to go again."

Preston thought about it for a second and doubted that Shannon Louise would ever want to go back there again. "I don't know. She has a lemonade business, so we can stop by and ask her; her house is on the way."

"Ok. I'll see you tomorrow."

"Ok."

"See ya'…"

"David!" It was Preston's turn to remember something. "Wait!"

"What?"

"Be sure to bring your swimming trunks. No matter what we do tomorrow, we'll want to go swimming for sure."

"You have a pool?"

"Yeah."

"Oh, tomorrow is going to be great."

"I can't even imagine a better day…"

Chapter 29

═ 1 ═

S hannon Louise's dad was not in the door five seconds before his little girl came down the stairs, hysterical. She had been having mood swings lately, and his wife attributed it to the little girl going through the first steps toward becoming a lady. He understood the biology of it, but he was never prepared for the fury that could occasionally erupt.

"DAD, WE HAVE TO GO TO THE RESTAURANT STORE RIGHT NOW!!"

"Hey, my day was great, how was yours?"

"I'm really not in the mood for the jokes today, dad."

"What's the problem?"

"Today sucked is the problem."

"Watch the language."

"Today was a horrible piece of turd muffins."

"Ok. Tell me about it."

"What is there to tell? I stubbed my stupid toe, and my lemons all went bad. I had to give people their money back today because they asked for it. I didn't even know that you could do that without a receipt. WHO ASKS FOR THEIR MONEY BACK?" She screamed this last part.

Stan Tate tried to stifle his laughter. No reason to make things worse. "How does your toe feel now?"

"I don't know, dad. It's not broken if that's what you mean. I don't even care about my stupid toe. I couldn't make any money today, and I actually had people who wanted to buy some lemonade for a change."

"That does suck."

Shannon Louise looked at her dad, her emotions thrown off kilter by her dad's attempt at humor. She could not help but smile. "It's not funny, dad."

"I know. I get that."

"I need a sign that says, 'All Sales Are Final'."

Her dad stood up and straightened his slacks. "I'll tell you what. Give me ten minutes to change and freshen up and then we can go get some more lemons so your customers won't want their money back."

"Yeah, about that, dad. Can we talk about the whole fresh-squeezed lemonade angle?"

Stan Tate looked at his little girl and smiled. He was proud of her for trying the good stuff, and frankly, he had been surprised that she had gone through a week of attending to her stand every day. He rubbed the top of her head. "Let's talk about that on the way there."

"Ok. Sounds good." Shannon Louise smiled at her dad. He always made things better, at least whenever he was not at work. "Thanks dad."

"You're welcome daughter. Get ready, I'll be right down."

Stan took about fifteen minutes, and when he came down the stairs his daughter was waiting. The ride to the restaurant supply store took a little longer than that, and Shannon Louise's dad agreed that the fresh-squeezed lemonade was a harder product to make and clean up after. He also agreed that the time she spent prepping the drink also amounted to a monetary cost because, as he had said on many occasions, time is more valuable than money.

By the time they were inside the store, they had agreed to *let fate decide* by comparing the price of a pre-mix powder with a case of lemons.

They checked the powder mix first, and both decided that it was not even worth a further look. For $30.36, she could get a case of six large containers for making lemonade, each one capable of making over a hundred servings! At last, her first victory of the day. She also bought four hundred more cups and as many more lids as she needed. Her dad convinced her to also invest in a small bag of lemons, convincing her that if she just cut up a few lemons and let them float in each batch, then technically she would not need to change her sign that promised to have some fresh-squeezed lemon juice in each cup.

Perception was more important than reality.

With her dad promising to buy any more lemons that she needed for the rest of the summer as she needed them, for just under $70 she had everything she required to finish the next seven weeks of business. From this point on, all sales would be profit.

For the first time all day, she felt her life coming back into balance.

Traffic was bad, so her dad took a different route home. Shannon Louise knew that she had gone this way before, with her mom the last time she could remember, but it was in no other way familiar to her. When they were about halfway home, she looked out her window and saw a sign not unlike the one that her friend had seen earlier in the week.

We Buy Used Marbles.

The sign infuriated her again, though she did not erupt at her dad; instead, she seethed quietly for the next several minutes, stewing over the whole thing.

She still could not believe how much money Preston got for his one marble. Although she felt bad for being angry at his good fortune, a thing that she knew was not nice, she also realized that the root of her anger was not in his victory but in her defeat. Going in she had not expected so much as Preston received, but she did have a hope that she would make more than she had. Plus, the whole way that the appraiser lady acted and spoke - her offer and her tone - made Shannon Louise mad just remembering it.

Why would all her old marbles be worth less than that one used shooter.

What had the lady said? We don't buy old marbles; we buy used ones. Is that what she said? That's what the sign said. Had the appraiser mentioned buying other things, too? Shannon Louise was too mad to remember.

"Dad, why would something used, be better than something old?"

Stan glanced at his daughter before returning his focus to the road. "You got me. Why would something used, be better than something old?"

"No dad. I'm asking, you."

"Oh, well, who says that it is better?"

The little girl did not want to tell her dad the truth, at least not the whole truth. "That sign said that they buy used things. Why not just say old things?"

"They probably just meant either one. If something is used then it's probably old, too."

"Yeah, but what if they were specific on purpose?"

Hoping to avoid the drama bullet he had already dodged once since getting home from work, Stan tried to imagine the question as if it was literal. "Let's think about this."

"I don't want to think about it, dad, I just want an answer."

"Well, that's how I get answers, sometimes," Stan said, "by talking it through."

Shannon Louise rolled her eyes at her dad.

"So, I guess a used tool might be better than an old tool; an old tool might not work anymore."

"I don't think they were selling tools, dad."

"What were they selling?"

Shannon Louise tried to think of a good lie. "Sporting equipment, I think."

"Sports memorabilia, well that's a big market. I guess that something used by a famous ballplayer would be worth more used than just something old. Like an old ball glove from the nineteen-thirties would be cool to have, but having one that belonged to Babe Ruth would be worth a lot of money."

"Why is that?"

"Because somebody famous was associated with it."

"And that makes it worth more?"

"Well, it gives the item more of a story, more of a history. A baseball glove worn by someone like Babe Ruth or Derek Jeter reminds the owner of those people who wore it, and that makes it worth something more than just something old, I guess."

"So, because people remember stuff, it makes the stuff worth more?"

"Kind of, I suppose. I guess it depends on your perspective. Would a ball glove worn by your grandpa be worth more to you than one worn by some famous ballplayer that you don't know?"

"It'd be worth less to a lot of people, but I suppose that to you, grandpa's glove would be worth more."

"A lot more." Stan smiled at his daughter. "Don't get me wrong, I'd love to have the money from selling a famous glove or bat or something, but I think that I'd much rather have something – anything – that reminds me of my dad."

Shannon Louise nodded. Her dad's example made sense, to a point. "What if the person wasn't famous, though. Would something used really be more valuable than something old? Would a stranger care about something that was only personal?"

"I mean," *where was she going with this*, "I feel like old things are usually more valuable than used things, to be honest, especially if there is no nostalgia attached to it."

"What's that?"

"Nostalgia? It's like memories of a thing."

"Na-stall-ja?"

"Close enough."

"And that means memories?"

Stan tried to think of a relevant example. "My dad was a huge Cleveland Browns fan, and he was at the stadium for the last game before the original team moved. I remember he came home that night with one of the seats from the actual stadium in his car. He said that everyone took them. Same with the seats from the old Riverfront Stadium down here; people bought those things, though. They were valuable not because they were old chairs, but because looking at them made people remember all the good times and memories they had from the stadium, from sitting in them watching the Reds or the Bengals or concerts or whatever. In grandpa's case, it was the Cardiac Kids."

"Kids having heart attacks?"

"Never mind. My point is that the seat represented something more to your grandpa than just a chair; it represented so many other memories he had from that place."

"So, nostalgia is like a memory tied to a thing?"

"Yeah, memories, feelings, emotional connections."

"And some people pay for that kind of thing?"

"Yeah, some people pay a lot for that."

"So, they're buying the memory of the thing and not just the thing?"

"Yeah, that's a good way to put it."

Shannon Louise thought for another moment before again speaking. "How can you tell if a baseball glove has nostalgia? Do they write their name on it or something?"

Stan smiled at his daughter. "Memorabilia is authenticated in some way, but I don't think that it's because Babe Ruth actually signed his name on his glove. There's paperwork."

"What if you don't have any paperwork?"

"There's something called provenance, which is the history of a thing. Some objects have proof that goes along with them, and some are so famous that people just know what they are already. Like a famous painting or the Crown of England."

"Provenance?"

"Yeah, it's the story associated with an object, and it proves ownership."

"So how does that work?"

"I don't know, honestly," Stan admitted to his daughter. "Either you have it or you don't, though, I know that. If you have Babe Ruth's baseball mitt and you don't have the provenance, then you don't have Babe Ruth's baseball mitt, you just have an old piece of leather."

"Weird."

"Yeah, I suppose it is kind of weird," Stan paused, "unless you have more money than sense."

"Yeah, or unless you're just weird."

"It's probably the money, honey."

Shannon Louise nodded, but she was not sure. On some level, what he said made sense, but that still did nothing to help explain how a marble had provenance or whatever it was called; it did nothing to make her understand why her friend's one marble would have any such nostalgia attached to it while hers apparently did not.

How could a person even tell that just from looking at a thing like a marble?

Chapter 30

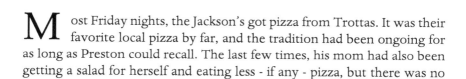

Most Friday nights, the Jackson's got pizza from Trottas. It was their favorite local pizza by far, and the tradition had been ongoing for as long as Preston could recall. The last few times, his mom had also been getting a salad for herself and eating less - if any - pizza, but there was no reason to think that tonight would offer any change in routine.

Preston's dad was the first to get home that night, and he seemed surprised that his wife was not already there.

"Your mom been home yet?"

"Not yet dad. Haven't seen her."

"Hmm." Haynes took out his phone and called his wife. No answer.

"Maybe she's getting the pizza, dad."

"Yeah, maybe."

After changing clothes, showering, and waiting another fifteen minutes, Haynes thought about ordering the pizza himself, but instead decided on a change of plans. "Get dressed, Preston, we're going out to eat, tonight."

Preston did not necessarily like it when he and his parents went out to eat, but he jumped at the chance to spend some time with his dad. He changed his shirt and put on some shoes and socks and was ready to go.

"Where do you want to go?"

"I don't care, dad."

"Ok," Haynes said, "I'll decide."

The route his dad went in driving to the local brewpub took them past both the Tate residence on Coronado as well as the corner of Glenway Avenue and Cleves Warsaw, same intersection that Preston had recently crossed to get to the building on the other side of the street. Looking at the building now, and not just following his friend, he did not see anything on the outside of the space that indicated the magic within. No one driving past would ever be able to imagine what was happening behind the anonymous facade, much less the value of a single marble to those working inside.

"Did you do anything fun today?"

"Swimming was fun."

"You really get our money's worth out of that pool."

"Yeah, it's extra nice on days like today."

"It sure was a hot one."

"Yep."

They drove in silence for a few minutes. "Did your mom mention what she was doing after work?"

"No," Preston said. "I haven't seen her all day. I slept in, too."

"She didn't wake you up when she left?"

"No, I guess not." For the first time, Preston considered the unprecedented action.

"Have you noticed her acting weird?"

"Mom? No, not really."

They drove the rest of the way in silence. Preston always liked it when they drove through downtown, and today he could see the tall buildings even though the place they went was north of the highest constructions. He was also intrigued by the old building that seemed spooky on the outside but felt warm and inviting inside. This place looked like an old warehouse, which was accurate, but the tavern inside was much nicer than the building or even the neighborhood itself would have suggested.

The menu did not really have anything that he liked, but his dad was able to get him a quesadilla without the onions and the peppers. Preston did not notice that his dad drank two beers. Unlike when his parents took him out together, they did not stay too long after eating their food.

"Remind me what time you have practice tomorrow," Haynes said to his son. They were driving home, and it was getting late, but the sky was still bright enough for golf.

"Twelve o'clock."

"High noon."

"Yeah," Preston said, thinking about his next day of practice.

"Remember, no swimming until after."

"I know dad; I know."

"Ok, well, plan on me taking you. I'll probably just stick around and watch practice and take you home, too."

"Ok dad. Don't forget that we're taking David home with us."

"That's right," Haynes said, reminded of the agreement made with their son. There was another commitment that he himself also made, but he could not recall exactly to what they had agreed. "Ok, sounds good champ. You guys can do all the swimming you want afterward."

"Oh, we plan to do that. I told him to bring his swim trunks."

"Smart."

"And he's going to bring his bike, so you'll need to make room in the back."

"I don't know about that."

"But he has to bring his bike," Preston pleaded. "That's how he gets to practice; besides, that's part of what we're going to do. I can't show him around the neighborhood by walking. Duh, dad."

Haynes relented. His wife's car was not in the driveway and Preston was apparently his only ally in the family right now. "Ok, ok. Good point, kiddo. I'll make sure there's room back there."

"Thanks dad!" Preston also noticed that his mom's car was not parked in the driveway or on the narrow street. "Where's mom?"

"I don't know."

Preston recognized that his dad thought it was strange, but he was not worried in the same way as his adult in the room. They walked inside and neither noticed anything different from when they left.

Each wished that there was leftover pizza to munch on.

"Hey dad, do you think we could go up in the attic to look for those marbles?"

"Right now?"

"Yeah, I thought that if we did it when mom wasn't here, then we wouldn't have to listen to her complain about it."

Haynes laughed at his son. *The kid had a good point there.* Without asking why his son had a newfound interest in marbles, the parent again relented to the wishes of his son. "You know what, let's go do this thing."

Preston jumped for joy but otherwise restrained his enthusiasm. He did not know yet if he was going to sell them, but he wanted to have the collection easily accessible just in case. All the better for keeping his options open.

Climbing into the attic was easy once his dad pulled down the stairs from the ceiling. Preston carefully watched his dad's actions, trying to cast each one to memory for future use in case he ever wanted to go exploring up above on his own. Nothing appeared complicated about what his dad did to make the stairs appear.

Haynes went up before his son, reaching through the dark to turn on the only light in the attic by pulling on the string. With enough light to see, he turned his attention to his son at the top of the stairs. "Watch your step up here. Don't step anywhere that you don't see one of these boards, either on end like this or laid out flat like that." He pointed to the different flooring options that would support his weight.

"What if we step anywhere else?"

"You'll go through the floor and your feet will be sticking out of the ceiling."

"Really?"

"Well, maybe not for you, yet, but definitely if I did it. I'd probably go all the way through, to tell you the truth."

"Straight to the basement, huh dad...?"

"Ok smart aleck." Haynes looked around the room before committing to a path. He turned back to his son. "You know what, just stay there by the steps. I know which box we need."

Preston watched his dad move carefully across the room, each step chosen by need. When he reached his destination, he moved one box before opening another. With few other movements, he removed a satchel and returned the lid to the box before crossing his previous path in reverse. The young boy could almost feel the energy of the bag as his dad approached. It was impossible to know how many marbles were inside or what their appraisal might be, but Preston could almost imagine the bag glowing with worth.

"Here you go," Haynes said, handing the bag towards his son. At the last minute, he pulled his hand back. "Actually, climb back down the stairs first. The steps were like those in a navy ship, and not as safe as normal stairs. He wanted his son to have both hands available for navigating back down to the floor below.

Preston did not immediately understand his dad's concern and wondered if he was going to take an inventory of the marbles inside. Once they were on the same page, Preston started down.

His heart stopped when he heard his mom's voice from behind.

"What are you two doing up there?" Her inquiry did not have the edge that he associated with getting caught in the act of doing anything disappointing, but he knew that could all change in an instant, and he figured that it would once she saw the bag of marbles and realized what was happening. Surely his mom was going to put two and two together and come up with 125 reasons for him to be in deep trouble.

"Getting some marbles down from the attic for our son to play with," Haynes said, holding the bag up as if it was proof of him being a good parent and not evidence of their son's guilt.

Preston swallowed hard. He wondered at what point his short life would flash before his eyes and if he would even know it before his mom killed him. Should he just take his chances and fall off the ladder on purpose? Certainly any distraction was better than what he was about to face.

"Oh," Janay instead said, her tone flat. As if that was it, she turned to walk back downstairs.

Still certain he was in trouble, Preston rushed down the steps to prepare for whatever his mom was about to say. *Was it so bad that she had to walk away?*

"Wait a minute," Haynes said, following his son down the stairs and handing the bag to Preston without another thought to its contents. "Where have you been?"

Janay turned around and looked at them both. Her eyes were red, but her makeup did not seem smeared or diluted in any way by tears. Her hair was still pulled back, and she was still dressed in her work clothes, but she seemed a disheveled mess. "I don't know. What do you mean?"

"It's after eight o'clock. Did you have to work late?"

"No, I got off at the normal time."

"Did your workout date with Kellen run long, then?" Haynes was clearly upset, but he was careful to keep his emotions in check, always as a habit, but especially now with his son watching.

"Kellen?" Janay's eyes widened as she said the name. "Oh my God, I need to call him. I've never blown him off before."

"What has gotten into you? You're worried about calling him, now? You didn't see enough of him the last three hours?"

"I haven't seen him today."

"What did you do after work, then?"

"I don't know," Janay said to her husband, her words sincere, "I guess I was just driving around."

"Trying to avoid something?"

Janay tried to recall why it had taken her so long to get home from work, and she realized that she could recall nothing except driving one way and then another and yet still more ways, around her target - their home - but never actually finding it until too many things came together at once for her to ignore. She easily could have been driving still if not for those little reminders. "Just thinking, I suppose."

"Just thinking," Haynes repeated, looking back at his son. "You might have time for one last swim before you need to get ready for bed. Big day tomorrow."

"Big day tomorrow," Preston repeated before disappearing down the hall and into his room.

Preston closed the door and ignored any conversations his parents were having or other sounds he may have heard. He was going to change into his swim trunks and disappear into the pool, but first he wanted to see what his new cache of marbles looked like. He first made toward his desk, but then he thought about the sound dumping the marbles would make; he switched his step and walked over to his bed.

Without ceremony, Preston dumped the marbles onto his flattened bed sheet.

His eyes were immediately drawn to every marble at once.

First, he saw a large boulder that was clear and had a red tornado through the center. Next, he saw a light blue shooter with a band of white and a swirl of red. Another marble had brilliant green and yellow hues. Still another was purple with many shades of violet and indigo all twisted and combined. There were little peewees and big boulders. Yellow ones and slightly black ones with a haze of clear gray; one solid iron biggie that looked capable of destroying all comers. There were more aggies than anything. There was also a long piece of string that was tied at the ends with the tiniest of knots. He did not know that was the circle used for the competition of the game named after the pieces used to play it: marbles.

Preston thought about counting the little glass balls, but there seemed too many to even begin.

The 10-year-old was impressed with the collection that his grandpappy had amassed in his lifetime; he was certain that none of these originally belonged to his mom. He had memories of the large man, and he knew that his mom had at least mentioned how her dad was a champ at collecting marbles around his neighborhood.

At first, Preston had assumed that she meant her dad used to walk around collecting marbles like discarded aluminum, but now he understood about playing keepsies and what that meant.

Almost without thinking, Preston knew that he could not sell all these gems. His mind was young, and his brain was still developing, but even he understood that some of these little objects were important to be saved in order to at least help in recalling that part of his grandpappy, a man he never really knew but a teacher who nonetheless left behind his own brand of lessons. Picking up one of the marbles, a mid-size beauty that could only be described as a galaxy inside a globe, Preston tried to imagine how his mom's dad had arrived at owning this treasure. Who did the man beat to secure this marble? Had he lost it before and won it back? Did the man even care about winning this piece?

It was easy for Preston to imagine all manner of stories for any of the little gems strewn out before him. Did he even want to sell any of these?

After what seemed like a long time, Preston selected five of the marbles to sell and put the rest back in their bag. He put the five expendable marbles under his pillow like important, discarded teeth, and he put the more comprehensive collection in his sock drawer.

The young boy felt as if a burden had been lifted from his shoulders. There were no more marbles to be found, now all that was left was to sell just a few of them, just these five; sell these five, that was all, for now, just five little beauties, one a champion boulder with a red twist and another a longshot peewee with the black dot, and three others equally random but only slightly less, nostalgic.

Preston changed into a pair of swim shorts and took his last swim before practice the next day, his last swim before learning about the depths of despair, his last swim before his mom's marbles were on the line.

Chapter 31

S hannon Louise was the first one awake on Saturday morning. Unable to sleep, the young girl, five months from being a teenager, was awake before the sun could rise on her street.

Though she did not get out of bed until over an hour after first waking, she spent the time thinking, dwelling on her actions of the past week. Her stubbed toe still hurt, not much, but just enough so that she could remember what a bad day was like, enough to decide that today was going to be different.

So far, in just her first week, she had earned $87.00, $123.00 if she counted the marbles. She had spent about $70, so she had profited $53.00. Not caring that she had only earned $17.00 of that total, the only reality was that she still needed $447.00. That was about three hundred cups away, much better than the four hundred she was prepared to sell.

A reason for optimism!

She understood that she would not have any more marbles to count on, but she also realized that she had missed out on a lucrative – not her word – Friday and had still not seen what a Saturday of business was like; maybe the weekend days would be her best opportunities for making money.

Maybe today would be the day that would change her life.

The young businesswoman did not think in those terms, but her mind was open to any possibility.

She had her lemonade stand set up and ready for business – the new powder mix was so much easier than squeezing lemons – before the first garage sale in the neighborhood had pulled open their own doors.

Shannon Louise did not really understand words like optimism or positive thinking, but her mind was focused on success, and she had an innate belief in things turning out okay for her in the end. She was not without doubt, but the precocious 12-year-old was ready to face whatever demons came her way.

Chapter 32

D avid Hardy was the next one to wake up that day. Like the older girl he was going to meet, David also woke up before the crack of dawn. Still dressed in his sweatpants and favorite football jersey, the little kid was almost lost in his oversized clothes. After a quick visit to the bathroom, David went back to his room, grabbed a blanket from his bed, and draped it over his shoulders like a cape as he made his way to the kitchen. He poured himself a large bowl of cereal – his family poured the milk in the bowl, first, before the cereal was added – and walked out to the living room couch.

Once the television was flipped on, he ate his cereal and watched SpongeBob and Patrick until the next person woke up. He was not worried about practice; he would warm up by throwing at his pitching net in the backyard for thirty minutes before leaving. He also had no care for packing his things. He had everything he would need for a sleepover already wrapped up and inside his bag, everything except his toothbrush; he would need to remember that later.

David was also not concerned about the marbles he had stowed away in his bag, the ones he had zipped up inside his bag's inner pocket. The marbles were plenty safe in there – no one was going to search him – and he really had not given any thought to the condition of the colorful glass orbs once they were in someone else's possession. Had the youngest player on his team - his baseball team as well as the trio he would fall in with later in the day - thought about the afterlife of the marbles once they were out of his own life, surely he would have assumed that whoever would pay for them would also show them a nice home.

Watching cartoons and eating his cereal wrapped all warm in his blanket and oversized clothes, David Hardy thought nothing about the marbles at all, in fact. He did not understand the concept of compartmentalizing, but that is what he had done. No one was going to miss the marbles. He was going to sell the marbles. The marbles were safe in his bag and not needed again until he was at his friend's house.

No reason to spend time considering marbles.

The Fry Cook Games, one of his favorite episodes ever.

David munched his cereal and drank all the milk when he was done. He did not know it, but life was about to throw the young baseball phenom a curveball.

Chapter 33

───── 1 ─────

N either the receptionist nor the appraiser slept the night before, the period of darkness between Friday and Saturday. Not that they required rest. Each had their different haunts that occupied their time when not at work, but neither discussed their time at home with the other when they exchanged their morning greetings – usually nothing more than eye contact or a nod of acknowledgement. She lived much further away from the job than did he, a circumstance that was also true at their previous post up the state in Toledo many years before.

Their daily commutes, however, were equally timed and almost instantaneous.

There had been many times when neither was able to leave work until after dark, a job requirement on rare occasions, the rarity of which did nothing to make such times any less of an annoyance. Each understood that such were the rigors of their obligation and complaining did absolutely nothing to better relations with those either above, or below, their own standing. One time, a customer had taken so long flimflamming over the sale of his Pokémon collection that they had literally ended up being trapped at work for nearly an hour after dark.

It was a literal, living, Hell.

Never, though, had one of them ever shown up at a time different than the other. Not even on his first day was this receptionist ever late. The man he replaced, her second receptionist, was lost when his home was burned to the ground by a lightning strike. He was also never late. Deb lived in an old stone home on a national registry of historical places – St. Gallen, Switzerland, in fact - so she had little fear of being lost in a similar way. The receptionist hailed from a less sturdy home life, and his prospects for continued employment were as shaky as dried timber. The company fire department did their jobs better or worse depending on the spirit one devoted to the business, though, so he was on good standing.

Tardiness had no place where they were concerned, and there was no greater priority in their existence than in executing the duties of their jobs, which was serving the thing in the middle of her office, keeping it full and keeping whatever was on the other side - her boss or her boss's boss or whatever layer of hierarchy there was beyond the appraiser and the receptionist – content if not happy.

Keep it full; keep it happy.

Besides, company-provided transportation was an unwavering benefit of their contract.

This morning, just like every other, the appraiser and the receptionist walked around the corner just as the first light of day was rising over Cincinnati. The phone calls would not start for at least another couple of hours, but as far as they were concerned, they were open for business once they walked inside. Any change in the routine was a welcome relief and preferable to a boring day from Hell, but then again, even the most boring day was better than an eternity spent in the deepest pit of that void they ultimately served.

Chapter 34

Preston again woke up late, but today it was his dad that got him up and going, suggesting a shower to get the day started. Preston was going to protest, but he could sense that his dad was not in a joking mood. He also told Preston to get his room cleaned up since he would not have any other time to do it before practice and his friend coming over after.

The 10-year-old did not argue or complain about any of it. He was happy to be having a friend stay over, and he was excited for his friend to meet Shannon Louise as well as the marble lady. Plus, he could not wait to get all the business part of the visit over with and then just have fun swimming and playing catch or whatever else they did with their time after that.

His morning went by quickly, and he was surprised when his dad yelled up the stairs that they had to leave in ten minutes. Preston was more shocked when he came downstairs and realized that both his mom and his dad were dressed and planning to take him to baseball practice, together. He could not recall the last time that his family was all together outside of the house like this, and he found that he had to go all the way back to last year and his very first day of practice to find such a memory.

"Morning, mom."

"Good morning, Preston," his mother said. Drinking her coffee, her hair all pulled back, she seemed normal except for some puffiness under her bloodshot eyes. "How did you sleep, honey?"

"I slept good, mom." Preston sat down and wasted no time before plowing through the bowl of cereal waiting there for him.

Janay watched her son eat. He would never ask how his own mom slept, but she had not slept very much last night. Jealous of the trainer she finally told him about, her husband was clearly upset, and their disagreement weighed on her mind. She knew that she had done nothing wrong –

he was the one who slept on the couch – but she was having trouble justifying to herself why it had taken her so long to get home from work.

She had a hard time concentrating on anything from the previous day, really. Even her time at work was a blur, and she was burdened by feeling as if something important was being forgotten; whether that something was work related or personal, she did not have a clue, but assumed it had to be related to her job. Current troubles and some apathy notwithstanding, she did not think there was much in her personal life to be forgotten, at least as far as duties or responsibilities. Her son had his practice schedule, she had her work schedule, and the next scheduled visits for the family were a dentist appointment for Preston at the end of July, and a general check-up for Haynes the second week in August. Her own next appointment was with her gyno, but not until October.

Whatever it was, it would come to her, eventually. For now, she was content just watching her little sweety eat his Apple Jacks.

Janay Jackson was not really a drinker. Every once in a while, at a party or social gathering, she would have a drink or two just to break the ice or to carry as a prop. The mid-thirty, mother of one did not have any problem with drinking but drinking sure seemed to have a problem with her. The last time she had tied one on, at a relative's wedding, Janay had woken up the next morning with large gaps in her memory from the night before. Though she would eventually watch video to help coax some of those memories into showing themselves, the way she had felt that next day was similar to how she felt this morning. There was no headache, not today, but everything else seemed less important, her own actions and thoughts seemed less closely associated with anything real, like they were happening or occurring to someone else, and she was just a viewer with a bad connection.

That's kind of how she felt now, like she had a bad connection within herself, disassociated from the reality of her life happening around her, yet somehow without her, too. She was not tired, but she felt sleepy, her body's attempt at suggesting another reset, a close your eyes and everything is bound to be ok later type of reset.

Janay was content to simply watch her angel eat his breakfast, but it was gnawing at her from the inside; something in there was missing.

Chapter 35

B aseball practice dragged on forever, for Preston and David on the field, and especially for Haynes and Janay watching in the stands. With no conversation to kill the time, the two hours and ten minutes spent sitting under the midday sun was, for the parents, a much longer sentence than the time had been for the two boys involved in the activity.

When practice was over, no one was in the mood to linger.

"Hey mom and dad," Preston said as he and David walked up to the Jacksons.

"Done already?" Haynes asked.

"I thought it was never going to end," Preston said.

"Yeah, that was a long one," David agreed.

"Dad, have you ever met David?"

"I don't think so," Haynes said, extending his arm down to the kid smaller than his son. "Nice to meet you. I'm Mr. Jackson."

"Nice to meet you, sir."

"And mom," Preston started, "you met David at tennis lessons before."

Janay looked at the young boy who did seem familiar. She nodded her head without extending any other physical greeting. "Nice to meet you, again, David. You can call me Janay or Preston's mom or Mrs. Jackson, whatever you like."

"Nice to meet you," David began, "Preston's mom."

Preston watched the encounter, surprised. His mom was always in a hurry to leave practice, and she always introduced herself as Mrs. Jackson to his friends and teachers. Today, it was her husband who seemed anxious to leave.

"So, Preston says we're hauling your bike home with us, too."

"If that's ok," David said. "I brought my bike lock in case it doesn't fit."

Haynes nodded his head, impressed, before shaking his head. "We will make your bike fit, even if Mrs. Jackson has to ride on top of the car to make room."

Janay smiled at the mention of her name, but she did not protest her husband's comment.

"Thank you, sir. I don't think my dad really would have liked me leaving it, anyway."

"No, I suppose not."

The bike fit in the back of the SUV with no problem, and the group was on their way. Preston's dad broke the silence.

"I was thinking that we would flip the script and get our Friday pizza tonight."

"Trottas!" Preston looked at his friend. "Have you ever had Trottas pizza?"

"I don't think so."

"It's the best pizza in town."

"Besides that brewery down on Spring Grove," Haynes said. "That place actually has the best pizza in the city."

Janay agreed with the assessment, but she did not offer anything to the conversation. She was trying to remember why they did not eat pizza the day before, on Friday, like always. *Did I even eat last night after work?*

"Anything you don't like on your pizza, David?"

"I like pepperoni and green peppers."

"I'll probably get two pizzas, then, one for you guys and one for us."

"Sounds good, dad." Preston liked the pizza the way his parents ordered it, with more toppings, but he liked pepperoni and green peppers just fine.

"When we get home, I'm going to knock out some yard work and you guys can go play for a few hours. I'll have to run to the hardware store and a few other places, too, so I'll get the pizza later, and then you guys can just munch on it whenever you want to."

"Sounds like a plan, dad."

"And what do you young men have planned for today?" Janay asked. Her inquiries were normally more terse, and there was never a zero percent chance of her vetoing any plans she heard that did not fit with her expectations of how her son should spend his time.

Preston looked quickly at his friend, nudging him with an elbow and winking. "I was going to show him around the neighborhood, first, then go swimming afterwards."

"You guys don't want to jump in the pool now, to cool down after that practice?" Haynes asked.

"No, it's no fun to ride your bike all wet, dad."

"Good point, son, good point." Haynes knew that his son had a closet full of clothes into which he could change, and he suspected that his little friend also had a change of clothes with him, but the dad did not really care how his son spent his free time playing today. He was proud at the success his little man was having on the field during practice. Clearly, one year to mature had made a world of difference in Preston's game.

The drive did not take long, and once David's bike was free from the confines of the car, the two boys raced upstairs to put away the young visitor's bag.

Preston closed the door while David opened his bag and retrieved the marbles. "Check these out. Do you think they're worth anything?"

Preston looked at the marbles his friend owned. Like his own collection, David had all different sizes and colors of marbles. He had not gotten a close look, but really both sets of marbles, his and David's, did not look all that different from the marbles that Shannon Louise had to offer. To him, it was impossible to even guess what the value would be. "They sure look cool, but I can't tell what she'll offer for them."

"The marble guy is a she?"

"Yeah."

"That's cool, as long as she buys my marbles, I don't care what she is."

It was not David's best choice of words; if he knew, he would care.

Chapter 36

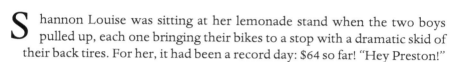

S hannon Louise was sitting at her lemonade stand when the two boys pulled up, each one bringing their bikes to a stop with a dramatic skid of their back tires. For her, it had been a record day: $64 so far! "Hey Preston!"

"Hey Shannon Louise."

"Who's your friend?"

"This is David Hardy."

David looked up, slightly bashful around the older girl, he smiled and mumbled something she could not understand.

"What are you two studs up to today?"

"We are going back to the marble store."

The expression on Shannon Louise's face changed; no longer smiling like before, she now had her lip curled up in a sneer. "Oh, that place."

David could tell the girl was less enthusiastic about the visit than Preston had been when talking about the experience.

"Yeah," Preston said, not really noticing, "I brought a couple more that I found, and David has some too."

Without needing to walk out from behind her lemonade stand, she pointed to the counter as she spoke to David. "Let me see what you got."

David pulled his bag out of his pocket and set it down on the counter. The colorful objects were visible through the clear plastic, and David did not think the girl really wanted him to let them roll freely on the counter.

Shannon Louise looked at the bag. In the same way that space is said to look the same no matter which direction you look – a concept that seemed ridiculous to the little science nerd within her – so too did David's bag of marbles resemble the one she had sold to the woman. She picked up the bag and examined them more closely. The little guy had about half as many as she sold. Not an expert, the young businesswoman inside her had spent some time looking these items up on the Internet, and she failed to see how they could possibly be any different from those she already sold.

"Pretty nice bag of marbles," she said.

"Thanks," David answered sheepishly. His cheeks felt warm.

"I brought five this time," Preston said, holding out his own little gathering in the palm of his hand.

Shannon Louise glanced over without leaning in for a closer look. The one thing she could tell was that Preston had five marbles, each one unique by their size as much as by the design of their colors. "Nice."

"So do you want to come?" Preston looked up, cupping his eyes from the afternoon sun.

"You know what, I do want to come. I would like to have a few words with that appraiser lady."

"You didn't like her?" David asked.

"Oh, she was nice enough, I suppose, but she didn't pay me crap compared with what Preston got for his one marble." Ready to close shop for the day, Shannon Louise started gathering up her things. "I can't wait to see what she says about your marbles, though."

Preston and David helped clean up as best as they could; Preston remembered how he had helped before and tried to repeat those tasks while David was impressed at the inside of the girl's home as he carried two almost empty pitchers of lemonade.

Once they were on their bikes and headed for the marble shop, it was a short ride to the busy intersection; this time, however, instead of walking her bike across the street, Shannon Louise led the way by staying on her bike and pedaling to their destination.

David did not think twice about following her, but Preston felt guilty about the act. In the end, after thinking at least twice about what he was doing, Preston brought up the rear without stepping off his bike. If he had stopped to walk across the street, he probably would have been forced to wait at the crosswalk for the next cycle of the traffic light.

"This is the place?" David asked, looking at the plain façade.

"Yep," Preston said.

"Come on, we can take our bikes inside." Shannon Louise was aggressive now in taking charge of the group; the closer they got to seeing the appraiser again, the more the young girl felt the need to hurry.

Walking through the door in the same order in which they arrived, Shannon Louise led the group inside, followed by David and then Preston. As before, they each walked their bicycles inside the business. Once they were all inside and the door was closed, the little window slid open.

"How may we...," the receptionist paused slightly as he looked at the three pre-teens, "help you, today?"

"We want to talk to the appraiser," Shannon Louise said. "We were here Thursday."

"And...?"

"And we want to talk to her."

"Do you have something you want her to appraise?"

"Yes." Shannon Louise looked at the two boys then back at the receptionist. "Well, they do. I just want to talk to her."

The receptionist squinted his eyes. Every interaction with the public was different, but nearly all fell into a predictable range of patterns. This interaction, this little girl, was already well outside the bounds of those norms. "And what is it that you have for her today, then?"

David was the first to pull out his bag of marbles.

"Marbles," the receptionist said, happy to again be on a familiar track. "Bound to be some good ones in there."

"You would think," Shannon Louise said.

Before sliding shut his window on the group, the receptionist looked again at the young troublemaker.

"This is the part where we wait for the appraiser," Shannon Louise said. "Cue the spooky music for when she walks in the room."

"You really don't like this lady," David said.

"She's just jealous that I got so much more for mine than she did for all of hers."

The tall girl shot her little buddy an unapproving glance. "Yeah, it did kind of suck, Preston, but not because I was jealous of you. I'm glad you took that lady's stupid money, and I hope that she pays you a lot for those five tweekers in your pocket, same for you little guy, but I just don't understand why mine were worth so little."

"I'm sure I just got lucky with that one," Preston said. "I went into it thinking eight bucks would have been good."

"I don't know what I expected, to tell you the truth, but something about it afterwards just left a bad taste in my mouth." Shannon Louise shook her head and felt a shiver go down her back. "No, something was off about her alright."

"I don't know," Preston said, trying to remember if he had felt one way or the other about the lady before she had dropped a stack of cash on him; after that he pretty much just remembered quiet elation.

David looked around and stuck the bag of marbles back in his pocket. Like all of them, like almost everyone who ever comes in, he was taken by the general plainness of the room. Drab white, one door, one window, and the sign explicitly declaring *All Sales Are Final*; that was the room. "I have a number in mind; I won't take less than that."

Preston looked at his friend. He really had not considered if he had a base price for the five marbles in his pocket. His brain had been assuming that he would make as much as before, maybe each, but he now supposed that it was more likely that the first one had been a fluke. Eight dollars each seemed like a better number to expect.

"How much?" Shannon Louise asked, looking squarely at David.

David's eyes were locked on the taller, older girl. Her personality was more forceful than his, but he still understood the value of hiding your cards. "I don't know if we should say that out loud. What if they listen to you while you wait?"

Shannon's eyes looked quickly about the room. She had not considered that possibility, but it did make sense. On their first visit, she tried to recall if they had said anything while waiting that would have cost them – her – money in the exchange. Maybe they didn't even need electronic equipment, the walls could just be thin.

"I apologize for your wait," the appraiser said, reeling off her lines as soon as the door opened and before the door had time to close behind her. She recognized two of the three immediately, and this time she was not surprised by their bikes parked off to the side of the room. "Oh, hello today."

"Hi," Shannon Louise said flatly.

"Have you brought a friend with some marbles for me to appraise?" She smiled at David. "Good afternoon young man, my name is Deb Vilitch."

"Hello, ma'am," David said. He pulled the bag back out of his pocket, extending it forward for her to see.

"Ok, let me take a look then." As she took hold of the bag of marbles, she also grabbed the tray from the hand of the receptionist, who wasted no time in sliding shut his window.

Shannon Louise noticed the exchange, and how the man seemed to open the window at the right time. It seemed like proof and she became convinced that the newest little guy, David, had been right about some type of surveillance being in use.

The appraiser poured the marbles into the tray and watched them spread to find their own place on top of the felt bottom. Her eyes were happy with the sight. "You have quite a few quality pieces here."

"I do?"

"Oh yes, yes indeed." She again looked back at the colors in front of her. This was not the most dazzling display she had ever seen, certainly not even the third or fourth best she had seen this week, but it was an adequate collection, representative of multiple sources, and worthy of paying tribute. Not even the most she had seen this week; she was still impressed enough to make an offer well above David's unspoken floor. "Ok then."

Shannon Louise noticed that the window again slid open.

"We are prepared to offer you one thousand dollars for your bag of marbles."

David's eyes almost popped out of his head. The amount was impossible to comprehend. Did his parents know what these things were worth? Was there a real chance that they could miss these little pieces of glass?

Preston reached into his pocket and pulled out his five marbles. Suddenly, his mind again raced back to thinking of them as worth much more than eight bucks a piece. He looked at them as if he could discern their worth.

"Wait a minute," Shannon Louise interrupted.

The appraiser did not like this little girl interfering with her pitch, and she looked at her to convey this displeasure. Her own anger, however, was blunted when she saw and became transfixed with the five marbles in this other little boy's open hand. These five were together as bright as was the entirety of David's sample, and each one was specific in its brilliance.

Having seen them, Deb Vilitch could not unsee them, and seeing them meant wanting them, needing to have them. "We could call it eleven hundred, just for the symmetry."

The receptionist produced a short stack of bills from behind his window.

"No. Wait." Shannon Louise put her arm up as if blocking the sale. Sensing that she now had the appraiser's attention, she continued. "How can you say that?"

"How can I say what?" the appraiser replied. At once, she was conducting business with the littlest boy, entranced by the handful of marbles being held by the other boy, and engaged in this vapid discussion with the little girl. She may as well have been juggling cats.

"How can you just say that his bag is worth over a thousand dollars and Preston's single marble was worth over a hundred dollars and my bag, MY STUPID BAG OF MARBLES, was only worth thirty-five dollars? Thirty-six with the kicker. How can you say that with a straight face?"

"Sour apples, dear?"

"Sour apples?" Shannon Louise repeated. "Are you baking a pie?"

"It's a saying, a phrase, it means that you are jealous of your friends," Deb Vilitch looked down on the girl. "That way of thinking will not keep you pretty for very long, little one."

"I'm just saying…," Shannon Louise began, not sure what she was going to say.

The appraiser raised her eyebrows in mockery.

"I'm just saying that I want my marbles back. I have your stupid money right here."

"All sales are final, in case you haven't learned how to read yet, dear." The appraiser pointed at the sign before looking again at the two boys. "I'm sorry that your friend interrupted us, now how about that offer?"

"Wait a minute," Shannon Louise again interrupted.

"No," Deb Vilitch said, the anger in her glare no longer diluted by thoughts of the cache within her clutches, "you listen to me, all sales are final. Your marbles have been processed; they are gone. I couldn't give them back if I wanted to."

This made the little girl furious. She had not really expected the lady to give her the marbles back but knowing that they had already moved on somehow made everything about it seem more final. "But it's not just final, is it?"

"What could you possibly mean?"

"After you buy them and we leave, that's when you get your payoff."

"We are a business."

"Your business is marbles."

"That's the deal. Sell us your marbles, and we will give you cash. Fair trade."

"Except it's not a fair trade. It's more than that. You don't want old marbles."

"And…?"

"And, and why not?"

"If you want to run your own marble business, then please feel free to set up a shop right next door if you like. Buy all the old marbles you want."

"Well, you can keep my marbles, but I'm not giving you any of the nostalgia from it. We never agreed to that."

Deb Vilitch's eye twitched, betraying the pang of doubt raised by the little girl's comment.

Preston and David watched the exchange, amazed that the little girl was holding her own with a professional adult like the appraiser. Shannon Louise noticed the woman flinch.

"And same goes for my friends there," Shannon Louise said, pointing at the boys, "tell her that you'll sell her your marbles, but not any of the nostalgia that goes along with it."

The appraiser raised to her full height, now visibly agitated. "That is ridiculous."

"No, no it's not. Without knowing it's Babe Ruth's baseball mitt then it's just a stupid piece of leather. You can keep my stupid marbles, and I'm going to keep your stupid money, but you can forget about me giving you the provident."

"You mean the provenance?" Deb Vilitch said, laughing away the threat. This girls' marbles had been void of any such regality. She had not yet been hit with the reality of her own arrogance providing the little girl with the term she needed to qualify the argument.

"Yeah, and same for my friend. Tell her Preston. Say she can't have the provenance to your marble." When Shannon Louise repeated the word, she did her best to mimic the appraiser and make it sound dramatic.

"Yeah," Preston said, "we didn't agree to anything like that."

"I gave you one hundred and twenty-five dollars for a marble! A marble! And you want to get smart with me?"

"All sales are final, but they really aren't final until after we leave, isn't that right?"

"You have no idea who you are talking to little girl."

"Do you mean just you or whoever you have listening to us in here?"

Deb smiled. "You have no idea who is listening in here."

"So you are listening to us in private."

"Someone is always listening, child." She looked back again at the two boys. She did not want to lose this sale. "Again, I apologize for your friend's interruption. Like I said, you both have exquisite collections there that we would love to pay you for. We will of course sell them to recover a profit, but you will be paid fairly, of course."

"Tell her she can't have the nostalgia that goes with it and see if she still wants to pay you for them."

"You are impossible little girl! Why are you still in my store?"

"If I leave, they're leaving with me."

It was a statement and not a threat, but Deb Vilitch bit her lip and tried to regain control of the situation. Like working for a check that was already spent, the appraiser knew that this week would not be a success unless she had this business with these boys completed and their marbles dumped into the artifact.

Not after seeing them.

The pile of cash that the receptionist provided for the offer to David was still sitting there, just like the offer to the young man.

David really wanted to leave his marbles behind and run out with the pile of money, but he knew that amount of cash would cause nothing but problems. If he did the right thing and told his parents about the windfall, they would punish him for stealing; if he sold them and didn't tell them, it would eventually come out that they were missing and then he would feel like a thief. Either way, the amount was too far above his floor for him to even consider. If the marbles were worth this much money, one way or another his parents would notice them missing. He could not do that to his mom, nostalgia or not.

"So, what do you say?" The appraiser looked at David. "Accept the offer and I can make one for your friend." Deb Vilitch looked at Preston and winked. "Five good ones there, too."

"I have to pass," David said, picking up the bag and helping himself to putting his marbles back inside the clear plastic.

"You have to pass?" Even after the confrontation with the young girl, the appraiser had never expected such a rejection. "Excuse me?"

"I can't sell them for that much."

"You want more?"

"I could never take that much money home without my parents knowing."

"You don't have to tell your parents everything, you know."

"He gave you his answer, lady," Shannon Louise barked.

Disgusted, Deb Vilitch looked away from David, slicing a glance at Shannon Louise before setting her gaze on Preston; she forced a smile. "Well now, just you and me, little buddy. I don't even have to look very close to tell you that I can offer you," the demon appraiser paused as she glanced at the stack of cash already in the window, "one thousand one hundred dollars. The same amount for your five marbles that I was prepared to offer your friend for his entire bag of glass."

"Don't do it Preston, she's not playing straight."

Preston recognized that was a lot of money, more than Shannon Louise had hoped to make by working all summer, but he was now spooked by the argument he had just witnessed. He didn't want some stranger to show up at their house asking his mom to explain the history of any of these marbles. She would kill him, for real.

"Do we have an agreement, Preston?"

"What if I just agree to sell them, but you can't have any of the stories or anything. I don't want my mom bothered."

Clearly off her game and now on the defensive, the appraiser muttered to find the words. "Well, well, why I mean, that is all just ridiculous. The agreement is straightforward. You sell me the marbles, and I give you cash. No need for clauses. No need for stipulations."

"But all sales are final?" Shannon Louise asked. It was obvious that she was mocking the appraiser.

"You are ridiculous!"

"Then agree to it if it's ridiculous."

"Who are you to come in here and make demands and try to change the rules of my business. If you don't like my rules, then you never had to sell me your worthless marbles!" The appraiser tried to recall the last time she had hated anyone as much as she now hated this little girl. If she were allowed, she would have strangled her right then and there, wringing her neck and twisting her spine until that stupid, self-confident grin was pulled right off her face.

That was not her department. The company had other ghouls for that type of work.

Without saying a word, she looked at Preston, her tone again softened. "What do you say, kiddo...?"

Preston looked from the appraiser to the money to his friends.

"Ask her if you're playing keepsies, Preston. Ask her that."

Everyone in the room looked at Shannon Louise.

The appraiser was the one who had the expression the little girl would be hard-pressed to ever forget, the one that would, from this day on, occasionally wake her from sleep screaming.

Clearly angry, her patience at its frazzled end, the professional woman was unsure exactly where this encounter had gone so wrong, and the blend of confusion and anger created a scowl of injured hatred that was as scary as any Halloween mask. "Of course we are playing for keepsies, little girl; such is life."

"But you never said that, and everyone knows that you have to agree to that before you start the game."

"Is that what you think this is, some kind of game?" The angry demon sneered at the 7th grader.

"You tell us, but you know that you're wrong."

The appraiser stood silent. The little girl was of course not wrong.

Preston looked at the marbles in his hand. Suddenly the whole thing, selling the family's stuff, crossing the forbidden street, all the things surrounding this place – except his new friendships – seemed tainted and wrong. He wanted the money, but he already had a lot of money that he did not know how to spend. Maybe he could always come back later if money again became a concern.

He looked up from the marbles as he slid them back into his pocket. "I think I have to pass, too."

Deb Vilitch wanted to scream and lash out, allow her true nature to expose itself, but she was a professional, and she was bound by professional constraints, rules in place to ensure that the business operated and functioned in the shadows without interference from unwanted attention. There were other ways to follow up beyond these four walls, beyond this time, not for her, directly, but for others either up or down the chain.

"Please stop back again when you are serious about making some money and not wasting my time." The taste of the defeat stung like salt on a wound, and the demon's mouth seemed filled with it. Having seen the marbles now leaving her grasp left her with an unusually severe sense of loss, a feeling to which she was generally immune.

David led the way out followed by Shannon Louise and then Preston. He felt like he should apologize or something, but then the taller girl leaned back and whispered in his ear. He looked at her unsure, but she nodded encouragement.

He turned back to face the appraiser.

"I'm sorry, ma'am, but I also want to say that I never gave you the provenance of that marble I sold you. I just sold you the glass."

"You sold me that damned marble and everything about it! Get over that, kid."

"What if it wasn't his to take?" Shannon Louise asked, her bike in the doorway blocking it.

"Then he shouldn't have sold it."

"The nostalgia and memories and stuff weren't his to sell."

"Then he shouldn't have sold them."

"Well then they shouldn't be yours to take."

"And yet we did." The appraiser seemed proud in her revelation.

"Well then, he just took it back the same way. Choke on that one."

"You never said we were playing for keepsies," Preston added.

"GET OUT OF MY SHOP NOW! GET OUT NOW! YOU WILL PAY FOR THIS LITTLE GIRL. ONE DAY YOU WILL PAY FOR THIS! I PROMISE YOU THAT!"

Preston scrambled to follow Shannon Louise out of the shop and onto the sidewalk. David was already back across the busy street.

Before the light changed for them to cross, Shannon Louise looked Preston in the eyes. "Whatever happens or doesn't happen because of that, it sure felt good."

Preston forced a laugh. It felt like something alright.

"We made that lady pissed off."

"*You* sure did."

"Me?" Shannon Louise said, acting surprised. "You're the one who really pushed her over the edge."

"Do you think she'll call the police?"

"Why, because we wouldn't take her money and sell her our marbles?" They would say that she lost hers." The two of them laughed and crossed the street. The pain of money lost was a real feeling, but as they caught up with David and pedaled away from the shop, the memory of the cash left sitting there became less real.

Chapter 37

P reston's mom was there waiting for her son when he pulled into the driveway. She was caught off-guard by the two friends with him. She recognized the boy but could not recall it was from baseball practice and tennis lessons, and now she was remembering a conversation about a friend staying over. Why had she ever agreed to that? What most surprised her, though, was the addition of the third wheel, the girl she did not recognize but who was clearly taller than either boy.

She addressed the group as they pulled in.

"Well look at the lot of you."

"Hi mom."

"Are you going to introduce me, son?"

"This is Shannon Louise," Preston said, turning to his best friend for a day. The rest of the summer they would see each other the two times that Preston again visited her lemonade stand, but after she earned her money and closed up shop for the summer in mid-July, their encounters were much more sporadic. The two of them would still see each other in passing, and occasionally during high school find themselves at the same parties on the weekends, but never again would their bond be as strong as now. "She's pretty awesome."

"Shannon Louise? Is that your last name?"

"No, just my name. My last name is Tate. We live over on Coronado."

"Oh," Janay said, smiling at the tall girl with the welcoming smile. Whatever feelings she had upon realizing her son was gone and she had no idea where her family had disappeared to, were now replaced by a joy that her son was making some friends around the neighborhood. "Well nice to meet you too, Shannon Louise."

"Nice to meet you."

She looked at the younger boy standing there, a young kid who clearly did less swimming than her son. "I'm Missus Jackson."

"Hi Missus Jackson," David said, playing along with what he assumed was a mom joke.

"Haha mom, you have met David like ten times now."

Janay Jackson looked at her son's younger friend. He did look familiar, and she did recall talking about the kid who also played tennis. It was all so familiar. Unlike before, when the confusion had been due to the missing pieces and routes to remembering, this time the information was crammed in and not yet sorted and back to a familiar place of reference.

"Are you guys going swimming?"

"Yeah, mom, if that's ok."

"It is."

Preston motioned for his friends to follow him.

"I don't know where your dad ran off to."

"He said he was going to run some errands and then pick up the pizza." Preston stopped walking and looked back towards his mother.

"Pizza? On a Saturday?

"We didn't have it last night."

Janay tried again to remember what if anything she had eaten for dinner the night before.

"Mom, are you ok?"

Janay squinted her eyes at her son, the light of her life. She felt the need to catch up with her husband, and she knew that she owed Kellen an apology for... something. Looking at her little man and his little band of friends, she saw nothing wrong with the day that would not eventually be able to work itself out.

"Yeah, babe, I'm ok." She rubbed her son's head and turned to follow him.

There would be one day in the future when, alone, she would feel an irresistible need to look for a lost marble, and like her son she would spend an afternoon going through every nook and cranny in their home: to no avail. Though she would not think about the shooter that was colored like a yellow rose with a beautiful brown swirl for quite some time, the memory of it, and everything associated with it, the nostalgia, was still there.

Chapter 38

Thomas Abell sat at his wife's bedside. His world having fallen apart in just a few days, the broken man sat holding his wife's hand, trying to focus on making sense of her condition while also trying not to be distracted by wondering why his daughter was not responding to any of his calls, texts, or even e-mails. She was a disappointment, and it was just like her to not be present when truly needed, now, in the midst of a family crisis.

The dad in the man could not help but think that a gentle and sincere visit by their daughter would awaken some attention or interest from Mabel.

To say that Mabel was delusional would be incorrect, there was nothing in her brain that was invalidating the memories she did still possess, and there were no phantom visions trying to lure her remaining thoughts down the darkest corridors of a human's imagination.

Describing her condition as catatonic was also a misnomer. The woman was awake and alert and aware, to a degree, but not so much as she was overwhelmingly distracted by the missing pieces. Without those bridges holding together and joining the framework of her mind, she could not get past the one simple task of trying to recall her daughter's name.

Mabel could hear and see all happening around her, and to say that she did not care would also be incorrect. The feeling of being in diapers was not lost on her. She could even hear her beloved husband speaking at times the very name she was in vain trying to recall, but so intent was she on getting over that lone hump of remembrance that she was oblivious to the truth she was seeking.

In her heart, Mabel knew what it meant to not respond, and she was fully aware that being in this place was certainly not where she wanted to be, but any attempt at anything else was now secondary to the simplest of tasks: remembering the name of her only child.

Thomas held his wife's hand, this room now like a second place of living, a place separate from the comfort of simply being at home, surrounded by the familiarity of, if nothing else, your own things; this was like a prison for his soul. At times he would mention that their daughter was worried, and on her way, even speaking her name aloud, but it was all to no avail. Nothing seemed to penetrate the shell of isolation that had engulfed his wife whole.

Their daughter was not coming any more than her mother was coming back; that first fact would be confirmed shortly. Each of his girls were gone, and each, like the father seated here now in this room, had a second place of living, their own life after life, their own living Hell; in two cases, their own fate worse than death.

Chapter 39

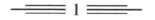

D eb Vilitch walked in her office and screamed, an uncharacteristic expression of emotion for the demon. The events of today would certainly be etched in her permanent record. She had job security, and being terminated was not a fear, not a real fear for her, anyway; she was skilled and had an eye for judging worth.

Besides, she was not just any ghoul; she was a demon.

She would never read about the other ills of today's world - like the body of yet another fentanyl overdose, Agatha Marble Whittaker, Aggie Marble to her mom, being found behind the wheel of a parked car - but the appraiser would have understood just the same, probably better, than most people would try.

Deb Vilitch walked over to the pit and looked inside. Not quite the sun on her face but something else, a different type of acceptance, even if only illusory.

Without notice, the fire bubbled and a small round ball, flaming and quick, shot out from the pit and exploded through her eye, lodging itself permanently in her mind if not her head. The shooter that was colored like a yellow rose with a beautiful brown swirl in the middle, and the defeat that it represented, would forever belong to her as a memory as well as a piece of her being.

Before the next seller arrived, her appearance would be fixed and her eye would be back to working its magic, but that little ball of a memory, her own keepsake, would be there burning, forever, an eternal reminder of the little girl who defeated the devil bitch at her own game of keepsies.

The End

Tales of Terror

Not One of Us Is Against Us

═══ I ═══

W elcome behind the curtain, the thick velvet pall that separates our life from your own inevitable ends. Hamlet lamented that final veil, the ultimate land from which no traveler returns unshrouded; indeed, we respect the finality of that crossing.

What lies on the other side of anyone's *true* final day is not our concern or purview; we have no stake in that fight.

Our currency-in-trade is soul-crushing, and as such we do maintain relations with a variety of characters and unsavory sorts - one in particular who is by far our best customer – but we are not evil. I would argue that we are in fact good and needed, a requirement for the proclivity of the life we all recognize; indeed, without fear what is there but death?

We, again, respect the finality – or not – of that final barrier, so we choose to have our fun – get our work done – on this side of that line, more or less. There are fates worse than death, and whether that time between is fleeting or forlorn, forgiving or fraught with torture, it is in that wedge where we find the currency we seek.

We, again, are not evil. Our associations may appear grim, but we are loyal to the nature that binds us all and we would never disavow our relationship with anyone whom we employ or with whom we do business, the good and the bad alike. We do use magic and spells and altered perspectives to achieve our goals, but such things, though uncommon, are not themselves evil.

At worst, we are guilty by association; at best, we were here first.

But we do maintain our privacy in a way that could imply some deeper level of guilt. Our headquarters, the last outpost of The East Erie Company, is a mere manor located on the outskirts of Patrick, Ohio, in the actual heart of East Erie County. Yes, we share a name with the county in which we reside, and that does at times make for a confusing paper trail, but we were here long before the incorporation of the state, not to mention any designation as a territory, settlement, encampment, tribal meeting area, or at the foot of a glacier more than a mile high.

We were here first, since there were creatures here who could think outside of themselves, that is, those beings capable of knowing fear of that world in which they live.

Our dwelling has been modernized, in a sense, enough so that we are able to operate globally from our little home here in Ohio. It is not as grand as it could be, certainly not like the gawdy outpost in Orleans, France had been, but for a home last renovated in the 1890's and polished to the highest standards of that time – an era that happened to also produce some of the finest houses in Patrick to this day – we could not be happier with it.

There are not many of us who live and work here – at the headquarters in Ohio - and it is rare when we receive a visitor. The grove of trees – the locals call it a woods - surrounding our home is protected from development by an easily enforceable spell; we own the land. Any miscast eyes that do wander across our manor are afflicted with a loss of any memory of that fact. This is done through a slightly more complicated manner of sorcery.

Shamira – currently – is the one in charge of the security we expect here at the last outpost of The East Erie Company. Though she is a talented and spirited demon, her loyalties as of late have been questionable. Some may consider it weakness to even keep her around considering some recent transgressions on her part, but the reality of it is that I do not have time to break-in a replacement for her position. She is competent and in her own cold ways personable and charming. I am not afraid of her temper, and the resistance she has displayed keeps me sharp in guarding against it.

Is keeping her around a sign of weakness?

Yes, perhaps, for one weaker than me.

I keep her around as a show of strength. She lives now in immediate fear of my inevitable retaliation, and in many ways, that fear alone is repayment enough for me. She is useful and she is not easily replaced.

But at the end of the day, we are all replaceable. Around here, I am of course indispensable, but a world could indeed exist without me or my brand of fear.

Not for long, but such a world could exist before winking out of existence.

We do have two spirits in the kitchen, neither of whom I would ever want to replace, but neither of which resides at the manor, either. Like most of our ghouls, they do have their nights and earliest morning hours to themselves and their haunts, but we ensure that their true residence is well-maintained so that it is they who return each day.

We also have a doctor on staff, my personal physician and nutritionist, Dr. Wren Wray. Making the most with what we have, she concocts daily teas and supplements to my diet, keeping me energetic, spry, and youthful. Unlike the couple in the kitchen, Dr. Wray does reside here on the grounds, coming and going as she pleases.

For the most part anyway.

I do not need her to exist, let me be clear about that, but I would say that Dr. Wren Wray is the one character around here I would rather not live without. Her companionship and dry sense of humor keep me honest and engaged. Unlike me, she was born of this land and is more attuned to the language it speaks, so there is also a practical benefit to honoring that relationship and blood connection running unseen beneath the skin.

Some would call it feelings; regardless, the obligation I am compelled to carry for my fine doctor may be seen as a weakness, and it likely is.

I do not care.

What am I going to do, fear it?

Ha!

In any case, she would never betray me, of this much I am certain.

Speaking of betrayal, Rippen is my servant, and I share his services with all who live in the house, including the only truly human part of our extended work-family, our driver Kellen Patrick.

Our new driver is a wonderful man who has had a tragic past. When our last driver received some bad advice from a local psychiatrist – another, longer story – we lost him and managed to trade up for young Kellen. Like our other friend from Ohio, Kellen is a writer who wants to one day publish a novel of his own.

We wish him luck, because that would give us some options besides the writer from Galion we have been using.

HEY!

I digress. Kellen is a great part of our team as a driver, and he has taken an interest in handling our social media accounts. We have always been late to the technology game – the Devil is in the Details, you know - and this is no different, but my human driver has some experience with social media and truly seems to have some ideas to help us extend our reach with a greater frequency of occurrences; we need no help finding new markets, for we are already in all.

And then of course there is me, your narrator for this short jaunt, Patrick de Molay. That is not the name I was given at birth, no doubt, but it is one I've carried for the last millennia. Though an honest being with an empathetic nature, I operate a business in a field that does not allow for mercy or forgiveness, and I run a tight ship. I am the Chairman of the Board, and we operate as a Board of One.

That is our team here at headquarters.

Modest, I realize, but we have many other operatives working in other places, a legion you could say, any place and anywhere you can imagine, really.

By numbers, we have more ghouls under contract than anything else. We prefer working with demons because they are more productive and have a better latitude for finding opportunities to succeed, but there are fewer of them around. Ghouls are fine though, hard workers and loyal, even if they will rarely evolve into true demons.

Really, we'll work with anyone; even fiends in whom we feign disinterest can be used to accomplish a goal. Let's be clear: We do harbor disdain for fiends; that is true; but we will work with them when it suits us.

Through these stories we have allowed into print you will learn more about us and what we do to keep this world of ours in balance. There may be other books, too, ones not authorized by us but perhaps written in a way that our involvement will be less than transparent to you, the intelligent reader. As far as the ones we are allowing, look for such enigmatic characters as the likes of Dr. Olive Huss and KC Chance to be featured in their own standalone tales sometime soon.

What about Kellen's story? Our driver's own work of fiction?

Until he can decide on a plot for his wavering pianist – and stick to it – then the symphony that is the story of Mason Paton will remain a work in progress.

Welcome to The East Erie Company, where not one of us is against us.

The End

Olds-Pancoast Funeral Home

"You're dead."

"I'm dead?"

"Yes."

"Then where am I?"

"This is The Olds-Pancoast Funeral Home. Your body has just been processed."

"Processed?"

"I am the caretaker, the mortician. I performed my task, well, all except this last one here."

"I've been here before, for a funeral."

"I would imagine so. This is a small community."

"So, if I'm dead, then does that mean that my funeral will be here?"

"Your calling hours are tomorrow at seven; the service is the following morning."

"How did I die?"

"You don't know?"

"No."

"What's the last thing you remember?"

"I was going outside to do some yard work. It was a nice day out, sunny. I'm older, and I know my hair has thinned, so I always wear a hat when I'm outside anymore. I remember it was hot, I was hot, and I took it off to try and cool down."

"You died."

"And now I'm here?"

"And now you're here."

"So, what happens next? Do I stay around until it's time for you to bury me?"

"Something like that."

"Is this normal? Do you talk to all of your, um, customers this way?"

"It is most definitely not *normal,* and yes, I do speak with all my guests like this. It is rare when one gets past me."

"Is this part of death, then? Do all funeral home directors, all morticians, know this secret?"

"This is part of your death, and no, I am one of the few with this knowledge, this gift, this duty you might say."

"Oh."

"Yes, it can be a burden at times."

"So, what happens next?"

"You have a choice to make."

"A choice? Even after death there are decisions to be made?"

"In your case, yes."

Swallowing hard, the vacant spirit wondered again why they were now special in death when in life they had been uniquely ordinary. "In my case...?"

"Not everyone has such an opportunity. Most of you die and then move on."

"Most of us? Does that not include you?"

The mortician smiled. "This is not about me; this is about you."

"Is this choice a punishment?"

"How you may or may not be judged after your death is not a matter of my concern, but your choice does not preclude such considerations."

"But I am here because of you?"

"I suppose that in a way, you could say that, but you are the one who led your life and died when and where you did. I was here when you were born, and I am here now that you are dead, before and after you there is me. But here because of me...? I can't take credit for that."

"But why did you choose me?"

"I choose no one; you came to me."

"Then what is my choice?"

"You can come work for my employers, or I can put you back in your body."

"Back to life? You can bring me back to life?"

"I did not say that. Everyone thinks I say that. I can put you back in your body, back in the box."

"But then what?"

"Then you are buried after your service."

"My body is buried, but surely my soul isn't meant to be trapped like that!"

"Your soul? I don't know anything about that."

"Then to what do you think you now speak?"

"You are a spirit, a disinterred consciousness; that is to whom I speak. What animates you still is not bothered by my business, by my duties, by my gift."

"Well then it seems I should be free to go on my way then…"

"And yet here you are, speaking to me."

"Am I free to leave?"

"You will notice I am not restraining you." The mortician put his hands in his pockets.

"Then I could leave…"

"You have nowhere to go."

"Surely there is somewhere I am meant to go; someplace beyond here, a final destination."

"Like Heaven or Hell…?"

"Well, yes, exactly like that." The spirit paused. "I should say that I have lived an admirable…"

"Save it. Please, I mean no offense, but any of that is beyond my reach or concern."

"But you can't stop me from going…"

"If you were meant to be in a pure place you would not be here talking to me."

"What are you saying?"

"Your next stop will not be one of those places."

The disinterred spirit began pacing the room. Though there were eyes casting glances at the only door in the room, there was no action taken to begin moving towards it. There was an urge to go for the door, but the compulsion to remain was undeniable. "I could go home."

"Well now, there's an option we can discuss."

"You can send me home? I'll take that option."

"But we haven't discussed the details of that choice yet."

"But it's an option?"

"Yes, of course."

"Then I'll take it."

"There are obligations associated with that choice."

"They can't be worse than being locked up in that box."

The mortician shrugged his shoulders.

"What are my choices then?"

"The first choice is to come work for us at The East Erie Company. You will work for us during the day, and then you will be free to return to your homely haunt at night."

"Sounds like a job."

"It's an obligation, and if you don't have a specialty then yes, it could very much be like having a job. Repetitive. Monotonous. Soul-crushing. You will be used here or there as need be, maybe find yourself as a steady receptionist for someone more specialized than yourself. This is really the role that most of the ones who come my way go. I don't see a lot of other demons on my table."

"Other demons? Are you one?"

"I am a specialist, so yes, I would rank as a demon.

"What you describe and do would seem more ghoulish."

The mortician laughed loudly.

"Why does that amuse you?"

"That is your fate."

"My fate?"

"To be a ghoul."

"Me, a ghoul? I don't see how…."

"Then you choose the box…?"

The spirit looked at the body it had once inhabited and animated with its presence. As a lifeless shell – now naked and stapled back together – there was no comfort in the husk that remained; no longer a welcome place, the corpse no longer seemed like home. "How long would I have to work for you?"

"When you no longer have a home to haunt then your obligation to us will be expired."

"And in the box?"

"Hard to say. I know some Egyptians who were pleasantly surprised to be freed after only a few thousand years…"

"A few thousand years!"

"Of course there are no guarantees. There was an entire generation of Parisians who only needed to spend a decade or less before they were exhumed and set free."

"Oh my Lord."

"No salvation here, I'm afraid."

"Where do I go then?"

"After the box? Like after the planet explodes and all things are made equal again?"

The spirit shivered at the thought before nodding in the affirmative.

The mortician shook his head once in denial. "I don't know, but it won't be back to me, that I can assure you."

The spirit did not know what to say.

"Have you made your decision?"

"It doesn't seem like much of a decision at all."

"It's really not."

"Does anyone ever choose the box?"

"You'd be surprised."

"Why would anyone choose to go back to their body and its tomb?"

"They assume there will be a peace found in that return; they fear being changed by the work if they choose us. Some find solace in holding on to their beliefs; some fear being made to do ghoulish things."

"Ghoulish things?"

"You will be a ghoul, most likely, so yes, by definition your actions will be ghoulish."

"My house won't last forever; at some point I will be free of your obligation."

"Your obligation is not to me – everyone always thinks that - it will be with our employer."

"Same difference."

The mortician shrugged his shoulders. "In your case, now, I suppose it is all the same. Either way, it is time to choose."

"I already told you; it is no choice at all."

"I need you to say it. Exclaim that you want to work for The East Erie Company."

"I want to work for The East Erie Company."

The mortician smiled and opened his arms for an embrace; the two shook hands, the ghostly apparition taking form to engage in the customary exchange. Their grip on each other was firm and tight, binding. "Welcome to The East Erie Company where our creed is, not one of us is against us."

"And what if I don't follow directives. What if I do end up against you?"

The mortician smiled. "Then we find a different body that can fit in a smaller box, and we send you there."

The End

Parlor Parlay

═══ 1 ═══

"Welcome to my home." Patrick de Molay said. Wearing his standard outfit, a dark gray business suit, vest, and a squat top hat made with the blackest beaver pelt ever seen, the old man did not seem annoyed but instead pleased. "I am not in the habit of taking appointments much less unexpected visitors."

"I know." The Ohio author was dressed in faded gray jeans, a white T-shirt, and a black hoodie. He was perfectly familiar with the setup of the front room in the manor, the office of the last outpost of The East Erie Company. Dark stone arches supported the floor above, and rich, dark wood paneling was cut to match nicely with the stone. The plain, leather-bound books filling the shelves were just right and free from dust. The writer even knew the contents of the desk drawers hidden beneath the dark wood and smooth finish, an area free from clutter and anything resembling technology.

The room appeared just as it had in his imagination, just as he described it in his most recent tale.

"Come, let's sit in the parlor."

"I don't need to follow you." The author left the room and walked around the corner to the next room. There was a curiosity to walk up the grand stairs or look at the dining room he knew was across the open hall, but he did not hesitate on his way into the next room.

The parlor was equal parts wood and stone, but the contents were intended for relaxation and release. The large billiard table with the attractive surface was the first thing to catch attention, but there were other options for spending leisure time. Past the side bar the writer noticed the opening across the room that led to a hidden set of stairs.

Beyond the billiard table there was a lounge area with a couch and some comfy chairs, but the writer chose to sit down at a small table pushed against the closest wall. The two chairs were ornate but not the most comfortable.

"You must know that once you came here, there would be no leaving."

"I know. I'm not interested in leaving."

"You want to stay?"

"I said that I'm not interested in leaving, but I am not beholden to stay."

"Is there a difference?" The man who embraced fear and employed it as a tool appeared confused. Not an easy task to achieve.

"Can we get to why I'm here?"

The old man was annoyed that his question was being disregarded. "Yes, of course, it's your life."

"I'm happy to hear you admit that."

"Don't read too much into the comment."

The neighborly author waved away the remark. "I need to talk about my team, the ones I paid to publish my stories and set up my website."

"How is that my business?"

"I believe they are a subsidiary of yours."

"Why would you believe that?"

"Because they are incompetent."

The old man's back stiffened as he sat up in his chair. "That is not a trait usually associated with The East Erie Company."

"Their incompetence is soul crushing."

"That does sound like us."

"Dealing with them has been like a fate worse than death."

"What do you know of fates worse than death? That is our specialty."

The author raised his eyebrows.

"Yes, well."

"I want to give them the benefit of the doubt, but after sending them the same changes for the fifth time I am past the beginning of having doubts. I still have a second book to put out with them not to mention the website. Sometimes I can't help but wonder if they are doing it on purpose."

"Seems paranoid."

"They keep assigning me to a new project manager who is there to fix everything."

"That happens."

"I'm on my third one."

"That could be us."

"Like I said…"

"Perhaps they are a subsidiary in one of our departments."

"Perhaps…?"

"Ok, they are a subsidiary in one of our departments." The old man adjusted his top hat. "What do you want me to do about it?"

"I want you to let me do it by myself. The publishing, the website, all of it."

"But you need us."

"Maybe I do, but I don't need them." The author adjusted his weight in the chair. "Besides, you need me, too."

The old man scoffed. "You are hardly our only writer."

"I know."

"What are you going to do, quit again?"

The remark hurt, and the author moved in his seat, not a squirm but a repositioning of sorts. "No, I will never do that again."

"Then what? Start writing romance novels?"

"No."

"Start writing about monsters that sparkle?"

"No."

"Then what. What leverage do you possibly think to hold over me? I have all the leverage I need here in this manor of mine. From this place I can leverage fear across the globe, as I have done, since there have been creatures here able to know fear."

"I know. You are the source for most of the horrors we feel and face, at least the ones I know about anyway."

"Then why do you suppose to come here and make demands of me?"

"I'm thinking about writing a sequel to You Wish."

"You wouldn't do that!" The old man slapped the table.

"Oh I would." The Ohio author smiled, the bags under his eyes disappearing for the moment. "I already have a title for it. *Be Careful 2 Whom You Wish.*"

"There's no reason to be rash."

"I don't think that one will have an ending you will appreciate."

"A happy ending?"

"Not for you."

"What do you have planned for me?"

"A fate worse than death."

"I am a fate worse than death. How can you possibly hurt me in that way?" The old man smirked and laughed a quick chortle. "I have no soul to crush, either."

"I'll make you the good guy."

"I've been the star in one of your stories already; I came out more feared than ever before."

"I'm not talking about you being the protagonist of your own story; I'm talking about you being the good guy; the one who saves the day."

"For others?" All color left the old man's face. "You couldn't possibly do that to me. It would violate and possibly nullify my contract."

"Yes, but I could. I already started editing and revising *You Wish* to get it set up for the sequel, twenty-three years later."

"You are despicable."

"You *are* in my life."

"What do you want?"

"I already told you. I want the power to publish my work – format it, submit it, all of it – and I want the same for my website."

"And if I agree then you will not write that sequel?"

"I will not write that sequel as my next project."

"Then I will agree to give your next two works the attention they deserve. I will give you a new team dedicated to your success. We will be your partner and inspire plenty of other books to make you forget about that nasty sequel."

"I'm not trying to be difficult. That's not my vibe."

"But you write horror stories."

"Are you judging me?"

"Do we have a deal?"

"We have a deal."

"Tell me about your next couple of projects?"

"One is about a demon psychiatrist who gives bad advice. Her name is Dr. Olive Huss."

"Sounds familiar…"

"You'll recognize the setting."

The old man raised an eyebrow. "And the other…?"

"The other is about a guy who wrecks his snowmobile, loses his memory, and ends up seeking refuge at a mysterious house in the woods."

"That sounds familiar, too."

"It is." The author looked about the room.

"He would never be able to find us, of course."

"I found you."

"Yes, well," the old man said, momentarily befuddled. "My allergy to sage brush only makes me sneeze, you cannot use it to kill me."

"That's good to know, but I have no desire to replace you..."

"Well, I suppose you want me to thank you."

"Not yet." The author smiled, knowing he had won this round. "You didn't let me finish: I have no desire to replace you, yet."

"And they say I am a monster."

"No one is saying that..."

"I suppose you want me to thank you, then."

"Yet. No one is saying that, yet."

The End

Super Brave Man

═══ 1 ═══

"**A**re you Super Brave Man?"
Built like and looking suspiciously similar to the Verb in Action from another comic depiction – that's what's happening - the tall and confident superhero looked down at the pale old man. Though slightly hunched over, this old fellow seemed spry and was taller than most other elderly folk; still, next to the towering figure of the man who did not respect fear and who helped others get past being scared, everyone was small. The older gentleman's squat top hat was not enough to make up the difference either.

"Yes, yes I am." The hero had a smile that was as genuine as it was warm and inviting. "Are you scared? Can I help you overcome some fear?"

"Oh, I am perfectly fine with my fear, I just want to understand yours."

"You are fine with your fear?"

"Yes, of course. Don't you embrace your fears?"

"No, I face down and overcome them."

"Fear can be fun; ride it like a wave."

"I don't see how."

"You don't enjoy horror movies?"

"I have no time for that."

"Indeed. That's too bad."

Super Brave Man could tell this gentleman was being genuine in his replies; besides the black nature of his top hat there was nothing ominous, all appearances instead suggesting frailty and harmlessness. The elderly man's hair was dark with gray tips, and he was impeccably dressed in a dark and gray three-piece suit. A professional man if not slightly old-fashioned, his mere presence presented nothing to fear. "I am Super Brave Man; there is nothing that I fear nor any fear I cannot overcome, and there is nothing you should fear, either."

"Certainly you fear aging?"

"I do not age like most humans, so I have no reason to fear that like a normal man."

"I have seen you fly up in the sky above me; I imagine you could be injured if you fell from that great height. Doesn't that ever bring you fear?"

The superhero blushed and shrugged his shoulders. "Sir, I can tell when people are being genuine with me, and I can tell you care and are not asking in jest, so let me assure you, I am perfectly safe when I fly."

"I did not mean to imply anything less."

"I believe you; trust me, though, even if I fell asleep in the sky I would not be harmed in my return to solid earth."

"So you cannot die?"

"I am super and brave, but as you already noted, at the end of the day I am only a man who is super brave."

"A man who does not age and cannot be harmed when falling from the sky…? A man who does not cower when faced with demons and ghouls…?"

Super Brave Man chuckled; everything was always easier when looked at from the outside. "Yes, I have lived a long life helping other people, but that nourishes me, keeps me young at heart. I know that one day I will die, but by that time I will have helped so many others overcome their fears that I like to think it will be more like an earned rest, my eternal retirement…"

"A reward for all your good deeds…"

"Yes, yes, I suppose that is one way to look at it. We can dream I suppose."

"And of all your strengths, which would you say is your greatest?"

"That's easy, it is the one that allows me to be super in every other way. I fear nothing."

"Nothing…?"

"As we already discussed, there is nothing that I fear. No fear that I cannot overcome."

"Indeed."

"Indeed, and in fact my greatest source of pride regarding my strength is my ability to help others overcome their own fears."

"You can really do that?"

"Yes, I have even helped people with whom I did not share a language."

"How did you communicate?"

"Fear does not need to be stated to be real, and it does not require words to be felt or overcome. Facing our fears usually begins with controlling our emotions, and those feelings transcend speech."

"Fantastic."

"It is what I do."

"Indeed."

"I could help you overcome your fears."

"You and I see fear differently, I'm afraid." The old man smiled and tilted his cap. "I embrace my fears and have no need to overcome them. I am an honest man, and I tell the truth; that can cause fear, at times, but again, such is life."

"If you ever change your mind, I am always on the lookout for someone who needs my help overcoming their fears."

"How noble of you."

Super Brave Man shrugged his shoulders. "I do what I can to overcome fear."

"Fear is a natural emotion, though, one born within every living thing who can sense the world outside of itself."

"There are a lot of things that feel fear, but only humans can overcome those fears."

"Oh, I wouldn't be so sure about that."

Super Brave Man had an unusual feeling of doubt overcome him, showing itself by twisting the smile downward ever so slightly.

"There's all manner of life that needs help overcoming their fears. The rabbit lives a timid life because of its fear; imagine the joy that little bunnies could bring if they felt free to roam as they chose."

"I do love bunnies."

"Who doesn't love bunnies?"

"They're just so cute and cuddly."

"Yet they are allowed to live in fear…?"

"I never considered…"

"No, no I suppose not…" The old man let his words hang in the air before continuing. "If you can help humans then you could probably help the rabbits, too."

"I can help anyone who feels fear, so perhaps you are right. I am fearless, and I can help others feel the same."

"And you certainly aren't afraid of a challenge…?"

"Certainly not!"

"Well then, perhaps you can start by unleashing those timid bunnies from their fears."

****

The old man made it a point to chance upon another meeting with Super Brave Man. Though it had only been a short while, the towering icon appeared in some ways diminished, drained of just a little bit of the superiority that allowed him to tower over the older man, over all men.

"Why do you look so tired, Super Brave Man? I have come to help you and yet I fear, no pun intended, that you do not appear up to the task."

"I am up to any task."

"But you look as if you've encountered a fright?"

"I fear nothing."

"I suppose you could just use some sleep."

"There are a lot of rabbits in the world. When you left me last, I thought about your words and realized that I could not live in a world where so many rabbits were afraid to be bunnies."

"So you took away their fear?"

"I did."

"Every rabbit in the world?"

"Yes!" Super Brave Man stood tall, the pride from his accomplishments boosting him.

"That must have been difficult."

"There are a lot of rabbits, to be sure, but they tend to live in burrows and patches. I was able to find several at once, usually."

"How did you communicate with them?"

"Fear truly is not bound by words or confined to language. Fear is an instinct that transcends the boundaries between life itself. In helping others, even the rabbits, I am able to do the same."

"Remarkable." The old man was impressed and repulsed. "That must make you feel just so wonderful. More good deeds in your ledger."

"Yes, thank you for helping me to consider it."

"No need to thank me." The old man paused. "But it does make me wonder…"

"About what?"

"About the deer?"

"Deer?"

"Yes, like Bambi. I just learned that deer are actually one of the most frightened creatures that roam the land; that's why I came to find you on their behalf. To them, everything is a predator, even that twig breaking under your foot is a thing for a deer to fear. Even their very name rhymes with the word. Deer fear."

"Everyone loves Bambi."

"She was an orphan."

"I just don't know if..."

"I'm sure you can only do so much, like living with knowing that you could make things better and not. I too would be afraid to try."

"Now that's not fair."

"You *are* Super Brave Man." The old man smiled. "Am I lying?"

The hero considered the old man. Again, except for his choice in fashion, there was nothing about him that would invoke a reaction against fear or indicate that the old man was being deceitful with his words. Were his tone different, then perhaps his words would ring more provocatively, but as delivered, the old fellow seemed to be sharing a genuine concern. "No, you are not lying. I agree that it is not fair for deer to have to live in fear."

"Especially if their bunny friends are living their best lives."

"They do run in the same circles, I suppose."

"And you could check on the bunnies while you are there."

The superhero nodded his head. "That is a rather good idea. Thank you again for bringing this all to my attention. You are a fine man."

"My pleasure, but I am only trying to help." What it was that he was trying to help he did not specify.

****

Patrick de Molay waited less than a week before again tracking down the superhero. This time, there could be no denying that the super brave man was off his game. "Good afternoon, Super Brave Man."

The hero looked down, but leaning as he was the two were nearly seeing eye to eye. The bags under one set were hidden behind large sunglasses. Any lack of luster in the twinkle bouncing from that same pair of otherwise super orbs was only apparent in his sluggish demeanor.

"My goodness, did the deer do that to you?"

The superhero did not shake his head, but he was also not quick to answer. "The deer were not easy; that was a task. Yet there are many fewer deer than there are – were - rabbits, they nonetheless roam a wide range and do not find a steady burrow to call home."

"Were rabbits?" The old man smiled because he already knew the answer. "Were rabbits…? Like werewolves…?"

Super Brave Man let down his guard and began to weep. "It was horrible. I went back expecting to see so many happy bunnies waiting to welcome their friends the deer, but instead I found a slaughter. There were so many dead rabbits that the predators couldn't even eat them all."

"Their fear was keeping them safe."

The hero wiped his eyes. "I refuse to accept that, but they refused to defend themselves regardless of the motivations."

"A rabbit's only defense is its fear. It has no weapon stronger than its own timidity."

"I don't know if I can accept that fear is ever a strength."

"Well, either way it's done I suppose, unless you want to teach them to fear…?"

"I could never do that."

"You could…"

"But I can't. You understand the distinction."

"I understand. I suppose it will work out better for the deer."

"They are a more intelligent creature. It will be different."

"Perfect. I love your optimism!"

Sensing the sincerity in the old man's words, the superhero felt his sense of purpose returning.

"It got me thinking, though - our last conversation, and your words just now seeming to introduce an element of Fate - there is not a creature more intelligent and misunderstood than a dolphin. They have no arms, no legs, they can't speak, yet their brains are as large and developed as humans. Imagine the fear they must face swimming around down in the darkest depths."

"Dolphins?"

"Yes, surely you've heard of them."

"Sir, I've swam with dolphins."

"Then how could you not sense their fear?"

"They seemed happy to me."

"They probably thought you were there to rescue them. You are Super Brave Man; your reputation precedes you."

The hero's head swelled even as it drooped at the thought of having let anything down. "And you really think they live in fear."

"I happen to know this for a fact. You are a superhero; am I lying to you now?"

Super Brave Man was exhausted, and he knew that the cause was his prior encounters with this old man, but now as then there was nothing about the man's words that rang as anything but true. This old man truly wanted the superhero to help these poor creatures. Never mind how the old man knew that dolphins sense fear or why he was interested in helping. "No, you are not lying."

"Your business is your own, but since you find yourself idle, I just thought perhaps I would bring it to your attention."

"I do not mean to appear idle; in that moment I was just too tired to go looking for people in fear."

"People can take care of themselves, but I will try to think of a way to help you with them as well." The old man snickered. "But now, the dolphins could really use a hand, so to speak."

"Your words are true."

"And this is a problem you could go and fix, not one that you have to spend time looking for."

"Finding someone in fear was never a problem."

"But you are limited."

"I am limited. I have to admit that is true."

"But this will give you a purpose. That always makes you feel better."

"You are a man fond of the truth."

"I have no need to lie. Why you could say I am as honest with the living as I am with the dead."

Super Brave Man understood the old man to be saying that there is no reason to lie to the dead so why try, and hence the same applied to his dealings with the living. The old man was certainly not lying now nor had he ever as far as the superhero was concerned. "Ok, let's talk about helping the dolphins then…"

****

"You are a hard man to find."

Super Brave Man was now a shell of himself. The suit seemed baggy and was hanging from his body as if it had been stretched. As he landed next to the old man, his feet hit the ground hard, his knees needing to buckle slightly to lessen the impact of the drop. His height was now less than the old man with his hat.

"I'm quite easy to find, I'm afraid." The old man smiled and tipped his cap. This time the superhero had approached him, but the encounter was only allowed to occur because of the will of one half of the duo. The old man was walking along the reservoir outside Patrick, Ohio, the adopted hometown whose existence he preceded.

It was because the old fellow had allowed it that the superhero was able to find him.

"I don't know where you hide, but it is a fine place indeed if I cannot spot it from the air."

"I'm sure if you did see my residence, you would just forget; my home is unremarkable in having that effect on people." The old man smiled a little more than usual. Though telling the truth, technically, it was about as close as he ever came to telling a lie.

Embellishments – or lack thereof – were not viewed by him as wholesale deceit.

"Perhaps one day I could be your guest and I could decide for myself."

"That could certainly be arranged. I warn you though: you will like it so well you may want to stay."

"I think I need to getaway to clear my head."

"You do look awful."

"And to clear my heart."

"Your heart hangs heavy?"

"I made things right with the dolphins like we discussed, and you were right: They are indeed intelligent creatures! I learned so much from them, and they were smarter than many humans I have saved."

"Did you give them hands?"

Though drained and lacking enthusiasm, the superhero smiled. "No. I am just super, not godly. I am just a man, remember?"

"It's hard to tell the difference sometimes."

"I know. Honestly, sometimes it's hard to tell the difference myself."

"You have a great power. That responsibility becomes its own burden."

"That is true."

"Yet all does not seem right in your world, if you don't mind me noticing."

"I have not slept since the last time we spoke."

"Really…?"

"Yes, like you, apparently, I cannot lie."

"Was it the dolphins?"

"No, they were easy, and all too eager to accept, actually. They helped me by gathering entire pods. I've never seen so much agreement about embracing and spreading my message."

"Curious. Did you stop to wonder why?"

The superhero paused, looking more dejected than his stooping form already implied. "No, I did not consider."

"Well, I certainly wouldn't worry myself about it. I'm sure they were just thankful to have someone helping them for a change."

"Yes, I'm sure they were grateful."

"So what's the problem?"

"The deer."

"Oh dear," the old man said, coming as close to mocking the superhero as decorum allowed him to dare, "what were the deer up to?"

"Every roadway I flew over seemed to have a dead deer carcass on the side of the pavement. I was always accustomed to seeing a few here and there, but they were everywhere."

"That is horrible."

"And humans were killed in some of those crashes."

"It's easy to overlook the human toll."

"Yes, it is."

"I guess the deer were no better off than the rabbits."

"The rabbits! What rabbits? There are no more rabbits that I can find."

"They've all been dispatched?"

"Yes, or they're in hiding…"

"Which they would only do if they had reason to fear…"

"I never thought of it like that. This has become a nightmare."

"You could always teach them to fear…"

"No, no, no I cannot imagine doing that."

"You said that you look at fear differently; we both know you could teach them fear…"

"I don't know…"

"I am not super like you. I cannot talk to deer any more than I can speak with the dolphins. I can talk to the living and some of the dead, but trust me when I say that I would be of no use to you with the deer or the dolphins."

"The dolphins…? I thought we agreed they were okay."

"That's right. Different problems for a different day. The deer. I really cannot help you with the deer."

"I'm sorry to have troubled you then."

"Since you are here, our last conversation again got me to thinking, and I believe I found a way to assist you in your cause with humans."

"How so?"

"What if I was able to give you a book that had a list of every human who was going to be scared this year...? With a list like that you could help everyone on it."

"To have such a list would be a dream come true! Fear would have no place in a world like that."

"Well fear always has its place regardless, but you could help all those people overcome their fears. Real people, not rabbits and deer and dolphins."

"If only there were such a book."

The old man looked at his car and nodded at the driver standing there. The disheveled driver walked to the trunk, opened it, and pulled out a large book. With little effort, the man who was not well-built walked the thick tome the short distance to the two men. He extended his arms, handing the book to Super Brave Man.

The superhero was tired and less than he had been, and the heft of the book surprised him, especially since the slightly built driver had seemed to carry it with such ease.

Still.

The possibilities began to make him feel a sense of his strength coming back into bloom.

But only for a moment.

Super Brave Man flipped the book open and immediately his eyes grew wide. The pages were thinner than tissue paper, a multitude of pages, and even still the writing was incredibly small and written in a fancy script.

"I trust you can make out the words."

"Yes, it is just hard, and there appear to be many entries for the same name."

"There are many Matt Smiths out in the world."

"I never thought of that."

"And who only gets scared once a year? Why, I imagine that some people get scared multiple times in a day."

"That's a good point."

"But if anyone can help them, then it's you, Super Brave Man."

The superhero nodded his head, wondering why this old man kept haunting him before remembering that he was the one who started this conversation. "Yes, if anyone can save these people, then I suppose it has to be me."

The old man reached out and touched the super and brave man's hand. "I believe in you to do your best and give it your all."

The hero stood straighter and started to fly away, but the weight of the book made it difficult. After a second try and a running start, he was up and away.

****

The death and funeral of Super Brave Man was not a well-attended event. He died helping others overcome their fears, everyone in fact, and at the end, he could not live with what he had done.

For one, the sheer physical toll was more than even his super form was built to handle. Everyone, it seems, has fears, everyone – save he and the old man, that is – has many things that they fear. He was able to open everyone's eyes the littlest bit and help all realize that their greatest fear should be not believing in themselves to overcome any other fear.

But there was never, truly, any last person. Once he had reached everyone on the list, it seemed that new names were being added as if born. It was all so tiring and exhausting.

But finally it was done, and for all his feats, Super Brave Man finished the book and felt proud. The pride gave him just enough energy to fly over the seas to check on the dolphins.

What he saw beneath the seas broke him like the waves upon it.

The water was littered with dead sea creatures of all sizes. The dolphins had banded together and used their intelligence to attack everything else in the water, quickly establishing dominance over all but the most isolated patches of ocean. The carnage was as repulsive as it was impressive.

Super Brave Man wept, loudly, his very real tears and sobs turning the oceans with their powerful drops, but it did nothing to scare the dolphins and in fact only made the other creatures left to wonder what was happening in their world to bring all this agony raining down on their heads.

Not wanting others to see him grieving, the superhero flew to the isolation of the forest; even there he could not find any solace. While most of the deer were now culled and gone, those that remained were angry and not willing to wait for death to approach them. The first violent attack from a deer shocked him so much that the blow injured him as it would any human.

It was a truth more real than supposed. He did not have the will to fight the deer, and it took him another kick to the head before he could gain his feet enough to run and fly away from the scene, battered and bloody. He was not afraid of the deer, and still he feared nothing, but he did find himself drowning in doubt as to the surety of his actions.

What had he done?

All of that made Super Brave Man less so of the first two and brought home the reality of the third part of his name. He had tried to help the rabbits and deer and even the dolphins and had made a mess of it all. He understood that it was folly for him to have even tried to help those other creatures who were not human. That had been his mistake, a painful lesson to be sure, but one that he felt could be learned from, recovered from, and built upon in the future. He had never been so low, but at least there was his success with humans.

Surely the people in that book – all the people, really – had been made better off by the deeds he had just performed. As he was flying to his place of rest, he looked down and noticed that the world was in turmoil. Without their fears, the people of the world were no better than the animals he had helped. Some were timid and meek, and some were unrestrained.

The chaos he instead saw gave him a start and literally broke that super thing in his chest that for you and I would be a heart. All he had wanted to do was help others, everyone in fact, but in the end, he found that cause was itself no cure.

He could make no sense of the result in his brain, and his body could take no more.

Some say that the fall from the sky is what killed him, but that was not it; indeed, Super Brave Man was dead and gone before his very human body hit the ground.

****

The funeral home was empty save for the only two names not listed in the guest book, the spirit of a man who had once been both super and brave as well as that older man, the one who wore the gray suit, black top hat, and outlived all. It was he who walked over to the casket and pulled the life out of the dead man's breath.

"I knew you would be here."

"I don't even know where here is."

K.P. MALOY

"This is the Olds-Pancoast Funeral Home, of course. We had your funeral here."

"Why here?"

"Patrick is the home of fear; it seemed like a fitting place for you to inspire us all one last time."

"There is no one here."

"Yes, well."

"Why am I here."

"Depends. Do you mean the you there about to be sealed away in that vault below the ground, or do you mean the you that is here now talking with me?"

"Is there a difference?"

"Clearly." The old man looked at the open casket, extending his hand as an invitation to look. "Is that not you, there?"

"It is."

"And am I not talking to you here, now?"

"You are."

"So then you see what I mean even if you are being obtuse about it."

"Obtuse?"

"And you really do not know why you are here?"

"Which me are you addressing?"

The old man turned quickly and let out a loud laugh. "Yes! I love your humor in the face of this situation."

"What is my situation?"

"You will not find immediate rest in your tomb below ground."

"I won't?"

"No, you will not. You are facing a fate worse than death."

"What?"

"A soul-crushing fate worse than death, in fact."

"Me?"

"Yes, you." The old man shook his head even though he was still smiling ever so slightly. "Am I lying now?"

Though dead, the superhero knew that the old man was telling the truth.

"Your actions resulted in more death and carnage than some asteroid impacts. The world may never again be right because of you."

"But I was only trying to help."

"You were trying to interfere."

"I wanted to help."

"It's funny, by removing fear you interfered, which ended up creating whole new things to fear. You did such a great job that people will be scared of things tomorrow that we haven't even considered yet today. Think about the irony of that."

"Am I a monster?"

"Oh, I would certainly say so. Yes. An entire new kind of monster the world has never known."

"But then you made me that way."

"Come now, are we children? Did I really make you do anything?"

"It was your idea for me to help the rabbits and the deer and the dolphins. It was you who had compiled the book of people and the fears they would face."

"It was your choice what you did with what I told you. It's not my fault you wanted to be the good guy."

"But I am the good guy."

"That was your intent, but how did that work out for you?"

"I'm here."

"Do you even know where here is?"

"The funeral home."

"That's right, the Olds-Pancoast Funeral Home. But after that, then what? You are an untethered entity with a tortured soul, dead yet still capable of affecting life; in other words, you're a demon. Your new life is going to be haunting this box you're about to be buried in. You aren't attached to any property. You can't be confined to one thing. Even your super suit is being buried with you. People have forgotten their fear, for the moment, and they have forgotten about the need for someone like you to remind them to face and overcome their fears."

"But that can't be…"

"Can't be true…? Am I lying?"

The old man was not lying, and it made the dead hero a little angry. "So how long am I here?"

"How much turmoil is in your soul? You caused a lot of grief. Just thinking about all those bunnies alone." The old man shivered as if a chill was running down his spine. He actually welcomed those. "And the dolphins; well, they're killing people now, as we speak."

"People…?"

"Yes, the people aren't afraid of the dolphins and the dolphins aren't afraid of the people. So, guess who loses that one…? I'll give you a hint, none of these encounters have happened on land, at least not yet."

"What have I done…"

"Pretty much ruined the world."

"There has to be something I can do."

"Perhaps there is."

"What? Anything! I'll do anything!"

"You would have to work for us…"

"I don't care. I want to make things right."

"I don't know if you have what it takes to make it right."

"I'll do whatever it takes."

"You'll need to sign a contract."

"Give me the pen. I'm ready."

"You don't even know what we will have you do."

"I don't care. I want to help. Tell me how I can help."

"You can teach them to fear again."

Super Brave Man was already dead, but even this demonic form of himself was turned cold at the prospect. He knew it was against his nature, but he also knew that it needed to be done. He was ready to give them back their fear.

It was the only way.

They needed to learn.

He was ready to become the monster they would never forget.

Super Brave Man would teach the world to fear.

The End

Love Racket

"**I**'ll say it again, but I cannot be more clear: If you use this racket, you will win this match. At the end of this day, you will be the Australian Open Tennis Champion."

"Is this one of those analogies?"

"Metaphor. No, it is neither an analogy nor a metaphor." The stern coach looked at his student, by far the most successful he had ever coached. The sport was not always tennis, and the object was not always a racket, but the effect was nearly always the same.

In every competition there was a crutch to be exploited.

Now it was make or break time; in this case, the two being one and the same.

"What are you saying? If I believe it, then it will happen? That's already what got me to this point. That's already the mindset you've instilled in me, coach." Sepp McGee looked at his coach, unsure what meaning the man was suggesting beyond words.

It wasn't the first time in the last year that the man had pushed ideas outside the bounds of tennis, but it was perhaps the strangest thing to cross his lips. Both men had heavy accents, and to the untrained ear or any American it probably sounded like the two men were from the same part of the world.

They were not even from the same plane of existence.

Sepp was from Australia, and his coach, well, he was from farther away, further than geography anyway.

In the moment, Sepp did not recall – nor try to remember - how the two had met, the chance encounter that brought them together. That really did not matter. To Sepp, what mattered were the results, and the tennis professional could not dispute that over the last year his coach had delivered those results, or at least put his player in the mindset to hit those goals.

Now, though, Sepp was standing at the edge of true greatness; the hard work was paying off. The time spent had already produced dividends; just to be here itself seemed a magical act.

Six weeks ago, after a strong push from his coach, he had found his groove and played in an open-field qualifier for the Australian Open, a tennis major and the ultimate event on his home continent.

Two years ahead of the schedule they planned, Sepp competed above his potential and played his way into the biggest tournament his country hosted. Just being from Melbourne and playing his way into the field was something he could have talked about his entire life. The player had already accomplished enough on his own merit to forever look in the mirror and not be ashamed of the competitor looking back regardless of the stage of life he found himself in as a person.

Through the luck of the draw, a late-round injury to a highly rated opponent, and the game of a lifetime, the young Aussie had already solidified himself as a legend in his own right; now was the gravy, the chance to etch that reputation in stone by maybe pulling off a miracle.

Or turning in the performance of a lifetime.

Either way, all he had accomplished up until that point had been on his own. His coach could be a demonic task master, pushing Sepp to train as hard as his humanly limits allowed, but until this moment there had been no hint or suggestion of assistance outside the bounds of hard work and intense competition.

As it was, without even playing the game, Sepp could forever walk into any bar in Australia with his head held as high as his accomplishments genuinely lofty. He had already made his parents and his country proud by advancing this far; he had already proven to himself that he could compete at the highest level.

Still, a victory would change his life in a way nothing else ever could.

A win at the Open of his country would be a victory no one could ever take away.

Or so he thought.

His new coach had some unusual methods, but again, he could not disagree with the results. He was willing to play along on most days, but now, after warming up and getting ready to step into the tunnel and onto the court...?

This seemed to be the time for motivational discourse that was serious and not a mishit attempt at humor.

"I'm saying that if you use this racket, it will ensure you of a victory."

"So it's like a magical racket?" Against his own feelings, the pragmatic Aussie laughed. "I appreciate you trying to relax me, but I think I want to keep my edge for this."

"And I couldn't be more proud of you, Sepp, but the choice is up to you."

"What choice?" Now fully annoyed, the tennis player snatched the racket from out of the hands of his trainer. It was a fine racket, but nothing about it seemed special. It was clearly not new, but it was also not so old as to be a relic of any sort. The weight was balanced, and the grip was comfortable, more padded than he was accustomed to, but firm. He took a couple practice swings while his coach continued speaking.

"You've done well, Sepp, exceeding my every expectation. You can go out there now, against the number two player in the world and give it your best shot, which, the way you've been playing, may very well be enough. I cannot lie to you about that. But what I'm saying is that if you use this racket, I can guarantee that you will not lose so long as you are using it."

"And again, I ask, what makes it so special?"

The coach looked once over each shoulder to confirm that they were alone before leaning in closer. "It's enchanted."

"I told you I need my edge." The player handed the item back to his coach and picked up his own bag of rackets before storming out of the locker room, through the door, and into the tunnel. Sepp was annoyed with his coach, but as he walked the short distance down the concrete corridor, he could hear the low murmur of the crowd as they sat anxiously waiting for the finals to begin. They had paid a small fortune for their seats, and they were ready to see a champion crowned even if few of them expected to see a close match for the local boy who grew up just beyond everyone's backyard.

Still, sporting miracles could happen...

As long as the local boy didn't embarrass himself...that was really all anyone could wish.

Except for Sepp, he wanted nothing more than to win. He was this close, and he was not about to be denied.

Tournament officials stopped him before he could exit the tunnel; they wanted him to wait for the announcers. Sepp could tell by the muted roar and polite claps that the crowd was welcoming the player they likely would have been rooting for had he been playing any other competitor. The number two player in the world was well-liked, much more so than was the current number one, but no one was going to get a louder ovation than their own native son.

And a ruckus applause he received.

Australians being a naturally vocal bunch, the crowd cheered for nearly a full three minutes before being successfully quieted by the officials. Sepp tried to ignore the applause and focus on his routine, but sooner than he would have expected, the match was ready to begin.

Sepp was given his choice of balls and the crowd grew quiet for his first serve. The silence was not an unfamiliar sound for the tennis player, but to realize that so many different voices were now quiet waiting for him to act, and on this large local stage, well that was a little much.

Still, even with all the pressure and his adrenaline pumping, Sepp took a deep breath and dropped a burner right down the middle of the court. The world's number two stood there and watched the point go flying past without moving a muscle. His second serve was hit, but it flew off the racket sideways and did not return across the net. After a light serve that was returned before being smashed back for a third point, Sepp was up 40-0. One last burner gave him the first game in nearly record time.

The crowd went nuts when the two players switched serves. Sepp could feel the rush of emotions and cockiness and adrenaline coursing through his body.

This was real!

This was really happening!

He lost the second game nearly as quickly as he won the first one. He then lost the third and fourth ones, too. He in fact did not win another one the rest of the set, losing it 6-1.

The crowd was quieted, sensing that embarrassing defeat that many had predicted, and even the player was humbled and mad.

The second set went much better for the native son, but after a loser return that didn't hug the line enough, Sepp lost 6-3. Down 2-0, the players were given 300 seconds for their break and for the television network to pay some bills.

The Australian looked up and locked eyes with his coach. The man was not allowed to mentor him during the match, but Sepp just knew that the coach was laughing at him behind that smug visage.

Sepp dropped his head and slammed his racket to the ground, cracking it at the neck. He tossed it aside and could hear the murmur as the crowd reacted to his outburst.

240 seconds left.

Sepp looked back at his coach and this time the man was raising his eyebrows at him. What was he trying to say?

Looking at his broken racket, Sepp unzipped his bag and reached for another one. He settled on a replacement but then his thoughts returned to the one his coach had offered down in the locker room.

The enchanted racket.

Sepp looked at his coach for the third time and now the man was nodding his head as if in agreement: *Yes, it's time for the special racket.*

The tennis player shook away the voice in his head, certain it could not be real.

180 seconds.

Sepp jumped to his feet and approached the chair judge.

"May I run to the locker room."

"You won't have time."

"I just have to grab something."

"Are you injured?"

"I need a new racket."

"You have a bag of them."

"I don't have the one I need."

"You're going to need a magical racket to beat him, you know."

"You don't have to be a jerk!"

The crowd, sensing that something was happening, began to murmur.

"Do you want me to get them involved?" Sepp looked at the crowd, most of them pulling for the hometown underdog. If he wanted to get them riled up, he could do so if he tried.

The chair judge shifted in his seat. "You only have 120 seconds. Any later and …"

Sepp didn't wait for the man to finish. He turned quickly and ran for the tunnel. His eyes tried to focus on the opening ahead, but it was impossible to not take notice of what seemed to be every face looking at him. The crowd had no idea what was happening, but they all began to cheer and clap, half standing already and the rest joining them, the men, the women, and even the children including a few babies. He could see all their faces and each of them looked as if they could be fellow Aussies. There was even one semi-local group pulling for him with a sign that read *Kiwis for Sepp.*

He could have turned around there and finished his day like a proud man defeated. He could have faced his challenger alone. That last thought before disappearing into the tunnel caused him to look over at the place where his coach was sitting, his special seat in the stands.

The coach was there cheering with the rest of the crowd.

The tennis professional who was lucky to even be in this tournament much less playing in this match looked down the short tunnel and began to sprint. What he was doing seemed crazy, but he felt that he could not risk living with any inaction. With his guard dropped, it was easier for him to believe in this enchanted thing than to continue having faith in himself.

Before he was down to 90 seconds, Sepp was in the locker room and standing in front of his locker. He opened the door and found that the racket was not there. Why had he assumed it would be?

"You knew I wouldn't tease you like that."

The tennis pro turned quickly as if returning a potential ace. His eyes widened as he saw first his coach and then the racket. "How did you get in here so fast?"

"I could not tell you I had this thing and then not have it for you when needed."

"And it will work?"

"Every time."

"What are you, exactly?"

"I am your coach."

"But what is this…?"

"Me or the racket?"

"Are you not one and the same?"

"This is not a thing of evil, if that is what you ask."

"Then what manner of magic is it? What type of prophet are you?"

"I am your coach, a trainer who is able to see the talent in others and bring it out, allow you to see it, give you the means to achieve that success. I have brought you to the brink of your greatest potential, now the rest is up to you."

"My greatest potential?"

"Yes. For you, what could be greater?"

"And that racket will help me win."

"Or the racket."

"Is that a yes?"

"You will not lose with this racket in your hand."

"Is there a catch?"

"You have already laid yourself bare before me this past year, and now you know what you can do when pushed. Nothing about using this racket will take away from what you are capable of accomplishing, but it may change your way of appreciating it, and in that way, it may of course change you, alter your perspective perhaps."

"So it will change me then..."

"Why assume the worst? Being the champion will change you, but there is nothing about the racket that will require an exchange from you."

"If I can win this match then I can do anything."

"Indeed. I have been telling you that from day one."

"Then I'm not going to risk it now if I can use this racket and guarantee victory."

"No one would blame you if you don't blame yourself."

"Why would I blame myself?"

"You have about fifteen seconds."

Sepp's eyes grew wide, and with the racket in hand he sprinted out of the room and down the tunnel. As he ran out onto the court, he could see the clock as it ticked from one to zero.

No one thought twice about the fact that he was carrying a new racket, not then; even the chair judge was busy checking his notes and setting his own cards in order. People did notice, of course, the entire world wondered, but in that moment, Sepp carried the racket like a booger in his nose, there but hopefully unseen.

The third set started on time.

There were moments of intrigue and great feats of sportsmanship during the next set, but Sepp won it going away, 6-2. He only lost the 2 points because his opponent was dominant on his serve all day and those shots were never touched by Sepp or his enchanted racket.

The fourth set was similar, ending 6-3.

The fifth set, the final and deciding set, was closer.

Sepp was up 3-0 when he was seated for a changeover. He had never before been more confident, and he felt on top of his game. He believed in his heart that he was winning because his skills were honed, his time was now, and he was indeed maxing out his potential.

But there was a hint of doubt that he allowed to creep its way into his thoughts.

How much of his success was his effort and how much was the enchantment of the racket?

Certainly, there was more to his winning than something that was probably not even a fact...?

He looked over his shoulder and did not see his coach seated there in the chair where he had been seen cheering him on before. Sepp set aside the racket that had delivered his success and he chose one of the others from his bag.

His first serve went wide, and his second was easily returned for a point. His next serve was crushed back in his face and past his racket, whiffing a miss. His next serve was returned, a volley Sepp endured for two of his own returns before again losing a point. He double faulted to lose the game.

The next game he did not serve, but the results went in the same direction. His confidence shaken, he went down with only one weak swing that sent his return shooting wildly off to the side.

Dejected, he took his seat as they again switched sides. Looking back to the place where his coach should have been, Sepp saw only a vacant seat. There was nothing wrong with the racket in his hand, and there was nothing wrong with his hands; there he had all he needed to move on and win, securing a moment of glory in sports history.

Without any further consideration to switching rackets, he took a quick drink of his water and rushed to his new side of the court, his determination steeled, and his enthusiasm heightened to succeed.

He lost the next two games in similar fashion to the previous two. His opponent, the number two player in the world – and a former number one – was now steamrolling his way to what would be his fourth Australian Open title with just two more games. He was only up 4-3, but the last four points were so dominant that it was hard to imagine a rebound coming for the local player who had already given the effort his all.

As the two men returned to their seats, there was a louder than usual round of polite applause for the homegrown finalist who had just lost his lead along with any momentum he had going into the last set.

Sepp slammed his racket on the ground, breaking yet another tool in frustration and anger. This time, as before but with less questioning, he grabbed the racket that his coach promised would return a guaranteed victory.

Sepp won the last three games with little problem and in short order. The only real drama occurred as the two competitors were again taking their seats before switching sides and it became apparent to the crowd that at 5-4, Sepp was in the position to win the tournament on the next set, and he was holding serve.

What had seemed impossible at the beginning and improbable fifteen minutes prior, was now turned around and going strong the other way.

With the guarantee of victory in hand, Sepp aced three of the next four points and easily slammed back the only return his opponent managed.

The crowd went nuts and Sepp was almost unable to believe it. He looked at the racket in his hand and wondered what had just happened.

Had it been him or was it the racket?

In what should have been his finest moment of celebration for his greatest accomplishment, his maximized potential, he could not help but feel that he owed his success to the racket and not his hard work and training.

Had he just cheated himself of this opportunity?

Overjoyed but upset with himself nonetheless, Sepp slammed the enchanted object to the ground, thus breaking his third racket of the day.

Throwing his arms next into the air, Sepp allowed himself the moment to find some enjoyment in winning the greatest match of his life. The crowd was chanting his name, and it would of course be their day, too. The taste of victory was all so sweet…

But there was another flavor there as well, one that did not leave a good aftertaste nor ever dissipate.

It was a bitter taste he would never be able to wash away.

****

There were not many times after that when Sepp had to pay for a drink anywhere on the continent of Australia. An instantly minted home hero, the tennis player was recognized in every tavern and backyard barbie-Q down under. He accepted their gratitude, and he was always happy to sign his name when asked.

Jumping through their hoops was easy, easier than actually talking about the match. Sepp preferred the hit and run approach with the public, always happier to encounter large crowds than one-on-one conversation with a fan.

Of course, people wanted to discuss the back-and-forth nature of the match, the command he exhibited on one hand and the steamrolling he took at others. It was an often-used metaphor for the parity of the game and the nature of competitive sports. He was held up as an icon; his opinion was sought every year when the tournament was played.

Sepp could nod and smile and pretend not to care, but the talk of his greatest game came to be a burden, a hardship that became harder as the telling of it became another layer making it heavier.

And of course, most everyone wanted to talk about the racket, the thing he ran away to retrieve and came back with after that second set. What was the importance of that instrument that he would run back to the locker room to get it? Why did he abandon it in the last set? Why did he smash it?

Sepp had told so many stories over the years that there was confusion. At first grabbing the racket had been an afterthought, his real intention being something else. That something else then became the focus and there was never any one thing that he told twice the same way. The racket, he would eventually say, was the one he used during training and was most comfortable with.

Was he upset then that he broke it at the end of the match?

That was the hard one. That was the question he could never answer. Better to discuss the coach who unexpectedly parted ways after the victory than to discuss his feelings about that.

Why smash the lucky racket?

He did not hate it at the time, no more than he disliked himself back then, but each day he hated both a little more. He was glad he smashed the racket; his disdain for it was real. Did he appreciate forever being the winner of his country's home cup, The Australian Open Tennis Champion…?

No, in fact he did not.

As much as he liked seeing his name in the record books, he was not proud enough to look others in the eye and speak about the victory. Especially awful, he learned, was talking with his opponent from that day. Looking that man in the eye was a feat more difficult than anything else he did in his life.

And every year during the tournament they were interviewed, many years together and in person when it was impossible to avoid eye contact with his opponent.

Had he stolen the match?

Yes, of course he stole the championship from that man, and likely kept his competitor from his own best chance at again reaching a number one ranking.

Yes, he was in possession of something that did not belong to him. Sepp was aware of this, and the guilt would always trouble him.

But what had he stolen from himself?

He never won another match. Competed, yes, a few times, at least in that first year, but the drop-off was complete. His greatest potential would in fact be found that day.

When looking back, he was always most proud of the one part of the match which everyone else – except his opponent, of all people – never discussed: the first game. When he had jumped out and won those first 4-points, he was on top of the world. In truth, he could have lost everything after that point and still had himself a seat at any bar across the Outback. He still could have been able to look himself in the eyes.

"Hey Sepp, can I buy you a beer?"

"Absolutely."

"Hey Sepp, can I get you to sign my ball?"

"You got it."

"Hey Sepp, can we talk about the racket?"

"In tennis, a racket is like love; it's nothing."

The End

Radio Gag

"WEEC Radio."

"Hey! I wanted to call in and answer their question."

"Randy and Rhianna in the Morning?"

"Yeah. I want to say what I would do for the money."

"The twenty-five grand…?"

"Yeah!"

"Ok. Tell me what you would do."

"Don't I get to tell them?"

Scott the call screener sighed. "You're being recorded right now, so we want you to say it like you're talking to them and then either way we have it. We might use it to promote an upcoming bit, it might end up being a radio gag, or we might just say thanks and hang up."

"Radio gag?"

"Yeah, gag, like a bit, a schtick. Us having fun."

"Oh."

"So, either way, kind of depends on you; let's hear it."

"Ok. I guess, um, ok, here's what I would do for…"

"Hold on. Stop."

"What?"

"Listen, I want you to relax. My name is Scott, I'm the call screener. What's your name?"

"Matt Simms."

"How old are you, Matt?"

"I'm thirty-four."

"Oh cool! I have a sister named Beth who just turned thirty-four a couple weeks ago. We always joke that now she's a year older."

Imagining a peer on the other end, Matt laughed into the phone.

The call screener mimicked the laugh. "Perfect. Now that you're all re-laxed, tell me what you'd do for the money. Start it off by saying something like, 'Hey Randy and Rhianna, know what I'd do for that money....' Say that, and then just say what you'd do. Trust me, that will give you the best shot at, well, something."

"Um, ok. Here I go." Matt paused, audibly cleared his throat, and then proceeded with a greater tone of excitement in his voice. He did not yell or sound crazy, but he did produce a recording that could have gone on the air if it had not been intercepted by the call screener. "Hey Randy and Rhianna, know what I'd do for that money...? I'd spend the night in a coffin!"

"Cut. Matt. That was perfect."

"It was?"

"Yes. You nailed it."

"Wow. Thanks a lot, for saying that and for getting me in the right frame of mind."

"Hey buddy, no worries. Life is all about finding that right frame of mind. So, tell me though, would you really do that?"

"Sleep in a coffin?"

"Yes, spend the night in a closed casket for money?"

"Like for cash?"

"Probably a check."

"I would totally do that for twenty-five grand. American dollars, right?"

"Obviously."

"Well, you know..."

"I know." The call screener did not repeat the unspoken question. "But you would really do it, if we had a real contest that we were planning to make from all this...?"

"Are you guys giving away twenty-five grand!?"

"Whoa, whoa, whoa. I didn't confirm that or start promoting anything, yet, I'm just saying..."

"I would do it, yes."

"That's amazing." You could almost hear the call screener smile as he paused. "Ok, why don't you give me your phone number, and we'll see what happens..."

★★★★★★★★

Matt Simms looked at his phone. He did not have the number previously saved, but his phone nonetheless recognized that the call was associated with WEEC RADIO. Though he had forgotten about calling in to the

Randy and Rhianna Show, Matt was quickly reminded of the challenge when he saw the call letters on his phone. With his next thought the money, he turned off his radio – he was listening to a different station, but that did not register with him until later – and the 34-year-old prep cook cleared his voice as he answered the call.

"Hello!"

"Hey Matt, this is Scott the call screener from WEEC. How are you doing?"

"Doing great, doing great. How are you?"

"Oh, I'm fine. Thanks for asking. But this call is about you."

"Me?" Matt did not want to assume anything, but the tone of his voice betrayed the hope that was rising in his heart.

"Yes, you. Listen, I have some good news and some bad news."

"Oh." Matt's mind locked onto the immediacy of the negative.

"No listen, this is all going to end up good. Trust me."

"I trust you."

"There we go. I mean, I've gotten you this far, right…?" Scott the call screener laughed out loud in a reassuring way.

"Yes you have."

"Ok. I can tell the suspense is killing you." The reassuring voice chuckled. "The good news is that they like your idea and Rhianna and I think it's the best one. The bad news is that Randy likes it ok, but there is another one he does like better."

"Oh, I guess that's hopeful. How do you decide? Are you the swing vote?"

"Me? No, I'm nobody, just the guy they trust to answer the phone."

"Oh."

"That said, here's the deal. The other caller, the one Randy likes, has a neat idea, but it will take some money to pull off. They also live out of town, so that's time and money. The producer doesn't necessarily care one way or the other, so if we can pull yours off this weekend then you'll be a wrap, make the choice for them, and get the money. How does that sound?"

"Are you being serious!?"

"Yes."

"Oh my God! I've never won anything before in my life!"

"Ok, well hold up for a minute. So far, all you've won is the chance to try and be a winner. You'll still need to show up and spend eight hours in a casket to win."

"To win twenty-five grand, right? Twenty-five thousand dollars, right?"

"Yep."

"Where do I show up? I work Friday and Saturday; I could come down there Sunday?"

Scott the call screener paused. "You know what, that's perfect. They want to make sure we're going to have a winner before they start promoting it as our seasonal feature, and if we had a wrap by Monday morning they would be pumped!"

"But I wouldn't be live on the air?"

"No, like the initial phone call, a lot of the theater you hear on the radio – the hosts talking, anything with people calling in and especially contests – is all scripted or heavily edited. That's why everyone always sounds so polished, and the contests all seem to work out."

"You guys know who the winner is before you actually run the contest?"

"Yes, but not exactly. We do things like ask the question, what would you do, then we get the info we need. You won't believe how bad some of the phone calls are going to sound when we run the comedy piece for the executive team's monthly meeting. I'll burn you a copy."

"Thanks. That would be cool."

"And that's the great thing about radio. We can do fun things like bury you alive for entertainment..."

"Buried alive...?"

"Well, you won't be buried." Scott the call screener laughed. "Not buried, buried, anyway."

"But in an actual casket...?"

"Yeah, that's what I was about to say. Being on the radio we can do this anywhere, anytime, and then build the piece around it. At some point, obviously, you'll actually be on the show, live, but that would be later in the month."

"But the money...?"

"Twenty-five grand. It will be a check, but they figure out the taxes for you, too, and then make the check high enough to offset that part."

"So the net pay is twenty-five grand...?"

"Yep."

"And this is real...?"

"If you can spend eight hours in a casket."

"For that much money...? I guess that's what got me here. I can totally do it!"

"Great. Love your enthusiasm."

"So how will that work...? Will you have a casket in the studio?"

Scott laughed into the phone. "No, the studio is barely larger than a casket itself. We have a warehouse where we do offsite things like this. I'm pretty sure we even have a casket that we used as a prop a few years ago when the Steelers were in town, if not, we run ads for a local funeral home; I'm sure they would help if needed."

"I guess I didn't think about the actual nuts and bolt's part. Thanks for not making me provide my own casket."

"We like easy."

"So where do I go and when?"

"Do you have something to write with?"

"Give me a second."

"Take your time. I have all day."

★★★★★★★

Waiting for the day to pass on Sunday was an easy stretch compared with his shift the night before. Matt slept in until after noon, so half of his day was spent before he had time to think. He then spent another 90 minutes wandering around the house trying to wake up and shake the slumber from his body. By far the biggest decision and amount of time was spent trying to decide if he should wear a collared shirt and jeans or something more comfortable like his sleeping clothes and favorite ball cap.

Working his shifts on Friday and Saturday without spilling the beans was a task more difficult to manage.

Scott the call screener had been amiable and agreeable about most points he covered in the follow-up, but his insistence on secrecy was stern and terse: Tell anyone and the whole deal was off. The radio station was of course going to use the entire affair as a promotional piece that would be sponsored by one local retailer or another, and having any part of it covered on a competing station was not going to help the program, The Randy & Rhianna Show.

The timing worked out great, because Matt could think of about a hundred ways to spend even half of the $25,000. He did not have time to listen to the radio much, so he avoided disappointment when he did not hear any promos or other details of the random question he was taking seriously.

What would you do for $25,000?

About thirty people called that day, twenty-eight to be exact. Some had silly answers like marrying a sibling and others had questionable offerings such as eating food they would not normally consume, a vegetarian willing to eat meat. Most of the replies were standard and filled the Randy & Rhianna Show with a couple segments of random quips and hand-crafted hilarity. Matt was one of the last to call, number twenty-seven to be precise, and his suggestion caught the call screener as being just the right choice at just the right time.

Not to be on the radio, no, not ever.

Just the right choice for something else.

Something wickedly wonderful.

That was, after all, kind of Scott's specialty; getting just the right people into place at just the right time; besides, of course, simply screening out the others completely.

A real go-getter, Scott the call screener was a ghoul on his way up the ladder to being a fearsome demon.

Matt had partied in the area of downtown Cincinnati known as Over-The-Rhine, cool spots built in renovated warehouses and other pre-Prohibition industrial remains. OTR had once been dominated by all things related to the sale of beer, and today it was a time capsule of buildings being repurposed as apartments and storefronts and even some modern breweries, the cycle in some instances having come full circle.

After six o'clock on a Sunday did not seem to be the happening time in the party neighborhood. The stores and bars were closing early to wrap up after the bulk of busy already experienced throughout the hectic weekend. Matt was not concerned in any way; he was a big boy; he could take care of himself.

Parking was also not an issue; the building had its own little lot with easy access. The pavement had a noticeable slope, and it was next to a government-type building that Matt assumed was a halfway house, but there were other cars parked there, so it felt safe.

Looking around the lot, though, he was reminded that this was going to be an overnight visit.

Was he ready for this?

The building itself was imposing. At least five stories tall, it was easily one of the highest buildings in the trendy neighborhood filled with brick buildings from the 1800's. There were bricked up areas on the upper face of the building suggesting windows or in some cases even doors had once been present, hinting in some ways that the parking lot itself was likely laid flat atop the remnants of a gone and forgotten sister structure.

How much would a bet cost for him just to spend the night inside this building…?

And he was going to do it in a casket?

Was he ready for this?

He again scanned the lot before looking around at the inside of his car. If he had not quit smoking three years earlier, then he supposed he would have been hot boxing about three cigarettes at once right about now. As it was, he was content with the CBD gummy he took before leaving home and the comfort of knowing that he had two more in his pocket.

Matt also brought a bag with his earbuds and some headphones just in case, and he was happy to see that he still had over 75% on his battery. It did not occur to him that his phone being taken may end up being one of the rules for the contest.

He supposed that in the best case he would fall asleep and be awoken to the sight or sound of someone announcing him as a winner. Worst case, he supposed, he would not make it the full time, perhaps even with the radio team trying to do things to make it worse, scratching on the outside of the casket, creating the sound of dirt being scattered on top as well.

The worst parts were all too easy for him to imagine that he was prepared for it as if it was an eventuality. What he knew would not happen is him backing down and not completing the eight hours. He was about to make over $3,000 per hour just for lying on his back.

Matt did not care that the casket was once used by the effigy of a Pittsburgh Steeler; he would not be deterred by the shady neighborhood with the creepy tall building; this was his moment to win for a change.

With his bag in hand, he locked his car and looked up at the building. While creepy or eerie were good words for describing it, Matt could tell by looking more closely that there was a lot going on. He wondered if Scott would be able to give him any history to consider.

As Matt began his walk toward the building, another man came into view from the near side of the building. This shorter man waved at him with one hand while his other hand was holding something slender, like paper.

"Are you Matt?"

"Yeah! Hey! Are you Scott?"

"I am." The call screener closed the distance with a smile on his face and his hand outstretched. "You're a big guy, aren't you?"

Matt chuckled. "Yeah, I guess I'm tallish. You'd be surprised how many people are taller, though."

"And I bet you notice them all."

"I do, actually."

"I'm a short fella, so it's pretty easy for me to imagine everyone just being taller than me." Scott smiled and released his grip, laughing at his own joke. "One of my best friends was a tall fella, though, and I remember him saying that he notices everyone who is taller than him."

Matt laughed. "Yeah, I guess that's kind of true."

"Anyway," Scott the call screener motioned towards the corner of the building nearest the government building next door, the side from which he had emerged, "we'll go in this side door over here."

"Does the radio station own this building?"

"No, we just rent out one floor, the fourth floor. We do some of our demo work up there and build our promotional items in the other half of the space. I don't usually work in this building, but they gave me a key."

"What did this building use to be?"

"It was part of an old brewery. There was an icehouse next door and a power plant in the parking lot. The whole operation had about a dozen buildings around here. Christian Moerlein Brewery. Dunlap Café one street over was the old horse stalls. In this building they stored ice and aged beer in the basement."

"That explains all the bricked-up openings."

Scott smiled and looked up. They were now standing at the corner of the front and about to walk in the side door, so the façade was in plane-view, its features extended on the flat surface and stretched at an angle more intimate and distorted than found when passing by. The image of it was anything but a plain surface. "Yes, this old place certainly has many stories to tell."

"Well, I'm ready to add one more."

The call screener opened the locked door, holding it for his guest to enter first. "We'll take the elevator there."

Matt looked at the thin cage partially exposed through the open wall greeting anyone entering the door. To the left a winding staircase made with a skeletal metal frame hugging the outer walls disappeared first down and then up and around the corner closest to them, and it was not an easy decision about which was the better, safest option, the stairs or the elevator.

"You can take the stairs, and I wouldn't blame you, but taking the elevator is part of the charm of this old building."

"Yeah, I'm good with it."

"I mean it's luxurious compared with the casket."

Matt laughed nervously. "Yeah, I suppose so, if you look at it like that."

"Well, I'm excited for you. We'll just have you sign some paperwork once we get upstairs, I'll go over the rules, and then we'll get started."

"Just like that, huh?"

"Just like that."

"Will you be here the whole time? And is it just going to be you?"

"I will be here the entire time; I'm kind of your eyes and ears on the outside, making sure you're safe inside. I knew you'd trust me, so I made sure to pull this shift. Normally I work days. I can't wait to see you get this money!"

"Well thanks man. You've been great."

The elevator required the manual closing of a gate that was more like a cage wall. There was no ceiling. Though short and with one hand holding a folder, the call screener secured the car easily. Once it was shut, Scott pulled on a rope that extended all the way up and down the shaft. The car started jerking towards going up before smoothing out for a less bumpy ride. Scott manually closed a little hoop after they were above the third-floor level. "This thing is janky, but you have to respect the mechanics of it all. People back in the day were quite clever."

At the fourth floor the closed hoop caught a ball attached to the rope, halting the car's momentum, and slowing it to a quick stop. Scott opened the gate and again motioned for Matt to go first.

This room was large, easily half of the entire floor space of this level. The lighting was decent, even with more than half of them now off. He saw some saws and lathes and other general woodworking equipment off to one side and another piece of equipment that he assumed, based on the two pieces of metal beside it, was for welding.

The space was not cluttered and seemed generally free from debris.

Scott led them across the room and towards a large sliding door that was closed.

"The prop guys – it's actually a husband and wife – work in this space and build things for us as well as our sister stations on the other side of the dial. They work for Channel Five, too."

"That's cool."

"Yep." Scott unlatched the sliding door and gave it a hard tug, pulling it open more than enough for them to enter. "Over here is where we do our magic, and where you'll be spending the night."

Matt looked around the room. With more light, it was easier to see the details in the room, small things like the peeling paint or windows covered with black cardboard held in place with tape.

The waffle-like insulation along three of the four walls at one end seemed normal considering they were here because of a radio station. There was some random equipment off to one side of the space near the acoustic padding, but most of it looked like musical equipment that a band would use when practicing and not anything resembling a studio table like you would expect to see in a radio or television station.

In the center of that space, however, was a casket with a short set of steps pulled up close and the two lids lifted open.

Matt swallowed the hollow pit in his stomach trying to escape out his mouth.

"You know, the producer wanted me to haul that thing down in the basement and set you up there."

"What?"

"Yeah, I said no."

"How would you even fit it in the elevator?"

"There's a larger elevator on the other side of that room we just left. Freight elevator, much more sturdy than the one we used."

"Well, I'm glad you didn't do that."

"Yeah, he thought it would make it scarier for you. I told him, Jeff, the only people you're going to scare, or inconvenience, are your own people, me and whoever else is here throughout the night."

"Oh. Ha. Well thanks. That probably would have made it a little weird."

"Yeah, the basement in this building is no joke; it's like thirty feet down. It would have freaked me out, too."

"Yeah." Matt again looked at the coffin.

"I'll take you down there in the morning."

Matt lifted his eyes from the casket just long enough to acknowledge Scott before returning his gaze to his bed for the night. "Cool. That'd be cool."

"I told them no to the worms, too."

"Worms?"

Scott laughed. "Yeah, one of the guys in the studio thought it'd be funny if you had worms in the box with you. I told them no to that, too."

"That would have been horrible. Thank you."

"Yeah, no problem. Like I said, I got your back while you're in there."

"I appreciate that. I don't like worms."

"Who does." Scott followed Matt's eyes and laughed. "I didn't test it out or anything, but it looks surprisingly soft."

Matt touched the smooth, cloth lining and he felt a shiver across his skin. "This just got real."

"Well, let's make it official then." Scott stepped over to a small workta-
ble that was being used as a second-hand desk. He laid down the folder and
opened it so that the contents were visible to Matt.

In one pocket of the slim folder was a contract, and in the facing pocket
was the check already made out to Matt Simms. Scott removed the contract
and handed it to Matt, but he made sure that the expectant contestant could
see his name on the check. "Here is the contract slash indemnity waiver for
you to sign. Basically, the station isn't responsible if you have a panic attack
or even have a heart attack in the box. It also says that you agree to our
stipulations; I'll cover those in a minute.

"The other part is the rock-hard rule that you may not try to leave the
box at any point in the eight hours. If you lift the lid, you lose. Also, a standard non-disclosure form; this is our story, not yours. And then, of course,
we also have the check. It's actually for Twenty-nine thousand and change;
that's the number accounting came up with to cover the taxes so you can
actually say you made twenty-five grand."

"You guys don't mess around."

"We don't, we don't, we don't mess around! Hey!" Scott laughed. "Old
gag from one of the shows I used to work on. Great guys."

"What about the bathroom? Do I get a break or anything?"

Scott chuckled. "No, and unfortunately everything in that regard is out
of my hands. There's a sensor that will activate when the lid shuts, and if
it opens at all in that eight-hour window, a loud alarm will sound and corporate will get a text or email or some shit and game over. Once the alarm
is activated, there's really nothing I can do; except keeping your check safe
to give you after or shredding it if you fail, I am really just here to make
you feel better about being inside the box."

"I appreciate that. So, no bathroom or snack breaks then."

"There is a restroom through that door over there if you have to go now
or after. As far as snacks or entertainment, you are welcome to take anything inside the box that you like."

"I'm allowed to have my phone?!"

"Of course, just don't call and tell anyone what you're doing or where
we're located."

"Mum's the word. I probably won't even call anyone, just listen to music."

"Yeah, you don't want to use up all your air."

"Is that a thing?"

"Well, that is one of the stipulations that we need to discuss. Someone at legal apparently did some research and they don't believe that anyone can survive for more than four or five hours on the amount of air inside a casket. You are a bigger guy, so I don't think that I disagree, at least as far as you're concerned. You're going to be given a mask that is attached to enough air to last you ten hours, so two more than we need."

"A mask? I couldn't stand the mask during Covid."

"I know. I know. I know. I get that. But this one will keep you alive through the night. It's some pure alpine air, or some kind of horseshit."

"I really never thought about the air being an issue."

"I know, me neither. It's not pure oxygen or anything, so you won't blow up, but I wouldn't recommend vaping in there or anything."

Matt laughed.

Scott smiled. "Why don't you go take a whiz or whatever business you need to do and then we'll get this show on the road."

****

Tucked away in the corner of the floor, the restroom was a box built inside the larger space. On the flat opening that was the top of the bathroom ceiling there were some boxes being stored, and that space seemed dark and cluttered.

Matt entered the restroom and closed the door as he was turning on the light, otherwise he probably would have left the door open. The bathroom was the worst one he had ever seen; compared with how clean the rest of the space seemed, he was shocked and disgusted at the horror he found once inside this separate place.

The most obvious and worst thing was the smell. The stench of rotting feces and decomposing flesh were heavy in the air, and it seemed likely that there was mold and mildew in the mix.

The toilet was clogged with dark brown water, but it was not close to overflowing. The sink had a dark shade of green growing along the edges of the discolored porcelain. The paint on the walls, chipped and cracked, was in places smeared with what was hopefully dirt. Even the ceiling was on the verge of collapsing on itself. This last detail made him wonder about what was being stored in the boxes above the festering restroom.

For the briefest moment, Matt thought he was going to get physically ill. Then, the thought of letting loose with his head anywhere near either the sink or especially the toilet was almost enough itself to make him hurl. He felt sick and considered his ability to hold out for eight hours.

Would I piss my pants for twenty-five grand?

Gathering himself, he only unzipped his pants and peed into the toilet because he knew that not relieving himself was going to be worse once he was past this moment. He had chugged two Gatorades during the day, and he knew they would eventually run their course. Matt was careful, though, not to create any kind of splash that could fly back on to his jeans.

He did not bother flushing the toilet, and he did not try to wash his hands in the sink.

Being in that bathroom seemed like it could possibly even be the worst thing imaginable…

****

"It's a better fit than I would have guessed."

"Yeah, even with this air canister, my legs have plenty of room to move."

"Perfect. Makes you wonder how much room a short guy like me is going to have at the bottom down there."

"I know, my feet and head aren't even touching."

"Well you can buy yourself one when this is all said and done if you want; we'd probably even sell this one to you at a discounted rate."

"I might take you up on that. Let's see how the rest of the night goes."

"You have your phone handy, and your headphones are good to go. Can you reach your bag ok to get whatever you might need out of there?"

"Yeah, I should be fine." Matt thought about the edible gummies in his pocket and he subconsciously reached up and tested his ability to reach that part of his body. "All good to go."

"Ok. Before we put the mask on and close the lid, let's cover a few things."

"Ok. Shoot."

"Once we close the lid, it won't be locked: You can open it at any time. The caveat, obviously, is that if you do then the game is over, and we all go home. I'm not staying here with you if you quit early, bank on that."

Matt mimicked Scott, smiling and chuckling slightly.

"This is the sensor." Scott the call screener held up a small device that was dark and seemed capable of doing what he was saying it could do. "It's magnetic, so once the lid is closed, I will clip this to the side of the casket along the edge where it opens. If the piece comes apart at all once it's activated, game over. It might sound loud when I set it in place, and it may take me a little adjusting to get it right, so I apologize for that ahead of time."

"No worries."

"And there's two of them, one for each lid."

"Yeah, I didn't really think about the bottom lid."

"They never do!" Scott started laughing at his own joke. "I'm just kidding. This is my first time for something like this."

"Funny."

"Yep," Scott reached for and grabbed Matt's arm, "here, hand me your wrist."

"Ok…"

Scott pulled out a plastic band and attached it to Matt's forearm, letting it slide easily down to his wrist before tightening it a bit more. "Is that comfortable?"

"Yes, what is it?"

"Two things. Once an hour it will vibrate. That is me telling you it has been an hour. It's automated, so not really me, per se, but you get what I mean."

"I understand. Very cool."

"Yeah, well, you have your phone, so it's not a big deal probably."

"Yeah, good point."

"Anyway, the buzzer will go off once an hour. It's nothing too crazy, so it shouldn't wake you up if you fall asleep, which would certainly be my goal."

"Good point." Matt looked at his new adornment. "I actually didn't even consider that as an option; I've been trying to think what all I can do for that long to keep from going crazy."

"Sleep." Scott laughed out loud. "Sorry, I couldn't help myself. Anyway, the second thing is that it has a monitor that keeps track of your heart rate and breathing…"

"More legal…?"

"Yeah, you got it."

"Ok."

"One more thing. I'm going to close the lid and I want you to push it open, just to get a feel for how easy – or hard – it actually is to do. Like I said, I didn't try this thing out beforehand."

"Ok. Sounds good."

Scott closed the lid, and it was a smooth action with a tight seal.

Because the bottom section was still open, the light sneaking past Matt's feet and hips made the enclosed space around his head and chest seem smaller and more constrictive than he would have thought possible. He did not panic, but for about the fifth time in the day the action he was about to take – even if it was simply laying still in one place – seemed more real than at any time before.

Like being on a scary rollercoaster, he did not see any way of backing out or turning around, not that he wanted to quit.

He pushed on the lid and was surprised that he had perhaps slightly more room than he would have expected, and the lid was not difficult to push open, but it was also not something which could get accidently kicked up in the middle of the night if he did fall asleep and get startled awake.

Not a likely outcome – and not his fate – he seemed relieved at the action of the lid. He did not anticipate needing to repeat that motion.

"All good?"

"All good."

Scott grabbed the air mask and helped Matt get it set in place. After getting the thumbs up, he turned on the airflow.

The air was immediate, cool, and clear, so fresh. There was not an odor to it, and there was nothing about it that reminded him of the ocean or any other such place where the quality of your breath could be guaranteed pure, but the steady stream was almost a taste unto itself, just clean and pure, like good water. The oxygen blend was also better than any fresh air; he did not need to stand there breathing it on a beach in high humidity sweating.

There would be time for that after he won this…

What was this? In what was he now engaged?

Was it a bet?

Was it a contest?

What exactly was he doing except competing against himself for $25,000, nearly $30,000 with the tax money included?

Scott the call screener snapped his fingers and Matt stopped daydreaming.

"You good?"

"I'm good."

"Okay, I'll see you in eight hours." Scott smiled and slapped the side of the casket before reaching for the lid. "You know, some of the guys wanted to come down here and mess with you by pretending to shovel dirt on top of the casket or even moving you around as if being transported some-where, but I told them I would not let that happen."

Matt's laughter was muffled by the mask.

"Like I told you before," Scott said with a wink, "I'm your eyes and ears out here; like my baby sister would vouch, you can trust me."

Matt gave him a standing thumb.

It would never occur to him that Scott had previously mentioned that his sister was older. A lot of truths – or lies – would never dawn on Matt.

****

Watching the lower lid close was not tough, but as the top door shut and sealed him in lightless black, he was unprepared for the immediacy of the complete darkness. There was no sense of panic when the black veil shrouded his sight, but the lack of anything made everything become more real. He could hear a sound that he assumed was the magnetic sensor being stuck in place, first somewhere along the top edge of the casket and again near the foot of the metal box. It was hard to pinpoint where the sensors would have been exactly placed, but Matt could picture them all set.

The countdown was on.

The urge to again test the ability to open the lid did pass through his mind, but he slapped the notion away as about the dumbest move he could have made.

The sound of his own breathing was also perceptible, especially with the mask and the steady flow of clean air being forced through the tube, but the consistency of it would eventually make the noise easy to overlook.

The mask and the fresh air it provided was not a bad thing, and it was more comfortable than any mask he had worn during Covid. The clean air, not sweet but simply fresh and cool, was refreshing, but the sound of him breathing echoed loudly through his head. It did not take away his ability to hear himself think, but it did eliminate the silence and it did take away from the range of sounds outside the casket available to him.

There was a sound like someone had slapped the top of the metal box, and he could hear a muffled voice on the other side of the thick-gauge steel. It was easy to picture Scott the call screener telling him he was on the clock and slapping the top of the casket for good luck.

He was on the clock.

Matt wasted no time reaching for his phone. It was not difficult to re-trieve it from his pocket, and although his elbow did bump against the side of his enclosure, he did not worry about accidentally bumping open the lid. He had enough space that he did not see that being a problem.

Accidently opening the casket lid would not be a problem, not at all.

Inside the closed casket was too dark for his face to open the screen, so he used his code to unlock his phone.

The light from his phone screen was brighter than he could ever remember it being, and the immediacy of it hurt his eyes. After lowering the brightness as far as it would go, he went to his alarm and started both an 8-hour countdown timer as well as an upward counting stopwatch.

The thought of sleeping seemed impossible, so Matt started by looking through his social media feeds. After doing this for what seemed like not much time, bouncing between Facebook and Instagram mostly but checking his Twitter posts and latest Threads, he felt a slight tickle on his wrist and realized it was the bracelet alerting him to the passage of the first hour.

Since it did not seem possible for the time to have passed so quickly, Matt immediately checked his timer and stopwatch, both confirming the passage of the first hour.

"One out of eight. Woo Hoo!"

The next hour did not go by as quickly, but he was equally surprised when the bracelet buzzed the second time.

The second hour started by going back to Instagram before checking emails and then finally going through and making sure all his text messages were opened enough to be read and no longer showing several hundred notifications. He took a screenshot of the empty icon, but when he tried to send it to Isabella Stine - one of the cuter servers at his job who recently joked with him about his notifications piling up on his home screen - the text and photo did not go through. He tried two more times before the buzzer shook his attention and made him again confirm the time with his own counters.

Two hours down, six to go.

Before he could ponder the passage of time working in his favor, his phone alerted him that he was at 20% charge.

Matt turned his phone off and the darkness seemed impossibly black. There was still a glow on his brain from the bright screen, but his eyes could register nothing. He knew that there was fabric in front of his face, and he knew that the air mask was around his nose and mouth, but he could see nothing beyond those tricks his mind or retinas were playing with his senses.

He opened his phone and saw that it was already at 19%. There was not enough light for his face to unlock the screen, so he keyed in his code and began closing his open apps. When this was done, he again tried to send the picture to his coworker Isabelle.

As before, the message was unable to be sent.

Confused, Matt opened his Instagram app and saw that it was working fine. He was pulled in to watching a message from Phoebe about the burden of being an attractive ginger and then he watched a couple videos of people behaving badly at work before he found himself sucked into scrolling for another five minutes.

Five minutes was all it took before he received a notification that his phone was now at 10%.

Slightly panicked, he again turned off his phone. The device was off, and he was in the darkness for about twenty seconds before he again turned it on, once more needing to use the passcode when facial recognition did not work. He quickly closed the few apps he had just opened and was reminded of the undelivered text before closing that app as well.

The darkness was again spoiled only by the square glare that was a figment floating in his brain and not one he could in truth see. He supposed that in some way the receptors in his eyes were still activated, but the result was the same.

He could see nothing.

The first two hours had gone by so quickly, but he had spent almost no part of that time in the dark. The thought of spending the next six hours without his phone seemed like a different level of commitment, a new challenge.

To be fair, though, he tried to convince himself the rules just as easily could have stipulated that he forfeit use of his phone, so the first two hours could be seen as a bonus. He was lucky to be able to kill two hours with it.

That would not make the next six hours any better. In truth, it would be less than that, now, five hours and a lot of change; still, a challenge on an elevated level.

He pulled out his phone and turned it on without unlocking his screen. By his calculations he had already killed ten minutes of the third hour, only fifty minutes to go.

Then five more hours after that.

Calming his mind never occurred to Matt, but he did find himself laying still in the darkness for the briefest moment. He brought his hand up to his face, and he could not see it even when his palm touched his nose.

The phone did not make it past the third hour.

But Matt did not realize it.

Laying alone in the dark with his thoughts, vacant and hollow as they were, Matt did not stand a chance: he was asleep before he again had the thought to open his phone.

Without dreaming, he slept the remaining hours away, not waking up until greeted by his eyes and ears on the outside, Scott the call screener.

"Matt. Matt, are you alive?" Scott the call screener was standing with one hand on the open lid. His smile appeared as genuine as it was wide.

Matt opened his eyes, the mask and air flowing as cool and clean as before. It did not take him any time to know where he was, though he did wonder if he was dreaming.

With one hand still on the lid, Scott used his other hand to lift the oxygen mask off the face of the successful contestant. "Hey buddy."

"What's wrong? Why did you lift the lid?"

"I can close it if you want to go another hour."

"What time is it? I fell asleep. Did I win?!"

"You did it!"

"It's been six hours?! Already?"

"Eight hours, buddy."

"Oh, yeah, right." Matt rubbed his eyes.

Scott was relaxed and smiling. He did not appear tired or disheveled from having been awake all night as he lifted the bottom lid too. "Did you fall asleep?"

"Yeah, I must have slept the last five hours or so. Wow. That was pretty easy."

"Well, I'm happy for you. I imagine you'll need to use the bathroom again before we get into all the paperwork and promos?"

"Promos?"

"Yeah, they just want me to get a few words from you while you're all pumped up. You know, standard stuff. I'm sure you can imagine…"

"Oh yeah, that makes sense." Matt sat up. His body felt tight and stiff, but not much more than he normally felt every morning. He had slept more soundly than he had in at least two years, but he did not feel groggy or light-headed; this he attributed to the fresh mix of oxygen and air. He also had not consumed any alcohol before sleeping. "And actually, I do have to take a piss."

"Ok. Let me help you out of there." Scott laughed and used his hands to assist Matt in stepping out of the casket.

"Thank you." With Scott assisting, Matt had no problem getting out and on his feet, but his legs did feel stiff and his back did feel tight.

"You know where the bathroom's at..." Scott pointed across the room, "I already have the paperwork laid out, so I'll be ready whenever you get back."

Matt shook Scott's hand before walking back to the door across the room. He was inside before being reminded of his prior visit.

As before, the smell of the small bathroom engulfed him before the light could fill the space. He was again greeted by the same disgusting scene as before, and again he wondered why a fancy radio station would allow for such a horrendous utility space. After breathing the purified air, the putrid aroma was almost enough to make his head swim. The air had a taste thicker than any cheese, and the contestant winner almost considered not using the toilet at all.

Having to go, though, he proceeded.

As he was standing there above the toilet, it was only after he started his flow that he considered the toilet had somehow changed. It was still nearly full of whatever foul liquid existed before, whatever combination of exhausted bodily fluids was there pooled, but there was an island grown up in the middle of the murky waters, an isle of solid waste poking above the surface.

It was also all the more decrepit because there was no visible toilet paper, within the bowl or anywhere in the room.

Had Scott really used this bathroom...like that?

Matt was positive that pile of poo had not been there the first time he used the bathroom. Trying hard to avoid breaching the island of excrement with any forceful streams, Matt finished his business and left the room as he found it. He did not wash his hands in a sink that would have undoubtedly made his skin dirtier. Hesitantly, he flipped the light switch off and walked back across the outer room and towards Scott the call screener.

"Twenty-nine thousand dollars! How much of that time in there did you spend thinking about how to spend it?"

Matt shrugged his shoulders. "I honestly don't know that I thought that far ahead."

"That's a lot of money."

"Life changing."

"Ha!" Scott laughed out loud. "Life changing indeed."

"You know maybe I'll do you a favor and pay someone to come clean up that bathroom."

Scott looked toward the dirtiest corner of the room. "Oh that. Yes, you know I just got so accustomed to using the one downstairs that I forgot how gross that one can be. I should have thought of that."

"You don't use that one…?"

"No, but there were other people here tonight. One of them must have used it."

"There were other people here tonight?"

"Oh yes, quite a few in fact. There was a lot of our company members with an interest in your quest who stopped by either coming from or heading to the station. Our station is just up the hill there, in Clifton. We'll have a dozen selfies ready to post and use once this thing goes live."

"Selfies?"

"Yes. Pictures of them with you. Well, you inside of the casket."

"So selfies with the coffin?"

Scott laughed. "Yes, exactly. You were probably sleeping."

Matt shook his head with a smile on his face, but it was weird and unsettling that others had been in his presence while he was vulnerable.

"Here." Scott extended two pieces of paper. "Sign a few things and this will be legal."

"Is that my check?!"

"You got it."

"Thank you again. Thank you so much!"

"Hey, you can thank me by signing this paper." Scott paused. "Actually, you could do me a huge favor by jumping back up in the casket."

"Back in the casket?" Matt looked at the open lid and the space within.

"Yeah, I forgot to get a picture of you inside the box."

"Oh, that makes sense."

"Here, just sign these first." With the check in one hand, Scott extended his other hand and motioned to the two papers and pen there.

Matt picked up the pen and quickly signed his name, twice. He was excited and giddy and any thoughts of the bathroom or his unseen visitors were evaporating from his mind.

Still waving the check, Scott motioned back to the open casket.

Matt looked back at his overnight bed and felt a mild annoyance. There was not a sense of fear or impending doom hanging over his head, looking over his shoulder or whispering in his ear, just a sudden sense of his time being better spent elsewhere.

Still, resisting his gut, he complied…

Scott helped Matt back up the short stairs and into the box. He was more cognizant of the air cylinder resting against his outside leg, but the fit felt familiar otherwise. Once settled and the bottom lid closed, Matt posed while Scott snapped a few quick photos before handing over the check. The call screener took a picture of the winner holding that, too. "This is all yours, buddy, almost thirty grand."

Matt sat up. Check in hand, the finality of it all swept away that previous sense of missing out on something elsewhere.

"You know, one of the visitors you had while you were in the box was the chairman of our board, Patrick de Molay. He couldn't wait for you to pop out of your shell, but he wanted me to relay a message to you." Scott had one hand on the lid and the way he was positioned above the open half of the casket, his body was blocking Matt from getting out of the box without the call screener stepping aside.

"He did? The big boss?"

"Yes, he did."

"And...?"

"He said he would double the money – already wrote you a second check – if you could stay an hour in the coffin without a mask."

"No air?"

"Well, you would have air, but like you initially proposed, in truth, with the same threshold, shall we say, of four hours. Sixty minutes is only a quarter of that time."

"So it wouldn't be safe?"

"Well...," Scott extended the word before pausing. "Listen, I haven't run this past Legal or anything, and I honestly don't think they would approve it, but there is a signed check in my folder that could be yours in one hour." Scott the call screener looked at his wrist even though he was not wearing a watch.

"I see."

"Plus, I'll leave the mask and cylinder of fresh air for you, in case of emergency or whatever." Scott winked and leaned in closer. His voice was almost a whisper. "I don't even care if you use it once the lid is closed. No one is going to check that."

Matt looked at the check in his hand. It was hard to believe that this was now his; to imagine two of them was almost too much. "Can I think about it?"

Scott squinched one eye while his smile dropped. "I'm afraid that my guy was pretty clear that this was a one-time-only offer. My directive was

K.P. MALOY

213

to proffer the offer and then either sit and wait and give you the check or else destroy it."

"So do I have to give this one back if I try and fail?"

"You keep that first one in your hand, no matter what."

Matt took a deep breath.

"Not to put any pressure on you, but the boss made out a bonus check to me if you even try."

Matt started nodding his head. Even without the nudge he would have made the same decision. The chance to double his winnings and walk away with almost sixty thousand dollars was truly life changing.

"No pressure at all," Matt said, laying back down, his smile wide, "let's do this."

"Thank you sir!"

"Hope he made it worth your while to stay another hour here babysitting me."

"Honestly, I would have been stuck here at least until sunrise, so it's pure benefit. Thank you."

"Happy to help a brother out."

"I don't know anything about being a brother, but I'll take this assignment over some of the others I've seen over the years."

"Some good ones, huh?"

"Define good." Scott laughed once.

Matt mimicked the laughter.

"I'll have a coffee waiting for you in an hour. I'll tell you a few of the doozies then."

"Let's do this then, again." Matt reclined and tried to prepare himself for what was about to happen. He had already done eight hours in the box, how hard could one hour be...

****

As it was happening, the hour was easily one of the worst in Matt's life – until that point - but at the end of it, he was alive.

Even before he realized that his phone was dead and useless, Matt was overcome with the aroma of the bathroom clinging to him like smears on the sides of the toilet. The odor was in some ways worse because of the confined space and the consideration that those particles of disgust were now intimately close and likely inside his own body.

He at first wondered why the odor was so bad this hour, then he remembered that the first time in the box he had been wearing the oxygen mask, a mask that was still inside the coffin with him, an option to be used in case of an emergency.

For the first time, Matt also thought about the floors in the bathroom area, and he could not help but think of the amount of stink coming from his shoes. He could not help but picture worms.

The thought made him squirm.

Alone with the aroma and a dead phone, Matt's thoughts were left to roam. He was not tired, and the chance for sleep was remote.

Most of his hour was spent contemplating how best to spend the money he would have at the end of this. It seemed inconceivable that he would be driving through OTR with that much money, and it was even more difficult to understand how his bank would respond. Would there be additional paperwork needed to deposit such large checks...?

Matt also considered quitting his job. The total amount was more than he made in a year, so taking extended time off was an option he saw in his future, but he wanted to be smart about it. Have a plan. The amount was not enough to start his own restaurant, and that was not even a dream of his, but it could be enough to help him start a new gig where he could be his own boss, maybe being a carpenter or handyman. With that much money in the bank he could buy some tools, take some low bids to get experience and start word-of-mouth, making a new career from scratch. Such a move would indeed be life-changing, and with these checks he could afford to do that.

Taking a vacation for a week somewhere tropical also sounded like a good idea; indeed, he even managed to see the time away as a benefit towards plotting the execution of his new business plan. If nothing else, it would give him the break and then start he would need to make the leap into his new future.

If nothing else, it would be a change of scenery, a place with tall drinks, tropical beaches, and fresh air.

The stench was not something that he thought about for the entire sixty minutes, but at any point in that one-hour span he was reminded of it and his thoughts would stray, first to the odor and then on to one of the other limited topics rattling in his brain.

But always was the stench present, always was it there waiting to announce itself as the transition between topics.

Was it getting worse?

He considered using the mask to get a reprieve and some clean oxygen, but the possibility of the usage being a violation of the rules was too much of a chance to take, regardless of Scott's assurances. The mask was there if he really needed it; if he started to feel woozy or light-headed then he would use the fresh blend of air before opening the lid, it would be there; in case of emergency, it would be there.

The darkness was not the problem he thought it might be.

The black existence of visual depravity allowed his thoughts to switch from one idea to the next. For the first time in a long while he allowed his imagination to fully roam, and he could start to see a lot of possible futures for him and his new money. Some investments here, a couple of bets there, stay with the plan on the tools but find other ways to supplement even that income.

Now that he had the cash, he could even afford to enter one of those high stakes' poker tournaments at the local casino…

The lack of sight also made his sense of smell all that much stronger and keen, but unlike the foul odor now haunting him, the darkness itself was clean.

The lack of light made him realize how few times in his life he had ever experienced such complete darkness; perhaps this was the only time he had ever perceived such purity from any of his many physical senses. He wondered what the experience would be like under the effect of a mind-altering hallucinogen.

That made him think about the uneaten edibles sitting in his top pocket, and he wasted no time in reaching in and munching down the two gummies waiting there.

He was hungry and thirsty, but the logistics of trying to eat and drink inside the box now seemed improbable and potentially messy. The feeling of satiation he would take from eating his apple would be less than the recognition of the sticky hands he would have waiting for the lid to open and then what, wash up in that disgusting bathroom…?

Scott said there was another restroom that he used, but it seemed odd that he would not warn away his visitors about the status of the bathroom so close by. It also seemed curious that the main boss would visit the location and him staying away from that restroom would not be at the front of Scott's mind.

Surely an employee would worry about the big boss seeing such a mess…?

And if he had, why not warn Matt too? At least the second time.

It made no sense.

And what had the man meant when he said he had to stay until sunrise? Hadn't he mentioned at the beginning that he was not going to stay any longer than needed?

But Scott was the call screener, and so obviously this was not his building nor his problem. As the friendly and helpful man said, he was conditioned to using a different bathroom and was likely unaware of exactly how awful that room had become even if he knew it was a place to be avoided.

Matt at one point wondered about the type of person who would have used that toilet, even squatting instead of sitting, much less without toilet paper.

What kind of visitors had Scott entertained...?

It was at about that time when the bracelet buzzed, marking the passing of one hour.

Unlike the first time around, this time he was fully aware of the hour and what it felt like to win.

Without consideration for the actual amount of time passed, Matt started to move his hands to push up the lid. As his fingers made contact with the soft cloth, he stopped.

There was no guarantee that the bracelet had been synced with the new start time. It was entirely possible that the thing was just set on an hourly reminder, one already predetermined by what happened the first time. Scott himself had said that it was on an automatic timer.

How long had he spent out of the casket?

Ten minutes?

Thirty?

Certainly it was not less and likely not more.

Not wanting to nullify his winning by any technicality, Matt brought his hands back down on his chest and waited for Scott to open the lid.

And he waited.

After five minutes, Matt began to feel uncomfortable. He waited for what he assumed was ten more minutes. That seemed like a reasonable amount of time between waking up to Scott standing there and watching that same man close the lid for the second time. It seemed reasonable in terms of being likely, but it was not a comfortable time spent.

The odor.

The aroma was still lingering, somehow failing to fade and go stale even as becoming more rotten. It was at this point that Matt became aware of himself holding his breath as much as possible, eventually lifting his shirt to breathe with the fabric as a filter when he did draw breath.

After that, he started counting, getting as high as 300 – five minutes – before taking a deep breath.

Lungs filled with stanky air, it was a breath he would instantly regret.

This time when his arms extended, he did not make the decision to stop himself. With the full force expected to open a heavy door, Matt's arms made contact with the firm resistance beneath the soft cloth interior.

The lid did not budge.

Matt tried again.

Nothing.

First slapping with an open palm and then tightly clenched fists, Matt struck out at the top of the lid hoping to make noise, draw some attention, wake Scott from his slumber, whatever stupor it was keeping the man – his friend and ally? – from opening the lid and letting him out.

What if the man had a heart attack? Then what? How would he get out?

But why was the casket even locked in the first place? Wasn't the point of the sensor to tell when he had himself opened the lid?

It didn't make sense. The edibles were clearly kicking in, Matt could feel their effects worming their way through his brain, but nothing about the box being locked made sense. He tried to come up with reasons for the lid to be locked, but he could find none that explained everything.

The buzzer on his wrist again buzzed.

Had a second hour already passed?!

Matt again banged his fists and open hands against the casket, this time kicking and screaming and using his elbows against the sides of the steel box.

His actions were of no consequence.

Two hours. How many hours did the legal team say was feasible…four hours? Was he two hours away from dying…?

Matt thought of fresh oxygen, the ideal blend of purified air, and when would be the best time to start using that sacred resource. Whatever was happening on the outside had to be a misunderstanding that would surely be remedied, but it did not seem prudent to use the mask so soon. The sweet escape of the fresh air still seemed like a luxury of last resort.

He again tried to imagine what misunderstanding or misinterpretation could have happened to keep the lid closed. It was not impossible to imagine that there was a misunderstanding about the time, even though Matt was positive that Scott had been specific in saying 60 minutes. A quarter of the time until his air would run out, that is what Scott had said.

Now Matt had used up half that time.

Nothing about his interactions with Scott the call screener suggested a nefarious intent, and it was hard to think of anything except the disgusting bathroom that seemed out of place.

The disgusting bathroom. That was another image that continued to haunt his time. The visual aspects were themselves hard enough to forget, even the past couple hours had done little to fade the disgust from his ability to recall the scene, but the odor was still quite real and, in its own way, all too fresh. The smell had not faded, and he did not feel himself especially immune to the effects of the nauseating aroma.

His mind kept being drawn to his shoes and the fact he was now sharing his precious air with them and all the stench they had inevitably carried into this confined space. Why had he not thought to take them off? Had the box smelled this bad the first time around?

By far the worst image that his brain could conjure was the thought of more faceless strangers standing outside the box and his helpless form inside. Was this all part of some ruse, some idea of revealing him to the world live and on the show?

Besides Scott simply falling asleep, it was the only explanation that made any sense.

It was the only excuse that offered an out, a plausible means of escape.

His wrist again buzzed.

Three hours? Already? Was he now three-quarters of the way towards using all his oxygen?

His head did feel light, and he had no doubt that the pervasiveness of the foul air did not help, the foul sense taking the place of something fresher and sweeter, clean air like he would find in the oxygen tank at his feet.

He wanted to save the tank as a last resort, but he knew that time was drawing near. He would again lose himself to thoughts and visions and memories of things that were and things that could – or in this case, now, may never – be, and then that fourth buzz would vibrate his wrist.

Would he even make it to that fourth hour?

He pushed again on the lid, again with his hands and feet, elbows and knees, all to no avail. There was no force behind his actions that would ever open the box just as there was no reply.

Distraught, for the first time he broke down and quietly started to weep. He felt broken, and he wondered if any amount of fresh air left in that tank would be of any use to him. If his watcher and eyes on the outside had not responded by this point, returned to finish his duty and end his shift, then what hope was there of another hour or two making a difference.

Slowly and with great deliberation to not pull anything loose, Matt found the mask and moved it into place, careful to place the straps smooth against his head. Whatever chance this was going to offer, whatever stop-watch on his life the use of this air would begin counting, the immediate freshness of it was going to make things okay if even for just the first few moments of breath. The sweet escape would at least be enough to allow him a calmer vision on which to hold his last breaths if and when they did come.

Eyes closed in the already dark tomb, Matt turned the handle at the top of the tank and started the air flowing. This new air came quick and hard, and its impact was immediate and decisive.

Coughing and actually retching into the mask, Matt was overcome with the concentrated and quick delivery of the same aroma he had carried with him from the bathroom. Whether his mind had been tricked that first time into accepting this rotten air as fresh or else the contents of the tank had been fouled, Matt would not recover to know.

Both checks would be his; money taken to the grave.

The End

Welcome Home Walker

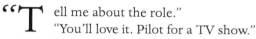

"Tell me about the role."

"You'll love it. Pilot for a TV show."

"TV show? Morty…"

"Julie, babe, trust me. This is going to make you a big star and then you can pick and choose your roles."

"I want to be in movies. My friend Meryl said actors never break the stigma of being cast in a television series."

"Oh, your friend Meryl said that, huh. Well then, what does your agent know about squat?"

"She's a good actress."

"What's she been in?"

"She was in Mary Poppins."

"Oh, that one. I should have known. I dropped her years ago; ambitious as all get out but way too picky about her roles. She missed her shot."

Julie Cutler knew that her agent Morty Sloan was being defensive; her friend Meryl was a great actress who was going to make it big one day. They were the two best students in their weekly acting class with Carol Rivers, and even the esteemed teacher had agreed that television could treat its actors harshly. It was the early 70's, and an Emmy was less prestigious than either an Oscar or even a Tony. There were some television stars who made a lot of money and did find a level of fame worthy of living large in Los Angeles, but even the best would always be in the shadow Hollywood cast over the town.

And Julie believed in herself, even dreaming that she was in fact better than her talented friend Meryl. She had been in her own production as a youth, and she had studied hard since then.

Her vibe suited the current decade well. Julie wore her hair long and free, often fuzzy from not being combed the 200 times her mother had advised as a child growing up in Illinois. She was taller than most actresses in her classes, and she occasionally towered over some of the actors. Built like a slender model, the amber-haired beauty looked good in a bikini even if she had trouble filling it out in all the right places.

Julie wanted to succeed, but she had principles; she had limits.

"Carol agrees. TV actors get pigeon-holed in their roles."

"Listen, Julie, baby. This is a win-win for you. There's a lot of push behind making this show a hit. You won't be the star so it's not like there's prominent association with your character, but it's a recurring role that is expected to have at least one scene per episode. That's some serious exposure."

"Yeah, but TV…? Morty."

"It will pay some bills. I'm guessing you could use some of that."

Julie looked out the window. Acting had so far cost her more than it provided. She enjoyed the craft of homing in on a character and bringing it to life, taking the rough idea and honing instead sharp edges. She could see how some current actors wasted their greatest roles by delivering lackluster execution, and she just knew that if given a starring role she could turn in a career-worthy performance.

"If the pilot clicks – and I'm telling you, the team that the company behind this has assembled will make it huge – then the first season is already slated for 22 episodes; that's at least six months of good-paying work. Are you telling me that kind of money alone doesn't get your attention?"

The actress did not answer right away. Of course she could use the money. She did not have any friends who wouldn't want to make that kind of income. Even the ones who despised material possessions required cash to fuel their own dreams.

But what would her career be in a year? What roles would this opportunity cause her to miss?

"What's it about?"

"It's a guy who's a teacher going back to his old neighborhood and school. A comedy, but some dramatic storylines, too. New thing: use comedy to get a message across."

"The show is going to have a message?"

"Yes, and I think you will appreciate some of the plots. They eventually plan to take on some real issues like women's rights and the place of race in society. It will all be told through a classroom, and again, using humor, they will actually be impacting the audience by delivering a message that hopefully changes some attitudes. And their politics align with your own, by the way."

"Yeah, but it's always the producers who…"

"Not with this project. New York is behind it."

"You make it sound altruistic."

"I mean, they aren't hosting Sunday brunch at Sally's house, but teen pregnancy and promiscuity will be a topic in one of the first episodes."

"Shaming the girl, no doubt…?"

"No, in fact she is the one who will be controlling the narrative."

"No shit."

"Yep. I told you. Perfect role for you."

"So, what would be my part?"

"The teacher's wife."

"In the classroom?"

"No, you'd be shown with him at the end of a day, reflecting and helping give him guidance at home."

"Sounds like I'd actually be the one helping steer the ship towards finding solutions to the problems. The classroom is all fun and games but then the enlightened wife is the one who gives him the good ideas needed to tackle the problem…?"

"Exactly like that!"

"It does sound intriguing. I'll give you that."

"I told you a thousand times: Trust me, babe."

"Who's the lead?"

"Some comedian that the New York people love. It will be set in New York. Brooklyn or The Bronx or something. One of the boroughs."

"New York? Do you expect me to relocate?"

"No need. Stock shots of the neighborhood and what not, but the studio will be in sunny California."

"And you think this will be done right?"

"New York is behind it. This comedian is a somebody to someone, and I hear there's one of the kids that they say will be the next James Cagney. We represent him, too."

"Seriously?"

"Yep. He's playing an Italian student who hides his insecurity about school and learning behind his neighborhood popularity. Lots of depth to play with, for lots of characters."

"Any back story on my character?"

"Blank slate waiting for the right actress to fill out the role. Great opportunity. Yours if you want it."

"Wow. I wasn't expecting all this."

"So, what do you say?"

"Let me think about it."

"Don't think too long, Julie. This role is yours today, but that may not be the case tomorrow." Morty paused. "Do you want to regret the chance you decided to take or regret the opportunities you turned down? Your choice. Don't think about it too long, though. You're already 27, people won't be calling you baby forever."

****

Julie took the job, and the pilot was a hit. The initial buzz was everything Morty had promised and so much more. Welcome Home Walker was a success, and the focus was not on her in any way that would make a mockery of her brand.

But there were problems, red flags that made her less than thrilled when the show was renewed for a second season.

"What do you mean you have doubts? Isn't this where we were a year ago?"

"Don't get me wrong, I appreciate so much about this show, but I haven't had even so much as a call back for any movies since. Meryl landed a part in a movie and has another one showing her interest, and I haven't heard anything. That and I'm kept busy on the days when I'm not shooting, so I'm doing a lot of work for free."

"And the powers that be - the New York team and we here at the EEC - are all thrilled with you, that's why they're giving you more money this next contract."

"I saw that, and don't get me wrong, I'm probably going to take it, but only because the money is so good."

"And I hear that you'll be featured more next season."

"I hope in a more meaningful way."

"Trust me."

"Like I said, I probably will."

"What are your concerns, anyway?"

"Besides the normal stuff I've already told you a thousand times…?"

"I know you aren't fond of your TV husband."

"He's ok, I like him alright,' Julie looked for the right words, "but he's not that smart."

"He's a comedian."

"Yeah, and not a very funny one."

"I've met him. I didn't think he was a stupid man."

"My character is named Julie because he couldn't remember the name they had written for me. He thought my real name was the character name and they just let him roll with it. Do you know what that was like for my preparation?"

"I can't imagine. What else?"

"The kissing scenes are just too much with his mustache."

"Less intimacy, we can talk to them about that. What else?"

"I would really like more say with how my character is written."

"That's a big ask."

"They don't know how to write women, and a lot of times they let me change my lines anyway."

"I'll see what I can do."

"It's also that my character isn't really the sounding board in the way I was expecting. The social issues haven't been there for me to work with."

"Ok. I'll bring that up, too. Anything else?"

"The episodes that end with us talking and him telling me a stupid joke about his family, any way we can cut back on those, too?"

"Oh, I love that part!"

"Well, they are horrible to film. Pretending to laugh at that is the hardest acting I've done in my life."

Morty laughed. "Ok. Noted. Is there anything about this show that you do like?"

"I like the money."

"And that's it?"

"I guess I do like the kid. I feel like he and I have a certain chemistry if you know what I mean."

"I told you; he's going places. He's a special project."

"He's not as dumb as he acts."

"No he's not, and neither are you."

"What do you mean?"

"Be careful what you wish for…"

"Just try to get rid of the 'Hey Julie' jokes at the end of each show."

"You got it, kid."

****

"Season three, here we come!"

"I don't think so, Morty. I don't think I can take it anymore."

"What? You can't quit now. You're having a baby this season!"

"I know, and I spent most of last season being pregnant. Portraying a mom was not my idea of discussing the issues that we face today as women. The role of mom has been played to death."

"Look, if this is a negotiation tactic, I don't think you want to play hardball with these guys. We ourselves have a strong relationship with New York, I don't think the EEC would like you quitting now."

"It's not a negotiating tactic."

"I don't even know why you waited 'til now to bring this up; we really should have inked this deal months ago.

"I don't even want to discuss it. Tell them I'm done."

"Julie, let's talk about this like adults."

"No, I'm done."

"You had a great storyline this season."

"I had a baby all season."

"And you killed it!" Morty paused enough to reflect. "Figuratively, of course."

"I'm still being shut out of movie roles. Meryl is on a roll now with a movie out and a new role. Now she's filming a movie with legitimate stars. I told you this would stymie my career."

"You're paying the bills. Taking trips, too, I might add."

"But think what I could be doing."

"TV isn't hurting the kid on your show."

"Yeah, well, I'm happy for Johnny starring in movie roles, but lots of good that does me."

"I already told you; that's not my fault. He was fast-tracked, but it shows you what is possible."

"Yeah, well, my problem with him is personal, not professional."

"That's between the two of you. Why don't you want to continue?"

"I'm getting less say than my first year, and that joke bit at the end of the show is every week now. There are some episodes where that's the only part I'm even in."

"Testing shows that is some viewers favorite bit."

"Well, it's horrible. 'Julie, did I ever tell you about my crazy uncle Lester? Julie, did I ever tell you about my great grandma Bearnice? Julie, did I ever tell you a joke that was actually funny?' It's all just too much, Morty."

"We can talk to them about that. I got the intimacy reduced."

"There is that, but I still ended up pregnant."

"Come on," the agent coaxed. "What's your price?"

"No more of the schtick."

"Monetary price if they say no to that."

"Fifty percent bump, and I want to see some more roles, more roles like Meryl is getting."

"You got it. So, we agree that you give consent to me accepting this deal for you, after doing my best to address your concerns, of course?"

"Yes, take whatever you can get, but I'm serious about trying to change the dynamic of this role a little this next year. And the money."

"You got it. I'm working hard for you momma."

****

"Julie, let's be adults here."

"No, this show has derailed my career."

"You're getting more roles than ever before."

"TV spots. Little parts for one episode here, one episode there. The Love Boat…? Really Morty?"

"Like you wouldn't be hounding me if you weren't getting roles like that. Lots of big-name people have been on The Love Boat. Rosemary Clooney's even been on that show."

"Even she's had recent movie roles that I'm not getting consideration for. Thanks for reminding me."

"Hey, you passed on at least one role."

"That film was basically one close-up away from having an X-rating. Did you read the script?"

"I read the script. You could have pulled it off with great aplomb." Morty paused. "Meryl could have made it work."

"Meryl! You know she's going to be nominated for an Academy Award. An Oscar!"

"You could pull off an Emmy…"

"Not the same thing Morty!"

"Easy. Easy."

"Don't tell me to be easy. This is my career. Get me off that show and get me some real roles!"

"Look, after this year the show will probably get cancelled anyway. Johnny's not going to stick around – it's a miracle he committed to this next season – and then you'll wish you had that role to play around with. You'll see."

"Another year of, 'Hey Julie, did I ever tell you about my sister…? Hey Julie, have I ever mentioned my cousin…?' Is that what you are asking me right now? Can I handle another year of that? Will I subject myself to another year of that?"

"You don't have a choice."

"What do you mean I don't have a choice. If I'm a citizen of this country, then I will always have choices."

"We signed a contract last year agreeing to do 2-years."

"What!? Why would you do that? You can't do that."

"I can and I did. You authorized it."

"No, I didn't!"

"You signed the contract yourself."

"What? I can't do it! Do you know how often strangers approach me on the street and just start in, 'Hey Julie, have I ever told you about this relative…?,' 'Hey Julie, have I ever told you about that relative…?', well it's a lot! Several times a day, in fact. I can't take it anymore, sure not for another year!"

"You'll get used to it."

"And another year of it will only make it worse."

"Come on. One day you'll miss that attention."

"Never! It's a fate worse than death."

"A fate worse than death…?" Morty laughed. "Why that's nothing. Julie, have I ever told you about my great uncle Patrick…"

The End

Horror on the Edge of Town

The Beginning

G ouging my name from off the wall did not help just as setting the
house on fire did nothing to stop…

What was it we had been trying to stop?

Wasn't it already too late even by that point?

Maybe for us – it was for David - but not for the others, certainly not
for the rest of those faceless names written on that wall, on that wall and
beyond.

Too late for most, but perhaps not for all.

Just like David to think of others before himself.

Again, what was it that we thought we were trying to stop? I know what
we convinced ourselves we were stopping - what David convinced me -
something akin to an abomination unfit to exist, a cursed house or unholy
deed; but now, without David here and me alone, I am not sure if that
makes it all more real or mere fantasy.

The trouble with my story is that I don't know what to believe myself.
The last hour has been like nothing I could have ever imagined, and the
fact that I just set fire to that old house on the edge of town would seem to
confirm my worst fears are indeed true; I have lost my mind, my grip on
reality, or at the very least my ability to reason.

But that is why I am huddled here now, dedicated to this self-siege until
I can sort through the last few days of my life, if not the pertinent parts
between the age of fourteen and now, me nearly forty-three. My hope is
that by writing out this, this, this thing as best as I can recall, then perhaps

by doing so I can make sense of what right now seems to make no sense at all.

The simple answer is that, like my two best friends before me, I have fallen victim to an inevitable curse of delirium and madness. One died by his own hand and the other, well, I don't know if I can say yet how David died, not because I do not know – I watched it happen less than thirty minutes ago – but because I cannot be sure that I did not just now cause it to happen.

I did not murder my first-best friend or willingly take his life, but I fear that when I look back on these relevant events from my own life, I will find myself more culpable than my own participation should have ever warranted.

To believe in that possibility for the downfall of my life - of our lives - then I need to go back much further in time, back to the days when being best friends meant something.

Even now it seems as unfair as it is hard to comprehend, but I need to find a way to accept that the end of my life was not going to happen because of a thing I did when I was fourteen.

Chapter 1

T he first thing I remember is that the idea of visiting the house on the edge of town came not from one of the three of us best friends but from Isabel, the girlfriend of my second-best friend, Neil. Neil and Isabel had been dating for about two months at that point, but the older girl had experience in ways that none of us had yet to understand, those of us being me and my first-best friend, David.

With Isabel, Neil had graduated from one club to that other one we all longed to one day join.

I would be succumbing to imagination if I posited how the conversation arose, but I have no doubt that Isabel had heard of the place because she had once visited it with a previous boyfriend. I'm not sure how I think I remember this point, but I don't think it matters in any regard; the more I write the more I am bound to remember.

She knew about this place, and she took us.

I'm sure it did not take much convincing. Isabel was the only one old enough to drive, but we were always up for adventure. That was true before that day and it would be true until each of our ends, I suppose.

Our hometown of Patrick, Ohio is not large, so getting to the house on the edge of town did not take long. Even starting from David's house, which was about as far away as you could get from two places in our town, the drive took only about ten minutes.

I don't know if I had ever noticed the house before that first visit, but if so, then it was certainly not like the way I would think about it every time I went past after that day.

Set back from the road just enough that it was not obvious, the closest apparent neighbor to the abandoned property was down the street, County Line Road, a lone house all the way near the intersection with Biddle Road.

The surrounding trees were a mix of tall firs, maples, and oaks. Though late in the year, the changing leaves were still clinging jealously to the branches, and they obscured the horizon as well as the totality of the house itself.

It did not occur to me at the time that people living on the street behind the property would be able to see the house, but I have since come to the realization that during the coldest months of the year at least one house on Anderson Road could see the eerie place.

Other than the overgrown grass and odd smell of decay, the only thing ominous about that visit was when Isabel pulled into the long driveway and parked her car there. Though we were not readily apparent, not like the car would have been if parked in any of our own driveways, we also were not invisible, and this was not our property.

It was not lost on us that we were trespassing, trespassing with the intent to vandalize, truth be told.

Of course we did not see it that way.

We were not rascals like that. Searching for adventure, we were more likely to jump from a hay loft in an open barn out on Beck Road than we were to break in and cause destruction or try tipping any cows. We liked to have fun, but none of us enjoyed hurting anyone.

Having been to the house once before, Isabel led us around to the back door and opened it as if just coming home with groceries. There was no power to the structure, and the entire place smelled, as I already noted, of mildew and decay. There was nothing overwhelmingly foul about the atmosphere, certainly nothing foreboding, but that sense of being trespassers and vandals did cross my mind.

It was immediately obvious that the house was old, but not in a way that indicated it had been abandoned for a long period of time. Clearly years had passed since anyone last lived in the place, but when it was inhabited it had been left in as good a shape as could be expected for a building probably built over a hundred years prior. There was crown molding in the kitchen and in the hallway, a dark wood that vividly marked the line between the lighter walls and the white ceiling.

The house on the edge of town was in many ways like a museum dedicated to wood. The paneling, the floors, the doors, and even the long wooden beam that would be waiting to guide us up the stairs: all beautiful wood.

Isabel and Neil were leading the way together, hand in hand. They were about the same height, and they were both athletic and rail thin. Her hair was as black as his was light, and she was still summer tanned where he was already winter pale. Despite all that and the two-year age difference they made a cute couple. I'm sure that Neil was imagining them breaking off for a few quick minutes to explore the bedrooms or something, but we were there for a different purpose, and his girlfriend seemed to be the one leading our group in that charge.

"I haven't made my wish yet, so I'm excited to do this too." Isabel looked back at David and me. David was taller and darker than any of us, darker than almost everyone else in town, truth be told. Back then I was stocky but eager, different from today, now slightly taller, heavier, and more broken. "You brought the marker, right?"

"A sharpie," David said. He did not have it in his hand or bother trying to get it from his pocket as proof, but he was confident. We believed in him too; David was our leader.

On most days.

Today, Isabel was leading us into the unknown; of this point I am entirely clear.

"Perfect."

"Why didn't you write your name on the wall when you were here before?" Neil asked.

"There was a group of us, and it seemed stupid to do it then, but when Lisa's wish came true then I had second thoughts."

"Lisa Tinch?" David asked. He always had a crush on the older girl.

"Yes. Do you know her?"

"What did she wish for?" I asked, interrupting my friend before he could reply.

"She wanted a new car, and her parents bought her one."

"Didn't she wreck her old one?" Neil asked.

"Yeah. So?"

"Well, her dad's loaded. It's a cinch they would have bought her a new car anyway."

"That makes sense," David said.

"She should have made a different wish," I said.

"Well, that's not the point." Isabel turned and continued by leading us out of the kitchen and down a hall.

"How many of you were here?" Neil asked.

Isabel glanced back at us before looking over at her boyfriend to answer. "It was a long time ago, months ago, in fact, at the beginning of last summer, like between the end of school and Becky's Fourth of July party. I don't remember. There was a group of us."

It was still the same calendar year, and the trees still wore a full coat of colorful leaves, but the seasons had changed at least once since then; her point was clear to me: When she was here it was before she and Neil had started dating.

"How many of you besides Lisa signed it?" David asked.

"I don't remember how many of us were here. Maybe four."

"Did any of their wishes come true?"

Isabel looked at her boyfriend before answering David. "Not yet, but they all wished for long-term gain. Scott Hicks wants to be famous. Bruce Barnes wants to be rich. Naomi Tyler wants to be a model. That kind of stuff. It'll happen; you'll see."

"I believe in this kind of thing." It was the first and probably only time I had ever heard Neil mention anything esoteric, and we stayed in touch through college. Neil had even stopped walking to make sure we understood the plausibility of his girlfriend's story. "I heard about this thing that happened here in town a couple years ago where some guy wished that everyone had to do what he said. Can you imagine how cool that would be...?"

I had agreed that it would be cool for a number of reasons. I don't recall what David thought, but Isabel was not a fan.

"That would actually be a horrible thing to have happen."

"Not if you were the one making the wish," Neil said.

"Well, no, but for anyone else who had to listen."

"Se la vie," David said. His parents had money and so he got to take a real vacation every year, and then a shorter one usually, too. My first-best friend did not speak French, at least not back then, but he did know a few words and phrases from different languages.

"I did hear about that, too, but I heard that it was a kid who buried something, made a wish, and then ran off a cliff because he thought he could fly." It was true, sort of; there had been a kid a couple years older than us who jumped off the cliff that was near the local swimming hole – and not far from the house on the edge of town, in fact - but not particularly close to any water. I had heard the wondrous details of the story about the time it happened because a kid in my class, Stu Talbott, said he knew one of the kids who made a wish that came true. Kids said lots of crazy things at that age.

"What was his name? He was only a little older than us back then," Neil asked.

"But younger than we are now," David added.

"Darren Henderson," Isabel said. "That was his name. He jumped off a cliff just down the street, actually."

"That really wasn't far from here," David noted.

"Yeah, the reservoir is right across the street."

"Makes sense," David said, "water and wishes would go together. Just an odd coincidence."

"Do you think he came here?" I asked.

"No," Isabel said.

"How can you be sure?"

"His name wasn't on the wall."

The living room or whatever the largest room off the kitchen had been used for was drabby. The space was in relatively decent condition from what I recall, but everything in this room was darker; the wood, the walls, the thick dust, all of it dark gray. Don't get me wrong, there was a classiness to the room, but the dark interior, lacking any polish, was not much to look at.

Plus, there were no windows in that room.

We continued down the hall without entering that large room. The hallway was slightly wider than most houses built now, and we passed one closed door that was made of a darker wood than the walls themselves. The hallway ended with another opening into that same large room as well as the foot of the stairs.

Isabel turned towards the bottom of the steps and stopped. "If anyone is frightened, they should turn around now."

"Why?" David asked.

Isabel laughed. "No reason. I'm just kidding you. There's nothing creepy upstairs."

She was right; conversely, she was also very wrong.

Chapter 2

The first time I saw the room, the forgotten bedroom on the second floor of the house on the edge of town, I did not notice the names written on the wall.

Not at first, anyway.

The first thing that caught my attention was the large window that was opposite the hallway door through which we entered. Not only was it larger than most any window I had ever seen in a bedroom, before or since, but its placement made it impossible to miss. Perfectly centered and framed in the same rich wood trim that molded itself around the top edge of the room, the shape of the elongated oval was as splendid as the window it framed. It was almost as if the room was built to accommodate or compliment the tall, shapely window.

Outside, most of the greenery had grown colorful, and even the tall firs seemed to be on the verge of losing a third of their needles, but the cloak was thick and there was not much to be seen except for trees. For reasons I will never understand, I was drawn to thinking that there was something more to see just past the barrier of those trees.

It was also easy to recognize that this house was once an amazing home. Based on size alone, this was likely not even the main bedroom in the house, and it was grand.

"Woah," Neil said from behind me, "look at that."

I had already walked past him and assumed he had finally caught up with the awesomeness of the window. "Have you ever seen one so big? Or that shape? And in a bedroom!"

"That's not what he's talking about," David said, pulling at my shoulder. Recalling the memory of that action sent a very real chill down my spine just now.

"I've seen a window," Neil quipped.

I turned around and for the first time I saw the names scribbled on the light plaster wall.

At this point I could have done what Isabel did the first time, watched and left without leaving my mark. At this point, I could have left and only been a witness to all that has since unfolded. I suppose if I had not written my name on the wall that day then all of this would have ended with the death of David, but that is not the choice I made; that was not the choice any of us made.

And would David even be dead if not for my involvement?

"There's not as many names as I would've thought." I don't know what number I considered, but I had been expecting to see more.

"Yeah, there's only like a dozen names up there." Neil guessed.

"Eleven," David said.

"What's your point?" Isabel asked.

"Is this a new thing?" Neil asked.

"Or is it tried and true?" I don't know where the words came from, but I imagine it was from some commercial on television.

Isabel looked at us all as if we were dumb and too young to drive. "I mean, this house hasn't always been abandoned."

"There *are* only eleven names," Neil said. He counted Lisa Tinch, Bruce Barnes, Scott Hicks, and Naomi Taylor as the names he knew from his girlfriend's story. He also saw Rob Cotton's name on the wall, and he knew that he and Isabel were rumored to have hooked up this past summer. Conveniently that guy was not mentioned in her story. Neil would later tell me that he understood not being able to be upset with her about something that happened before they met, but he was also unable to remove the image of them from his brain.

"I know most of those people," David said, "at least by name."

"Yeah, and the rest look faded and older."

"Yeah, I see what you mean." It was obvious.

"How did you guys hear about it?" Neil asked.

"I don't remember," Isabel said. In hindsight, it was clear her answer meant that Rob Cotton was likely the one who had suggested they all come here, a summation that would prove to be true.

"It looks like Rob Cotton and his brother Brad signed their names next to each other," David noted.

"That's right. He was the one who told Bruce Barnes about it, but I don't remember if he was here then. He probably signed it with his brother."

Even now, today, all these years later I can recall thinking that she was lying. It was obvious to me that Rob Cotton's name was dark and fresh, unlike that of his brother Brad whose own signature was covered by a thin layer of dust. None of the others ever mentioned that specific detail, but I remember it just the same.

"So, what do we do?" Neil asked, ready to change the subject.

"You close your eyes and then write your name on the wall while you make your wish."

"Do we write our names with our eyes closed?" David asked.

"They all did."

"So, pick a spot, focus on that spot, close your eyes, wish, and write?" Sometimes Neil *sounded* like the smartest of us all. He was the one who had snagged the older girlfriend.

"Yeah."

"Sounds simple enough."

"There's probably some trick to writing your name with your eyes closed," David said.

"It is harder with your eyes closed." Isabel knew because she had practiced it like a thousand times since that day; she mentioned that to Neil later, sometime after that day. "But you get used to it pretty quick."

None of us questioned how we would get better between our first and last names.

"Who wants to go first?" David asked, holding the Sharpie for everyone to see.

"Isabel, why don't you go first," Neil suggested.

"Ahh, lady's first," David said, "Aren't you just the gentleman."

We all chuckled; I can recall that like it just happened. We were all so young and stupid.

"I am a gentleman, but I was thinking more along the lines of she has actually seen other people do it."

"Either way," Isabel said, "I don't mind; I'll go first."

"Do you know what you're going to wish for?" Neil was asking his girlfriend, but his glance in our direction opened the question up to me and David as well.

Isabel nodded her head vigorously. "I do know! I've been thinking about this a lot."

"I already know mine, too," Neil added.

The way he was looking at Isabel, I was convinced that his wish had something to do with her, or, more specifically, with them. David and I just looked at each other. I had no idea what I was going to wish for, and I don't recall what I thought David was going to consider with his own wish.

We all watched as Isabel took the pen from David and walked over to the wall. It looked like she was deliberating, trying to find the perfect place to leave her name. Once she found the spot to her choosing, she wiped the wall once, took the cap off the marker, closed her eyes, and then wrote out her signature. The letters were tight and loopy, and the last letter of her last name swirled all the way around the entire name, but her handwriting was impeccable, like she had practiced it a thousand times.

Isabel Collins.

When she was finished, Isabel opened her eyes and looked first at her name on the wall before turning back to look at each of us. Her eyes were alive and charged, ready to see anything happen, anything that could be wished for was possible. She otherwise appeared the same as before, but we all believed that she was now different; she had made her wish; it was our turn to join her on the other side of that reality.

I'm sure she wasn't really thinking about anything when she handed the marker to me, and I certainly did not infer anything from her actions except that it was my turn to go next. Even though I could think of nothing original, I took the pen from her hand and walked over to mark my presence on fate's ledger. Once I found a suitable place, I too wiped the wall once and then closed my eyes before signing my name on the pale plaster.

Chapter 3

W e first heard the story about the house on the edge of town on a Tuesday after school. There hadn't been a lot of thought put into the visit, so there weren't – at the time – any real questions to ask.

The four of us were all sitting behind the local community center smoking cigarettes when David mentioned that he wished he could be in two places at one time. Because of the context – my friend was going to be a doctor and wanted to be able to help multiple people in many locations – we all laughed at him as not living in the real world.

We were young, but back then we were taught to believe that there was nothing gained without some kind of sacrifice. That was before the tech bubble later that decade or before the word IPO could make the average investor rich.

But then Isabel mentioned the house on the edge of town and the wall of wishes inside. We laughed at first, but then when she said that she knew people who had done it and had their wishes come true, well, we were kind of hooked. She never mentioned at the time that people referred to one person, and that the wish in question was one that would have likely come true regardless of where the person had written her name that night.

To be fair, we had never asked.

At the time, we didn't know any of that. We didn't know anything back then or else we probably would not have proceeded as we did, without thought or regard for any consequences.

No, we certainly would not have proceeded.

But that is not a fact, I suppose, and my goal here is to get at the truth by focusing on the facts.

I don't know if I can say to what degree any of us believed the notion to be true, but I can attest that we all thought it possible. We were younger then, much younger indeed, and surely it was easier to believe back then that something good could come from a wish than it would be to believe the same thing now; conversely, it was nearly impossible back then to believe that anything dreadful could happen because of signing our names on an abandoned wall.

Because it had so far proven to be true, that thought was all too easy to believe now.

Facts.

David had been talking about wanting to be a doctor; the only one of us smart enough to not be smoking, it was a pursuit each of us could picture our friend making with success. His lament, though, was that doctors are limited to seeing only so many patients and he had the desire and hope to help so many more.

David really was that much better than all of us. He was back then, and he was that way as an adult too.

He was that way until the end.

David was the one who brought up the idea of making a wish to be able to be in more than one place at a time.

Wrong.

David was the one who had said that he wanted to be able to be in multiple places so as to be able to help on different fronts at once. Neil was the one who made a wise crack about not all your dreams and wishes coming true. That was when Isabel had jumped in to agree but also concurring that at least one of your wishes could indeed be made to come true.

Yes, that was how it happened.

David had presented the problem.

Neil had proposed a solution.

Isabel had suggested a resolution.

And what part did I play? Who was I but the one dragged along behind the gravity of this topic the other three had breached.

I knew it was more than that, my part, even if it was nothing more than to be the last – figuratively – to tell at least our part in this story.

Facts.

Those other three were involved in the kernel of interest that became our involvement in this endeavor; that was a fact.

As that bystander pulled along, those hands buried deep in my pocket were clean; I had nothing to do with all that would follow.

Certainly, that must be a fact…

Chapter 4

I sabel went first, and I followed her in going second.
Like a practiced celebrity, the older girl's name was emblazoned with curves and swirls and all the flair one would expect from a glossy 8x10. When she opened her eyes, the young beauty seemed happy with what she saw. Although her eyes immediately switched over to Neil, she was polite in handing the marker instead to me.

My signature never looked great, so there was not much of a difference between writing my name with my eyes open or with them closed. A forensic detective might have had trouble deciphering the scribble – more so now - but my mom would have certainly recognized the name as mine. I wrote my name close to Isabel's, but not so close as to crowd her own fantastic imprint or to make Neil feel jealous.

David was the next to write his name, and his handwriting was about as bad as mine. He was quick about it, but I knew that he was not making his secret wish so flippantly.

Neil finished up, signing his name so close to Isabel's that their lines at one point crossed. When he was done, he put the cap back on the marker and returned it to David, who stuck it in his pocket.

At that point we all looked at each other in silence and then left the room the same way, quiet, like leaving church.

None of us asked the other what they wished, and no one seemed eager to talk about any of it. Neil did not even joke about finding a reason to explore the room at the end of the hall or any other part of the building alone with his girlfriend.

We were probably less solemn than I remember, but from there we went back downstairs, returned to Isabel's car, and drove down the road to the reservoir where we parked, talked, and smoked cigarettes before getting dropped off back at our homes.

There was no celebration or high fives.

It was a school night, and none of us had wished for anything that would keep the rules from applying to us.

Chapter 5

I t took me about a week to realize that my wish had not come true and to forget even having made it. Years later - after graduating high school and attending college, and sometime after we lost Isabel - the subject of the house on the edge of town came up when Neil and I were camping with other friends.

"What did you wish for?" Neil had asked. "And when did you know that it wasn't going to come true?"

"I wanted to fly, by myself, with no suit or technology being responsible. I just wanted to be able to fly like Superman."

"Like the kid who jumped off the cliff…?"

"I guess I couldn't think of anything better."

"Oh man," Neil had said, "I can picture you jumping off the roof now."

"I'm not the dumb one, not like that kid all those years ago. I started on the ground and tried to fly up to the roof, not the other way around."

"Yeah, anyone can fly down to the ground."

We had a good laugh over that one. "So, what about you? What did you wish for?"

"I wished that I would always be man enough for Isabel."

"You what?"

"Yeah, stupid, right. I wanted to always be able to keep her satisfied, you know, more than anyone else ever could."

"Yeah, I know." I paused, deliberating my next words. Though a best friend is with you every step of the way, offering comfort and support during the rough times, like when your girlfriend cheats on you with two college guys at the same party, they are also the ones best at ribbing you. "Guess we all know that didn't come true."

"Nope, I guess not."

"How many seconds did it take *you* to realize that your wish didn't come true…?"

"Very funny."

"I guess she got her wish, though." I knew I was pushing it, especially since life had been pulling us apart by that point, but again, that's what best friends do.

"Ha ha. Very funny asshole." Neil was smiling, so I knew he was along for the joke. "Actually, her wish was to be a famous movie star, and that's probably not going to happen now."

"No, probably not."

"I guess that just leaves David," Neil had said. "Do you know what he wished for that day?"

"You know what…? I don't think he ever did tell me; I feel like he wanted to be able to help more people."

"It was either to be in two places at one time so he could help more people or to be able to stop world hunger. You just know he made one of those kinds of wishes."

"Yeah, you're probably right."

"Maybe his wish did come true."

"I mean, he hasn't even become a real doctor yet and he already has that website up and running. Maybe his wish did come true."

"We should go make our wishes over again."

"Ok, next time we're both back in town we'll go back and try again."

"Bet."

We had a good laugh about it, but we would never have that chance.

Chapter 6

T hough she had a two-year head start, Isabel and I went to the same college down state in Cincinnati. She was in the design program that the university was renowned for, and I started off in the engineering department. Neither of us would graduate from those esteemed programs, and only I would earn a degree and leave college sane; Isabel did neither.

By the time I was living on campus, Isabel and Neil had been broken up for a year and our paths rarely crossed. The one time we did run into each other in Cincinnati, before either of us took our educational wrong turns, the meeting had been brief and cordial.

With barely any time for catching up, our adventure inside the house on the edge of town did not even come to mind.

At least not mine.

Looking back, it's hard to avoid speculating what thoughts were in her head at this point in her life.

Like all people do, we promised to keep in touch and parted ways. I would only see her one more time after that; it was, however, the last time we ever spoke.

I heard stories, of course.

Though I wouldn't hear about it for almost six months after the fact, it wasn't long after our meeting that Isabel did the first of many things that could only be described as crazy.

She started attending church, which was not crazy in and of itself, but she apparently became overly religious, attending services every day. She also dropped out of the art program, which made no sense because until then she had, by all accounts, been an excellent student. She had also left Cincinnati and moved back home with her mom.

Once back in Patrick, she switched to the Catholic Church, St. Patrick's, because they were the only group who met every day.

Oddly enough, this was not her most outlandish act of religious devotion. That would occur at the Episcopal church across town, the one she had attended as a child when her parents were still married, back when she had no choice in the matter. Apparently, she had started attending multiple services on Sundays, going to as many as three churches to honor the Sabbath.

One Sunday Isabel crossed a line in some ways more permanent than any marker written on an abandoned wall.

After the pastor at the Episcopal church, Malcolm Tollbridge, finished his introductory passage, Isabel stood up from her seat and addressed the congregation. To this room full of strangers, Isabel admitted to every manner of sin she was holding in contempt within her heart.

There was partying and underage drinking. There were the standards, like not taking religion seriously or not listening to her parents. Most of the top ten.

Murder was obviously not weighing on her heart – thankfully – but she did confess to worshipping false gods though without specifying or ever mentioning the house on the edge of town, wishes, or the wall covered in names.

On that day, in front of all those strangers, local parishioners just wanting to scrub away the sins of their own week, Isabel also confessed to her many sexual escapades, wanton acts which horrified many even while arousing a few. There was her first time with Jimmy Grants. There was the drunken sex with boys whose names she could not always remember. There was experimentation with other females and the story about the frat party, that deed itself having also happened on two other occasions with various partners. There had been an abortion.

And all of it out of wedlock.

Her mom and stepbrother did not attend church anymore, so there was no one in attendance to be ashamed when Isabel finished her confession and calmly sat back in her seat.

But Patrick is a small town, and word gets around. People talk.

That day was not the end of Isabel's odd behavior.

Some of it I would hear about, later, but not necessarily as it happened. News of her got passed around at parties - apparently like the way she herself used to get passed around down in Cincinnati – and you would hear stories. It was not hard to imagine the tales that I did not hear.

None of it sounded like her, like the Isabel my friend used to date, like the girl who drove us out to the house on the edge of town.

None of it sounded like her, but truth be told, none of her actions made me ever once question our names still there on that wall. There was nothing in my brain that ever thought to associate the stories about Isabel acting crazy with the time we closed our eyes and made a wish.

Back then, that was never a possibility; now, now that seems entirely possible.

Chapter 7

1

F acts.
Not all of Isabel's odd behavior was centered around church.

Isabel had a hard time keeping jobs. I never heard this from her directly, but our hometown is small, people talk. Being a cute girl with a smile hard to resist, she had little problem finding a job and getting her foot in the door.

No, her problem was staying employed.

I know that she worked at LeModels Hardware store over on Chester Street. There was also the hotel, the Patrick Pride Shoppe, the Yogurt Barn, The Dairy Cottage Chicken Shack, the local YMCA, Craig Asher Auto, Bainbridge Marketing (easily her best job near as I can imagine), and of course Teeters Sports Bar.

Although I was in town on the Friday night when she walked out of her job at Teeters, I was not at the sports bar to witness the scene. I certainly heard about the drama from others over that weekend, though.

Probably not an uncommon situation, unfortunately, but one of the patrons at one of her tables made an inappropriate comment about duties beyond serving food and drinks. I don't know if the manger did not handle it properly or just not at all, but regardless Isabel walked out that night and caused a scene. This one was less a confession of past wrongs and more a screed against those who would do wrong as well as against those who would allow it to happen.

Her meltdown was epic and the thing of legends. It was the kind of incident that you hear about from so many different people that it almost seems like you were there and a part of the action.

At the time, I never stopped to consider that the reputation she had in fact gained, the new persona she had become, Crazy Isabel, was an indication of her being less than sane in a clinical sense. I certainly did not associate it with the time we all signed our names on that wall.

Neither of her two big manifestations had been experienced by me in any kind of firsthand way, and in fact the only person I ever talked to that had even been present at either the church or Teeters Sports Bar incidents was Alice Wheeler. Alice and her twin had been at the sports bar and Alice told me that the room started quiet, trying to hear what was happening. Once it became apparent that the disgruntled server was raging against the crowd of patrons and not just the establishment, that was when the booing and other verbal hissing began. She said that one drunk customer had to be restrained from violence against Isabel.

Except for the boldness of it all, none of it matched the Isabel I had known, not the one who so confidently led us into that driveway and up those stairs so many years prior.

Isabel was only two years older than us, but that day she may as well have been the adult holding our hands. Then, at some point between now and then, at some point between when I last spoke with her in Cincinnati and now, she was lost to us in more ways than one.

Chapter 8

T hroughout college and until after our tenth reunion, Neil and I stayed in contact about as much as two single friends living in different cities can keep in touch. He lived closer to our hometown, moving over to Mansfield where he was an industrial engineer for a laser cutting and etching company. He had been with the company only about two years at that point, but he was already making more money than most of us attending the ten-year reunion.

David had been in the first year of his residency at the OSU Hospital down in Columbus, and he had been unable to attend that weekend of reunion activities. It put a damper on the get together, but Neil and I managed to carry on without him. After the sanctioned festivities of the first night came to a close, too early for most of the partiers in our class, Neil opened a tab at one of the local pubs down on the main strip of our small town.

Orange Bar served food, but it was the kind of place you came to drink. There was a good chance that most of the food eaten there was also deposited back in the bathroom before leaving, but, long and narrow and always seemingly busy, the place had a cool vibe for just hanging out whether there were seats at the bar or if the room was jampacked and standing room only.

On that Friday night, it had been jampacked and standing room only.

Neil only kept the tab open for one round of drinks plus twenty-nine Orange Bar Shots - served in a disposable plastic shot glass, it was the only fancy shot you could ever expect to get at Orange Bar – and throughout the night people were thanking Neil, some repeatedly.

One of those was Tara Tate. The petite cheerleader had never really stood out as one of the attractive girls in our class, but over the last ten years she had grown into a beautiful woman. After the second time of her stumbling up to Neil, touching him on the arm and leaning into his body while thanking him for always being a cool guy, it was obvious that the two had some chemistry if not a hidden history of which I was ignorant.

Though perhaps not verbatim, even now I can recall the conversation that followed as if it was still ongoing within the space between my ears.

"What was that all about?" I had asked, impressed.

"She's just drunk."

"Did you and her bang or something?"

Neil had laughed. "We hung out one night, but never went all the way."

"When was that?"

"Right before I started dating that crazy bitch Isabel, actually." Even then, almost eleven years later, Neil was still bitter about the way the relationship had ended.

"I never knew that."

"It was one night at Bruce Royer's house, towards the end of the summer. You were in Canada fishing with your dad."

"I remember hearing about that party. I remember because I never hung out at his house before, but I always wondered what the inside of it looked like."

"It was nice."

"Figures. What happened?"

"We were partying and ended up being the last ones awake. I don't think either of us ever saw each other as anything more than friends, but we still had about as much fun as you can have without really having fun, if you know what I mean."

"Maybe you'll change that tonight."

"Maybe." Neil was upbeat until that point. I remember the change as if a switch was flipped. "We probably would have wrapped it up that following weekend, but that Thursday is when Isabel and I hooked up. She put out on the first night – go figure - so I guess the rest was kind of lost to history."

"Worked out good for you."

"Until it didn't."

"Yeah, I guess not."

"I take that back. She probably did me a favor. At least no one associates me with her craziness."

"Well, maybe only one or two people anyway."

He knew I had been joking, but his smile was small and sad. "Imagine if I had stayed with her. I'd probably be the long-haired Jesus freak riding on the bus selling spiritual healing to the masses."

"What do you mean?"

"Crazy Isabel. She left town with some travelling ministry like three or four years ago. Right after she had her blowup at Teeters."

"A traveling ministry?"

"With its own bus."

"What do you think happened to her?"

"Who cares? Probably dead in a ditch somewhere down in Texas."

"I could see her flipping the script on him and taking over the bus. Maybe he's the one left in the ditch and she's the one leading the flock."

"She was too far gone for that."

"What do you mean?"

"I saw her about a month before her thing at Teeters. It was unexpected, and I really didn't want to talk to her at all."

"What happened?" I remember thinking at the time that my friend Neil had a lot of secrets.

"She wanted to apologize for any heartache she caused me, and she asked my forgiveness."

"Seriously...?"

"Seriously."

"And...?"

"And?"

"What did you tell her?"

"I wished her well and told her to fuck off."

"Hard to do both."

Neil had laughed. "I suppose. Easier than forgiving her."

"I suppose."

"What do you think happened to her?"

"I think she was probably always a slut."

"That's not what I meant."

"Why did she go crazy?"

"Yeah." I thought the question had been obvious the first time.

"I don't know. Probably because she didn't get her wish."

I laughed, but Neil remained serious.

"No, seriously. I think she was really butt-hurt that she didn't become famous overnight."

"You think so? That's kind of crazy."

"Isn't that what we're talking about?"

"I guess you have a point."

"We all put our faith in something that day, something that turned out to be nothing. I guess the joke was on us."

"Yeah, but it didn't drive us crazy." I laughed; Neil had not.

Neil was way too serious, and he was not quick to answer. Once he did find the words for his reply, he spoke them and then walked away from me and straight up to Tara Tate and a minute later the two of them left the bar together. I didn't know it at the time, but his parting words would be the last he and I would ever talk about a topic related to the house on the edge of town.

"Maybe our crazy just hasn't caught up with her crazy yet."

Chapter 9

N eil and I didn't talk much the next night at the reunion, but at the end of the evening he did leave again with Tara Tate.

When the two of us did talk, we also managed to get ahold of David with a facetime call. Neil was happy on the phone and I'm sure that David thought he was missing a great time with old friends.

It was an okay night with some people who used to be friends.

David wasn't missing a thing.

In fact, he was a participant in the best part of the night.

That Facetime call was the last time the three former best friends were all together, if even through the magic of a phone.

Not counting our names on that wall, of course.

Chapter 10

F acts.
Between that weekend at the reunion and when we lost Neil, lost to death and not whisked away on some spiritual bus, I saw or talked with him again maybe a dozen times or just more. It was a period of about seven years, and the first couple were more regular than were the last five, including a bachelor party weekend and his wedding to a beautiful woman who was not Tara Tate, Kristy Belkish.

The last three years of his life we saw each other twice and spoke again maybe three times on the phone.

By any objective measure we were barely still friends, but being best friends meant that – to me – the relationship never felt distant or strained. There was always the belief that we could at any time pick up and start where we left off.

The last time I saw my childhood friend - the last time we spoke, not just me hearing his dead voice on the recording of his outgoing message - I knew that something was not right with Neil.

It was at Thanksgiving and like a lot of other Patrick transplants I was in town to see my parents for the holiday weekend. I was at the Duchess Shoppe Gas Station filling up and a car pulled in next to me kind of fast. I'm not the type to comment to random strangers - my mom had raised me to avoid conflict – so I was not planning to say anything to the driver who was about to be pumping his gas from the other side of the same pump tower as me.

My eyes were paying attention to see who was driving, though.

The angle had made it hard to see, but as soon as the door opened and the driver stepped out, I immediately recognized my friend. My first thought was that Neil's hair was a mess and looked as if he had just re-moved a sweater. He wasn't wearing a sweater – was in fact just wearing a collarless shirt – but the weather was already cold outside, and it was just my first thought that the driver must have been warm inside his car and had maybe just finished a long drive.

It is funny how the brain can think so much in such a short second. I had an entire scenario for this stranger built from just my first quick glance.

The second thing I thought, and it was a feeling that was so close behind the first one it is hard to believe they were separate ideas, was that I felt bad because it had been almost two years since the last time we spoke; I wasn't positive at the time, but it had been almost that long, two Christmas Eves past. That time was itself a bridge between a period of a year, and it was the foundation of a broken promise to try and stay better in touch.

He did not see me; that was seemingly obvious to me because even though he looked my way he just started pumping his gas without a word of acknowledgement. I couldn't see his actions, but it seemed apparent to me that he had some difficulty getting his gas cap off or something. I could hear him swearing to himself but still loud enough for at least me to hear on my side of the pump.

My hands were free, and I had already entered my PIN, so I leaned around the gas tower to speak.

"Neil!"

"How's Cincinnati?"

If I am truly dealing with facts, then it is a fact that I fully recall thinking that my friend had in fact seen me before I said his name. He did not turn to look at me, but he obviously knew it was me.

"It's fine. My job sucks and I need a new career, but it's keeping me busy."

"What's it been…two years?" It was at this point that he turned his head, and we were able to truly look at one another face to face. My friend looked wretched. His eyes were dark and hollow as if he had not known sleep for a long while, and his once youthful appearance was dissipated, gone and replaced by someone who looked older than I ever knew my friend's own father to be.

I know I did not reply. You would have thought I was the one who had been approached with his back turned.

"It was Christmas Eve leaving church."

"That's right." I moved closer so we could shake hands or embrace, but the way his body was turned towards his car he did not seem open to such gestures of friendship.

"Holiday rush got us both running around I guess."

"Yeah, I had to run out and get some ice cream; gotta have the right kind of vanilla ice cream for mom." I paused to laugh, sure that my friend would laugh as well at the reference to my mom's habitual preference for French vanilla ice cream. I personally liked natural vanilla bean better, but I thought my friend would at least think of my mom and laugh at any of the fun times she took care of us or made breakfast for our tight-knit group.

Instead, Neil had just nodded his head and turned his attention back to his car, or at least whatever was on the distant horizon on the other side of his car. Nothing special that I could see, just he lost to a daze.

"I'm heading over to the parent's house, too. Got the wife and kid there; not sure how much more I can take, honestly."

"The holidays do that to us, that's for sure."

This remark seemed to get his full attention, and he turned his head as well as his body towards me. Neil was never our largest friend, but I could now see that there was less of him hiding beneath his bulky coat.

"The holidays? I'm just talking about life." He shook his head. "It's just never enough."

"What do you mean?"

"It's just never enough. There's always someone wanting more. More of this, more of that. More of my money, more of my time, more of me."

Not sure what to say yet positive that my friend was just talking about the basic frustrations of life, I smiled at him and shook my shoulders. "Life just has us chasing our tail in the dark sometimes."

"Yeah, compared with that, writing your name is easy." With that, Neil turned his body back towards his car.

Now unsure what next to do, the click of the gas pump caught my attention and I returned to my side of the tower and replaced the gas handle back into its slot, replacing my cap and closing my lid. It took the receipt maybe five seconds to print, and I walked back around the tower to say goodbye to Neil.

He was already in his car and pulling away. I could see that not only was his cover open, but the cap was still hanging out and dangling by the plastic strap. I had waved, but it was no use; he sped out of the parking lot and into traffic as if late for something important.

That was the last time I ever saw Neil, my best friend, my second-best friend, dead or alive.

Chapter 11

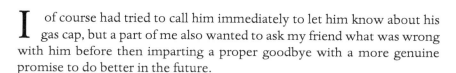

I of course had tried to call him immediately to let him know about his gas cap, but a part of me also wanted to ask my friend what was wrong with him before then imparting a proper goodbye with a more genuine promise to do better in the future.

He did not answer; I had ice cream in my warm car, and it was not until after we ate and were watching the third football game of the day that I again thought of calling Neil, at this point just to say goodbye and let him know I cared.

He again did not answer, but this time I left a quick message of friendship.

It was then three weeks later, when I was making plans to come back to Patrick again, this time for Christmas, that I next thought of calling my old friend. I was not about to let another year go by or wait until the next awkward conversation before reaching out on my part.

Once again, though, he did not answer; this time his mailbox was full.

It was maybe an hour later that I received a phone call from a number I did not recognize but from an area code which represented my hometown's general region of coverage.

Without too much hesitation I answered, not honestly sure who I was expecting to be on the other end.

"Hello."

"Hello?" The voice had not been calm.

"Who is this?"

"Who are you?"

"You called me?"

"You called first."

"I called you?"

"Yes, you called Neil's phone."

"Oh," I had said, now recognizing the voice as belonging to Neil's wife. "Hi Kristy. I was just going to be up from Cincinnati during Christmas and wanted to see when Neil was going to be available to…"

"Neil's dead."

"What? No!"

"I'm sorry I didn't recognize your name when it popped up on his caller ID. I'm sorry to be telling you this way."

"What happened? I just saw him three weeks ago."

"You saw him then? I'm not surprised he didn't mention it; he was already past losing it back then. It's all so obvious looking back, you know…"

"What happened. What battle did he lose?" It was at this point that I distinctly recall being positive that my friend had succumbed to a terminal illness that I, as a horrible friend, had been unaware of. The anguish of imagining my once best friend – second-best friend – going through such agony made me feel even more guilty for not keeping in touch.

Life is just so much to juggle sometimes, and truth be told, when he was married, Neil was the one who took that first step away from our little group. For better or worse, when he got married was when we lost touch.

"He lost his mind. Neil lost his mind."

"So where is he now?" I remember thinking that perhaps I had misunderstood her shocking remark and perhaps Neil was not dead in the literal sense.

"On my mantle, Neil's in a jar on my mantle.

The worst *was* true. "So how did he die?"

"Suicide. It wasn't pretty. The cemetery wouldn't have him, so we didn't have a service. He lost touch with everyone outside of work, so I didn't bother calling anyone. I figured if anyone cared then they would call. You called. I should have expected that. I don't know how often you guys kept in touch, but he always had stories about you two back in the day. You two and David. Whatever else was wrong with him, your friendships meant a lot to him at one point in his life."

I did not really need her to tell me this any more than she required my own expressions of sympathy for her loss, but I appreciated her reasons for what she was trying to say, and I followed suit by reminding her the ways that I also could have done better.

"If there had been a service then I would have tried harder to reach out to everyone."

"Kristy, I'm so sorry. It's so hard when you're so far apart. You try to keep in touch, but then life gets in the way, obligations seem overwhelming, it all just seems like too much."

"He said all that?"

"I'm sorry?" I was talking about me and my reasons for not having done better at being a friend to Neil.

"I guess you did talk with him before, at the end. That sounds like how he was talking before…, well, you know."

I was nodding my head, but I felt detached from the comment.

"I was right here watching it happen and I still don't know what I could have done to stop it, to stop any of it. It all happened so slow; until it all happened so fast, that is."

"Kristy I'm so sorry."

"Don't be sorry. It's not like you had anything to do with it."

Chapter 12

O ur call that day was brief and not much more was said.
Neil was dead, and if I'm writing about facts, I don't know that I should include her last statement as a fact.

Though self-inflicted, did I have something to do with Neil's demise and eventual death?

His wife attributed it to depression, specifically seasonal depression that she said he got every year around the holidays but that this time had never seemed to have gone away from the previous winter. By the time his family became aware that he was having a real problem, something more serious than usual that required a different level of attention, Neil was past the point of wanting help.

His wife had mentioned that he attended therapy sessions; but only a few times and even then, she was uncertain if he even went to any appointment other than his first one.

I had no reason to suspect anything about what she told me, and as before but with a much heavier burden, I again felt guilt for letting such an unbridgeable gap build between us. I felt guilty for not being there to help Neil when he really needed it; I felt like a horrible friend.

I felt guilty for a lot of things, I suppose.

We all go through dark periods in our life, and I would be lying if I said that the news of my friend's passing did not cast a shadow over my own perspective for the rest of that holiday season. It really didn't help that David was also unavailable, not in the same way that Neil would never again be available but just busy being a good doctor.

We did of course talk, and he was as stunned about Neil's passing as I had been. We found several reasons to call each other the next four or five weeks after that, and even found a weekend – a Thursday and Friday week-end – to hang out in Columbus and catch up.

The two of us talked about a lot of things.

We speculated on what happened to our friend.

We talked about being two older guys who were still single.

We talked about the future and made promises to keep in touch.

What we did not do that weekend was talk about the house on the edge of town.

Chapter 13

D avid and I kept in touch more frequently between that hollow holiday and our twenty-year class reunion. He was able to get away from work that time, and it was not lost on me that there I was, ten years later, with the one friend who had missed the last reunion and us instead both missing the friend who had been there ten years prior.

We had of course discussed Neil, and I for the first time retold to David as much of my conversation with Neil's wife as I could remember. I am certain that recalling and saying that for him then helped me to remember that same dialogue again when I wrote it just now.

"Did she mention the house?"

"No. He had a good job, but they hadn't been there too long. If I had to guess, I'd say…"

"I'm not talking about their home."

"Oh. Did they have a second…."

"I'm talking about the house on the edge of town."

I was taken aback by the mention of the place. In hindsight, in the last ten years I had maybe driven past the old house a half dozen times, but none of those times was my imagination anywhere near walking the grounds. I did not have to be reminded of the significance of the place a second time, but the image of it then, coming as it was from David's mouth, jarred me into a different, slightly altered reality.

Whenever I had thought of the house on the edge of town, I associated it with the other two already gone and not my first-best friend standing with me here still, then.

Certainly I did not associate the place with me.

Not before then, anyway.

"No. Why would she mention that?"

"I don't know, just a hunch."

"Nope."

Unlike Neil, my talking partner at the last reunion, David the doctor did not start a tab or buy a bunch of drinks. We interacted with others, but for the most part we were a couple throughout the night.

"Do you remember Darrel Rutty?"

Although I had not thought about the man for a while, I did recall the little guy who was actually a year older than either of us. "Yeah, I remember him."

"Last night before you showed up at the country club I was talking to Jeremy Georges."

"Yeah, they were good friends."

"Yeah, well guess what?"

"What?"

"He's dead too. Like Neil."

"He killed himself?"

"Yeah, a couple years before Neil, actually. He wasn't exactly on my radar."

"We can't talk; Neil was hardly on our radar."

"That was on him."

"And us."

"And us." David had paused; he seemed distracted and concerned about something related to our conversation. "That's what I'm saying."

"What?"

"The house. The house on the edge of town."

"What about it?"

"They were there too."

"Who? Jeremy and Darrel?"

"And Tina Maples and Susan Grove."

"They all went there...? To that same house?"

"Yeah. It was after we went. He said he saw our names up there. Asked if we went with Rob and his brother."

"Talk about crazy." I was made to remember the two brothers, Rob and Brad Cotton. Their names had been on that wall, though I know that they did not go there at the same time. The thing about them that stood out, however, was not that their names were on the wall or the fact that Isabel had hooked up with Rob sometime before she and Neil became an item.

No, the thing I remembered most about the brothers was the way they died.

Though each passed at different times, about eighteen months apart, each of their lives ended in basically the same way.

Rob, the younger brother and older than us by a year, was messing around in his car and was then chased by a local cop, Nick Abalone, an old veteran who would retire in less than two years. The chase ended when Rob lost control of his car, wrapping it around a telephone pole at the southern end of York Street. Eighteen months later, Brad, the older brother, was speeding through town when he was himself chased by the local police, again the same officer, Nick Abalone, and again the same street. Though they were headed in opposite directions, the long road through town was straight until it ended with a curve, each end the same, the road as well as the Cotton brothers.

Brad met his end against a tree on the northern bend, but the result was identical.

"Yeah, I hadn't even really considered that, too."

"What do you mean?"

"They all wrote their name on that wall hoping for a wish and they all ended up dead or crazy."

David had always been the realist amongst us, level-headed, and even now in my state of shock I know that I was caught off guard then by my friend suggesting something ominous related to the silly ritual we had once performed.

"And?"

"Come on. You have to admit that's a bit of a coincidence." The look in his eyes burned themselves into me, and even though I had not been present for any warning signs coming from Neil, I was not heeding any similar appeals from my friend at that time. David was the sane one, so I did not associate his words with the state of his mind. "Rob. Brad. Isabel. Neil. Darrel Rutty. Susan Grove…"

"What happened to Susan Grove?"

"Drowned her kid and ran away from town. Probably dead like Isabel."

"What? How did I never hear about this?"

"Bro, that happened when we were still in college."

"I guess I was drinking that week."

"We never really ran with her, and she was living over in Galion when it happened, I think."

"That's weird."

"That's why I asked if Neil ever talked about it."

"Not with me, and not that I know of."

"Brad and Rob had a sister. She might know something."

"Are you going to talk to her?"

"Of course not. I'm just saying."

"Well Jeremy and Tina are still out there, don't forget about them."

"And you and me." His look was different than any I could remember my first-best friend ever before sharing.

He was being serious, and he was scared.

Chapter 14

I had my own health scare the year I turned forty-one. David and I made jokes about me making it to the next reunion, the big twenty-five, but I generally felt pretty good about lasting the couple more years needed to get there.

With no real assets or attachments holding me in southern Ohio, I took the opportunity to move back home with my parents. They were getting old more quickly in the last few years of their lives than they had in the first seventy, and it did not make me feel better having them worry about me when it should have been me taking care of them.

Dad had worked a good job at a local factory, and he was still in the generation that earned himself a nice pension from his union employer. There was a studio apartment above the garage where my grandfather had spent the last years of his life, and I know that his death left my dad with a tidy inheritance.

Living in the room above the garage was where I had wanted to stay, but my mom, always protective, had insisted that I stay in my old room inside the main house, where it would be easier for her to pay attention to and take care of me.

I spent about ten months there, living in the familiar bedroom down the hall from them, but during many of those restless nights I spent my time alternating my thoughts between two other rooms: the studio apartment above the garage as well as the room with the tall oval window in the house on the edge of town. The one room offered me the notion of a different level of freedom and rebellion than a 41-year-old man should have to consider, and I wondered if I would find myself first moving back out of town or out to that studio apartment above the garage.

I knew that I could not spend any long-term length of time in the small bedroom inside the house. Whatever comfort was gained from being inside where all the physical creature comforts like a big tv, a stocked refrigerator, and a pool table lived, the need to be mindful of each late-night step and door closing was sometimes too much to bear.

That other room, the one with the names on the wall, represented a different kind of escape, something deeper, submerged just under the surface of whatever escape that other notion offered. It held sway over my imagination with unseen fingers that I could not identify yet knew were there, much like the room itself there in my head, as real as need be to steer my other thoughts around it.

I knew that I could not go back to that room, not alone anyway, but safe in my own room thinking about returning there for no other reason than to look once more out that tall window held me in its own grip. Convinced I did not care about the names written on the wall, my thoughts were always on that special window.

Back and forth my imagination was torn between two rooms that were in some way each ripping my attention between them.

Both suggested to me a departure from within the confines of my mundane room, an extension of my broken body, I suppose.

The room above the garage was most clearly identified by the trinkets still collected there, gathering dust yet still fresh as if lived in. I visited that room often, for it was not hard to access it from the garage below, and looking around, it would be easy to list off all the items that made this room special to my father. Every trinket was a memory of his own father, and the place was as much a tomb for the memories of a man as a real-life grave is a final resting place for that same bodily form.

For me, that same room was an escape, a place of wonder with things like a hand-carved wooden soldier, a porcelain bust of a sailor made in Portugal, a Soapbox Derby car that was itself a memento from the dead man's son. It was a place I felt secure and safe, a place of refuge, a place to find wonder but also a space where I could always come to gather my thoughts.

That other place offered a different escape, and it was not one that was always welcome there in my head yet was hard to shake away from my brain.

It was easy for me to picture the other names on the wall. I could not remember all of them, but there were almost a dozen, eleven I would later be reminded.

Though I could not at the time imagine going back to see my name written there on the wall – much less write it again as Neil and I had once proposed - I would allow myself to consider sneaking back in for another peak out that large elongated oval window. I could recall seeing trees, but I knew that there had to be other details which my young eyes had missed.

My time living back in Patrick and inside the house of my parents was nice and therapeutic; I was able to use the months to heal, but my imagination grew more restless with each passing day.

Chapter 15

I started driving again, mostly short trips to one of the two grocery stores in Patrick, and I would be lying if I said that I did not find reasons to drive past the house on the edge of town. It was out of my way to do so, but I justified it as being a peaceful route that skirted traffic and kind of snuck into the grocery store from the lazy side of the street.

Each time I drove past I was secretly hoping to catch a glimpse of that window. I thought that it would be smaller than I remember and that seeing it would put one of those rooms out of my head for good, allowing me to focus on moving on, and eventually in, to the more attainable and important venue above my parents' garage.

The house on the edge of town was desolate and its privacy well-protected by so many trees growing near the street that it was impossible to see much past what little opening the narrow driveway provided. There was never any sign of cars parked on the gravel, and the grass needed to be mowed. I could scarcely even see any part of the house at all below the top of the roof.

Each time I drove by the isolated house I tried to catch a glimpse of the property before I was actually upon it, even trying to sneak a peek from behind while driving on Anderson Road. This road had been a cul-de-sac back when originally built, but an extension at some point after my birth and before our visit made it easy to drive around behind the property in the hopes of catching a glimpse of that large window.

Even from the top of the hill over on Biddle Road nothing was visible.

Each time and from every angle I was confounded to see that it was impossible to catch anything except perhaps the slightest speck of the slate roof or the brick chimney.

It did not help that the western side of the property was bordered by woods which themselves ran the length of the street across from the reservoir. These were the woods in which Darren Henderson had once jumped to his death. The next street that way was past the railroad track on the other side of the city's water supply, Harley Township Road, and at that distance the house was barely still a memory much less visible.

From what I could see, the only direct neighbors were trees and overgrown brush.

The closest house was actually the one directly behind it, a large Victorian manor with a decently sized yard. I drove past that house a couple times before figuring out that their backyard abutted the property of my interest; the thick tangle of trees nonetheless blocked any chance of them seeing that house there alone or the big oval window facing them like the all-knowing eye of a dragon.

This Victorian house had neighbors, but only on one side, two houses between it and Biddle Road, but here the houses were not so close together. No house felt alone, but neither did anyone likely have to worry about their neighbor overhearing the details of their affairs.

The house on the edge of town did now have closer neighbors down the street than I remember, and the newer construction style – faux facing and likely faux foundations as well – was clearly built in the last twenty years. But these houses were still on the other side of Biddle Road, and none of that made the house seem any less on the edge of town.

Across the street were more trees, part of some land owned by the county and managed – if not maintained – as part of a network of reservoirs spread around each township in the county. The reservoir was a popular place for kids to go and swim, adults to go and fish, and teenagers to go and drink beer. The water drained out over a spillway and then under the road and into an old quarry. Here there was another hole for kids to swim and, more importantly, jump from off a twenty-foot cliff. No one fished here, and for some reason, no one drank, either. This was the local spot to jump into the water and swim over and do it all again. There was no time for drinking on this side of the street. There was also a higher place from which to jump, as well as an old rope that most kids no longer trusted to get them out and over the water.

This spot was also not far from where Darren Henderson jumped to his death a generation ago.

I was not sure why pulling into the driveway, even just to turn around, seemed like an impossible task to me, but I did consider it at least a half dozen times.

Surely if Isabel, then a new driver, could be so bold as to pull her car with us into the desolate lane, then it should not be impossible for me to do the same.

Facts.

She did not know then what I know now.

Facts.

I suppose if this is an attempt to stick to the facts, then it is most accurate to say I did find myself drawn to the house on the edge of town more than I realized, and I did drive past it often and consider pulling into the driveway on several dozen occasions.

It was an act I was never able to do, not driving, not on my own.

Chapter 16

My stay with my parents lasted longer than I would have predicted; it was also more pleasant than I would have expected.

Spending that time with my parents, though sappy, did help me to appreciate the depth that their upbringing had given me. We were able to talk about grandparents and I was able to learn some facts that gave me a new understanding of my family and how I came to be me.

These were not facts pertinent to this narration here. Like my health, these personal tidbits were in some way representative of me, but they were not me as relates to that house on the edge of town. Some of the details were sordid – my grandmother, mom's sweet nana, ran a bootleg bar and casino from her own grandmother's living room – and some were charming – my other grandmother was a nurse during the war – but these things are just background noise; these are not the facts which I now need.

I appreciate these mileposts, but these are not the facts I need.

Not now.

I did continue to speak with David, sometimes as regularly as once a week for some stretches, and I did mention to him my observation that the town itself was edging closer to the lonely house where one time we went. He did not seem surprised that I was talking about the place, but he was concerned as to whether or not I had in fact returned.

I assured him that I had not, at least not in the sense he had meant.

Before moving back to Cincinnati, I did drive past the house on the edge of town one more time, but as before, I could not bring myself to find the courage to pull into the driveway.

It was several times, and that's the fact.

Chapter 17

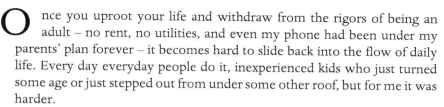

O nce you uproot your life and withdraw from the rigors of being an adult – no rent, no utilities, and even my phone had been under my parents' plan forever – it becomes hard to slide back into the flow of daily life. Every day everyday people do it, inexperienced kids who just turned some age or just stepped out from under some other roof, but for me it was harder.

I believe it must all come down to perspective.

Or expectations.

Or maybe the assumptions that our perspective gives us about those expectations.

That's more likely.

I suppose in a perfect world I would have been able to first move into the room above the garage before stepping out completely on my own. In my head, that had seemed like a good plan. I could move up there, feel as if out on my own, use that as the start of saving some money, making a real plan, and then going from there.

The biggest trouble for me was that there was no adequate work around Patrick, Ohio. My small town had opportunities, but most were related – literally – to youngsters running third and sometimes fourth generation businesses. There were jobs and I suppose careers to be found here, but none seemed a suitable fit for me and my past experience.

I was too old to find my break here, so I moved back down to Cincinnati.

David had suggested I come stay with him in Columbus, but I didn't want to put that burden on him. I also did not want to be put in a position to feel obligated to discuss all my own personal woes.

In hindsight, it may have been better if I had put that burden on both of us, better for both of us.

I suppose it was on some level pride, but at the time I remember thinking that I really had to prove to myself that the only way to get back on the saddle was to get back on the horse.

It did not occur to me that I was instead more than happy to put my elderly parents in a hard place. They of course insisted on helping me move back down, and they each made the drive, separately, down and back all in one day. It did not obviously kill them – they are alive and well and probably in the house, blissfully unaware in their dreamless slumber – but I know it was a long day and I could have avoided it all by simply moving in with my friend down in Columbus.

Or just staying put and moving in above the garage.

Money was not an immediate issue – mom and dad put up for my deposit and got the utilities turned on – so I was fortunate, but it took several exacerbating phone calls before I concluded that without them, I was truly alone.

Again.

Unfortunately, even with help, the head start, and the old contacts who I knew like friends, my return to The Queen City did not go well.

For starters, I missed home. Being around mom and dad for that time less than a year had brought me closer to them even as it ultimately drove me to leave.

I saw that was a mistake.

Even the little town of Patrick was something that I missed.

Ultimately, however, none of that really made the decision; that was made by my inability to keep the job I had procured prior to the move. That new job lasted about three weeks.

Mom and dad paid for the next month of rent too, and the three weeks' pay I got kept me in groceries, but then by the end of that second month and before the complete end of the third, the experiment was over and I moved back to Patrick, again, this time more broken than I had been the first time.

I had my second chance at freedom, and I let it slip away.

Chapter 18

U pon my second return, I had suggested just moving my stuff directly into the room above the garage, but my father did not think that was a good idea. I was not happy about the decision, but I did not argue or pout. I was a middle-aged man living with his parents, living off his parents; I did not need to add acting like a child to the growing list of regressions in my life.

I did find a job working at one of the two local grocery stores here in town – not the close one - and the labor of it helped put my spirits in a good frame of mind. My interactions with the public were limited to shoppers, most of them in a hurry, but the people I encountered all seemed friendly enough. I wouldn't say that I loved my job, but some of the cashiers were cute and liked to flirt, even with an older guy like me.

Nothing ever became of any of it; they were all just way too young and I didn't have the interest.

The other thing about this second stint back home was that I did not once drive past the house on the edge of town. I think it is safe to say that I did not even think about it at all during that time.

Not until two days ago, that is, when I started thinking about it again and have since thought of nothing else.

If this is a collection of facts, then that too was one of the facts.

Chapter 19

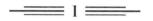

I think it is possible that I fell asleep. My head is groggy as if I slept. I am not yet sure if the authorities will be able to figure out that I am the one who started the fire, but there is a good chance that they will eventually trace David's car back to his first-best friend in town, me.

I still feel safe in this room, and so I will try to finish this tale before I am interrupted or next fall asleep.

I know when that knock at the door comes, whomever or whatever it is there to take me, I will not be coming back.

Chapter 20

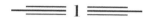

T his last time I've been living here, at home anyway, this time, has been for the last eight months. Though the work was not what I was skilled to do, and though I had only idle hobbies to exercise my mind, I found a stasis living and working as I was, staying at home under the roof of my parents and bagging groceries thirty-six hours a week.

It was not much, not like I had been accustomed when in my heyday down in Cincinnati, but it was peaceful and without stress and I was content if not happy.

Then David showed up two days ago.

That was when everything changed.

That was when this story really takes off.

Chapter 21

$$=== 1 ===$$

"**I** should have called first."

"David, you are always welcome in our home." My parents loved David like a second son, and they were sincere in their expressions of hospitality.

I came out of my room, and we all sat together and talked. We were getting ready to eat an early supper, and David was invited to stay. He had declined, saying that he had eaten on the drive up from Columbus and would have to be going to run other errands.

He looked pretty good. It was apparent that he was not missing any meals because he had gained about twenty pounds, but outwardly he was the same old David, pleasant and thoughtful of others. Like me who was already losing his, David's hair betrayed hints of his age with gray streaks formed by many tight curls fading like a wave. His forehead had perhaps gained more ground, but almost not worth mentioning.

I did notice that my friend was fidgeting, something he was not prone to doing. Though most of his gestures were slight, his hands never stopped moving. Tapping, twiddling, scratching, and even picking at his nails, something he never did. These were not the sole focus of my attention, but once I noticed them, they were impossible to ignore.

We talked with my parents for about thirty minutes when David said he had to run. Before leaving, he asked me to help him with something out in his car. I grabbed my jacket while he passed out parting hugs and we stepped out into the chilly late-day air. It was what we in Ohio call football weather, when the leaves drop and the air is cold enough to see your breath, but not so cold as to keep you from standing in it for three hours cheering your local team.

I was about to make a comment about the local football team being good again this year - almost having made it to the state playoffs; their only loss coming to the team that eventually won it all - when David dropped the pretenses and opened up about there being a reason for his visit.

"I need like ten minutes to talk to you."

I was caught off guard by his abruptness, and my first instinct was to think that he was going to give me a pep talk about my current situation. "David, I'm fine."

"You don't understand," David shivered once and looked to the garage. "Can we step in the garage to talk?"

"The cars are parked there, but we can go sit upstairs. That room is warm and has chairs and a couch."

"Just like the old days."

"Just like the old days. Did you bring some pot?"

David did not laugh, but he did allow a quick smile.

"Maybe you could write me a prescription for the medical-grade stuff I hear about...?" I was joking; my insurance would never cover that.

David again smiled without laughing, first opening, and then holding open the side door leading into the garage for me to lead the way inside.

"Listen, seriously David, if this is about me, I'm fine."

"This isn't about you, not like that anyway, I guess, not directly, but none of us are fine."

"What do you mean, like with Covid?"

"Us, all of us who signed our names on that damn wall."

Chapter 22

T he room above the garage was always one of my favorite spaces. A sanctuary from my room in the main body of the house as well as the last place my mom ever thought to look for me.

The last place anyone would ever think of to look for me.

The expansive room had originally been the apartment where my grandfather lived back when I was a baby. By then, my grandmother the war nurse was gone, and the old guy had liked living in that separate space that was yet so close to family. He liked being close to his tools, too, the same fine set that my dad still used to this day in the spacious nook in front of the parked cars below.

When my grandfather was alive, the room was supposed to be off-limits. When he died, I was still young. Because of the tall ceilings on both floors and the fact that there was a ladder for access to the roof, it was not a place I was supposed to be as a child. In reality, mom and dad never really cared if I came up with my friends, at least as long as we were respectful and did not trash the place when we were done, which we never did.

Though I knew it would not be cold, I was surprised at how warm the room felt once David and I had climbed the stairs and were seated.

"This place is exactly the same."

"It is the same. Unlike us it hasn't had any reason to change, I guess."

"We were changed the minute we signed our names on that wall."

"Jumping right too it then."

"This isn't a joke. I started thinking about it after the reunion, and then earlier this week something happened and now that stupid house and that damned wall are all I can think about."

"David, what happened?"

"First of all, you and I are the only two left."

"Left? What do you mean?" My first thought was of Isabel and Neil, but that was pretty obvious and did not make sense as an explanation. "Are you talking about Neil and Isabel?"

"Them, The Cotton brothers. Scott Hicks. Bruce Barnes. Lisa Tinch. Tina Maples. Susan Groves. Marie Thome. Even Lettie Lund. All the names that were there when we signed our names – Aggie Bretherd, Teri Marks, Tim Breckman, Naomi Tyler - all gone. They all went crazy, and some went crazy and died or just plain missing like Lettie Lund; and, I suppose, our own Isabel, I guess. I couldn't find out anything about those two."

I could not help thinking about my own health issues. I had not lost my sanity, but continuing to deal with the limitations of the condition were starting to drive me crazy.

"How do you know all those names? Did you go back up there?"

"I remember them from when we were there, that and talking to Jeremy Georges at the reunion."

"David, that was so many years ago."

David gave me a genuine expression of disappointment. "Really?"

"I know. I know. You were always the smart one."

"But I am going back out there."

"I retract that last statement."

"As soon as I leave here."

"Maybe you are crazy. Why?"

"Listen, first of all, it is a fact that everyone else on that wall from that day is gone, Isabel and Neil as well as all those people I mentioned plus the others. Crazy, dead, or both. Or missing, I guess, in the case of Isabel and Lettie Lund."

"You checked that out?"

Again, that same look. "Yes, I checked them all out."

"But Jeremy Georges is still..."

David just shook his head no.

"That has to be some kind of coincidence."

"Coincidence? There were fifteen names on that wall..."

"Fifteen...?"

"Eleven before us and then us four. Fifteen. Thirteen of them are gone."

"That's a pretty high average."

"Eighty-seven percent."

"Again, though, what's your point? People go crazy, sure, but people also die. Kind of the one thing we all still have in common."

"Not the same thing."

"David, you're supposed to be the level-headed one."

"There's more."

"Okay, what?"

"More names."

"On the wall? Have you been back there or are you going back there?"

"I'm going back. That first time was the only time I was ever there."

"Then how…"

"I was doing my rounds last week and I noticed on a chart that a patient was from East Erie County, so that caught my eye, and then I saw in her file that her address was actually on Parcher Township Road…"

"That's basically Patrick."

"Exactly, so I stopped back in to see her after she woke up."

"What was her ailment?"

"She tried to kill herself but had not succeeded. When I came in the second time, she was awake; I introduced myself, and we started talking. After just not even a few minutes of talking, I asked her what had driven her to do what she did, and she said without skipping a beat that she was convinced it was because she once wrote her name on a wall in an abandoned house and made a wish."

"She said that?"

"Yes! You can imagine how surprised I was."

"So did you tell her?"

"Of course not! I did ask her why she was so specific in laying blame on something she did as a teenager ten or so years prior."

"So, she wrote on it like fifteen or twenty years after us?"

"She and four of her best friends."

"How many of them went crazy or are dead?"

"Or both?"

"Or both."

"All of them."

I tried not to react with anything more than a blink. "That ups the percentages a little bit more I guess."

"Add in Darrell Rutty, Jeremy Georges, Susan and Tina and we're just under ninety-two percent."

"Funny but it seems like that number doesn't add up as quick as the body count you just laid out."

"That's the power of numbers."

Makes us a little more special, I suppose."

David did not smile.

"I just can't believe kids kept doing that." Looking back, I had before questioned what I was thinking on that day way back when. I guess I was just thinking that maybe I had found a life hack for being able to fly. The ridiculousness of having any expectations for that wish possibly coming true when it had in fact not come true was still something I could recall. It had seemed silly and at no time something that could end my life or condemn me to a fate worse than death.

"Little kernels of knowledge like that get passed on. Remember all those games we used to play with string?"

I laughed. "I couldn't tell you what we did or why, but of course I remember all those little time killers we performed with string. The one I remember is you stick your hand in and pull the string to undo whatever pattern the other one just did."

"There was also one that caught your hand like a trap when you pulled the string."

"Oh yeah! I remember that one, too."

"I think writing our names on the wall was more like that last one."

"Like getting our hand caught in string?"

"Exactly like that…it's a trap, except it's not just our hands and it's certainly not string."

Chapter 23

I walked him to his car. It never occurred to me to ask to go with him. Looking back, I know he was protecting me by not asking that I join, but I can't help wondering if he wanted me to ask. No one really wants to tackle that kind of unknown by themselves. No one really wants to face their fears alone.

Not even one of the good guys, like David.

And he was the best.

I suppose I have been a bad friend for the last fifteen years; I suppose I could have been a better friend going all the way back since high school, in a lot of ways to a lot of people.

"What do you hope to accomplish by going back?"

"I want to get more names to follow up on."

My friend's idea sounded scientific and involving a process; exactly the type of action I had known to expect from David. I still found it hard to believe that he thought there could be some kind of connection between an action we took as teenagers and our fates these many years later. I was perhaps not entirely well, but I was certainly not crazy.

Certainly not at this point of the story, anyway, I don't think...

Chapter 24

W hen my friend left, I found my mind drawn not to that room and that time far away; I spent the majority of my time trying to imagine why my parents were so adamant about me not moving into the room above the garage. It was a perfectly fine room; there was a sitting area for hosting friends; there was a bed and small kitchenette to support living; and there was a little writing table for thinking and sorting out my life.

I had each of those comforts inside the main house, but not all in one place.

A part of me was amused thinking of myself rebelling like a teenager and just moving my things into that room anyways. It would be disrespectful, and they would not be happy, but what were my parents really going to do about it?

I put the thought out of my mind and tried to not think about it any longer. That cycle of thought repeated itself until I was given something else to think about.

David did not ask me if I wanted to join him on his research trip, and I am not sure how I would have responded if he had. I suppose that based on my reaction when he returned two days later and did ask me to join him, I probably would have gone.

Chapter 25

M y mother and father looked at each other. I had seen the glance between them shared perhaps a thousand times, maybe more. It was the look of agreement and acknowledgement between themselves that they were unsure what to say or how to proceed, but that they were agreeing to remain unified and on the same page.

They used it most of those times while I was still in school and living under their roof, but it was one that I still witnessed by upsetting the apple-cart every now and again.

Lately it was more now than again.

My mother was the first to speak. As they grew older, she seemed to grow larger as my father had seemed to shrink. This was in regards more to their stature than to their sizes, but anymore it was usually her leading the charge in both regards.

"I thought your father and I made it clear the last time we talked about this," she again made a quick look at my dad for a show of support, receiving it by the slightest nod of his head, "but your father and I can't get up the stairs in there like we used to, not every day to check on you at least."

"But you won't have to check on me every day. I'm better now."

"We know that son," dad said. "But you can never be too safe."

My mother was nodding. "You can never be too safe."

"But my problem in Cincinnati was not my health, not this last time, it was just that I didn't have a backup plan when that first job fell through."

"We still don't understand how that happened." She did not need to look at him for reassurance on this point.

"It was a misunderstanding. We talked about this too."

"Yes, like the room above the garage; we already talked about that as well, remember."

"Of course I remember, mom."

"Don't get upset with her," my dad said, trying to defend his wife, my mom, "this is a decision we both made."

"But dad, you couldn't look after me when I was in Cincinnati, so how is it really any different if I'm just out there above the garage here in Patrick?"

It was dad's turn to look at mom, not for reassurance for what he was about to say but instead for guidance as to the tone of those words. "What is this all about, really?"

"What do you mean?"

"Is this something you're going through?"

"Going through?"

"Let's at least get to Springtime so we can pull one of the cars out of the garage," my mom suggested.

"We aren't parking a car in the driveway."

"You don't need to move the cars. I don't even need to move that much stuff up there."

"It's not a good idea."

"You won't have to help at all."

"It's not a good idea now," mom said.

"But why?"

"Because we said so, ok. Is that better?"

"Dad, I'm not a kid anymore, and you can't really give me the under your roof argument because I'm trying to move out from under your roof." Like any child arguing with a parent, there were holes in my logic.

"Well, you are kind of acting like a kid now."

"But dad…"

"No."

"Why not?"

"That was my dad's room."

"Your grandfather died up there you know."

"My biggest regret is letting him live up there."

"But dad, I'm not grandpa."

"I know son."

"So…"

"So what?"

"So can we at least agree to discuss this rationally one day."

My mom and dad again shared that glance. "Yes, when we can discuss it rationally."

Chapter 26

I probably spent too much time pouting afterward about not getting my way. I skipped dinner and went to bed earlier than usual. If they wanted me to wait, then I would wait, but I was not committed to following through on the part about talking through the idea again first. I had not entirely decided on a course of action, but I was certain that when the time came, I would not again ask for their permission before displacing myself into that other space.

I also tried to call David. Unlike when I had tried to call Neil all those years ago, David's phone did not ring before going straight to voicemail.

I thought that was odd, and I started to have my first nagging suspicions that all was not okay with my friend.

Chapter 27

I slept in later than usual the next day and considered not going to work. My body felt heavy, as if I had not slept a wink, and I really wanted to do nothing more than pull the sheets back over my head and hide under the covers.

That wasn't so crazy.

I did try to call David and he did not answer, his phone again not ringing before his voice requested that I leave a message.

The day was uneventful, but I guess I could not help thinking about those two rooms, the one above my garage and the one out there on the edge of town. The one room I wanted to move into and the other one I wanted to escape.

I curiously had no thought either for or against my own bedroom, the one I had been able to call mine since birth; that room with my physical belongings was no more a consideration than the dust gathered in either of the other two places where my mind now resided.

Chapter 28

Despite my parents' inability to release their grip on me while living on their land, and regardless of my father's feelings about parking a car in the driveway, they had fewer qualms with me driving to and from work. The car was not mine, so I had to borrow one of theirs – always dad's because he was the one least likely to drive anywhere himself – and they were generally lenient about most other things, which was why their resistance to my seemingly simple request for changing rooms made little sense. They were fine with the cars being driven, too, and I had my own set of keys for both, so having the vehicles leave the garage was a ridiculous prerequisite for anyone to bring up.

The explanation about my grandfather and his death did make some sense, and I could understand now – and especially now! – that the room above the garage had not changed at all in the last thirty years, and really probably not even that much in the last forty. To me, my grandfather was in that room as the pictures on the wall, the furniture, and the little nicknacks that were all so curious, each still in their own place. I had memories of the old man, of course, but I was not his son.

It was not that hard imagining my father looking at the room and seeing the man himself.

We simply had different perspectives; to him, the room was a shrine for a memory he held partially attached to that space; to me, it was a place of escape that I would respect but which was already a part of my being.

It did not matter at that moment; I had to work from three until nine.

The grocery store I worked at was different from the one where my parents shopped. Driving past the house on the edge of town was in no way on the route to my job, but I left early enough to be able to drive slowly past anyway.

Even with the trees bare, the thick brush allowed only the slightest improvement for seeing any part of the house. I could see the driveway quite clearly, and there were no cars parked there. I had no idea how to tell if any cars had recently driven up the path, but I could see my friend's car was not parked there, at least not where Isabel had parked all those decades ago.

On the drive to work, I tried to think about all the people my friend had mentioned who were now gone, and I took stock on the current fates of both he and I. As far as I could see it, he was doing great, and I was at least getting by; even averaged out we were way ahead of the game compared with the other couple dozen or so names on that wall.

Being human, I was able to consider two things at once, and my mind could not get away from thinking about the autonomy I saw when I pictured myself calling that other room, the one above the garage, my home. It held its own attraction and sway over me.

Mesmerized by both rooms at once, I also thought about not just the many names but also the large window in that less tangible room, and I found myself trying to recall what it was that I had seen when my attention was first there drawn. The window was tall and circular, an elongated oval that in my mind was half of the wall.

And what of the view, what through that glass had I seen?

Was it only trees?

Surely now with the trees thin I would be able to see something besides only more trees…

Any idea was beyond me, just as was the reason that room above the garage compelled me to transplant my life there.

What was there through that large window in the sky to so capture my imagination?

What was it about that room above the garage that would seem to complete me?

If only I could get a sense of living in the one and again looking out from the other then I know I would be made complete and at peace regardless of my outcome, be it insanity, death, or some worse combination of those two basic choices.

Daydreaming about hopes and wishes I now know to be false worship, I missed the turn for work and had to drive an extra mile both ways before I could get back on track, making me late.

Chapter 29

W ork was actually fun.
　　We were busier than usual, and I spent the majority of my time on Aisle 12 with Carmen Ashleigh. The high school junior who should have been a senior was not always the nicest cashier, but tonight she was in a better mood than usual, which made work more enjoyable than normal.

I really did not even think about either of those two rooms during my shift.

If I am being truthful, then I guess I should clarify that I did not think about either of the two rooms until Carmen made a joke during a respite when there were no customers able to hear.

"Jesus, I swear people are either crazy or fucked sometimes."

Her laughter at what she said and the way she shook her head lightened my heart and is a shared moment I will probably take to my grave, but it did get me thinking again about those two places separate from my body but perfectly present right there within my head.

I knew there was a third option: Both.

Chapter 30

— ‖ —

W hen I left work, I was in a good mood. Off for the next two days, I pulled out of the parking lot and did not even think about driving past the house on the edge of town until I was already pulling into my own driveway and looking at the slim, tall windows of the room above the garage. At that point I was tired and never considered pulling back out to drive around just for another pass at the lonely house.

I opened the garage door with the controller attached to the visor, pulled in, turned off the car, and then used the clicker to start the large door closing shut.

The light inside stayed on long enough for me to gather my things, lock the car, and take three steps towards the inside stairs before realizing I had to leave this building and go inside the actual house. The light stayed on until I was outside and standing at the door of the house using my key to get inside the main home.

Before going in, I turned to look at the garage.

It was always a unique building to me, but at that moment it seemed especially grand. Built in a day when carriages were in use, everything about it was larger than was typical for a detached garage. The ceiling was large and the space above was just that, spacious. From the outside, the size of the building now impressed me, more like three stories than just two, and I wondered why my brain thought to consider if a fall from that height would result in my end or instead only deliver me into the arms of a fate worse than death.

A fate worse than death…?

Had I thought of that on my own?

This thought tore me away from the imposing structure in front of me and sent my mind instead to imagining the room with all the names on the wall. Back then there had been fifteen names, what would there be now…? At least two dozen that David seemed to know about already.

So, forty…? Fifty…?

That number seemed like a lot, but four a year would place it well over one hundred.

How many names would David track down if not all of them?

If I was a betting man, I would say he would want to follow-up on all of them, but my friend's limit would probably be thirty or forty more names scribbled on a piece of paper.

Done with my thoughts of fancy, I withdrew inside the main body of the home and retreated into the shell of the room where I slept and from whence my first dreams had been borne.

Chapter 31

T he next morning – this morning(?), the last morning I awoke – I slept in until almost noon. Like the day before, I felt lethargic and tired, but this I attributed to me having too much sleep. I was asleep before eleven and slept past that late in the morning, so I had more than twelve hours of rest.

After going to the bathroom, I decided to take a shower which helped reset my attitude about the day ahead. I had the day off and I had big plans that did not include either of those two rooms. A light lunch at the local ice cream shop, a walk in the park, a trip to the store – the other grocery, for shopping – and maybe even a trip to the Walmart over in Mansfield for new shoes were all activities on deck for an ambitious day.

I dressed, styled my thinning hair, and even put on my shoes before I once thought to pick up my phone.

There was a message from David as well as a text telling me to check my messages.

His message was short and hasty, his words like his tone quick and rushed, and I did not delete the message when done. His words touched me like a cold specter and reset my hopeful day.

"I don't care what you have planned tonight, but I'm picking you up at six o'clock and we're going to end this thing, together. We aren't the only ones left, but we gotta be the only ones who can stop it. Six o'clock. Be ready and don't tell mom and dad."

Chapter 32

6:00 came and I had accomplished nothing on my list besides lunch, which was late more than it was light. After hearing David's frantic message and the sense of desperate urgency in his voice I could think of nothing besides musing about what he wanted to tell me.

I must have listened to that message a dozen times.

If we weren't the only ones left, then that seemed to indicate to me that the percentages would have shifted in our favor, but the timber of his voice made me question that assumption. I was never good at math, and I tried a few times to look for my high school calculator, when I thought about it, but I did not care enough to use the power of my phone or follow-through on the search when the obvious places yielded no luck on the first try.

I did not spend much time thinking about the garage or the room above it, but that room with the large window and names on the wall provided enough volume to fill the space of my thoughts.

I spent the day antsy and fidgety, and if I'm being truthful, slightly nervous.

I have never been one who had a great intuition, but I would be lying if I did not admit to then having a sense of impending dread barreling its way towards me.

Something bad was not going to happen, something bad was already happening.

David being thirty-nine minutes late did not allay my concerns or ease my worries.

Chapter 33

D avid called before he pulled up, and he asked me to meet him at the street. I didn't question him, and when he pulled up, I was waiting. The sun was already close to setting, but we still had maybe half an hour of good light left.

"I didn't want your parents to ask a bunch of questions."

"They were already getting set for bed. I doubt they heard me leave."

"Good. That's good." He pulled the car out, not squealing the tires or anything dramatic but with an urgency that was undeniable.

I looked around the inside of the car and was surprised to see that it was a mess. Not the kind of unkempt car I had when I lived in Cincinnati, one with dirty windows and burn holes in the seats and thick dust having bonded with the interior plastic. David's car was still immaculately sanitary, as far as I could tell, but it was cluttered with crumpled up food bags on the front floor and a backseat covered in papers that had spilled out of a shoe box.

David himself looked rough, clearly having not shaved since the last time I saw him. Though his hair was short with tight curls and never seemed to change much, it was not styled and in place like I was accustomed to seeing my friend as an adult.

"I'm guessing from your appearance we aren't going out for a late supper."

David did not laugh but instead shot me a quick glance. Whatever was on his mind and keeping him from being jovial, he was at least sane enough to pay attention to the road while driving.

"Listen, we have to make one stop first, but I have a lot to share."

"What are we doing?"

David looked at me, this time longer than I would have liked. Traffic was light, and he was not driving too fast. He looked back to the road before he began talking.

"There's more names, a lot more names, and I've been tracking down all that I could find. Tim Rush: murder suicide. Martin Hughes: in the asylum up in Toledo. Jeanne Franklin: drove her car the wrong way on the highway down near Columbus; she killed a family of five. I remember hearing about that one, but they didn't mention where the driver was from and I never made the connection that she was the little cousin of Danny Franklin, not that he and I were ever friends, racist prick. He's still alive and doing great, by the way."

"Was his name on the wall?"

"No, but since I was checking I thought I would see what that shitbag was up to. I needed a personal break." David again looked at me but this time his face did break into a wide grin, and he did allow some deep laughter to escape.

"Anyone else we know up there?"

Kristy Hilvers. Maggie Thrush. Billy Jasperson. Rich Mainette. Danny DeNardo."

"All younger than us."

"All dead or crazy or both."

"I thought Kristy Hilvers had a really good job working on movies or something…?"

"She did have. Went bankrupt. Dead."

"Wow."

"They aren't all dead; there's some like us who," David looked at me but only for the quickest glance, "who are probably fine for now."

"Probably?"

"We haven't been fine since we made the choice to believe in that thing."

"The wall? Writing our names there?"

"Yes, the wall. The room. The house on the edge of town. I don't think it's just confined to that one wall."

"Are there names throughout the entire house?"

"No, still just that one room. Many more names and some general graffiti now, too. Not much graffiti everywhere else, the other rooms, but some. Warnings, I guess, knowing what we know."

"Oh."

"But it's not just one wall of names. I checked as many names as I could the last two days and it didn't matter where they were written in that room. Dead, crazy, or both."

"Or the ones like us…"

David stopped at the light and turned to look at me. What I saw in his eyes was not the sane, level-headed man who was my first-best friend, now my only best friend, my only friend; instead, I saw only someone else whose energy was driving all action and thought.

In a flash just as quick, he allowed a slight grin and chuckled.

"Or the ones like us."

Chapter 34

D avid had a nice car with lots of bells and whistles and I could not easily see his gas gauge but when he pulled into the gas station, this one a Marathon across the street from the Duchess Shoppe Gas Station, I simply assumed he needed to refill. He pulled up next to a pump, used the fob to pop the trunk, and tossed it back in the cupholder before exiting the car without saying anything.

Although I had heard the trunk pop, I did not really pay attention to what David was doing back there.

It did not occur to me at the time that the last place I saw Neil was at the gas station across the street.

I wish I could say that I filled the time with deep thoughts or ruminations on what it all meant, the room, the names on the wall, my obsession with obsessing, but the truth is that I got lost looking out the window, staring off into the distance, looking at something that was really just nothing at all.

Before I realized it, my friend was back in the driver's seat.

The smell of gasoline carried into the car with him.

"Alright, let's end this."

"Your story? Maybe you should go wash your hands first."

David's energy had changed, and he was more jittery than I had seen him the other day. He was excited and he was nervous, like he was the time at our old swimming hole, before he jumped off the cliff and into the water. "Nah, I got just as much on my shoes and pants as I did on my hands."

"Was the pump broken?" The smell of gasoline was nearly overpowering. "How did you get it on your pants?"

"It spilled out of one of the gas cans."

"Gas cans? What are you going to do with gas cans?"

"We. What are we going to do. We have four of them in the trunk."
Seemingly very happy with himself, David started the car and rolled down
the window.

"Are you asking me?"

David sat back and found a way to contain his energy. He closed his
eyes and took a deep breath. When he opened them and looked at me, he
now appeared calm and peaceful, as if the hardest decisions had already
been made.

"We're going to end this thing; we're going to end it for good."

"End what?"

"End this curse; end this ritual; end this cycle of insanity that we are on."
Before he put the car in drive, he looked at me with no reason to quickly
look away. "I already feel better, like the real burden has already been lifted.
Now we just have to follow-through and do this thing."

"Follow through on what, David? What are you talking about?"

"The house on the edge of town, we're going to burn that mother
down."

Chapter 35

I was about to tell my friend that his idea was itself an act of craziness, but before I could speak, he was turning out of the gas station and towards the direction of the reservoir. With a lot to say, he did not give me much of a chance to speak.

"Listen, before we get there, I think you need to know a few things. I'm not crazy."

"Clearly you're completely sane."

"Here's some facts for you. We are special, not because we are alive or sane or even about to do this thing, but because we were really near the front of the line on this one. I mean, I would pay anything to get off the ride – maybe even a little bit of that sanity you were talking about – but there were only eleven names before us. We already knew that five of those before us were Lisa Tinch, Naomi Tyler, Rob Cotton, Scott Hicks, and Bruce Barnes, so taking them out brings us down to six. It doesn't take a genius to know that when Rob's brother Brad went, he was with Tim Breckman, Lexi Marks, and Aggie Bretherd."

"And then there were two."

David's head whipped over to look at me and his eyes filled with joy. His laughter was quick, loud, and in many ways disconcerting. He looked back at the road, the smile still in place as the silence crept in.

I looked at David, not sure what to say. Did he forget what we were talking about or was there no point to his story…? "So, who were the first two?"

David again looked at me, his face still lit from the previous round of laughter. As we locked eyes, though, his serious demeanor again set in. He looked back at the road. "Marie Thome and Lettie Lund."

"I remember Marie! She was older than us by what, like three years?"

"Four, I think. She was a senior when we were freshman."

"Wow, guess she made an impression, because I feel like I saw her a lot."

"You just thought she was hot and noticed her every time you saw her."

"Well duh." I paused to consider the old flame, but thinking of her now as she was then did nothing for me and was in fact hard to even recall. I remember that I thought she was attractive like a college girl might be, but that was it. The other girl was not familiar. "Who was the other one?"

"Lettie Lund. Her family owned the house."

"That's weird thinking of that place ever having owners."

"I agree, but it had been abandoned for a few years before the next set of names were written down."

"So, the first two did it while they lived there?"

"While Lettie lived there. Marie must have been a friend; she and Lettie were the same age, within a year at least. The family disappeared when Lettie was eleven, so maybe six or seven years before you remember Marie and so about seven or eight years before we entered the picture."

"And how do you know they made wishes?"

"I don't know that, not for certain. I just know that they were the first two names on that wall."

"Are they alive?"

"Like I said, Lettie and her family disappeared. Marie is dead."

"Ouch. That one hurts a little."

"Yeah. If I had to guess, I'd say that Marie lost her young friend, Lettie, in a weird way, perhaps something she thought involved them making wishes. Maybe didn't think about it for a while or all the time, I don't know, and then one day she spilled the beans about the wishes. Maybe she thought they did come true."

"Like Lisa Tinch getting her new car?"

"Yeah, I suppose something like that."

"That's reaching."

"It started somehow, and they were the first two names."

"Good point. So, she tells someone…"

"Likely Lexi Marks."

"They were neighbors!"

"That's right. That's right. Marie probably mentioned it to Teri and then it made its way from there."

"That all seems to make sense, I suppose, at least the order of things, anyway, if nothing much else about the place."

"It's almost irrelevant."

"I suppose, but it's still nice to know. Did the family ever show back up?"

"No, and that's a weird part, too. They were involved in a dispute with the county, at least that's what I thought."

"What do you mean?"

"There was a dispute about a property line and where their land started and ended. Pretty straightforward stuff, I suppose."

"Except for the disappearing family."

"That and their foe in the dispute. Remember I said I thought it was the county; that's because I saw an entry for The East Erie Co. mentioned."

"Co...? So, like county?"

"That's what I thought, but then I saw in one of the legal filings that the suit was Peggy and Lawrence Lund v. The E. Erie Company."

"The E. Erie Company?

"Yes."

"That sounds like East Erie County."

"I know."

"So, are counties incorporated sometimes? Maybe it's just something legal like that."

"Maybe, but it was an odd thing."

"So, the family just disappeared, left without a trace, and abandoned their home?"

"Appears that way."

"So, who owns the house now?"

"The E. Erie Company."

"Shut up!"

"I wish I could."

"So, our county is up to some shady shit?"

"I guess we'll find out."

"What do you mean?"

"A county can't haunt your life the way that damned room has ruined so, so many."

"I'm not trying to be funny or set you up for a joke, but can a company really be responsible for the type of misery you are describing?"

"Maybe so. Maybe if it's The East Erie Company."

"E. Erie...?"

"Yes, eerie."

Chapter 36

D avid pulled in the driveway and did not wait for me before getting out of the car. He did not need the keys to silence the engine, doing so with the push of a button, but retrieved them from the cupholder long enough to pop the trunk before tossing them again back into the same place.

David did not see me shrug my shoulders, but I did so before following his lead and getting out of the car.

"Here you take two and I'll take two."

David was looking at me from behind the open trunk. I walked around to him, and he was so eager that he was already holding two gasoline containers and was waiting to hand them to me. Each one was large and filled to the top and it was easy to see how my friend had managed to get his pants splattered with gas while filling them. Even now the outside of at least two of the cans glistened from unevaporated remains of the flammable liquid.

"There's still enough light that we'll be able to see what we're doing." David made eye contact and I almost did not recognize this version of the man, my first-best friend. He was no longer fidgety, but all that energy was dancing and twinkling behind his eyes. He was not smiling, per se, but his lips betrayed perhaps a hint of delight at what was about to happen. "But not much. We have to hurry."

"Wait a minute, you are serious about this." Even as I took hold of the cans, or perhaps because of that weight, I knew the act itself was not simply one of insanity but certainly an illegal one that could allow for the possibility of real jail time. I may not be completely lucid, but even I understand that some actions have consequences, even the minor ones sometimes carry aggressive penalties, things like writing your name on a wall when you were fourteen.

His expression did not change but he instead picked up the other two gas containers and turned to leave, the trunk still open. "Let's go do this thing."

"David…"

He stopped and looked at me, any trace of a grin now gone. "I understand if you don't want to involve yourself in this part of it, but I can't turn back now, not after everything I dug up. The death, the insanity, the missing family, the little girl making a wish and then the other one who believed it to be true. The E. Erie Company. Is that just The East Erie County? If so, why is the county named like The Ohio State University? That's the part I keep getting hung up on."

"I don't get it."

"You didn't see it the way I did. There are legal entries for East Erie County, and there are legal entries for The East Erie Co. There's even one I found for The E. Erie Company."

"So, what do they do?"

"I don't know. They don't exist."

"How can they not exist?"

"I just haven't had enough time to find out, but it's obviously something."

"Maybe that's just the title the county uses when dealing with legal matters."

"Maybe, but that doesn't explain this place and what's inside."

"And you really believe this place is what… cursed?"

"It's something."

"So, what would a company have to do with curses?"

"I don't know. Maybe they deal in fear. Maybe they are all about soul-crushing and fates worse than death."

I looked at my friend and considered his words. Of all the things he said, this last part was somehow the easiest for me to believe.

"Whatever you want to call it, this house is killing people and haunting lives, and unlike the family who used to reside there, the lure of that wall is not going away. Clearly kids are still talking about it and going up there and…"

Either way, I was not going to let my friend do this thing alone, and I did not need to hear more. "Ok. I get it. Let's do this thing and end it once and for all."

Chapter 37

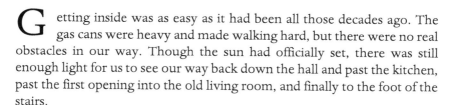

G etting inside was as easy as it had been all those decades ago. The gas cans were heavy and made walking hard, but there were no real obstacles in our way. Though the sun had officially set, there was still enough light for us to see our way back down the hall and past the kitchen, past the first opening into the old living room, and finally to the foot of the stairs.

I was surprised at how much the place seemed the same, and although it looked as if a squatter or two had at one point made the living room a home, there was not as much damage as I would have expected, either from nature or from the many generations of teenagers that had followed. David stopped at the bottom of the steps and set his cans on the ground, reaching then for one of mine.

"I can carry it."

"I'm setting them here, so they are ready to pour out after we start the fire upstairs."

"I see you've given this some thought."

David looked pleased with himself. "We're going to leave two down here and take two upstairs." He took the can from my hand, leaving me with one. Walking into the room just a few steps, David set the first can down and opened the lid."

"You aren't going to pour that out now, are you?"

"God no; the fumes would kill us." He chuckled a little louder and more than I would have liked. He walked back to me and took the last can from my hand, removing the top, and setting this one at the bottom of the stairs. When he was done, he picked up his two cans and started straight up the steps.

The place was still as dusty as I expected, and I could see streaks on the wall where the dust had been disturbed and then resettled, many smudges of imperfection and nuanced layers indicating different hands at different times.

David, having just taken this walk in the last couple days, did not seem as interested in looking around at the place; even carrying the heavy load he was up the steps and starting down the hall before I was on his level. He set one of the cans down outside the room with the names and continued down the hall, opening the door to the next room where he disappeared into. By the time I was standing at the doorway of our room, the room with our names there written, my friend was walking out of that other room empty-handed.

The aroma of gasoline followed him down the hall.

"We have to hurry!"

I picked up the can of gasoline and walked into the room, setting it down almost as soon as I was inside the threshold of the doorway.

My eyes paralyzed my body with the sight they beheld.

The first time I walked into this room I was taken by the sight of the large window, and even now I was aware of that window – how many times during my drives had I tried to see it from the other side – but my attention was fully drawn to the names on the wall, the names as well as all the foreboding graffiti that was seemingly everywhere.

I remembered thinking at the time we were first here that I had expected more names than the eleven that were there waiting for us. This time, however, even knowing that David had prepped me for more, many more, I was totally unprepared for the multitude of names there now to see. Not only was the original wall covered with more names than I had expected, but those signatures now extended down the adjacent walls with even more than a few written on the ceiling.

"I told you there were a lot." David picked up the can and was quick to start spilling its contents about the room. "Get your look in now. This is about to happen."

I looked at the wall where we had signed it. I did not have to look hard to see our four names right where we had written them. They were crowded out, but they were still there, more faded than Rob Cotton's brother's name had been all that time ago. I walked closer and reached out to touch my name, trying to remember making that stupid wish all those years prior.

Regardless of the nature of the consequences, natural or supernatural, that one action had brought me to this point now. I hated myself for getting myself into this mess. Without much thought, I reached out and started scratching at my name, first just a little and then a lot. Once I saw that it could be done, I knew I could not stop until my name was gone from that wall.

"Come on, we have to go!"

I did not answer but continued scratching at the place where my name had been. I only stopped when David pulled at my shoulder.

"It's gone my brother."

He pulled me back without my regard and I followed. He was bigger and his body had never betrayed him, so I complied without resistance. He got me to the door and pushed me down the hall, trying to give me a head start. He turned and ran back down the hall to the far room where he had taken that first can. Standing beside the open door, he pulled something from his pocket, sparked it, and tossed a burning flame into the room, quickly turning his back and covering his ears.

The sound was incredibly loud, but David was moving before the flames blew out through the open door at the end of the hall. He ran past the room with the names, stopped just past it, and again reached into his pocket. This time I could see that he had a lighter and a book of matches, which he wasted no time in lighting and tossing in the room.

I was frozen, but David again started moving before the roar and flames came rushing out from the room. The sound of shattering glass was barely discernible through the reverberations of the explosion, but to my ears it was crystal clear.

As David rushed towards me and the roar inside the rooms settled into a rapidly building fire, I was suddenly overcome with the realization that I had not taken the time to look one last time out from that large oval window, a large piece of glass that I knew was gone but a view that would still be present, at least until the room and the house itself were gone.

I had to see it one last time.

Faster than I had moved in a long time, I ran back towards the room and collided with David.

"What are you doing?"

"I have to see it! I have to look out the window one last time!"

"We have to go!"

"Please," I screamed, twisting out of his grasp and back through the door, "I have to see!"

I was past him and into the room before he could stop me. There was fire everywhere and the room was hot, but the smoke had not yet begun to build and there were random places on the ground that were free of fire and clear to step upon. All I needed was one glance, one quick look to see what was out there. For all the things I could recall, that one detail seemed to elude me; at that moment, it had seemed like the most important one.

Getting to the window was not hard, but the rapidly building heat was already making the place uncomfortable. All in the manner of just a few seconds and I went from heading down the hall to standing at the opening where the large window had once been.

The air being sucked in was cold and it was eager to feed the flames.

Looking out I could see that the sky was growing quickly dark, and I could see the top of the old Victorian over on Anderson and the top of a high window. *I knew it.*

Except for being more forceful and jarring, the pulling on my shoulder was the same motion that my friend had used to pry me from the window all those decades ago.

The flames were now closing in, and I could see the smoke beginning to roll down the hallway.

"We have to go!" David spun me around in front of him, pushing me as we went. I stumbled and nearly tripped, and I could feel my foot interfere with David's own stride.

I was out the door before I heard the thud, which was quickly followed by the screams.

When I looked back, David was on the ground and covered in flames, his pants ablaze, the fire was already working its way along the rest of his body. He stumbled to stand and get to his feet, but that only allowed his burning pants to more efficiently catch the rest of him on fire.

"David!" I moved to grab him while at the same time ripping the heavy coat from off my body and down my arms. Before my hands and the smothering coat could reach him, David's longer arms were pushing me away and I stumbled backwards and out of the room. He was moving, tromping towards me, and I again moved to help.

"Run!"

My eyes had to have been wide, and I know that I had to be crying, but I heeded his words and immediately started walking backwards because I did not want to stop my friend's movement. The ground was already lit in flames and there was no area both large and clear enough for him to stop, drop, and roll. I looked up the hallway and that end of it was ablaze, the heat already making me want to run as quickly as my broken body could take me.

David staggered into the hallway behind me, and I wanted to help, my coat still in my hands and ready to help suppress the flames on his body, but his speed was gaining on me.

"Get downstairs!"

I turned and almost missed the first step, and then I was down quicker than I thought possible. I could hear David behind me, and I turned to look.

Also moving quickly, he was just starting down the stairs and the flames did not seem as widespread as they had at first appeared. He was waving his arms and patting his chest, but his face did not look to have been touched. I started to turn my head back but then did miss the last step, causing me to land hard and out of control. The gas can at the bottom of the stairs was in my way, and we tumbled over in a heap together, me on top of it.

I scrambled up with the gas spilled everywhere but little of it one me that I could tell. Coat still in hand, I turned to flee down this lower hall and I heard a similar racket as David also missed a step and fell sprawled on the floor.

Almost instantly his body was engulfed in even more flames than before - so many more - and he struggled to get up, but this time could not.

I screamed and ran towards him, my coat and my hands stretched out before me ready to put out the fire burning my friend. As I neared, David again tried to stand and I tried to help, wrapping the jacket around him as I also swooped in to lift. I could feel my own pant leg catch fire, and even worse, I was forced instantly away from David when the coat I was holding and had just used to cover his burning body itself burst into flames, the rapid intensity of which took me by surprise.

The coat must have absorbed some of the spilled gasoline when I had fallen from off that last step.

I had just wrapped my best friend in his own death.

He dropped to his knees, and as I tried to move back in to again do what I could to help, and hopefully not make it worse, David was past the point of being saved by me. His body slumped over and now fully ablaze began convulsing, his life's last spasm shaking loose its mortal coil.

I swatted at my pant leg and got the flames to stop, but then I heard a loud crash and just turned to run.

I ran down the hall and out the door and around to the front yard. Without thinking, I ran straight to David's car and jumped in the driver's seat. I needed the key but as shocked as I was, I knew that I did not need to find it. I stepped once on the brake and then punched the ignition button and the engine started on the first take.

In front of me, the house on the edge of town was beyond saving.

Fire was blowing out and up from every upstairs window. From this side of the house, I could only imagine what the large window must have looked like right now. I wondered if the Victorian house on Anderson could see the fiery image I was picturing, an elongated oval glowing red like the eye of a dragon.

I pulled the car back onto the street and peeled the tires getting away; the trunk eventually slammed itself shut.

Chapter 38

A nd this is the tale of the house on the edge of town.

I drove David's car back to my parents' house – I had only been gone for about thirty minutes – and I parked it on the street. I guess on some level I understood that I had only been gone for about thirty minutes, but that David was now gone forever. I suppose that on some level - maybe that subconscious floor that directed me to try and make sense of this madness by recalling it here - I had my doubts as to whether I was ever really there or if any of this had actually happened.

I assure you; it did, and it has.

Upon return, my first thought was to run inside my room, my real room inside the main body of the house where I lay myself down to sleep, but then my mind turned to that room now on fire. If only I could drive by from behind and look upon it from Anderson Road, then perhaps I could truly put the matter to rest. With David's car away from the scene if not off the road, I did not see any harm in driving my father's car past the action. If I was not in David's car, then there would be nothing about my vehicle to connect me with the crime.

I walked into the garage through the side door, got in my dad's car, and started the engine. I was about to reach for the garage door clicker when I was given pause.

That's when the urgent idea arose in my brain to write down these words and tell my tale.

Without taking the time to turn off the motor and no need for the keys, I ran upstairs to this room above the garage to record my deeds.

I suppose I thought that it would not take me long, and I really did want to drive back past the house we set on fire, but this telling took longer than I ever could have imagined and now I am tired, deathly tired.

Perhaps when I wake up and read my words then it will all make some manner of sense, at least more than it seems to make to me here now.

The hour must be late if not early.

I can no longer keep my eyes open; perhaps it is best if I just drift off to a quiet sleep; with any luck it will be a dreamless slumber. If this tale has not cleansed me and I must relive that sight of watching my friend burn, I don't think that I would want to survive the night.

I don't think I should want to survive with that horror living like a worm inside my brain.

Before I pass, my head settled on my arms crossed, my last thought is that I never did ask David what wish he made that day; anyway, I feel confident that whatever it was we just did would surely make his last wish come true: No more of us on that wall would go crazy or die.

Or both.

The End

Lund Land

T his is not a story that requires chapters to tell but is instead just some
of the extra stuff, the little chunks that exist there to form the whole.
A look behind the curtain as it were, or, in modern terms, an end credit
scene. In any case, it is not a story that can fully be told in one sitting or
even from one perspective; but the idea of it can be conveyed as such.

At its heart, this is a tale that has been ongoing from the time life could
think outside of itself: The ability to become aware of our surroundings
and the near-limitless possibilities that abound.

Joyous wonder, to be sure, is not a hard thing to imagine.

But fear, indeed, is much easier to consider.

Once a thing is aware of that world outside of itself, well, then all bets
are off in terms of fear. Fear of loss. Fear of attack. Fear of death. Fear of
those fates worse than death.

Until she and her family disappeared, Lettie Lund remembered the moment she became aware of a life outside of her own.

Lettie was seven the first time she was tall enough to stand close to the
large oval window in her bedroom and look out through the thick glass.
She had obviously looked out the window before, many times in fact, but
she had never just stood there with the intent to look. It had been in the
middle of winter, just past the new year, and the snow was thick on the
Ohio ground. The fir trees too were made thicker by the snow gathered
upon their limbs, but the rest of the trees were bare, and Lettie could see
that behind her home and through the woods there was another house as
big as her family's own.

In the four years between then and when her family was dispatched,
Lettie became best friends with the little girl who lived in that house, Marie
Thome. Marie was a year younger than Lettie, but isolated on the edges of
town, the two girls were like close cousins. Walking back and forth often

between the two houses to play, the distance through the woods was easily traveled in just a few minutes.

The Lund family had lived on this land since before the town of Patrick was officially settled, and initially it was not as large as the property that Lettie's father would come to inherit.

Patrick, Ohio became incorporated as a city in 1831, and the plot of land that Edward Lund claimed for himself the decade prior to that was on the edge of where the new town would be. His property was also at the boundary of the county, East Erie County, with its southern neighbor at this point, Crawford County. The land that Edward owned was modest, but behind it ran a nice stream that would allow for decent fishing and hunting until he could establish his business as a woodworker. He knew he was on the outskirts of town by a fair measure, but the land was affordable, and it offered plenty of trees.

Edward was a distant ancestor to young Lettie Lund, and she never knew the man who was himself born over two hundred years before her birth. It was doubtful that her father, Peter Lund, had even heard stories about the old pioneer.

But not hearing the stories does not make them less real, and not being remembered does not mean that a life is without impact on the future.

The trouble all started - the issue that would one day result in Lettie's family facing a fate worse than death all began - when the county decided to damn the stream and relocate Edward Lund and his family. The pioneering woodworker was not happy about the prospect of his dreams being altered, a major source of his food supply being attributed to the stream, and he expressed his dissatisfaction to the county's first chairman, a man whose name has been erased from history but who was known to dress in gray and wear a vantablack top hat.

For his inconvenience, the county generously offered Edward a similarly sized plot of land across from the county's new reservoir and the road being built alongside it. The road would be called County Line Road even though the reservoir across the street was part of county property, too.

To sweeten the deal, the county agreed to give Edward half of the timber that was cut down to accommodate the new reservoir.

Edward obliged – what choice did he really have – but he soon found himself questioning if he would have been better just moving along and starting over elsewhere, maybe joining his brother in Tiffin.

For starters, the number of trees the county had to thin out was staggering, and Edward Lund was almost buried in timber. He saw this as a good problem to have, but making space for it all did keep him spinning his wheels for three full years before he was finally able to come to grips and start milling it for use in his craft. It was a trying time, and more than once Edward Lund had considered just packing up and walking away from it all.

But he persevered.

The wait and patience and the toil had been worth it; Edward persevered his own fate worse than death and found a way to come through it all without his soul being crushed dry. Raising a child in a modest pioneer cabin, he was never able to build for himself the house that he always wanted for his family, but before his death he was able to help his son build a beautiful home in the 1880's.

The house was a museum of wood, with every piece of molding and trim being carved by hand.

There were many detailed features of the house – cabinets that rolled out from within walls, floor safes, a secret door between two closets – but the one feature Edward prized the most was the large round window in one of the bedrooms on the second floor. An elongated oval, tall and the focal point when entering the room, the window was a thing of beauty.

It would be the room in which he would sleep until his death just a few years after the construction of the home. Though he would never see the large Victorian that eventually sprang up and occasionally in view from beyond the glass, when Edward looked out that tall window, he always knew that, at least figuratively, something else was out there to be seen. Something was beyond the flat glass, something silently calling for him to hear.

It was after his death that the family again ran afoul of the county and more specifically the entity around which the area was named.

Edward's grandson – Peter's great grandfather – wanted to build his own home just after the turn of that next century. Things in Patrick were doing well, and the family wanted to sell some land behind their home to help fund the building of a house on the adjacent lot.

The buyer of the property was Awesome Anderson.

Nobody in Patrick knew what Awesome's real name was or even if he had another name, but that was how he introduced himself and he rarely gave others any reason to question it. Awesome agreed to the price, even agreed to build a connector street to Biddle Road, and he and Edward's grandson went to the county office to sign off on the new boundaries and the terms of the deal.

When the records were broken out, the maps were consulted and amended. A plot of land that did belong to The East Erie Company was mislabeled as E. Erie Co./ Lund instead of Land. Though it wouldn't be noticed for over a hundred years, a clerical error was made that would bring misfortune upon the fortunate and a fate worse than death to the stoop of an innocent little girl.

Awesome Anderson built an awesome house, a big Victorian manor that sat behind the Lund's original homestead. In the summer, the two houses were isolated as if alone, but in the thinnest months of winter the two could be seen, one from the other.

Time passed and the town of Patrick grew larger, but that original Lund home would never be closer than just being a house on the edge of town.

Anderson Road was slightly closer to Patrick, and it connected the old Anderson property along with a few neighboring houses to Biddle Road. Near the end of the latest century, the county decided to extend Anderson Road a half mile and connect it with Harley Township Road to the west.

The only roadblock was the Lund land.

For some reason, the county had a memory that the land was most certainly not Lund land even if the records said so. None of the county officials were alive back then, but as if a bug was put in their collective ears, they fought like they had been there from day one. It was one thing to pay Peter Lund for land to build the road and move on from it, but the county did not want to accept that he also owned the remaining acreage.

So desperate were they that an offer was made to swap the acreage for the plot neighboring the family home on County Line Road, a much larger parcel that stretched all the way to Biddle Road.

Peter was not content to sit still, so the lawyer who was also distantly related to a woodworker ventured out to explore the acreage in question. He had not been one to play in the woods as a kid, and he had not been especially close with his father before that man's death, but as the last Lund male alive he felt an obligation to see why the county was so adamant about wanting the land that was not to be used for the road.

After a couple trips in the woods, he was finally closing in on the dark secret.

On the day before the night the Lund family disappeared, Lettie was outside playing alone when a black sedan pulled into the driveway. The driver exited the vehicle and walked around to open the door for the passenger in the back seat.

The little girl was only eleven, but she understood that this person was probably important.

"Hello young lady. Is your mother or father around?"

Lettie had been taught to avoid talking to strangers, but this man seemed important; besides, if he was parked in their driveway, was he really a stranger?

"My dad's out playing in the woods. My mom says he's been doing that too much lately."

"And where is your mother?"

"She's taking a bath. She says that's her escape from this place."

"We all need an escape now and again."

Lettie shrugged her shoulders.

"You have a place you escape to in your imagination, don't you? A place where no one can get you and no one can harm you?"

Lettie liked the sound of the man's voice. He was old like her grandpa - her mom's dad - but she knew that this man was not the same. His hat was kind of tall and funny and it was blacker than she knew possible; still, she nodded.

"We all have that place, even if it's just pulling the covers over our heads. Your place is probably way safer than that, though."

"I suppose."

"And you know that if you ever had to, you could keep your family safe in there as well...?"

"I can?"

"Sure, why you can take the entire family to that safe place and just stay safe there forever."

"Forever? They'd really be safe forever?"

"If it's a safe space you take them to."

"Are they in trouble?"

The man looked around and laughed. "Oh no, of course not, who would ever want to hurt your wonderful family? Trouble with the county aside, that is. I'm just saying; you could do it, and then there would be no question of them being safe and sound."

"How do I do that?"

"You just have to wish for it."

"I do?"

"Sure."

"But I can't snap my fingers."

The old man laughed, a genuine laugh at the innocence of the child. Though he detested her family he could still appreciate the tender moment. "Can you write your name?"

Lettie nodded.

"Fancy writing, like your mom and dad use when writing a check, not the letters your teacher makes you use...can you do that?"

"You mean my autograph?"

"I mean exactly that!"

"I can do that!"

"Well, to get your wish, all you must do is close your eyes and write your name on the wall of your bedroom. If you do that, you can make a wish to keep your family safe."

"I can do that?"

"You can."

"And it will come true?"

"Sure, as it rains it *will* come true."

"That's neat."

"You know what?"

"What?"

"If I was you, I'd run inside and do that right now, just to keep them safe before you forget."

"You would?"

"I would. You don't even have to tell them. Just make your wish and sign your name on the wall and tonight you can close your eyes and drift off to sleep knowing that when you wake up both you and your parents will be made safer."

"I'm going to do that!"

"Good girl." The man turned and nodded at his driver. "Please tell your mom and dad that the man came to read the water meter."

"Okay!"

Lettie did not waste any time and ran straight to her room, the one with the tall, round window. She had plenty of markers, and the only trouble was trying to figure out which color to use. She saw the pink one but thought that would be too light. The pink one did, however, make her think of her best friend, Marie, who lived in the old house behind her own. She and Marie played together a lot in the summertime, and Lettie knew that her friend was afraid about her parents breaking up. The little girl didn't know what that meant or how adults could come apart, but Lettie knew that it was not good.

Exactly the kind of thing her parents were going to be safe from ever again facing.

Lettie called Marie, explained the plan, and the friend was there in less than ten minutes.

Before Lettie's mom was out of the bath, both girls had written their names on the wall and made their wishes.

★★★★★★★★★★★★★

"How did you ever convince him to sign?" The female voice did not sound as surprised as her words would otherwise convey.

"I didn't have to convince him. I convinced the little girl."

"Is that binding?"

"She is a Lund. It is binding, and it is done as much as we need it to be. Once the family all closes their eyes to sleep tonight, they will be taken into the safe land of that little girl's dreams."

"Gone for good?"

"Gone from us." The old man could not help but smile at the duality of his comment.

"What about the other one?"

"The other one?"

"The other little girl who wrote her name?"

"Oh. Her wish was for her parents to remain together. Either that will happen, or it will not. Either she gets her wish, or she is disappointed. The torment will either drive her mad or to an early grave."

"Or both...?"

The old man laughed and adjusted his top hat.

"What if she tells others?"

"Same for them. Regardless of the outcome, once they sign that wall then their fates will be in our hands. Disappointment. Agony. Soul crushing."

"Fates worse than death."

The old man smiled and tipped his cap. "Yes, fates worse than death."

The End

Milton Keynes UK
Ingram Content Group UK Ltd.
UKHW020423131223
434231UK00014B/819